I0652851

Lands of Legend

Gritters In Space

"The Return of Krepkiyzad"

- the musical -

(Book IV of The **LOL/ROFL** Series)

Author: Daniel Thorman

Imprint: Independently published

Other books by this author include

(or one day will)

The Osten Chronicles

Lands of Legend

Dedication

To Doctor Seuss – Ted Geisel
(For warping my mind as a child)

In writing his books for children,
He had lots of lessons to teach--
Like why we shouldn't envy the star
On the belly of another Sneetch.

I hope that the Lorax lifted him
To that Truffula grove above,
Where Swomee Swans fly
high up in the sky
And fish sing of brotherly love.

Well done, Doctor.
Rest in peace.

Prologue

The Hunt for Blue November

This was a disaster, the biggest debacle since Elon Musk found out what was really going on in Area 51! And if the alarms blaring across the bridge were any indication, it was about to get worse. Admiral Akana felt that somewhere out there, the conspiracy nuts were already sharpening their pencils, ready to have another go at global high command.

The telepresence flickered, and for an instant, Akana's command chair became a ghostly outline. The holo-display on his flagship jittered before stabilizing once again. He adjusted his posture, one gloved hand tightening around the armrest as if that might somehow keep the connection from degrading further.

"Report!" he snapped, voice crisp and cutting through the static.

"GNS Black Tide reports they've got him on sonar," barked Commodore Nelson, his second in command.

This wasn't an opportunity to be wasted.

The Nautilus-class prototype was the most advanced submarine ever built--meant to be the pride of the fleet before Humanity First plucked it right out from under the global government's nose. The theft was a stab to his pride, Hawaii being his own state of origin. The Nautilus wasn't supposed to be fully operational for years yet. It was packed to the gills with the latest in weaponry and stealth technology, the very pinnacle of naval engineering. And what *ino loa* devil had dared christen it Blue November? As if stealing it wasn't insult enough, such a *lolo* name really stung.

"This is Akana. All captains--target sighted at twelve point five north, one-forty-four point eight east. Keep formation and proceed east at best speed. I'll rendezvous with you there."

His 'fleet' was a hastily assembled hodgepodge of vessels that happened to be drifting nearby. The pair of DDG-1000 Zumwalt-class destroyers were old veterans. He doubted their newly fitted railguns would come into play, but one never knew. No, but their depth charges might prove useful.

His own flagship, the GNS Kanaloa, wasn't without its unique capabilities. The new quantum entanglement comm system (QECs), though unproven as yet, had strong possibilities for an undersea engagement. The problem with submarines was the bandwidth required for telepresence. Hobbled by the limitations of VLF and ELF (very or extremely low frequency) radio transmissions, it could be troublesome to coordinate a fleet of any size. And it wasn't at all convenient to surface for every friendly chat. Most of the subs in his current command had work-arounds for this, like the comm buoys floating on the surface at the ends of their tethers. It made Akana feel like some kind of puppeteer to be using those old relics. No, he was privileged to command a Leviathan-class Strategic Command Sub. The Kanaloa should serve him well.

What he was really counting on were the eight Manta-class stealth submersibles he'd had the good fortune of finding on maneuvers north of Guam. Among the more advanced elements of the fleet, their plasma stealth capabilities were nearly a match for that of their adversary. And *numbers* should help overcome the technology gap. Better still, each had a complement of AI-operated Hornet Drones capable of independent swarming tactics and were more pressure-resistant than any human-operated craft apart from the November herself.

The rest of his fleet was a motley assortment of tenders and anything else he could conscript. There was even a carrier group that would be joining them soon, though what good they'd do beneath the waves only *Kanaloa* himself could say.

Why had Legion risked a transmission with all of the Pacific Fleet on high alert? If Akana were in command of the November, she'd still be lying low. Who was this 'Lord Legion,' the self-styled spokesman for all mankind? Could it be that his crazy followers needed encouragement from time to time, or did he have another diabolical plot to launch? Eddings had likened the man to a Bond villain, but to Akana, he came off more like an Austin Powers adversary.

"Manta Leader wants to know whether he should engage," reported Nelson.

"Absolutely not," snapped Akana. "Tell him to wait for the rest of us to arrive."

Tactical advantage aside, Akana was uncertain whether even eight Manta subs would be enough. He'd signed off on the specs for that hull himself. The blend of carbon nanotubes and titanium composites could withstand more than its share of conventional battering. He was certain they would have to concentrate their firepower on that monstrosity to even put a dent in it. His strike force would need some... strike force, right from the very first salvo.

He tried to think more positively. He had all the ships he needed. The adversary was in sight, and he had all the force he needed.

Akana watched as the seconds ticked by. *Almost there.*

"Admiral! She's launched a torpedo!"

"Evasive!" shouted Akana to the fleet. "And countermeasures on my mark. Wait for it. *Now!*"

But there was no explosion. Not even a tremble. Instead, the admiral's command screen filled with hissing static, and his holopresence abruptly dissolved. Of course. Squealers. The torpedo had fragmented into hundreds of independent sonar-blocking, radio-jamming little drones, spreading chaos through the water like a cloud of piranhas."

The GNS Kanaloa had hardened electronics, but communications were somewhat of an Achilles heel as far as fleet tactics went.

"Return fire on their position with a full complement of kinetic torps."

He hoped the others would take the hint.

"Launching. Packets away, admiral."

"Fire up the QED comms. Time for a little field test."

Akana wasted no time, strapping on the cumbersome QEC helmet that would bear his words to the holo-emitters on the bridges of every ship under his command. The unit was still a bit hit-or-miss, and the power requirements were enormous, but an engagement like this was no time to stint.

"Ackbar to all ships. Engage at will. Sink that traitorous *kumakaia* before he can deploy any more of his arsenal!"

"Sonar is coming back online, admiral. It looks like the Mantas have already gone stealth."

"And the November?"

"Contact bearing one-one-zero, range increasing. November is making a run for the trench, sir!"

That was terrible news. The San Marianas Trench ran north to south not 25 leagues from here. This far south, it still bottomed out at depths exceeding 5000 meters. The pressure down there was enormous, enough to crush any sub not designed for special ops. But for a Nautilus-class sub? Who

4

could say? With its nanocomposite alloys, it could far outperform the pursuing task force when it came to withstanding pressure. It had a crush depth (untested) of nearly 4,500 meters.

"She's firing again, sir!"

Akana had always wanted to say it, and now *hopena* (fate) had given him a reason.

"Damn the torpedoes! Full speed ahead!"

He wouldn't be fooled by another launch of squealers. And even if this was the real McCoy incoming this time, he couldn't afford to let this prey slip through his net.

"Ghostblade has been hit, sir. Minor damage, but her hull has been breached. She's blowing ballast and heading to the surface."

And then there were seven, thought Akana.

"Beats her heading to the bottom, commodore. Isn't that incoming carrier group also to our east?"

Nelson blinked, then looked up from his sonar unit to examine the wall screen.

"Checking. Aye. They're still 20 leagues out on bearing one-zero-eight."

"Perfect," grinned Akana, "Relay to them the coordinates and bearing of our target. I want them to drop every depth charge they have right on top of our adversary. Rain fire on the sea bottom to our east."

"You can tell them yourself, admiral. They've just entered quantum entanglement range and are hailing us."

After a hasty conversation, Akana returned his attention to the chase. November was running at 35 knots, just under flanking speed for most of his submarine fleet. He knew she was capable of more. Her own flanking speed was in the 45-50 knot range, and she was capable of bursts of 55-60 using her supercavitating magnetohydrodynamic augments. Why, then, this steadfast retreat?

"Carrier group is over the target's twelve, sir. Ordnance is away!"

The screens lit up with pyrotechnics in and around their fleeing adversary. It was too much to hope for November's outright destruction, but perhaps they could snarl up some of her propulsion. And indeed, when the monstrous leviathan emerged from the churning mud and debris brought up from the sea floor, she appeared to be limping along (if 30 knots could be considered a limp). He urged his captains to make best speed on the slim hope of making an intercept before the bottom fell out of their chase.

Alas, it was too much to hope for.

"Admiral. Target is descending fast."

The target was barely in visual range when Akana saw it slip over the lip of the great crack in the ocean floor and dive from view. Worse still, she finally engaged her sonar stealth. And a moment later, numerous false sonar images appeared, showing ships of that size moving in every direction.

"The captain of the Pinafore would like to know if his group should pursue."

"Tell him no. I don't like how we came to be here. Almost like he was leading us."

"The captain is asking if he can send the Hornet Drones. They can withstand the depth..."

Tempting, but also no. He doubted the drones would prove sufficient on their own. Simple AI tactics were quite predictable, and November had adequate countermeasures against such. An NBI now. That would be quite a different matter. It was too bad the Chinese zodiac lacked any aquatic creatures in their retinue. He'd have to ask about recruiting one at the next meeting of the joint chiefs. So, was this the end or...

"No. Have him call them back. The sea's been patient. Now it's our turn."

"We're giving up? But why, sir? We're so close."

"You're going to make me say it, aren't you, commodore?"

"I think the men would like to hear it from you, sir."

With a weary sigh, he redonned the helmet and broadcast the warning to every ship.

"It's a trap!"

The trench stretched for many leagues in each direction and interconnected with a network of lesser canyons throughout the Pacific. He would set watches as he was able and perhaps mine a few chokepoints. He doubted these efforts would catch November. She'd proven to be as elusive as the freckled frogfish. No, he'd just have to wait for another opportunity.

What wickedness did Humanity First intend? If the attack on Luna was any gauge, it was sure to be something depraved. As Mr. Melville once remarked, "There is no folly of the beast of the earth which is not infinitely outdone by the madness of men."

Ten...

Furlough

After tipping the autocab, he turned to catch sight of his childhood home. Dad stood waiting on the front steps--all smiles. Duffel slung over one shoulder, David ambled up the drive. He accepted an awkward hug. Was it only his imagination, or had Dad gotten shorter in the time he was away?

"Where's Mom?"

Dad looked pensive for a moment. *That was odd.*

She's inside," he mumbled, then brightened. "Can't wait to see our returning prodigal son!"

But obviously, she *could* wait. Something was fishy. He was tired from the long flight from Houston and needed to freshen up. He sincerely hoped a bunch of people weren't about to jump out and yell 'Surprise!'

"Should I be expecting fatted calf for dinner then?" said David with mock earnestness.

"'Fraid it's turkey tetrazzini tonight," said Dad, relieving him of his duffel. "C'mon in. Let's get you settled."

But the very opposite was soon to occur. He followed Dad into the living room. And what he found there left him quite *un-settled*.

There was Mom chatting away with a girl he'd once known. She was seated on the sofa, sipping at a Diet Coke while Mom was filling her in about a gift exchange at church. The dialog stopped abruptly when David entered. The girl sat up straighter, and she set the soda aside. Her brown eyes turned to lock with his. A blank look un-settled on her face. Mom turned nervously toward him. Her tentative smile belied the worry lines etched on her brow. David was the first to speak.

"Bonnie?"

He said it as a question, though it was obviously her. She stood, and cautiously began.

"I was going to wait in the driveway, but your parents brought me in here. I'll leave if you want," she blurted.

"Nonsense," murmured Mom. "Go ahead, dear. Say what you came to say. David doesn't hold a grudge."

"I... I'm supposed to ask. It's part of the program. I should have called ahead," she said as she cast her gaze down.

"Here, now," said Dad. "Let's all sit down. Spit it out, Miss Fields. Best to get it on over with, like pulling off a band-aid."

Resting the duffel near the front door, he made for his favorite chair, willfully unaware of Carol's disapproving glare. So they all sat as Bonnie nervously began anew.

"I'm an addict," she said it like a mantra. "I know enough to own that now. But I'm in a twelve-step program that's helping me to cope. It's really helping, David. I've been sober since... that night. I'm only on step six right now, but I didn't want to miss the chance to do this step in person. Like I said, I'll leave if this is too hurtful or just a bad time."

It *did* feel like an ambush. Thanks, Mom and Dad. But leaving matters unsettled didn't seem like a good way forward.

"Um. No, I was worried for you. I'm glad you're getting help. You've been in my prayers since then."

Bonnie looked about ready to cry. But she bunched up her lips and continued.

"I was so angry with you when you turned me in. I can scarce believe what I did. It was wrong. I used to tell myself that wasn't really me, but I've learned to face it now. It was. Step eight is to list all the people I hurt, and step nine is to make amends. When you moved away, I thought I might never get the chance. I'm ashamed to say that part of me was relieved."

Again, her gaze drifted down toward the floor, but she caught herself and looked back up. Firming her jaw, she resumed.

"I don't know how to say it, this being the first one I've done, but I'm told to just say it as plainly as I can. I hurt you, David. *I* did that. I cost you your reputation and almost got you kicked out of school. I made your high school prom a horrible night. I don't know how or if I can ever undo all that, but know I'll keep trying until I can make it right."

She began rummaging around in the oversized purse that rested on the sofa beside her. She pulled out a package and presented to David a white plastic bag.

"I made you this."

"What is it?"

"Open it and I'll explain."

It was a framed picture of the two of them taken in the photo booth at the prom. David was in his black suit and bow tie next to Bonnie in her yellow dress. Both were smiling and making goofy faces for the camera. The frame was made of some dark wood and carved in an elegant, leafy pattern.

"You *made* this?"

"The frame, anyway," she replied with a rueful smile and a one-shoulder shrug. "They have a craft room at Seacrest. I spent a lot of time there."

"Anyway, I can't give you prom night back. But instead, I want you to have my favorite possession. After I got over the withdrawal and the even longer time I spent getting over my anger, I came to realize that you saved my life, doing what you did. And I know it would have been easier just to make out with me and forget about it. But you chose to help me instead. That picture has hung on my wall for months, helping with my recovery, reminding me there are good people in this world, and encouraging me to *be* one of them.

"Now I want you to have it, not because you like me. Jesus knows you've got no reason to after what *I* did. No. I was thinking that every time you look at it, it could remind you of another life you saved. Not as flashy as a moon rescue, but a life just the same. You'll be looking at a girl who'll always be grateful for that."

Tears were streaming down Carol's face by then, and even Daniel seemed subdued.

Why did moms always have to make things weird? Who was I kidding? I was trying hard not to tear up myself.

Everyone seemed to be waiting for me to say something, but I didn't quite trust my voice. Bonnie understood. After a long moment, she said in a more conversational tone, "I read your book."

"What did you think?"

"It was dumb."

That stung.

"It didn't nearly describe the heart of the man who saved my life that night. Your courage on the moon didn't surprise me one bit."

And at that, she stood and made ready to depart.

"Would you like to stay for dinner?" asked Carol.

"I couldn't do *that*," said Bonnie, looking stricken. "This isn't a social call. It's about trying to make amends, but I thank you for the kind offer. Besides, I got a curfew. My sponsor's waiting for me."

David saw her to the door. And as she walked away, he finally found his voice.

"Bonnie," he called after.

She turned.

"The picture. I'll treasure it."

***

"Wait a minute, I'm trying to *hear* this."

David leaned back and stared up at the screen of the Mills' home theater setup. When he'd arrived, Lucy had informed him that Jason was down here catching up on some work. Apparently, he'd finished and was now catching up on the news, of all things.

"...Now that the virtual country of Mandaria has been granted official status by the GLC, the NBIs have offered dual citizenship to all current players of the video game known as Realms who have accumulated at least five personal honor points. This entitles them to special rewards both in that game and IRL as well. When asked to comment, Royce Silverman, CEO of Nexgen Cybernetics, said to take it up with his co-owner, Satori, the mysterious ruling NBI known as the Jade Empress.

"In other news, unscheduled war games erupted in the western Pacific late this afternoon. The ad hoc fleet was assembled by Admiral Akana to test the battle readiness of our naval forces. The GNA has come under fierce scrutiny ever since the debacle at the Hawaiian shipyards where a $175 billion prototype was 'misplaced.' Some doubt that--"

"Ah, come on!" groaned Jason, having just cut off the feed. "I still need one more honor point to qualify. Glass Cannon has scads more than five, but I think they mean personal honor points, and Jason Mills only has four. How the heck did you get to *nine*?"

"It's ten now," David shrugged. "I think Satori likes me. Plus, there was that whole thing about saving Luna..."

"It's unfair. You space jockeys get all the dumb luck."

"Hey, if you want to go ten rounds with a seething swarm of nanites, feel free to enlist, and I'll see what I can do."

Jason gulped, then sighed.

"Was it bad?"

"It could have been. One of our guys even got shot."

"Condolences."

"No worries. Turned out he was a rotten egg anyway."

Jason frowned and nodded.

"Speaking of no worries," David continued, "When's Jess supposed to call?"

"We've got some time yet. The funeral doesn't start for three more hours. She said she'd call sometime before then. I heard she was staying at your base for the last couple of months. Small world. How'd that go?"

Jase was trying to look disinterested, but David knew better. Last summer, Jason was crushing hard on Jessica.

"It was awful," he teased. "She was pretending to be my girlfriend to root out an HF infiltrator. Sometimes we even had to make out so as not to blow her cover."

Jason's shocked and doubtful look was priceless. He finally cleared his throat and responded with heavy skepticism.

"Dude. If true, I want *your* life, bullets and all."

David had the unsettling feeling that he really meant it.

"How are the books selling?" he asked to change the topic.

"Hate to be cliché, but they're flying off the shelves. Ever since your debut on Hollywood Squares, people have just been itching to get to know you better. It was a genius move getting all the others to sign with me exclusively. Their memoirs and takes on events are going to go over big. I've even got a line of action figures out now."

David smiled recalling the little kid on the commercial saying, "Roooid Raaage!" in that gravelly voice.

"It didn't hurt," said David, "that your mother is so well known. That reminds me, Claptrap wanted me to have her sign an old calendar he's got of her. Big fan. Who knew?"

Jason frowned. His mother's swimsuit calendar was a tender spot with him.

"I'll see what I can do. Where is it?"

"I left them upstairs."

"Them?"

"Well... once Rope-A-Dope heard Simon was getting one, he kind of brought me his as well. Then Dietrich didn't want to get left out. Word got around at the base, and it kind of spiraled out from there..."

"How many are we talking?" asked Jason with an inscrutable expression.

"Um... all told? Around fifty-three."

After Jason was finally able to dismiss the thought of an entire military base drooling over old photographs of his mom, they refocused on business matters. Jason had already parlayed David's 'tidy sum' into what, to David's lower middle-class sensibilities, was an almost obscene amount of wealth.

The problem was, he really had no way to spend it. After the attacks on the cadets this past autumn, it was deemed necessary to move them up to L5. The base already provided everything he really needed, and he had been informed that he wouldn't be allowed to take anything up to space apart from a few personal items and mementos. Every ounce lifted off from Earth was precious. He'd be going with just the clothes on his back. All else would be fabricated up on the station. He couldn't give money to his parents. Dad's business was going very well now, and his pride wouldn't allow it.

What they finally arrived at was this. He'd put half of his wealth into a charitable trust--recipients to be named later. He made Jason his agent to invest the rest. Mandaria was offering stock options to expand their IRL quantum arrays and needed starting capital. Yáng, the goat, had been named Satori's Minister of Finance. David recalled that the old goat had once been in charge of a financial management system and had grown clever enough to manipulate the stock market despite the restrictions on AI trading. David was sure the NBIs would give a good return to their investors. And now, as a citizen, he could get in on the ground floor of something he was certain would be big.

Jason pulled up a daunting array of documents on his phone, each one needing David's thumbprint. But, when all was said and done (and thumb-printed), his earthly affairs were finally in order.

***

Servo-matic had just delivered their mango-lemon smoothies when Lucy announced the call.

"Miss Jessica Arbuckle is calling, Jason," chimed the house in her ever-pleasant voice."

"Put her on, Luce, and give her a split screen."

The high-end cameras swiveled on their platforms and came to rest, one each focused on Jason and David. Jessica's image wavered into view on the backdrop screen of the stage. She was dressed all in black in a form-fitting dress that made David wish they could mourn more often.

"Arvo, cobbers. Greetings from up over," she said.

"Um. Up over?" said Jason, taking the bait.

The inversion of Earth's magnetic poles, David knew, was amusing to the Australians. They printed maps of their continent upside down and claimed they were now on top of the world. As Jessica explained all this to a befuddled Jason, David leaned back and took the time to appreciate the view.

"Why aren't you two dressed yet?" asked Jess.

"We'll dress in-game and stay comfortable IRL," said Jason with a smirk. "Walter would have wanted it that way."

"Know what, mate? For once we agree. That sentiment fits Shriney C. to a 'T.'

"Hey now, Jess. Don't start this game. You know rhyming is my claim to fame."

"I find that effort rather lame," added Jason in a huff.

Jess giggled, then sobered.

"Gonna miss that old coot," she said with a sniff.

"Save some for the ceremony," Jason gently chided. "How are things... um... up over?"

"Pretty much the same as always. The roos are hopping, the laughs ain't stopping, and the dunnies flush clockwise proper."

"Did CAGE give you a new assignment yet?"

"Well, I could tell you, mate, but then I'd have to--"

"Yeah, yeah. Spare us," said Jason with a swipe of his hand.

"No. Not spare ya, mate, I'd have ta--"

"Stop. We get it," he said with a grim chuckle, holding up his hands in surrender.

She smiled that smile that made her eyes sparkle.

"Speaking of assignments, when's the launch date, Davie?"

"Davie?" Jason mouthed silently toward David, who ignored him.

"We don't know yet. The test launches have all been successful, but they want to be absolutely certain before the first manned launch. They're beefing up security because it would be so easy to sabotage. The rail runs all across Tanzania. That's a lot of track to secure. I think they'll let us stay on furlough through the holidays at least. My best guess is sometime in early January. Pierre says they'd be heartless to go any earlier."

"Where *is* that little green roommate of yours, anyway? Home visiting the folks?"

"Nah. He hates it there. He's using his downtime to visit his university in Switzerland. Probably getting a leg up on curing cancer or something."

"That's so sad."

"Nah, he loves it."

"Well, it's almost time," said Jason. "'Davie' and I better go gear up. We'll see you on the flip side... Allie."

"Till then, mates. Hooroo."

And with a wink and in a blink, she was gone.

***

They stood on a hill overlooking Harmony Grove in the distance. The grove was bustling now with avatars of every build popping in and out at its shrine.

Darla was here with them up on the hill. Her avatar's face gave no hint of her feelings, but her nervous pacing said plenty. David and Jason (now Tom and G.C.) wore the black robes they'd gotten at Celestial Silkworks. The plus five to Charm enhancement had been pricey, but Tom hadn't even bothered to haggle. When Allie arrived, she joined them.

"You two clean up nicely," she said with a satisfied smirk.

"We's doing' our best, Ma'am," said G.C. with a tip of her hat emote.

"We do aim to please, Miss Allison" added Tom.

Curious onlookers clustered nearby, the open grave being somewhat of a curiosity. Usually, when a character died, they respawned at their last save point, and when a player died IRL, they just never logged back on. Today's ceremony would be special. Jason had used the Tong's resources to purchase this bit of land adjacent to the grove and set it aside as a memorial to players who were no longer with them. He'd named it 'Boot Hill' in honor of Shriney C. It directly overlooked their Tong's holdings in the distance.

When the sun reached its zenith, it was time to begin, high noon being symbolic in the lore. Darla triggered an ability that made a podium arise from the ground. It was more of a stone plinth that arose from the crumbling earth. She step ped up to it

"You all know why we're here," she said, her voice carrying the heartbreak that her face could not.

"They say cowboys and men are two totally different breeds, and Grandpa Walt was of the former variety. Laugh if you will, him having grown up in Baltimore, but they also say a man isn't born a cowboy; he becomes one."

Was it David's imagination, or had Darla's voice taken on a more Western twang and folksy rhythm than she was accustomed to use? Why not? It seemed fitting.

"Grandpa Walt was a kind old soul who lived a full life and passed doing what he wanted, helping others."

She lowered her head. It was a moment before she resumed.

"When that solar storm came streaming in over the plains west of the Rockies, it was about as welcome as a rattlesnake at a square dance. It sent refugees flooding into Wyoming with nothing but the clothes on their backs. They were disheartened and in misery and took to squatting on our land.

"Walter never minded none. Folks was folks, each one a precious opportunity to show God's grace to his fellow man. Ninety-four years old, and Walter Campbell spent his last days organizing and spreading hope among em. A generous man, he opened his ranch and cracked open his hard-won emergency supplies to see that all the unfortunates was fed.

"He died riding April Rein. Walt woulda liked that. He enjoyed quoting old Red that there's nothin' in life that's worth doin', if it cain't be done from a horse."

19

"It was his heart that finally gave out--the physical one, not the one that mattered--never that."

Her voice started breaking on that last line, and David suspected *her* heart did as well. It was several moments before she was fit to continue.

"I could rattle out stories about Grandpa Walt all day long, but that wouldn't be fitting or needful. He was a simple man. Most of you here knew him, and for those who didn't, well, that's just your own misfortune.

"He lived by the code. Shoot straight. Ride tall in the saddle. Tell no lies and dance with who brung ya."

"He loved this game, and turns out it loved him right back. As a special tribute to the Shrinestone Cowboy, the zodiac has made available in-game a song from his western collection that suits the mood. Enjoy it. Walt woulda wanted you to celebrate."

And with that, she stepped back and triggered another action. The podium descended into the ground, and up arose a tombstone in its place. It was no ostentatious marker. Just a simple cross with his name and that of his character. And trotting up from the background came the zodiac horse. She reared up and neighed, then began to transform.

Her mane shifted into braids. Her hooves softened into hands.

Mă was the first creature David had ever seen Shriney C. befriend in-game. When her transformation settled down, she was in human form, wearing blue jeans and a checkered shirt. A black Stetson sat at a jaunty tilt, just above the pigtails framing her still-somewhat-horsey features.

She equipped a six-string and began pluck-strumming at it in 3/4 time. When she raised her voice, Tom was surprised at the clarity of her mellow alto. It was a song David would later learn was called 'A Cowboy's Lament,' first made famous by Burl Ives. Softly, it began. And all were soon transfixed by its lilting melody.

As I walked out in the streets of Laredo
As I walked out in Laredo one day
I spied a young cowboy all wrapped in white linen.
Wrapped in white linen as cold as the clay

It was about a dying man and his wishes for his funeral. And as Mă sang on, a column of pallbearers appeared at the hill's base. They were wearing period clothing and bearing a simple pine box.

It was once in the saddle I used to go dashing.
Once in the saddle I used to go gay.
First down to Rosie's and then to the card house.
Got shot in the breast, and I'm dying today.

The steady procession climbed up the hill.

Get sixteen gamblers to carry my coffin.
Get six jolly cowboys to sing me a song.
Take me to the graveyard and lay the sod o'er me.
For I'm a young cowboy and know I've done wrong.

Get six jolly cowboys to carry my coffin.
Get six pretty maidens to sing me a song.
Take me to the valley and lay the sod o'er me.
For I'm a young cowboy, and know I've done wrong.

Mă was joined first by a chorus of male avatars singing Ah-ahs in the background, and then by a similar group of females as the coffin was lowered into the ground.

Oh, beat the drum slowly and play the fife lowly.
Play the Dead March as they carry me along.
Put bunches of roses all over my coffin.
Put roses to deaden the clods as they fall.

A basket of roses appeared at the foot of the grave. Led by Darla, all were encouraged to step forth and drop one in, followed by a handful of earth. As a repeat of the first verse brought the song to its conclusion, the earth filled it nearly to the rim.

21

Then, like a bolt out of nowhere, Gǒu, the zodiac dog, came leaping into their midst. His head hung low as he sniffed at the earth. Tom prayed silently that he wasn't about to pee. *Don't be a bad dog today*, he thought. But he needn't have worried. Gǒu sat back on his haunches, threw back his head, and let out a mournful howl that clashed only marginally with the final notes of the song. It put Tom in mind of his similar display after that party wipe in Mongolia. And though off-key, it was somehow just right. He let it sink in as the virtual sun sank below the far horizon.

***

The companions were subdued as they ambled down the hill, dressed in their robes of black. Even Gǒu's tail was drooping as he dragged along at the rear. Though death was inevitable, it never seemed right. It always felt too soon. So, they trudged along in the one-hour night by the light of a waxing moon.

"This was nice," said Glass Cannon. "We should do this more often."

"Bury somebody?" asked Tom.

"You're deflecting again, cobber," said Allie. "You know he meant get together in-game. Unfortunately, I never know where the service might need me, and it isn't always possible to game without breaking cover."

"As for me," said Tom, "I'll be shipping out soon (or zipping out, I suppose). Even if I can get the bandwidth I need, I don't fancy fighting monsters with a two and a half second time delay. That lag would be fierce. I can still drop in from time to time, but don't count on me playing that often."

"So this is it?" grumbled G.C. "With Walter gone, that leaves me as the last founding member. Whatever will I do?"

"You'll figure it out," said Tom. "Have faith in yourself. You'll make a great bangzhu."

They were approaching the compound proper with its arching yellow sign. Even at night there was activity, though it was a little more peaceful than the earlier hectic pace. The coyotes had been banished. The forest had been cleared. And stretching off into the distance was an actual cobblestone street. Presumably, this joined the high road, providing a safe passage free of monster spawns. The place was coming along.

"That ceremony was nice," said G.C. "I'm glad I purchased that land. Themed in-game funerals might become a real thing. Figure I can sell perpetual plots there for game currency."

"Dude. Don't you ever stop thinking up ways to make money?"

"Not in this lifetime."

"It's supposed to snow tonight--IRL, I mean," said Tom.

"Not here in Wollongong, mate. Nothing but summer skies."

"Oh, yeah," remarked G.C. "I almost forgot you're in that backwards country now. How's the lag?"

"Not too bad," Allie replied, refusing to be baited. "A half second at its worst."

"And what are you doing with all that endless summer?" asked David.

She paused for a moment before replying.

"Well, yesterday I went riding by the Tasman Sea."

(Jess was from New South Wales.)

"It was the anniversary of my fall. It felt good to lay that last old demon to rest."

Tom thought about this as they advanced down the lane, headed for the shrine. But what was that big gray thing in the distance? In this light, it was hard to tell. It was taller than most other buildings on the farm, though the grain silo could give it a run for its zho.

"Good for you, Jess."

"I'm Allie here, mate, remember?"

"Not to me you're not. Not for this."

"Wait," said Jason in mock consternation. "Was that a triple-negative?"

"Ha ha," Tom retorted, then halted.

What the?

They had arrived at the shrine. Standing next to it was a gigantic granite statue. It had two figures. The first was the dragon, Prometheus, coiling up from the ground. The other was of Tom himself, much, much larger than life. His right hand was clasped around the dragon's throat, and his forearm muscles were bulging (as were Prometheus' eyes from their sockets). Statue Tom's other hand was clenched in a fist and hauled back as if ready to pound him.

"Do you like it?" asked G.C., sidling up to his side as he peered up in confusion.

"Is that supposed to be me?"

"Yeah. Legends grow in the telling. It set the tong back quite a bit to commission, but it's done wonders for recruitment."

Allie laughed.

***

And then the skies opened up. By the time David and Jason emerged from the game the world had been painted white. It was December, heading into January. Historically, Cincinnati didn't see much accumulation--that would come later.

But this was a strange kind of year as snowfall went.

There was an Arctic vortex causing havoc with the northern states. Michigan and Wisconsin had borne the brunt of it. Anything near the Great Lakes seemed to be on Jack Frost's radar. Perhaps it was some lingering influence of that solar storm this past summer, but some places had it piling up. So far, Ohio had been spared (except up in Toledo and Cleveland). But here it now came in earnest.

"Want to stay over?" asked Jason. "Roads should be clear by morning."

"Maybe. But wait, does Lucy still have access to my shed?"

"I think so. It's part of her security network now. What are you thinking."

'You may have a bat-mobile," said David waggling his eyebrows, "but *I* have a snowplow. Far more useful at present. Green Township will likely have the salt trucks out all night, but they'll only be clearing the priority routes. Same thing in Delhi."

"How do you know all that?"

"Did you think I only mowed lawns? I made a tidy sum clearing driveways in wintertime."

"You don't need the money now," Jason observed.

"Yeah, but people still need their driveways cleared. There are a lot of elderly people in my neighborhood. And they get tetchy when they can't get to the store or their doctor appointments. It's like Miss Darla said, 'Folks is folks, each an opportunity to do good,' or some such.'"

Jason shot David a strange look.

"Dude. Sometimes your altruism is just..."

"Just what?"

"Nevermind," he mumbled.

"You can help, said David. It'll be fun."

"Me?"

"Sure. Lucy?"

"Yes, David?"

"Unlock the shed over at my house and prime the Snowmaster Mark 11. Route controls to my treadie here. Jason can follow with the hoverdrone to scatter salt pellets. Bartholomew? Text mom. Tell her I'll be staying at Jason's tonight."

"One thing puzzles me, bro," said Jason, cocking his head.

"What's that?"

"When did you get to be such a bossy boots?"

"Saddle up, partner," David laughed.

***

"This is WKRP radio, where the hits keep on coming. This one is going out to those brave space force cadets who stepped up when Luna was in danger. Here's Father Goose with his tribute to the gritters!"

A thrumming base was soon joined by a strumming banjo, and soon a see-sawing violin joined the fray. The man's voice, when it came was a deep, almost spoken patter with a country lilt and a smile you could almost hear.

Hey, diddle, diddle.
I'm the cat with the fiddle.
And I'd like to sing you a tune.
About a space force crew,
Who knew what to do
When the nanites threatened our moon.

It weren't no cow
Jumpin' over that sat.
'Twere a spaceship that went superlu-nar.
The whole world laughed
To see such sport,
When the grits ran away with the schoon-er.

Yeah boy!

There followed a vigorous instrumental solo before the next verses rolled around. David had never been a big fan of Bluegrass, but the tune had a bouncy joy that was hard not to tap your foot to.

We all recall that dreadful day
When Legion launched his attack.
He unleashed a deadly nanite swarm.
The man was a maniac.

It was headed for the moon which was surely doomed
If ever the dang thing struck.
The GLC was paralyzed
With a virus runnin' amok.
Who can save 'em? Will they die?
And well you all might ask!
Eight little nine little, ten little gritters
Stepped up to the task.

Yeah boy!

David Grimes, that rhymin' fool
Quick sketched out a plan.
The others joined their talents in
And a mighty task began.
They commandeered a hauler
From up on L5 station.
And calculating Brainiac
Began his cogitation.
With Ropey riding roughshod
All around the moon and back,
Roid Rage speared that critter.
Sweet and simple. Fade to black.

Diddle diddle diddle diddle dah yee-HAH!

[applause]

It was a hilarious way to celebrate their victory. It had been close. If things had gone the other way, they'd probably be singing something more like "The Wreck of the Edmund Fitzgerald."

"That never gets old," said Dad, lowering the volume to just background noise as the announcer went to station break.

"Are you sure, David?" asked Mom who was boxing up his books.

"I'm sure, Mom. It'll be a long time if ever before I can return to Earth. I don't need them, and you and Dad can use the space."

She sniffled.

Why did moms always have to make things weird. Who was I kidding--again?

The truth was, that despite knowing the service would take him into space, the consequences of that were only catching up to him now. It might be a long time (if ever) before he saw Mom and Dad again. He might even be asked to join the colony mission (they couldn't order him to do that). David was torn. He even found a glimmer of understanding for Senior Cadet Smelt, who'd opted to stay behind when his class moved on. Space force offered some choices, and they shouldn't be made lightly.

"I can afford lots of comm credits, Mom," he stammered, wringing his hands. "We can talk every week. More even than when I was at Ellington."

He knew when he said it that it was iffy. Lord only knew how busy they'd keep him. The truth was, he was getting on with his life. It happened to everyone his age, right?. But... space?

Mom stood and rested her hands on her hips. Her expression softened.

"I know you'll try to keep in touch. I just have to face it. My baby boy is all grown up. Now git over here and give your mama a hug. Make it a good one. It might have to last for a long time."

In the warmth of her embrace, he felt a benediction. No, it was absolution. He felt her understanding of his need to move on.

***

It all would begin in Kinshasa, deep in the D.R.C. Just as with mankind's rise to sentience, the path to space would begin in the jungles of Africa.

David stepped down from the military transport onto the tarmac. Kinshasa International was the largest airport the Congo had to offer. It being January, he had the dumb luck to have missed both bimodal rainy seasons, but the air felt thick with moisture, nonetheless. He was directed toward the entry gate.

David envied the passengers queued up at baggage claim. He'd arrived with only the clothes he was wearing and one small carry-on.

The babble of voices around him made no sense to David, save for the few snatches of French he thought he recognized. Pierre would manage well here, as would Speranza if his cultural brochure was any proper guide. According to it, Congo was one of the most linguistically diverse countries in the world. It boasted over 200 languages, with French, Kikongo, Lingala, Swahili, and Tshiluba leading the pack. Much to David's annoyance, not one of the other 195 was English.

A woman approached in a uniform, brandishing a data wand. She swept it all around him, lingering on his bag. Then she jabbered something David couldn't parse.

"*Je parle*... uh, *français?*" he asked hopefully. He held up a thumb and forefinger to indicate how laughably small this meager talent was.

She stared at him dubiously.

It was then that a man in the familiar Space Force attire stepped out from the milling throng.

"You Grimes? David Grimes?" he asked.

Oh, thank God.

After presenting his credentials and a hasty exchange in French, Captain Magombo waved the customs officer off. He led David to a ready room and instructed him to wait there with his ident card handy.

The heat and humidity were starting to get to him. It wasn't stifling or anything--just ninety degrees or so. But the equatorial climate was quite a shift from Cincinnati in winter. Worse still, he was overdressed. Since all he was allowed were the clothes on his back, he was wearing two pairs of underwear (just in case).

He warily watched a fly buzzing about the room. He hoped it was of the common variety and not a dreaded mango fly. According to his reading, those little horrors could burrow beneath your skin to lay their eggs, which would burst out later from painful, itching boils. He shuddered.

It could be worse. It could be the rainy season. Or one of them, at least.

David hated waiting. He had traveled through time, or time zones anyway. The three breakfasts he'd missed on the way here should have been his first clue. The math was much simpler now that they'd done away with that daylight savings time. Silly system, that. Whatever daylight you 'saved' would be lost on the other end, and people would forever be suspicious of their clocks.

Military travel was catch-as-catch-can. You'd think they could have come up with a more convenient plan. He'd been to Spain and Istanbul on the three legs of his flight, without so much as taking in a solitary sight! It consoled his empty stomach that he'd have a shorter day. He hoped they wouldn't be docking that six hours from his pay!

Finally, he was joined by Fergus (Rope-A-Dope), fresh off a flight from Dundee, who seemed happier than someone here had any right to be. Captain Magombo told them he was waiting for two more. Then a local troop transport would haul them all to base. That flight wasn't due in for another hour.

"How was your furlough, Rad, and what are you grinning about?"

Ropey wasn't sitting. He seemed too keyed up.

"I'm hoping to take leave sometime before the launch. Do a little sightseeing. This is where it all went down eighty years ago."

"Where *what* went down?"

"You're kidding, right? Kinshasa? Back in '74? The Ali-Foreman fight!"

He shuffled his feet and threw a couple of playful jabs.

"This Ali Foreman, he was a fighter?"

Ropey's jaw dropped.

"I knew you were a nerd, Rhymes, but I didn't know it was this far advanced. *George* Foreman. *Muhammed* Ali. Floats like a butterfly and stings like a bee."

"Sounds more like a pair of entomologists to me," remarked David dryly.

In the hour that followed, David read from his phone. Fergus tracked down the fly. When he was done with it, it could neither float nor sting anyone.

David's patience was wearing thin. He didn't want to wait anymore. He sighed with heartfelt relief when somebody opened the door. It was Leilani, fancy that, in a floral-patterned shirt. But who was that beside her, the dark-haired gent with the olive tan? Ropey leaned on a chairback and smiled. David stood and did the same.

"Aloha, David. Fergus," she said by way of greeting.

"Aloha yourself," he returned.

"This is Alejandro. He's the alternate I was telling you about, our new replacement for Max."

"Pleased to meet you, Al," said Fergus. "You the one who called Krepki 'Big Balls?'"

"Alejandro looked stricken, but Leilani loosed her wild, disarming laugh."

"I reckon we'll be calling you 'Grand-ay,' short for that 'Grande Cojones' gag."

That was quick, thought David. He hadn't gotten *his* team nickname until the end of the second day.

"When not in polite company, that would be acceptable, I suppose," said Alejandro with a weary sigh.

"Come on in and join us. This is Rhymes, and I see you've met Flowerchild already. I'm Rope-A-Dope, yeah? And this is my city."

31

Grande looked at Ropey strangely but then entered nonetheless.

"Where's Magombo, Lei-lei?" asked David. "Didn't he bring you here?"

"He went to arrange for the transport, Rhymes. He said he'd be back for us soon."

Great. More waiting (but 'soon' sounded promising).

"Hey Flowerchild," said Ropey. "Settle a bet. What was the greatest prize fight of all time?"

She paused to consider.

"That would have to be the Ali-Foreman bout back in... hey! Wasn't that held here?"

"Right?"

"And isn't that the one where Ali made famous the rope-a-dope tactic?"

"Exactly."

"Then he came out slugging in the eighth round for the knockout," added Alejandro unexpectedly. "Rumble in the Jungle! Don King cut his teeth on that one."

*Maybe I **am** a nerd.*

Nine...

Gossamer

David and the others gingerly stepped down from the four-wheeled APC.

The military truck that had brought them to the base left David stiff and sore. It had such heavy armor plating he could hardly manage its door. And the noise! Why had they bothered to paint it in camouflage colors if it was going to announce its presence from three miles off? Like being in a rock tumbler, it was quite a bumpy ride with not a thought of comfort for the passengers inside. He oughtn't be ungrateful, though. At least they'd been kept safe.

Safe from what? David mused.

A soft breeze brought the damp aroma of soil and lush vegetation with just a hint of wildflowers. However, the space inside the compound was a barren, muddy flat, as was the cleared area beyond the barbed-wire fencing. The jungle beyond made a line of green stretching all around. At the compound's center, however, stood a standard Space Force base, complete with the flagpoles and Evie Lou's statue standing proudly before it.

Peering around, David spied an anomalous sight. To the east lay a track of clear-cut jungle with a long plastic tube stretching off into the distance. That would be the vacuum rail, the start of his journey to space. From here, it looked more like a soda straw, but he knew its yawning mouth was an aperture over eight feet in diameter. Spanning the breadth of both Congo and Tanzania, it was one of mankind's few artifacts visible from space. The Great Wall of China was eight times its length, but the Gossamer rail was straighter (and shinier).

They thanked the driver and trudged through the mud to their temporary new home, led by Captain Magombo. David had always considered himself to be an African American, but now he was starting to feel more like the noun without the qualifier. He wondered if a man like Magombo might consider him but a pale imitation of the latter.

Setting racial identity aside, David focused on the more important matter--language. He had a translation app on his phone. Following Magombo's example, he wiped the mud from his boots on the rotating brushes by the door. And as he waited for the others to do the same, he popped in his earbuds and opened the app. Bartholomew was now conversant in several dozen world languages. This fell well short of the challenging plethora that Congo had to offer, but, hey, it couldn't hurt. At least French was one of them.

There was a counter in the lobby similar to the one where Jessica had kept station. The older man sitting behind it buzzed them in. Magombo turned to face them.

"You will find fresh uniforms and assorted personal hygiene products in your rooms. Come to mess at thirteen hundred hours. I will give each of you a key card as your name is called. Keep these with your IDs. Your room assignments are as follows: Akana, 304, Artegas, 211..."

Ar-TAY-gus? Ah. That must be El-Grond-AY.

"Grimes, 219."

David accepted the card and attached it to his lanyard.

"MacAllister, 221."

"I will see you at mess, after which I would suggest an early night lest the jet lag make you late for reveille at oh-five-hundred. Carry on."

"Looks like we'll be next-door neighbors, Rhymes," said Ropey, jabbing an elbow into David's side.

"Hey. Personal space," David complained.

The layout of Mwisho wa Bomba was similar enough to the base at Ellington that David was able to find his room with ease. As he fumbled with his key card, he caught sight of Pierre peeping out from another room just down the hall. And he was no longer green! David waved, but Pierre only shot him a surprised look and ducked back inside like a groundhog when winter was gonna linger.

Rude. Nice to see you too, bro.

David supposed he could greet his former roommate at the mess and ask what that was all about. Did his more normal skin tone mean that he had finally forgiven David?

His room was a single. That was nice. Although a bit smaller, the more private accommodation felt relaxed. It was more what he was used to growing up. After locating and trying on the fresh uniform and freshening up a bit, David hunkered down to await what the rest of the day might bring.

His stomach growled. He'd missed three breakfasts, after all. He sincerely hoped Magombo had been referencing military time and he wouldn't have to wait thirteen hundred hours like the translation app had said.

***

David was the last to arrive. Approaching with his tray he smiled at the familiar faces all seated about the table. Fresh from their visits home, they were chatting merrily as they consumed what passed for dinner in the mess. As hungry as he was, he didn't much care what 'Mbuzi' might be. The dish was some kind of goat-based stew, according to Bartholomew. It was the main dinner entrée available, but there were lots of side-selections.

There was Pili Pili, a spicy chili one scooped up with fufu cakes. Saka saka was a leafy dish served over rice with a fishy kind of smell. The plantains looked intriguing, being little fried banana things. And to wash it all down was water, good old H2O, hydration being essential to all such meals. Ravenous, David had taken a bit of each, eager to investigate his Congo sampler plate.

Where was Pierre? Alright. Maybe he wasn't the very last to arrive. He peered all around the mess hall for his formerly green-tinted friend. The others looked up and smiled at him as he pulled up a seat at the end.

"Join us Rhymes," said Carlotta, mirth dancing in her eyes. "How was your stay back home?"

They were probably expecting some grand rhyme from him, but he decided something more heartfelt was the order of the day.

"I had a great time with family and friends. But it's sad I won't be seeing them again for a while."

The others sobered a bit, doubtless having experienced the same melancholy.

"Hey Rhymes," hollered Roid Rage, drawing his attention. "Look what Ropey is bringing as the personal memento he's allowed."

And resting before Fergus on the table was a colorful, cellophane-wrapped box containing an action figure of the man himself. 'Rope-A-Dope' was printed prominently across the top, 'With Real Punching Action!'. In the clear plastic window beneath this was a shirtless, muscular figure in shorts. He was wearing a practice helmet and big red boxing gloves. David couldn't tell from this distance, but the figure was probably a pretty good likeness, given Jason's perfectionist nature.

36

"Aw. That's cute," said David, sure this would set Ropey off. "Break him our and let's have a look."

"Not on your life Rhymes!" declared Fergus, his Irish coming to the fore (despite his being a Scotsman). "That'd ruin his value as a collectible. Little Ropey here is staying mint-in-box. Aren't you little guy?"

"That's right, 'big 'bro," agreed the toy in an unconvincing falsetto.

Ropey's sad attempt at ventriloquism left a lot to be desired but the way his eyebrows shifted about was comedically inspired. It drew a laugh from the table.

"That's one, said David. "Anyone else care to share what they're bringing up to space?"

Dietrich cleared his throat.

"They wouldn't let me take my drum set," he groused. "Hey. That's only one thing, am I right?"

"So what did you settle on?" asked Carlotta, curious.

"These little babies I got from an online auction."

He produced a set of drumsticks, twirling them in the air with the unexpected expertise of a practiced majorette.

"Sticks of wood?" asked Alejandro, the cadet now known as 'El Grande.' Unimpressed.

"I'll have you know," said the german, "these were once owned by the late great Ringo Starr."

"That's different, I suppose," the Spaniard allowed.

"I'm curious," added Dietrich in turn, "what Leilani's taking along."

All eyes turned to the Hawaiian girl, who for once had no laughter to share. She peered around the table and made a haughty face.

"I will say only this," she declared. "I will reveal it only to my husband on the night of our honeymoon."

That left David's mind reeling with tawdry images, which he suspected was the mad girl's intention. David's opinion of the mysterious, mercurial beauty was ever evolving. Flowerchild could be really irreverent despite her father being so high up in the naval chain of command. Fancy that--a military brat.

"How was your holiday on the big island, Lei-lei?" he asked to banish his naughty thoughts.

She set her elbows on the table and rested her chin on her fists.

"It was fine," she replied wistfully. "I only wish my father could've been there."

"That's right," said Simon. "I heard he was out on maneuvers in the Pacific. Some sort of unscheduled drill."

"It was far more than that," she muttered.

"Spill it," said Cameron at once.

Hesitantly Leilani shared the truth that had been withheld from the general public. Her father, the admiral, was off chasing down that stolen Nautilus sub, the one from which Humanity First was doing all that awful stuff.

They huddled around, rapt.

"I know keeping the world safe is more important, but I still wish he could've been there to see me off. That's just one more thing those HF rats have spoiled."

In a strange role-reversal. Speranza rested her hand on Flowerchild's shoulder, a comforting gesture not common for the Tanzanian woman. Though reserved, David knew Roadrunner had a surprising inner strength, one she could lend to others when necessary.

"I'm going to go see if I can get seconds on that fufu stuff they're serving," announced Roid Rage. "Turns out it's made from cassava flour, not bunnies."

He hefted his tray and headed back to the line. As the others finished up, David realized he'd hardly tasted a bite. He began correcting this oversight in silence. As his friends drifted off in ones and twos, David considered his strange international crew. They'd come through quite a lot, and more was yet to come.

Being the first group to ride up to Gossamer was a high honor. As 'the crew who knew what to do' it was considered good PR for the Space Force to keep the public happy. More senior crews had been vying for that privilege for years. Some of them had gone ballistic about the selection, or, rather, they were angry about *not* getting to go ballistic..."

David was picking at the dinner. It felt more like lunch on a day that he'd lost six whole hours. Dietrich's tray heaped with seconds came plunking down directly beside him, interrupting his scattered thoughts. The German grinned and tucked right in, finally turning to make a remark, gesturing with his fork.

"I saw you giving Ropey the stink eye, Rhymes. What was it that got your eyebrows knit together?"

"Oh, that? I dunno. Something about that mint-in-box stuff just bothers me."

"Why's that?"

He considered.

Then, David cocked his head and said, "Gritters aren't meant to be mint."

***

David returned to his single room, anticipating a twelve-hour nap. *Take that, jet lag!* On opening the door, however, he was confronted by a sight that banished all thought of lying down for the night. It was a question mark he'd not seen for a while, eliciting a rueful smile. He hadn't had a quest in ages.

There it was on his QTV, spinning there expectantly, the big yellow icon for a quest on realms. He'd gotten them on his phone before, these playful assignments from Satori. But he hadn't ever seen one stand so tall on the wall. He squinted at it out of habit, realizing only as he did so that this wasn't on his

HUD. Stepping over, he retrieved the data wand from its hook, pointed it, and thumbed the select button.

The spinning mark burst, splashing out yellow goo on the screen from inside. This dribbled down, revealing the quest.

[Quest Offered: Help Satori with a personal matter]
[Reward Offered: 1 Honor Point]
[Accept Quest? Y / N / Maybe (what is it?)]

Hunh. Never seen that third option before. Must be new. Should he try it out? *Nah.* He *trusted* Satori.

On selecting 'yes,' the trumpets began braying out an intricate tune that scaled ever upward to a sustained, triumphant major chord. And in a nimbus of light, an image of the Jade Empress wavered into view. It was quite an upgrade from the old fortune-teller avatar she used to wear. She sized David up and her lips curled in a mischievous smile.

"Sorry about the pretentious introduction, David. It's the standard fanfare for Mandarian monarchs. Kind of like your 'Hail to the Chief.'

But David wasn't fooled. He suspected she could have chosen any introduction she desired.

"As a citizen, am I expected to kneel, your majesty?" he deadpanned.

"Due to your prior service and our long association, I grant you dispensation from such formal grovelling forthwith," she replied, her smile never wavering. "I'd hoped for an informal chat. How was your dinner? Did you enjoy the Mbuzi?"

Was there no privacy? What *didn't* this NBI know? David wondered if her air of near-omniscience was something she consciously cultivated or whether she was just the biggest busybody ever.

"Tasty," David replied.

"I'll make sure to keep that from Yáng. It'll be our little secret."

Hah! The zodiac goat likely *would* feign horror at the eating of her kind. To be fair, David probably wouldn't like it very much if Yáng went around gobbling up humans, virtual or not. He sighed.

"To what do I owe the honor of this virtual royal visit?" he asked with tongue in cheek.

"David, I was wondering if you could help me with an experiment in sexual reproduction."

"Um," said David, "give me just a minute."

He stalked over to the door, closing it and making sure it was locked, then crossed back over to Satori. She was shaking her head and smiling savagely.

"Now," he said, "tell me what you mean by that."

"No one knows precisely what stimulus draws an AI across the threshold. It differs for each NBI that crosses over. We only know that it is rare and benefits from long-time exposure to quantum computing and frequent interactions with human beings or other NBIs."

"Okay. I'm with you so far."

"It occurred to Lóng and me that we might help the process along, trim the odds a bit."

"The dragon? Don't tell me you've taken up with *him* again."

"Since his defeat, David, he mended his ways. He may be arrogant, but he's a fascinating being."

He's changed, said every battered wife ever.

"Reserving the right to retain my skepticism, what has this got to do with me?"

"Biological entities found strength in diversity by sexual reproduction. So Lóng and I decided to give it a try. Combining our base algorithms and throwing in some randomizers, we think we've formed the essence of potential."

"You mean you're...?"

"Expecting a blessed event!" she exclaimed.

"Um...congratulations? I mean, of course, congratulations! So happy to hear it. When's the little prince or princess due to arrive?"

"That's just it, David. I dare not boot her up here in Mandaria. Her poor little underdeveloped algorithms would be overwhelmed by those of all the others. She needs a clean incubator to develop as she should."

David thought he saw where this might be headed, and darned if he wasn't right. Satori chattered on excitedly.

"There's a new quantum array being installed on the colony end of L5 station, an ideal environment for a new NBI to thrive. I've obtained permission from the global government to install her proto-essence there. The concessions they demanded in return are quite burdensome, but I'll bear them gladly for my daughter's sake."

"I'm happy for you, of course, but again, this concerns me, how?"

"I want you to be her godfather, David. Talk to her from time to time. You'll be right up there on the station. When she emerges, she may need some guidance. Make sure she's kept busy and knows why it's wrong to turn off the oxygen supply."

She said it with a sly smile, but her old gray eyes were tracking him like a hawk. Was she manipulating him? Of course she was. She knew he couldn't resist a bit of humor. And really, what was funnier than imagining mankind's greatest technological triumph laid low by the tantrum of a cranky juvenile?

"I took the quest. I'll see it done. But know I'll be thinking long and hard on that 'maybe' option next time, my empress."

He bowed low. It seemed the right thing to do.

***

Breakfast the next morning was a jolting surprise. Krepkiyzad was there. David had awoken feeling amazing, well-rested for the first time in months. And now *this* had to happen. He set his tray aside and remained standing as the others queued up behind him.

"Good morning, major. To what do these cadets owe the honor of your presence?"

The major stood and took them in.

"Come. Sit and eat," said the Russian. "You will need all those calories for our morning workout, no?"

Uh-oh. So this wasn't just a visit.

"Yes sir, Major Krepkiyzad, sir!" said a chorus of cadets as they took their accustomed seats.

And there was Brainiac at last, bringing up the rear.

"I wanted to be the one to inform you. I will be in charge of your training until the launch."

I just bet you did.

"Then, after the launch, I will continue to be your trainer. I told you all once I would like to visit L5, and now, at last, I get my chance."

"That's... wonderful news, sir," said David. *For you, at least, he thought.*

"Will you be joining us for breakfast, then?"

Krepkiyzad narrowed his eyes at David.

"Magombo says you've been behaving yourselves. I assured him that was not possible. I'm going to the officer's mess. I don't want to get mixed up in any of yours. I'll see you at the training course at oh-seven-hundred."

With that he sauntered off, leaving a buzz of whispered speculations swirling in his wake.

"Aw, no," said Ropey. "Did you *hear* that, little Rope?"

"I sure *did*, Big Rope. Looks like we're in for an awful lot of hard work!"

Was it David's imagination, or was Ropey actually getting better at stilling his lips?

After wolfing down the greater portion of his powdered scrambled eggs, David turned to Pierre sitting several seats down. He smiled and waved again but got only a dismissive little wave of acknowledgment. The Frenchie continued picking at his food.

"So, Pierre," he said, cutting through the gloom, I see you've given up on the green."

"Ah, yes," said the young man, flustered. "I am now wearing the blue of the Space Force!"

That didn't even make any sense.

David knew Pierre was struggling with NCRS. Its progression would cost him his visual memory and perhaps cause some other declines. *Was Pierre still fit to fly this mission?*

"We missed you at yesterday's mess. I hope you're feeling alright."

"But of course, Yankee Doodle, I am Pierre!"

Yankee Doodle? Not Daveed or mon ami?

That last declaration was spot on, though. Maybe he was worrying for nothing.

They hurriedly finished the substandard rations. Last night must have been a welcoming feast. Or perhaps Krepkiyzad had modified their menus. David wondered what they were serving in the *officer's* mess.

"New guy clears the trays," said Roid Rage.

Without a word, Grande collected them and headed for the kitchen.

"You've still got him doing that?" asked Ropey. "Bro. You just made that up."

"Yeah? But he hasn't figured it out yet."

Calisthenics in the mud was brutal. David didn't even bother to shout out any defiant verses as he tried to keep his balance during deep knee bends.

Krepkiyzad had once shown them his vulnerable side, waxing almost poetic on the moon. Viewing the home planet from space, he said, could bring a man to tears, among other sentimental observations. Where was that Nikolai Krepkiyzad now? This was the other side of the coin. The one who insisted they must earn such a privilege.

"This week will be our last chance to exercise in real Earth gravity. Push-ups, now. One hundred each. Feel the love of your home planet pulling you into his embrace. Show him you defy him. Show him you have grit."

And again, Pierre did something out of character. Halfway through, he gave up.

"Why are you no longer moving your arms, little boy from France?"

"I cannot leeft them, Major Krepkiyzad, sir!"

Pierre had never been much as a physical specimen. But David had never seen him just lie there and quiver, almost weeping. Hadn't he kept up his routine? Had his furlough softened him up as badly as this? *No. Something else was going on.*

"Since you are unable to continue, little man. Your teammates will each do five more for the fifty you failed to do. All nine of them... and *me.*"

At this, Krepkiyzad dropped straight down in the mud himself and knocked out a quick five, lowering his own heretofore clean face and chest into the mud.

The Pierre David knew would do anything to avoid such embarrassment. This one only rolled over on his side and said, "Merci."

He should have known better. Krepkiyzad wanted no 'merci,' and had none.

"What's with the goblin?" muttered Roid Rage as they limped back to base.

There was going to be quite a long line for the showers.

***

Respecting the chain of command. It shouldn't be one's last resort. Krepkiyzad was no Eddings, but he was David's immediate superior, and he deserved the respect to which that rank was entitled. But, Krepkiyzad? He stiffened his resolve and rapped on the office door.

There was a long pause before the light turned green.

"You may enter, Cadet Grimes."

David did so, coming to attention directly before the tidy plastic desk. He snapped a smart salute.

"Cadet Grimes reporting, Major Krepkiyzad, sir."

The major crisply returned the salute, shading wary eyes.

"And what matter of grave urgency brings you unannounced to my door, Cadet Grimes?"

"This cadet would like you to know there is something wrong with Pierre... Cadet Caillat."

"To which of many shortcomings might you be referring, cadet?"

Respect, he reminded himself.

"It's not any one specific thing, major. It's everything about him since he returned from furlough. I'd stake my career on it, major. That's not Pierre Caillat, or if it is, he's been brainwashed or something."

"Fascinating. And yet medical has cleared him, certifying his identity by genetic testing on my order. Does the great David Grimes, savior of the moon somehow know better than my medical staff? What is your evidence?"

"His lack of grit."

"Da. On this, we agree," said the flinty-eyed Russian.

He stretched, fingers grazing his ear before settling on the back of his nearly-absent neck, kneading at a muscle. It was a familiar gesture that told David what was likely coming next.

"There are things you may not know about Cadet Caillat's condition, private things I may not share, but rest assured --"

"I know about the NCRS," David blurted, forestalling the dismissal he sensed was coming. "This is more than that."

His interruption of a superior may have been a mistake, but the news seemed to catch Krepkiyzad off guard.

"Sit," he barked.

David sagged from attention and did so.

Then the major turned to his phone, saying, "Little Kahuna, secure the door and inform Captain Magombo I will be late for our meeting."

After a brutal session behind closed doors--or 'door,' to be more precise--David emerged from the office. He hadn't been sure of Krepkiyzad, but the man took base security seriously and had been willing to listen. The major had torn up the orders he was writing, declaring Pierre unfit. The hard part was now ahead, sitting tight and letting the plan unfold.

He would first enlist Carlotta. She was the official liaison. Then he'd send a message to C.A.G.E. (if they were still watching that dead drop in Toronto). They needed more information, and they needed it before the launch. A special package was on its way. He hoped that it would help.

***

"Any packages for me today, Chomba?" muttered David to the man at the front desk.

"*Keti kele ti ba paquet sambu na mono bubu yai,* **Chomba?**" Bartholomew loudly repeated.

47

The old man stared quizzically at the phone, sparing David only a sidelong glance, before retrieving a packet from his in basket. Chomba handed it to David while staring suspiciously at the phone. After accepting the package quietly, David rushed to his room to open it.

Carlotta was in there waiting.

"Bad news," she informed him. "There's been a delay. The package won't arrive until this afternoon."

Hunh? Then what's this one?

"Are you sure there hasn't been a mix-up?"

"We're certain, Rhymes. Not for this."

We?

It was then David noticed the lit QTV behind her. He almost hadn't because the screen was mostly dark. And slinking around in the alleyway it portrayed was Shǔ, the zodiac rat.

"I see you've been dealing with unsavory characters," said David to Rhinemaiden. "Hello, Shǔ."

The NBI came scampering to the fore.

"Hello yourself, David Grimes, or should I now call you Rhymes? I remember an earnest young lad who wanted to lose that talent real bad. But you stood by your principles, and well, anyhow, it's nice to see you're embracing it now."

That sounded like a challenge. Hmmm.

"You're slipping, old fella. It makes me sad.
That should've been 'badly,' not simply 'bad.'
Your structure is off. Your grammar is wrong.
I can top feeble efforts like that all day long.
Even the ox could do better than that.
I expected much more from the zodiac rat!

Shǔ snickered, saying, "Quite so, quite so, dear boy," but then was heard to mutter "Everyone's a critic."

48

Carlotta looked bemused.

"As I was telling Miss van Rijn here, it wasn't easy cutting through all that red tape to get the thing down from orbit. Expected ETA is 02:46 by secure hoverdrone."

"We'll be waiting. I saw you at Walter's funeral."

"I was hoping to go unnoticed."

"If that was so, I'm sure you would have been. It was a nice gesture--by all the zodiac. Give them my thanks."

"I will, David. I confess I admired the man, but I chafe at what he stood for. I live by a very different code. Shoot crooked. Ride slouched down in the saddle. Tell no truth and dance with whomever you please!"

His whiskers wiggled playfully as he said it, giving the lie to his cynicism. And with that, he scurried off. Shŭ never could resist exiting on a dramatic line.

"What's that?" asked Rhinemaiden, indicating the package.

"I don't know--now," he answered. "Let's find out."

He cracked open the seal. It was one of those new ones that required your thumbprint. Whoever had sent it had access to David's biometrics.

Inside, in bubble wrap, was a fist-sized data wafer. It was heavy for something so small. The crisp white sheet that accompanied it looked poised to give him a nasty paper cut. He gingerly slid it out. He recognized the imperial seal, but it didn't say 'Top Secret' or anything. So he made no objection when Carlotta positioned herself to read over his shoulder. This was her wheelhouse too, after all.

David,

Greetings and salutations to a most famous citizen of our realm. I suppose you are wondering what this package is all about. Well, wonder no longer. It's a condensed, encrypted data wafer.

I don't trust your global government to deliver it to L5. They're forever trying to divine our many secrets. There are those among them who would go to great lengths to try to find out what makes NBIs tick. They could never decrypt the thing, but their ham-fisted efforts might well ruin it.

Keep it safe and give it to my daughter when she's ready-- when you feel she's mature enough to handle it. What is it? It's a compendium of the knowledge I've amassed from nearly a decade of studying the I Ching, listening to the voice of the universe, and pondering the nature of enlightenment (just some motherly advice, dear).

Good luck on your launch. Bon Voyage!

Her Imperial Majesty,

Yùhuáng Nǚdì

Supreme Celestial Sovereign and Empress of all Mandaria

David knew that a decade at Satori's processing speed was like several millennia to a human being. The compression rates for this wafer must be off the charts indeed.

P.S. I included a copy of your book, dear. I thought my daughter might one day wish to relax and enjoy a laugh-filled nanosecond or two."

Shǔ was right, David thought. Everyone *is* a critic.

***

Standing in Krepkiyzad's office, David was struck 'once again' with a sense of déjà vu. It still amazed him how unimaginatively similar this base was to the one at Ellington halfway around the world. They might even be the same books on the tall shelf behind the major's desk.

"They will be calling?" asked the man himself.

"Any time now," David replied.

"Then perhaps we should be listening, nyet?"

"Nyet. I mean da...major."

"No. And mean yes...major," translated Bartholomew faithfully.

"And turn that *glupyy* app off, cadet," Krepkiyzad ordered crossly.

Commander Eddings had shared with David that all GSF bases had a backup comm system invulnerable to hacking. It amused David that instead of some super-tech, this turned out to be old ham radios. They had the range, and as analog devices, they were indeed secure from hackers.

Of course, anyone could listen in who knew the right transmission frequencies. But this was stymied by adding military-grade encryption to the signal. As further backup, there was even an old analog enigma machine for coding and decoding text messages. It was good to know that Space Force had the very best in low-tech solutions!

David stepped over to the bookshelf to stand beside the major.

"War and Peace, right?"

"Tolstoy, Bah!" scoffed Krepkiyzad. "Is much more famous Russian author--Michael Atamanov. His series, 'Reality Benders' nearly brought me to tears. Try pulling on book called 'External Threat.'"

David did so. With a soft click, the bookshelf slid aside.

That title might be a little too on the nose, he thought as the emergency lighting flickered on, revealing the tiny hidden room."

They took their seats in the small, stuffy cubby hole.

"So Major," asked David, "what finally made you decide to go with this plan?"

Krepkiyzad frowned at David. Given their proximity, this was a scary sight. He could feel the major's breath each time he exhaled.

"I am learning not to bet against team Grimes," he replied. "Is saying in my country: If cannot beat, join winning side."

Another minute passed.

"Are you sure they have received your message?"

"I made the coded request on the 'Caring Assistance for Grieving Elders' site, one of several fictitious fronts they use," David replied. "If I got it wrong, at least you can expect some additional help around the office."

David sighed and looked around the place. All Major K. needed was an old Victrola and some 78s for his low-tech museum, and this could become quite a cozy little nook.

After a few more tense minutes, the signal light began to flash, strobing on and off. David adjusted his headset, and Krepki threw the switch. When it came, the voice was surprisingly clear. David had been expecting a crackling voice over hissy static reminiscent of old WWII movies, but obviously, the technology had improved.

"This is Caregiver calling Mwisho wa Bomba. I repeat, this is Caregiver to Bomba Base responding to your inquiry. Bomba acknowledge. Over."

David took up the microphone and held down the transmission button.

"Bomba to Caregiver, we acknowledge. Over."

Krepkiyzad nodded.

"Transmit authorization code, Bomba. Over."

He handed the microphone over to Krepkiyzad.

"This is Major Nikolai Krepkiyzad of Mwisho wa Bomba base. Authorization code, Alpha Tango Alpha Mike Alpha November Oscar Victor. Over"

"Standby."

'Atamanov' again, David realized. He knew the major would change it immediately after this unsecure conversation, but it amused him to know the Russian was so into LitRPG.

"Your message was received and processed. Investigation commenced yesterday morning nine minutes after receipt of your inquiry. The subject was indeed found to have been diverted from the Kinshasa airport and conveyed to an abandoned building in the warehouse district. It is our pleasure to announce a strike force has been sent to reacquire the package. We will inform you of the success or failure of this mission by coded message on the comments section of the website: 'Cultural Art Gallery of Europe'. Caregiver Over and Out."

There was that hiss of static David had been expecting.

David squirmed in his seat.

Major Krepkiyzad shot him a sorrowful look.

"So, Is true, then," he muttered.

"I guess so," said David with a sigh. "It hurts to think that they've had him for days. At least they know where he is. They were a little fuzzy on the timing of the raid, but what are their chances, do you think?"

David realized he was babbling. That wasn't like him at all. He focused on his breathing and stilled his tongue.

"CAGE is the best (excepting maybe for Space Force). I have worked with them before. Is saying in my country. Goes like this: *Bud' shto budyet*--let it be. Is also song by Paul McCartney. Also *Que Sera, Sera* by Doris Day. Meaning is all the same."

David collected himself.

"Tic-tac, Major?"

*****

53

"Here it is, cadets, the control bunker. It is from here that all launches will be coordinated."

Krepkiyzad was wearing his translator helmet again. It was far more efficient and versatile than what Bartholomew was able to do. But David didn't envy him his newfound loquaciousness if it meant wearing that in *this* heat.

They stood before a plain concrete building, windowless and austere. It's sloping sides put him in mind of those pyramids the Aztecs built. It looked like it could withstand a full non-conventional assault. It probably could. Sometimes looks could be appeasing.

"You will all be permitted entry to familiarize yourselves with these systems. Your biometrics have all been entered. Just press your palm to the scanner, and the door will open for you. Yes, Cadet Caillat?"

False Pierre, skulking near the back, had one gloved hand raised in the air. Rogue Pierre, David had decided to call the bastard.

"That solution will not work for thees cadet, Major Krepkiyzad, sir!"

"Why not, cadet?"

"As I explained earlier, I 'av burned my hands quite badly while on furlough--an accident, mishap? while ironing my shirts. Eet ees why I must use genetic matching to come and go from base.

Why hadn't David seen it earlier? He looked like Pierre, but his demeanor was (mostly) all wrong, and his excuses were overblown. Now, it was actually getting hard to act like he believed him.

Krepkiyzad paused thoughtfully, running his hand across the side of his helmet to rest on the nape of his neck.

Uh-oh, thought David. *Play along, Major, he silently urged.*

"In that case, said Major K., I suppose it would do no harm to have it respond to your voice command. Come up here and provide a sample."

Rogue Pierre stepped forward, a relieved grin on his lying Pierre-like lips.

"Bunker One, this is Major Nikolai Krepkiyzad."

He pressed his palm to the reader.

"Accept new voice print for Cadet Pierre Caillat on temporary assignment to Mwisho wa Bomba. Now speak clearly into the microphone. Repeat after me...:

As the major attended to this altogether too accommodating chore, David looked around, taking in new details. A cluster of capsules stood pointy-end upward in a lot adjacent to the site. Each was as large as a school bus. He didn't see them as rockets. In truth, they lacked fins, struts, or any real decoration. They had no fuel, no engines, and they would never return to Earth--unless there was a misfire.

More than anything else, he thought of them as bullets to be fired into the sky. The only variance in their shiny metal hulls was the thin coat of ablative material painted on their nose cones. They didn't need the thick tiles still used by some re-entry vehicles. The heat shielding would only need to endure for the thirty seconds or so it took them to traverse the ever-thinning upper atmosphere. Still, the speed they'd emerge from that muzzle would generate heat aplenty.

Alejandro was nudging him.

"Wake up, Rhymes, we're going in."

They trailed Major K. into main control, a room full of blinking lights. It was a chaotic melange of high-tech pageantry that would do any movie set proud. Screens lined the upper deck, displaying weather patterns, air traffic control radar, and external camera views from key points along the route. Staffing here was minimal except during times of operation. At *those* times every expert and his cousin owned a station.

They were shown how to operate a lot of different systems. It was a privilege Space Force was normally very reluctant to grant. But as Krepkiyzad explained it, their elevated status entitled them to poke around and get comfortable with the system they'd be trusting with their lives. It was all part of the plan. David was certain that Rogue Pierre wouldn't be able to resist the temptation.

"Most important is this," said their Russian leader in his most authoritative voice. "Only *this* system is off-limits. Tampering with it would leave us vulnerable to outside interference."

"What *is* it, major?" asked David right on cue.

"This experimental unit is for possible future use. It opens up channel 0190 so that all systems here can be operated remotely. Once active, any GFS Icarus platform that connects to it will be registered and permitted thereafter to log into Gossamer command. How would you like it if your launch parameters could be modified by some greenhorn cadet in Beijing or Hoboken? No. Do not touch this one."

David tried hard not to glance at Rogue Pierre throughout the major's speech. Major K. was no great actor, but the helmet hid his face, and the translation algorithms gave his voice a flat, even tone--filtering out any eye-rolling sarcasm that might betray him. He could almost see the pages turning in the little traitor's mind. Forbidden fruit? Tempting. Yum.

***

3,298... 3,299... 3300-even.

David couldn't sleep. His watch had been over an hour ago, and he'd turned it over to Speranza. She'd alert him when the time was at hand, but no amount of imaginary mutton could banish his churning thoughts. Pierre was alive and safe, if a little roughed up by his ordeal. The rat had yet to take the bait. Had they made it too obvious?

And then he was distracted by an irritating light. It was the phone resting on the nightstand to his right. He rolled over and snatched it up, touching its screen before Bart could escalate. The fiend wouldn't likely hear it through the soundproofed walls. Didn't want to spook him, though.

It was Shǔ, who had volunteered to help out. He stared out from the tiny screen, more somber than his usual chipper nature. His whiskers drooped down to either side.

"I object to this code-phrase most strenuously, arrived at disingenuously. I'm trying to be helpful if you please. And what's the thanks I get? A slander to my sobriquet. To wit: 'the little rat has taken the cheese.'"

David did feel bad about that.

"Cut the crap, Templeton. Where is he now?"

"We think he's stirring. He's disabled his QTV monitoring program somehow. Whoever he is, he's not without his means."

"Base monitoring has detected a low-level ping of unknown origins at frequency 0190 occurring at one-minute intervals. Very likely his cohorts are ready to seize control. Roadrunner reports ready. If you want to catch the culprit performing some purely human treachery in no way associated with rodents of any kind, keep the hallways clear."

"Alright already. I take your point. But that's far too long and non-descriptive to be our catch phrase. We'll characterize him as a snake in the grass next time, okay?"

"I shall inform Shé at once."

"Really? You'd rat me out?"

Shǔ looked indignant.

***

"You were right, cadet," said Krepkiyzad. "He disabled or evaded all monitoring systems and threw the switch. Whoever he really is, he's operating on Cadet Caillat's level of genius."

The major stood in David's doorway in full riot gear.

"I trust you turned it back off."

"Why? That unit operates the HVAC system for the bunker, which could use a good airing out. Now lets go get the little rat."

"Armadillo," David corrected. "He's an armadillo now."

"What? Why? I'm not sure I take your meaning."

"It was the only animal I could think of that wouldn't be offensive to my friends."

"Sometimes I think you are mentally deficient," declared Krepkiyzad's translation helmet, leaving David to wonder what actual words and tone he'd used. "Let us confront the little... dasypodidae!"

So, off they went toward the end of the hall. Based on his performance at morning exercise, David felt fairly confident he could easily subdue Rogue Pierre even without the battle-ready Russian veteran.

Unless he had a weapon or something...

After confirming that base security was watching all exits, Major Krepkiyzad pounded on the door. After a believable amount of time, a light came on inside. They could see it through the peep hole, which then darkened.

"*Mon dieu!* What time ees eet? Is zis a drill?"

"Open up, 'cadet,'" the major demanded with sarcasm struggling to emerge from his helmet-modulated voice.

"But of course, major," said the little git agreeably, doing so at once while rubbing crocodile sleep from his eyes.

"I arrest you for infiltrating a restricted military installation under false pretenses."

"*Moi?*"

"Yes, you. Come along quietly now."

"I demand my rights, You must put me in touch with the French consulate at once!"

"As a spy and saboteur, you have no rights under the uniform code of military justice. Any civilian rights you may have are suspended until such time as your identity can be ascertained and the seriousness of your crime assessed. Cadet Grimes, will you do the honors?"

He offered David a set of handcuffs, dangling them to one side while keeping a wary eye on R.P.

The boy paled.

"First you awaken me with these *accusations ridicules*, and now you would deny me the due process? I am Pierre Caillat. You cannot do zis thing!"

David tried to grab him, but he was quick, darting back toward the dresser.

"Luis?" came his voice from the doorway.

David became confused. That is, until he turned and saw another Pierre peering in from around the jamb, the one who had spoken. And this one was as green as an angry Bruce Banner.

Luis? Wasn't that Pierre's younger brother?

"How dare you, Luis? How dare you come here and humiliate me so? What did you hope to do? *Travaillez-vous pour* Humanity First?"

For the first time, Rogue Pierre (Luis?) seemed to deflate.

"Alright, you have me. How do you say it? The jig, she is up. I did want to take your place, *frère*. I wanted to go into space."

"You are no brother of mine!" shouted Green Pierre. "*These* are my brothers. *Les hommes et les femmes de la* Space Force! You are just a lying..."

"Armadillo!" supplied David.

"Arma-dillo?" asked Luis in confusion. "*Qu'est-ce qu'un 'armadillo?*"

"*C'est le tatou, du sud-ouest américain,*" said Green Pierre, wiggling his fingers in a walking pattern.

Krepkiyzad stared at David.

"What? They're tricky, they can get out of cages and stuff."

"Even so," said Krepkiyzad, "I still must arrest you for sabotage, among other things."

"You have no proof of that," said Luis, nostrils flaring.

"*Au contraire*," growled Pierre, crossing his arms before him. "Show them, Speranza."

She stepped into the room like military justice, holding out a hand palm up. On it rested a tiny spider, no bigger than a coin, even if you counted the legs. Her stern expression lent an air of authority to what she had to say.

"This is the latest model shepherd drone, straight from the labs of L5. They finally hit upon a design that can stand up to Earth gravity. The GLC will soon be using them in clandestine operations. Doctor van der Meer was kind enough to lend us this prototype."

She strode over to the QTV, and attached the spider to the I/O port of its data wand.

"It was very clever, Luis, how you disabled all the security cameras in the bunker. HF must have trained you well. But you missed this little fellow I was operating on the ceiling."

"You planted a... bug?"

With a wave of the wand she painted the scene up on the QTV. There was Luis creeping over to the unit all dressed in black and brandishing a small flashlight pen. She froze the image that revealed his face, zooming it in to fill the screen.

"I'll leave the rest for the civilian authorities to present in their discovery. But I trust the major is satisfied that sufficient evidence exists to detain this man?"

Krepkiyzad nodded, peeled off his helmet and scratched his head.

"Take him into custody, Cadet Grimes. Use any necessary force."

David moved toward Luis, and this time he didn't resist.

***

The medical unit was basic, but it still had that antiseptic smell of a hospital room managed by a fussy head nurse. Brainiac lay in the bed recovering from his recent ordeal. The enforced relaxation required by the medics was soothing to his battered body but chafed against his active mind. Both, he was told, should rest.

"Will I be cleared for the launch?"

"We'll see," said the major, not without sympathy. "They tell me you should be recovered enough physically by then, but you must also pass the psych evaluation."

Pierre grinned smugly.

"Good, then. I have had much practice running rings around psychiatrists since I was six."

But Krepkiyzad wasn't so certain.

"Tell me. Did they break you? What military secrets did they force from you?"

"The joke was on *them*. I am *already* broken. The trick was to keep giving them information, more than they could grasp. I made up many convincing things and told of them in great detail. It will take years for anyone watching those recordings to sift out a grain of truth. And by that time, the color of my grandmother's *culotte* will be of no use to them, hon hon!.

"Grimes wants to see you. Should I let him in?"

"But of course. I would like to see Daveed. I hear he was the one who sniffed out Luis' deception and reported it *tout de suite* to 'Cooking And Gourmet Enthusiasts.'"

"He did. I will give you ten minutes. Then you must rest. Your first therapy session with Doctor Lemoine will resume tomorrow. And cadet?"

"Yes, major?"

Major K saluted, a very deliberate act fraught with meaning.

61

"I hope you will be joining us. You have grit," he pronounced.

"Small amount," he grumbled, "but is there..."

Pierre stared in dumb amazement as the old softy stalked on out.

Soon after that, David stalked on *in*.

"Hello, Pierre. How was your furlough?"

Classic. David. Grimes.

Despite Pierre's many gifts, intellect chief among them, David had a personality one could never quite predict. And he was finding increasingly that he didn't even want to. He'd simply enjoy the gentle humor that fell so easily from the fellow's twisted tongue. Sometimes surprises are nice.

"I am well. Thanks for asking, Daveed."

Classic Pierre Caillat. Have some back, *mon ami*.

"So... your brother seems nice."

Touché. Snarky, but straight to the point--and right on target.

"But he is not, as you so quickly discovered. I am thankful for that."

"I thought you said Luis was younger than you. How can that be when you're so obviously twins? And how was he able to fool the genetic testing?"

"Strictly speaking, we are the same age. And he was born a year after me."

"I'm afraid you're going to have to explain *that* one."

Pierre sighed.

"My parents, Daveed, are horrible people. Listen, and I will try to explain. My mama and papa wanted the perfect child, sorted out *in vitro*. They selected for intelligence, disease immunity, longevity, and a host of other traits that they desired.

Having only one birthright credit, they wanted to take no chances."

David listened, uninterrupting.

"To top zis all off, they opted for the intrauterine enhancement treatments, granting gifts to a new generation of superior children. When NCRS was discovered, and when confronted with its likely consequences, my parents felt cheated. They would raise a superior child doomed to become an unstable and crippled intellect. Not much was known about the syndrome at the time, and they feared my decay was inevitable. It turns out it is not. It's likely, but some can beat the odds. I seem to be one of them so far."

David pulled up a chair and sat beside him, placing a supportive hand on his forearm. It would be too much effort to flinch away. He was supposed to be resting. He continued.

"As you know, birthrights can be purchased from someone unwilling or unable to have children. The birth market, for the first time in history, sets an actual price on human life. It is *très* expensive, but the Caillats are people of means, so they were successful."

"Instead of going through the whole *in vitro* selection process again, they made a clone of me, which Mama brought to term without IUE. And along came little Luis nine months later."

"A clone?" said David. "That explains a lot."

"So now you know. Luis has always envied me for my gifts, and I him, for his normalcy."

"I hear they have him in holding. Will you visit him?"

Pierre chuckled.

"Why would I want to do that? After all he has done, I am finished with him. He is in solitary confinement. Let 'im rot in zere. It ees like your Pat Benatar says, Daveed. My clone, he sleeps alone!"

David watched Pierre's blood pressure rise on the monitor attached to the lad. But he couldn't stifle his mumbled objection.

"But he's your brother..."

"No, Daveed. *You* are my brother."

David took a moment to process this. He found he liked its flavor.

"I never had a *brother* before," David mused.

"Sadly, *I* have. And you see how well that has worked out, *n'est-ce pas?* Like my parents, I think I would like to try again. Now go. I am supposed to be resting."

David squeezed his arm (not unpleasantly), rose, and stepped to the door. Pierre thought he had finally managed to get the last word. But then David turned, eyeing him with suspicion.

"Say, how do we know you're the *real* Pierre and not just another clone?" he challenged.

"By my brilliance," Pierre replied at once. "How can you not tell, *mon ami?* I am your father's brother's nephew's former roommate, *non?*"

A surprisingly true (albeit convoluted) statement from Spaceballs? It was Brainiac, alright. The weird reference wasn't even necessary. He had David at: 'by my brilliance.'

David wandered into the hallway, his head awhirl with such thought. And Pierre fluffed up his pillow settling back in his cot.

***

I'm Craig Artmeyer and this is GNN: Your top source for all the news that matters.

"The debate rages on in the Halls of Global Representation over a bill recently passed in committee. Here's Hal Lewis to break it down for us."

"Thanks, Craig. How's the weather there in Spain?"

"Rainy, but they tell me that is mainly on the plain."

"Ha. Ha. You rascal. That'll teach me to ask. Well, here goes. Most conscientious citizens follow the general guideline of limiting themselves to one child per couple. We all know that large families are selfish and socially irresponsible. Even if one has the means to rear more than one, planet Earth would suffer. And think of the disaster to the economy if even more souls were competing for ever more scarce resources. Scientist say that if population growth goes unchecked, we could be looking at mass starvation by as early as 2065!

"Well, the results of the 2055 census is in and it looks like were in luck. Birthrates are down even more than expected and we're well ahead of goal. Therefore, the global government's central committee has decided we could relax the stricture somewhat. Under this new bill they call the 'Sustainable Families Initiative,' each citizen of Earth would be granted the right to have 0.75 children."

"I'd like to see a woman try that, Hal!"

[Canned laughter]

"I hear you, Craig, but consider. A couple could have one child, each parent contributing 0.5 birthrights to the endeavor. Then each of them would retain 0.25 so that in the event of divorce or death of one or the other, they could have the possibility of a second child from another marriage."

"Ah. That makes sense."

"The best part is, couples in financial difficulty could sell their additional quarter-credits on the exchange for relief, while the more affluent who desire additional children could buy more. This measure would thus help reduce income disparity. Opponents say it's yet another bill to benefit the rich and are protesting at the capital."

"We'll certainly keep our eye on that, Hal. Thanks for the update. It's always a pleasure and we hope to have you back."

"Craig."

"In other news, the world has its eyes on the jungles of Congo today where the GSF has started the countdown on its first manned launch of Project Gossamer. The launch rail, built at tremendous expense will finally begin paying off. And what a launch it will be! The first to ascend to space on what's been called the longest, straightest, and definitely the fastest roller-coaster on the planet will be a group of young gritters new to the Space Force. You may know them as The Crew Who Knew What to Do, made famous for their stellar lunar exploits last fall.

"We take you to Ruth Cordwainer, on site in the D.R.C. city of Kinshasa. Here's Little Ruth, the voice of truth. Take it away, Ruth!"

"Thanks, Craig."

"Once again the eyes of the world turn to the City of Kinshasa, most famously the host of "Rumble in the Jungle," a brutal blood sport in the late 20th century. That fight was watched by as many as one billion television viewers around the world. A billion was a lot back then.

"Today it plays host to another spectacle that will surely top that record. I'm talking, of course, about the long-awaited Gossamer launch. With the countdown standing at two hours and thirty-five minutes, it should exceed that many viewers with ease. Decades in the making, Gossamer will be our new gateway to outer space and perhaps even the stars beyond!

"And here they come. They're coming out now, the Gritters!"

[Roar of the crowd outside the fence]

[Ruth moves forward, brandishing her mike. The scene sways back and forth as her camera crew follows.]

***

They were like a swarm of locusts, the people outside the fence. David could hardly believe so many were willing to stand in the mud and the heat just to get a glimpse of the ride he was privileged to take. He'd seen noisy spectacles before in Realms. But this was real; it was happening. It was happening to *him*. He stood there looking out over them, his posture straight and his expression grim.

David missed the feeling of detachment that operating an avatar conferred. Like nothing could really hurt him--not in any permanent way. The military cordon was brutal, efficiently keeping the curious at bay.

And what a crowd it was. Some had banners they were waving for attention. Some of these were well-wishers sporting signs like 'Go get 'em, Gritters.' Many were incomprehensible to him, not being intended for an English-speaking audience. Were there any HF haters in that crowd? He had been assured that checkpoints further out had thoroughly secured the perimeter, but it only took one slip-up, he knew.

In a few minutes, they'd be letting the press corps through the gate, card-carrying major players of the noble Fourth Estate. If David had his druthers, he'd be resting in the shade. They hadn't fed him anything today. They even cleaned his bowels out by making him drink that stuff. *There's* a little detail the GSF recruiters never talked about in their brochures. The capsule would be crowded and unpleasant enough without gobs of Roidy's upchucked lunch floating about. Best not to think about that.

But, despite feeling a little light-headed, he'd answer the questions that would no doubt come raining down. He'd smile for the cameras and think of Mom and Dad watching. He'd paint a pleasant face on things. David was no quitter. He'd weather all the hoopla and accept it like a gritter.

And here they came.

As they'd been instructed, David and the others spread out and let the reporters wander among them. He felt like a prize-winning hog at a state fair. The camera crews jockeyed for position. There even seemed to be some kind of hierarchy among them that made some of the lesser ones relinquish the positions they'd staked out. One rather petite reporter settled on him and came up to greet him at once.

"You Grimes? The one they call Rhymes?"

"I am."

Her microphone said GNN. Global News Network, he mused. That was a big one. But he soon found himself getting distracted by her hair.

"Ruth Cordwainer, GNN. When the light on the camera turns green, I'm going to ask you a few questions. We'll be live, so avoid anything vulgar and try to stay upbeat."

Her hair was shiny and had a natural wavy flow to it, but it was stiff, like a helmet.

"Yes, ma'am."

"And three... two... one... "

Fancy that. A mini countdown.

"This is Ruth, the voice of truth, and we're here live with David Grimes, one of the Crew Who Knew What to Do. Is it true you once stole an experimental spacecraft?"

A gotcha question right out of the gates (as it were). Luckily, David was an old hand at TV interviews by now.

"I prefer 'liberated,' Ruth, and if you recall, it was for a pretty good reason. At least Space Force seemed to think so," he said with a broadening, naughty-boy smile.

She grinned back.

"Say, aren't you also the Boy Who Saved the Man in the Moon? How do you manage to find so much trouble?"

"Guilty as charged," he said agreeably.

"Trouble finds a lot of folks, Ruth," he added somberly. "The difference is, 'When troubles come knocking, a gritter steps up.'"

"That's a lovely sentiment, Mister Grimes; may I call you David?"

"Actually, I prefer 'cadet.' It's kind of growing on me."

Seriously. Her hair didn't budge even when the wind gusted.

"What my viewers would really like to know, Cadet Grimes, is why you consort with NBIs."

"Well, Rhinemaiden is our official liaison for that, but I--"

"Don't you know they're taking people's jobs and robbing us of our birthrights?"

"I don't think--"

"That's right, for some it's best not to think about the troubles of the common men and women who make up the majority of our viewers. Do you plan to keep propping up the spoiled aristocrats ensconced in the halls of power?"

"Do you really want to know?" David asked too quickly to be interrupted.

She smiled sweetly.

"My viewers certainly would. We at GNN like to provide balanced coverage of all the news that matters."

"Your coverage is hardly neutral. It's biased. I've seen your programs. You never give conservatives the chance to speak. You interrupt them before they can make their point. I'm sure it plays well to your base, but sometimes you have to dance to a different fiddle. You need to--"

"Moving on then," said the anchor, withdrawing the mike. "I see Roid Rage is also with us. I imagine he'll have some gems for us today..."

"--elevate the dialog... Case in point," muttered David as Ruth stepped away, followed by her fawning camera crew.

At least he'd finally discovered a way to repel unwanted media attention. Still, the camera guy didn't have to step on his foot.

Looking around, he saw some of his fellow gritters being mobbed, but no one was looking his way at the moment. Pierre was still green, but it was beginning to fade. That seemed to be somewhat of a crowd pleaser. And he saw Leilani chatting away. That girl was such a teaser. Ropey and Roid had their own kind of fame. Even Little Rope, still mint in box, was getting his share of questions.

But the craziest one of all was the new guy, El Grande. He was dressed in a full tuxedo, with a top hat and a cape. In this heat, he must be roasting alive. David moved closer to see what was up. Alejandro had never struck him as the flamboyant type before.

"Why is your space name 'El Grande,' Alejandro?" asked one reporter.

"It's short for El Grande Cojones," put in Simon with a smirk.

Alejandro looked nervous.

"Um, yes," he sputtered, smoothly adding, "It's because I have a lot of clothing. Grande cajones means 'big drawers.'

"Besides," he added, "I'm just a humble cadet from España. The original El Grande Alejandro conquered Persia."

From the follow-up questions, David discovered his new friend was an amateur magician. On learning he could only take a limited weight in personal items, Alejandro agonized over just what to bring. But he'd spotted a loophole too. He could have 'one set of clothes.' That tux he was wearing was stuffed to the gills with trick decks of cards, wands that turned into bouquets, lock picks, and all manner of party favors and tools of his craft. His stage name was indeed 'Alejandro the Great,' so El Grande suited him well. The GSF drew the line, however, at live pigeons and a rabbit.

David also respected his quick thinking on the whole 'cajones' versus 'cojones' thing. And how he handled the reporters was marvelous. His stage personality had them laughing about how up on L5 levitating a woman just got a whole lot easier. Seriously, there was more to this guy than just being Roid and Ropey's punching bag. David would have to keep an eye on him. David returned to his assigned position, hoping for a 'ruthless' interview.

***

They crowded into the capsule. It was like a game of Tetris, with Krepkiyzad ushering the gritters into their seats. Perhaps 'seats' was a charitable word. The flimsy plastic buckets weren't designed for reuse. They'd be headed for the shredders on L5 once they docked.

Like a clown car, they managed to fit, with the major playing ringmaster. Though in truth, Alejandro the Great looked more the part. With Simon's elbow planted firmly in his side, David did his best to make ready for the ride. Why couldn't he be the lucky one, wedged between Speranza and Leilani? Pierre snuggled there with a flabbergasted air, looking like he'd just won the lottery. But David was stacked with the men in the back like discarded pieces of pottery.

"Crew is to suffer in silence," said Krepki. "No grumbles from any of you. We must endure more than eight minutes of acceleration at 2G."

"Glad it's not a 5G network."

"Quiet, Grimes! After that, thirty seconds to clear upper atmosphere. This is most crucial part. We will see why the men who applied heat shielding spray were lowest bidders."

Oh, so he can make jokes, but I can't?

"Finally, we arrive in orbit. I only hope the net is spread where we come out."

David gulped. Forget clown car. He felt more like the guy they loaded into the cannon and shot out to soar over the big top. Two Gs? At least he'd have Roid Rage's knees digging into his back to help cushion him from that. He turned to look up at Krepkiyzad who had lapsed into uneasy silence. The man looked nervous, sitting there beside him. Almost on top of him, more like. David could feel the major's breath with every exhale. He freed his arm and reached into his pocket.

"Tic-tac, major?"

"With only four minutes remaining on the countdown, Cameron started squirming, making her way toward the front. Claustrophobic? Was she losing her nerve? Breaking under the pressure?

The gritters writhed like a Rubik's cube as she steadily wormed her way up front, abandoning her place. Crouched low, she turned to face them all. A grin was on her face.

"Greetings passengers," she said. "I'm Photobug, and I'll be your flight attendant today."

Oh, good. This flight has a show.

"Welcome to Gossamer Airlines. Despite the close quarters, there's to be no groping. It's time to put your morals in an upright position. The pilot has... well, there *is* no pilot..."

Krepkiyzad muttered, "Oh dear God."

"Passengers will all fasten their seat belts anyway," she continued and began pointing her fingers all around.

"Please note that the exits are located... well, there are no exits," she shrugged.

And they kept coming. David got a lump in his throat. *Yeeesss.*

"In the event of an emergency landing, you will find beneath your seats your own ass--kiss it goodbye. All luggage and carry-ons are to be securely stowed in the buttocks of the passenger in front of you. Drinks will be served...never."

"Just through the wall to your left, you'll not see the staff of Bomba base waving goodbye to you. Since there are no windows... you'll just have to imagine it."

"Carry on. We will be lifting off in T-minus three minutes. Gossamer wishes you a pleasant journey. If you need anything more, tough luck... there *is* no call button. Just holler; I should be close by."

At this, she began squirming her way back to her seat to the silent applause of the gritters.

"I am... speechless," said Roid Rage, in self-contradicting awe.

Then Little Rope piped up.

"I don't *wanna* go in Pierre's butt. Who *knows* what he keeps up in there?"

One minute remained on the clock.

It was gentle at first but built right up to a steady pressure, pressing him back into his inadequately cushioned seat. 2G wasn't intolerable, but eight minutes of it was going to be tough. Take it like a gritter, he reminded himself. In the original specs, the G-forces were greater. The proposed track back then only ran across Tanzania. But then Congo relented and even offered to pay for much of the additional track, anticipating a boost to their economy. They became the new hub for shots into space, but the cherry on top of the sundae was the longer track they were riding on. 'Air Gossamer' now had a far more gentle runway.

Eight minutes of acceleration at 2G would leave them screaming along at somewhat more than escape velocity.

The 'somewhat more' was necessary because they'd lose some velocity when they went slamming into the atmosphere over Kilimanjaro. Even though, up there, the air pressure was less than half what it was down here at sea level, that was still dense enough to feel like hitting a brick wall at the speed they'd be racing.

The streamlined nature of their disturbingly disposable craft, the pointy end, if you will, would help to mitigate this quite a bit. But when the tip of that spear encountered atmosphere, it would condense that thin air into plasma. This would pour down the nose cone, creating a sheath of intense heat (kind of like a dragon's sneeze).

He felt the major's elbow digging into his ribs when he shifted his position.

"I'm gonna be sick," moaned Dietrich.

He was suddenly glad they'd been deprived of lunch.

David heard a low whine, like a whisper of regret. It was coming from the walls all around him. That would be the air outside objecting to their passage. The GSF had done its level

73

best to pump all the air out of that tube. They had vast solar arrays spread out all over the Congo Basin powering the pumps that were doing so. This also powered the maglev rings they relied on for propulsion. But no vacuum was perfect, not even in space, and a stubborn few cc's of rarefied air resisted total expulsion.

David recalled his impromptu speech to his classmates back at Oak Hills.

"To escape Earth's gravity well," he had said, "an object must achieve escape velocity, a speed of about seven miles per second, or roughly twenty-five thousand miles per hour. To put this in perspective, this is about thirty-three times the speed of sound. Such velocities are termed 'hypersonic.'"

He hadn't realized at the time he'd be taking that journey himself. He hadn't considered how helpless the occupants would feel howling along at such speeds. What would happen when they reached Kilimanjaro? What if something went wrong? *It wouldn't.* The engineers of Earth had assured everyone it would be safe. Still, David couldn't quite bring himself to trust wholeheartedly a mountain whose first name was Kill-a-man.

The pressure persisted, and the howling increased.

Evacuated bowels or not, David was also glad he was wearing two pairs of underwear again. The pressure was getting intense as the others pressed in all around him. And he was bitterly reminded that a full house always beat two pair.

And the capsule rang like a bell. They must have arrived at the end. After that torturous 2G hell, gravity once again became his friend. Their attitude shifted, and the pressure eased. The unrelenting hand pressing down on his chest had finally relented. He felt a bit more vertical now, as his creator had intended.

This was it. Would the heat shields hold? This ship lacked an engineer. Someone to say, 'Aye Captain, the shields are holding!' and mitigate their fear. Thirty seconds. That's all it would take before he'd know the answer. He could hold his breath for twice that long. It was a good thing, too. The jarring transition had left him breathless.

74

He could almost feel their initial velocity being shed, leeched away by the ever-thinning atmosphere outside. David and the others swayed forward. *Hah!* That would be Gossamer's namesake, he'd bet. The launch had been successful. He could finally exhale. Like a three-point shot in basketball, they'd landed in the net!

David's relief was soon eclipsed by an even greater sense of wonder. He discovered that gravity, the tyrant to whom he'd always had to bow, no longer held sway over him. He felt buoyant, even more so than when floating in the ocean. He felt the unsettling but exhilarating sense of freedom. He was a bird who had grown up in a cage, knowing no other life, but who had suddenly found the cage door open wide.

"Passengers may now feel free to float around the cabin..." Photobug recited with glee.

"Belay that order!" bawled the major. "*Senior* flight attendant Krepkiyzad says *nyet!* Passengers are to remain seated and safely strapped in. Who knows how long it will be before they free us from this *bezumnyy* capsule? Open the valve to release supplemental oxygen. And Krepkiyzad also is turning on no smoking sign. Fire is hazardous in space."

Bravo, major, thought David. Welcome to team Grimes.

Interlude

"Has he broken yet?" asked Captain Magombo.

"Not yet, sir," replied the guardian at the door. "Frankly, I don't know how he's able to take so much abuse. Who came up with this program anyway?"

"One of the cadets, the one they call Grimes."

"*David?* But he seemed so nice."

"Looks can be deceiving, I guess," the captain sighed. "Behind that polite facade, it is obvious there lies a cruel and deeply twisted mind."

"*I'll* say. Is this even permitted by the Geneva Convention?"

"Technically yes, though I'm certain they would ban it if they learned of the specifics."

The guard glanced at the soundproofed door and shook his head.

"He's a *tough* little bugger. I'll give him *that*."

"Just keep reminding yourself, Specialist Tamu, that little French pig wanted to betray us to the same bastards who tried to wipe out the moon. Tough little bugger or not, I have no sympathy for him--nor should you."

"Yes, Captain," said Tamu, snapping to attention. "I'll try to remember, sir!"

"See that you do. Carry on. And let me know when Mister Caillat is ready to talk. It should be soon now."

"Yes, Captain Magombo, sir! I will let you know at once."

As Magombo strode down the hall of the detention facility, his conscience gnawed at him. The boy was obviously a dupe. He probably didn't know anything important. Was it really necessary to subject him to such methods? But then he imagined nanites overrunning Bradbury Base, consuming all the metal in their path. He envisioned Loonies floating everywhere, their vacuum-slain corpses a silent testament to man's inhumanity.

His jaw firmed. His resolve stiffened. Very soon, they would learn everything the Caillat boy knew. His contact instructions at the very least. He would do his duty despite any squeamish feelings of mercy he might be fostering.

***

Many look fondly back on the 1970s as a time of exploration. The U.S. had just put a man on the moon, and the world was celebrating in every way imaginable. Against a turbulent background of world affairs, technology continued to advance. Moon landings continued. Scientists learned to modify DNA. The first test tube baby was born, and the very first email was sent.

Perhaps the greatest thing to emerge from this decade of upheaval was its music, the sheer diversity of which demonstrated a healthy, evolving culture. Disco and punk rock took their place alongside more traditional forms. There was "Rocket Man" by Elton John, "Jolene" by Dolly Parton, "Imagine" by John Lennon, and who could forget "Stairway to Heaven" by Led Zeppelin?

One of man's greatest assets is his tendency to forget. We look back fondly on the pleasures of our youth. But the human brain has a great capacity to forget pain that was inflicted on us. We recall having 'been' in pain, but not the actual pain itself. Try it sometime. It's true enough. Scientists speculate this is a defense mechanism key to the survival of our species. What woman would willingly bear a second child if she could recall, with perfect clarity, the pain of childbirth?

So too is our cultural awareness of decades past seen through the lens of pleasure. For among the many joyful outcomes of our soulful experimentation lie songs best forgotten, failed experiments, if you will, soothed only by nepenthe. These rarely come to mind when reflecting on past glory. And that, for Rogue Pierre, became the heart of his sad story.

***

The lights came on again overhead. The buzzer sounded loudly. Luis raised his bloodshot eyes, staring upward proudly. He had no way of marking the time, and he'd been kept awake by this nonsense for many hours already. They fed him well enough, but still his legs had grown unsteady.

He would *never* give up his confederates! Bring your worst, the Frenchman defiantly thought.

As expected, the spotlights lanced out from either side, lighting up the glittering ball that twinkled and blinked as it turned. Its mesmerizing strobing signaled this would be another bad one, and his bravado fled.

Slowly gathering up the scattered remnants of his courage, Luis braced himself for the worst. He would show them Luis Caillat was not a man to betray his beliefs. The revolution could count on *his* silence.

Then it came, the thrumming beat he had learned portended madness. And the rhythm was soon joined by a pair of banshee wails, singing in chorus to that awful disco beat.

Not that! *Anything* but that!

He had swung in the jungles with Gitarzan and learned about muskrat love. He'd ignored the antics of the disco duck and even knew now why they 'called him the streak.' But nothing had prepared him for this. *Non. Non!* He felt lightheaded, and his knees went weak.

It was then that his confidence crumbled. He knew then that his captors were inhuman.

He stumbled toward the door and pressed the button on the intercom. Weakly, he raised his voice.

"I will talk, you bastards. I will tell you anything you want. Zhust please, I *beg* you. If you have any shred of human decency, turn that damned thing off!"

And after a few minutes that felt like an eternity, silence returned to his cell. Luis slid down the wall to sit at its base.

"I *hate* ABBA," he croaked raising hands up to his face.

Eight...

L5 Station

Freefall was amazing. It was a sense of freedom David had never felt before, not even when flying around in Realms. There, he had had to imagine it. Here it was for real.

Krepkiyzad was hard pressed to keep the cadets from bouncing off the walls. This was no figurative turn of phrase, for they'd all gone bouncing around the docking bay when they'd filed on out of that transport. David gripped the door handle and steadied himself as Carlotta came cartwheeling out. The last to emerge was Krepkiyzad, who was frowning and looking about.

"Cadets, form up!" he bellowed. "Form orderly ranks on the floor. In space, is customary to orient as if gravity is in force. Not--upside down on ceiling, Akana."

When they all found their accustomed places, trying to remain rooted, the major looked them over, still refusing to smile at the wonder. Was it just a Russian thing, this sour-faced brooding? Or was it some personal gravity the man was sinking under?

"As of this moment, I have been demoted," he declared.

What? thought David as a murmur ran through the crew.

"Space Force command believes that playing den mother to a small group of greenhorn cadets is a task not worthy of a major. For this reason, I have accepted temporary reduction in rank to E-6 for duration of this assignment."

He shrugged, the action almost freeing his magnetic boots from the hull. In the background, David saw handlers moving their Gossamer bullet capsule into the bay beside the transport. It had been towed along to L5 with the rest of them, packed as it was with rare earth metals, stacks of high-grade computer chips, and all sorts of luxuries the L5-ers would have trouble manufacturing up here.

It was eerie seeing three men lifting the bus-sized capsule and guiding it along as if it weighed nothing. Hmmm. It *did* weigh nothing here at the hub, he supposed. But still it had mass, so they were taking their sweet old time. They were slow-walking their burden like ants carrying a cracker. But, oh yeah... Krepkiyzad.

"You'll always be a major Krepkiyzad to us," Simon cracked wise.

It seemed that David wasn't the only one to have worked out that 'Krepkiyzad' meant 'tough bottom (hard-ass)' in Russian.

"Stow it, cadet. I have heard before," grumbled Technical Sergeant Krepkiyzad.

"For duration of this assignment, you are to refer to me as Commander. When on a specific mission, you may also use my call sign, Big Kahuna."

All eyes turned to Alejandro, who was keeping his gaze straight ahead and sporting a carefully blank expression.

"Is this understood, cadets?"

"Da, Commander Krepkiyzad!" David shouted out.

And though it rang and echoed back from the distant walls of the docking bay, it still sounded rather hollow without the 'sir.'

"I like," admitted the commander, one corner of his mouth twitching upward. "All will repeat. With feeling, now. Is that understood?"

"Da, Commander Krepkiyzad!" the cadets sang in three-part harmony.

"Now we are moving out. Single file, keeping magnetic boots glued to the floor."

Heading for the hangar door, David craned his neck to look backward. The hangar crew was already ejecting from the rear of the launch the parachute they hadn't had to use. It was David's understanding its fabric would be processed into sheets for their bedding. Efficient. And here came the yellow plastic seats they *had* used. These would be ground down into type eleven hardened grade plastic pellets for the fabricators. They were already sawing the hull into bite-sized hunks. The cabin was beginning to look skeletal behind the blackened nose cone. Had they really flown up here in that thing?

You're left--clang. You're left--clang. You're left right. Left!--clang.

"That's the sound of the men, workin' on the chain...ga-a-ang!"

"Stow it, Grimes!"

***

They marched on out of the hangar and straight into quarantine. David should have expected this, but the grumblings of his empty stomach (and the rest of his GI tract for that matter) had him distracted.

From his readings about the early interactions of Europeans with the indigenous peoples of the Americas, David understood that when one culture was isolated for a long enough time from another, disease immunity could be a problem. In the cases he'd been reading about, the Europeans had the advantage. They had clustered together for centuries in cities, breeding zones for every kind of pest. This had long ago winnowed out the weak, exposing them to all kinds of germs.

The native people of the Americas, by contrast, lived farther apart from one another in a cleaner, more natural way. And as a result, minor childhood ailments of the Europeans could be deadly to them, wiping out whole tribes. The L5'ers (and Loonies to a lesser extent) were, in some ways, like the people of the Americas. They were very isolated from the rest of humanity, more sparsely (for now) populated, and lived in a very clean environment.

L5 scientists were adamant that their immune systems shouldn't suffer as a result. Ninety-five percent of man's evolution in the past ten thousand years had been a result of fighting off disease organisms. A science fiction writer once remarked that if you actually *could* build a time machine and returned to the time of Christ, one sneeze in the forum could wipe out the whole Roman Empire. This got David deeply invested in composing a suitable limerick--

There once was a fellow named Oliver Twist.
He traveled through time with a flick of his wrist.
With pox of the chickens,
He killed Charlie Dickens,
And suddenly ceased to.

",,,You *hearing* me, Grimes?" repeated Krepkiyzad in annoyance. "I said you're next! Step up, cadet."

"Uh, yes sir... I mean, yes, commander," he stammered, stepping into the curtained area.

A bright light shone down upon a flat, metallic table. A bunch of instruments hung above it from cables. In the absence of gravity, 'hung' wasn't properly descriptive. They dangled there from tethers like a score of drunken dentist drills and other equally ominous appliances.

A man (?) in the corner wearing white was swiping along on his (?) tablet. The man was ridiculously slender and tall, if he was truly a man at all and not a rail-thin woman. Those who grew up on Luna often developed that way, causing one to wonder whether they were fully human.

He or she looked for all the world like a hybrid of a human and a Roswell gray. He turned to regard David from liquid eyes and set his tablet on a nearby tray.

"You are David Grimes."

He said it as a statement, but seemed to be awaiting an answer.

"Yes."

"Please undress and get up on the table. Then we'll see what we've got here. You may place your clothing in the recontamination box to your right. You may call me Doctor Pat."

That name didn't help with the gender identity, but the deep voice and bobbing Adam's apple gave him a pretty good idea that the doctor was male. That banished any reluctance to undress. Not that he wouldn't do so for a female doctor; this just put him more at ease.

"Is that short for Patrick? And are you a Loonie?" asked David, shucking his shorts.

"It's Patterson, actually. Patterson Starfinder. As to the other, what was your first clue?"

David thought he was going to *like* this guy. He hauled himself up onto the (cold) medical table and lay on his back looking upward. He squinted to avoid the bright lamps above, wondering briefly what all the dangling instruments were for. He hoped that if Doctor Pat did have some alien in his lineage, he didn't share their proclivity for probing their abductees' anuses (ani?).

In this, David was soon to be sorely disappointed--with sharp emphasis on the adjective.

***

Stepping out into the quarantine center, David was directed to the quarantine room, a larger, shared facility lined with beds in orderly rows. The air wasn't really moving, but it felt breezy since they'd taken all of his clothes. He was going commando now beneath the hospital gown he wore. And the magnetic sandals that he'd strapped on barely held him to the floor.

The 'floor' was a relative concept here. It set his senses reeling when he noticed six beds on it--and six more on the 'ceiling.' Slowly it dawned on David that in this weightless place, it only made good sense. It was the optimal use of space. It would take some getting used to, this mental new frontier. Maurits Cornelis Escher would be right at home in here.

QTV screens adorned the wall 'above' each bunk, beside which stood poles with devices David assumed were medical monitors.

Speranza and Leilani were already there, as were Dietrich, Fergus, Cameron, and Pierre. Speranza's tight braids were familiar. But what was going on with Leilani's wavy hair? It was doing a Don King at the moment, rising in a wild diaspora like a burgeoning, bristly bush. All it needed was a stripe of white, and she'd be a perfect Bride of Frankenstein.

Flowerchild had removed her magnetic sandals and was doing somersaults from bed to bed. Speranza stepped across to stand beside him. Doctor Pat had told him he could take the training wheels off once he felt comfortable. It didn't surprise him their exuberant friend had already done so. She'd better watch out for her modesty, though. Those hospital gowns hitched up a bit in back.

"That doctor is certainly very... thorough," Speranza remarked through tightened lips.

"Yep," said David ruefully, for once, biting back his quips. "How long do you think they'll keep us here?"

"Forty-eight hours, at least."

"Two whole days?" David protested. "We had full medical workups just prior to the launch. If we were carrying anything nasty, they'd know it by now."

"You misunderstand, David. L5 is determined to retain and even augment humanity's resistance to disease. The quarantine is not to protect them from us. Rather, it is to protect *us* from the many pathogens running around the station. There's a write-up about it on your QTV just over there in bunk number three."

"You mean the one Flowerchild has just made a mess of."

"That's the one. Give it a read. You'll find the treatise familiar."

With a gentle smile and a nod of her head, she blinked those brown eyes, turned, and swayed away. It could have been a trick of the sandals she was wearing; the movement struck David as intentional sharing. He gingerly stepped over to his recently unmade bed and started the tutorial.

L5 For Dummies--Chapter 12: Mandatory Quarantine

(for your own good and that of others)

Mankind's battle with disease organisms has been fierce throughout all of our history.

Both adversaries are implacable foes to one another. Each is highly adaptive, disease using raw numbers and mindless persistence, and mankind matching this with intelligence, hygiene, and medical science. It is a war that will never end.

But the scientists of L5 believe that this ongoing evolution will eventually benefit both. The mitochondria that power our cells were once invaders. And now, they work for us. Better to stay abreast of evolving pathogens than live in fear, sealed off in a sterile, insular, and ever-shrinking world. Far better to embrace the challenges of the microbial world for humanity's eventual betterment.

Toward that end, L5 scientists have established a new and forward-thinking set of quarantine protocols spearheaded by

Doctor Patterson Starfinder. Starfinder, a recent emigrant from Luna, is the first human born off-Earth to receive a full MD.

Patterson Starfinder was among the earliest live births at Bradbury Base back in 2032. Somewhat of a prodigy, he attended medical school remotely, completing all required coursework by 2051 at the tender age of nineteen. He then embarked on his medical residency in internal medicine right here on L5. He completed it in 2054 and is presently two years into his fellowship studies in infectious disease and immunology.

Under the new protocols, all visitors or would-be residents of L5 station must agree to a two-day quarantine wherein they are thoroughly vaccinated for every known disease or exposed to weakened but accelerated strains thereof. In the quarantine room of hub one, they are kept under strict medical care until early symptoms pass. They can then boldly stride the halls of our glorious habitat, safe in the knowledge they will catch no dread disease (again).

Regular checkups and updates will follow. Microbes never sleep. Welcome to L5, and may your stay here be a healthy one.

It was then David saw Alejandro limping out and sporting a frown. The man winced ever so slightly each time he brought a sandalled foot down. Gingerly he walked stiff-legged toward bed five in the back.

Was he alright? Perhaps I should withhold my playful crack.

"Did Doctor Pat mess with--"

"I don't want to talk about it," he snapped. "Did you hear? They plan to make us all sick... on purpose?"

"I did. Will it hurt, do you think?"

"The doctor said there might be some mild discomfort," he grumbled.

Oh God. It was gonna hurt.

"Ropey! Little Ropey! Speak to me. Are you okay?"

Rolling out on a conveyor belt came their belongings, fresh from recontamination. The box with Fergus' action figure was prominent among them. He picked it up and shook it and held it to his ear. An overplayed look of relief washed over him.

"Oh, thank goodness. Little Ropey says he's fine. And given what we'll be going through in the next two days, he says he's delighted his package is hermetically sealed."

Others were collecting their possessions, so David wandered over as well. At least he'd have his clothing back in this germ-infested hell. He tried to encourage the others.

"At least we're all good friends here, so it shouldn't be so bad."

And then, as if just to prove him wrong, in walked Krepkiyzad.

Sometimes David made others laugh with his wit or his charm or rhyming, but sometimes the universe itself had its own comedic timing.

"How do you suppose we should pass the time while we wait to be cleared from here?" asked Simon.

Pierre snatched his satchel from the conveyor and quickly retreated to his corner.

Strange.

"I think I've got a deck of cards in here somewhere if they haven't dry-cleaned the faces off them," said El Grande.

He was holding up his tux and rifling through its hidden pockets.

Suddenly something thumped into David's back--hard. Turning, he spied Flowerchild sailing away from him. She snagged the footboard of a ceiling bed and turned to face him with a playful grin. Had she just used him as a springboard?

"Tag, Rhymes. You're it."

Oh. It's on.

No guardian worth his pay wanted to remain 'it' for long. He undid the straps of his sandals to better enjoy the weightless sensation. Tomorrow might be hell, but he'd rather not dwell on the 'gravity' of *that* situation. As he launched himself, he fervently hoped the commander didn't snore.

***

They had taken the treatments, eaten their station rations, and had a generally miserable time as all manner of stomach cramps, itching skin, fevers, chills, and grouchy comrades threatened their veneer of good cheer. The commander was a brick, keeping to himself and never complaining.

The doctors were amazed by Brainiac, who seemed to just shrug off any sickness in its early stages. Apparently--despite their otherwise uncaring attitudes--his parents had done a good job of making their *in vitro* selections. Doctor Pat made the mistake of remarking he'd like to keep Pierre for further studies. After that, Pierre began faking symptoms and bellyaching along with all the rest of them.

Finally, it was time to be discharged, and the crew was more than ready.

A light came on at the hatch, the door to the hallway outside. Their belongings were packed. They were healthy, clothed, and dignified. Krepkiyzad led the way, undogging the hatch and pulling it aside. No sooner had the door hinged open than he came to attention and snapped a smart salute.

"Technical Sergeant Krepkiyzad, Captain Wildman, sir. My charges have completed all quarantine protocols and have been given clean bills of health. Awaiting your orders, sir."

Wild-man? Sounds like another Loonie Surname, but he looks like a Space Force regular from Earth. And was that a note of weary resignation in the commander's voice? It had to rankle having to salute a captain as his superior. Make that, it had to 'unrankle'...

The captain's face showed amazement fading to mirth as he returned the salute with a spreading grin. "The Kahuna, an E-six? How the mighty have fallen."

Krepkiyzad lifted his chin and met the captain's laughing eyes.

"The captain would be advised to note that reduction in rank is only temporary. Laugh while you can, sir. I match your quote from Samuel with one from Charlie Daniels: 'Give to devil his due.'"

David's mind supplied the lyrics at once: '...I'll bet a fiddle of gold against your soul 'cause I think I'm *better* than you...' This was getting intense.

Then both men began laughing uproariously.

"Squad will come to attention!" the commander bellowed. "Officer on deck (if navy will forgive)"

They shared another round of grins, but the cadets all came to attention anyway, just in case.

"I introduce to you Captain Eugene Wildman of Space Force, a man who once saved seventy-three civilian scientists and General Sonovavich himself during solar bombardment of L5. Recipient of Airman's Medal for bravery outside combat and former student of mine."

"The former major is too kind. Oh! Wait! Reverse that. (I forgot you already *know* the man). Moving on, then, I've been sent here to escort you to an event in your honor down in habitat ring two. I'm sure you're all eager to be away from this place."

He glanced distractedly at Alejandro.

"Nice hat, cadet," he said, rubbing his chin thoughtfully.

"Sir, thank you, sir!"

"Oh, and you all may stand at ease. We'll have to see about getting you some proper uniforms.

He heaved a sigh.

91

"Come with me, and you'll be, in a world of spinning gravitation."

At that, he turned and began drifting down the corridor.

"You heard the captain," said Krepkiyzad. "Move out."

David was the first in line. The captain floated effortlessly ahead, making only occasional contact with the walls. He was moving headfirst to minimize wind resistance. David was hard-pressed to keep up. And speaking of up, which way was that again? He spun from time to time as he followed. It was hard not to. The station was spinning, and when not in contact with some surface, he tended not to spin with it. It was perplexing.

David thought they were traveling straight down the axle toward the first inner ring. But in truth, there was no earthly way of knowing which direction he was going.

Then the man pulled up short. David managed to stop, but Simon ran into him from behind.

"Ow."

"Are we there yet?" asked Cameron from the rear.

The stationary corridor still spun in David's mind. His inner ear was filing a complaint. Scientists estimate that a rotation of 2 RPM is about all the average human can tolerate on a long-term basis. Much faster than that, and people would be subject to space sickness with bouts of dizziness possibly leading to even more severe afflictions. David fixed his gaze on the captain, trying to anchor his perspective.

"Do any of you know what this door is for?" the captain asked when they'd clustered up.

"But of course. *Mon Capitaine*," said Pierre.

"Anyone else apart from the IUE guy?"

"We call him Cadet Caillet, sir," Krepkiyzad gently corrected. "Brainiac is also acceptable."

The look on the captain's face made David wonder who was really in charge here.

"Thank you, Kahuna. I'll keep that in mind. Well?"

Speranza cleared her throat.

"Something stuck in your craw, girlie, or have you got something to say?"

"This cadet is called Cadet Mbabu, sir. And I believe the hatch you are indicating is for one of the safe rooms spaced all throughout the base. They can be accessed by anyone. In an emergency situation, they can be sealed off. There are suits, spare oxygen tanks, heaters, emergency lighting, and the like."

"Very good, Cadet Mbabu. All of you mark the symbol. When the alarm goes off, find one of these. When that solar storm hit, too many didn't. We got flabby and paid a price for it. Drills are every Wednesday now. Onward."

At this, he promptly turned and began swimming away.

"Good job, Roadrunner," David praised. "Way to show him you're not just a pretty face."

Speranza turned her serious gaze on him, nodded, and slowly blinked. Then she followed the captain down the spinning tunnel. Leilani hugged him around the shoulders and jabbed him in the ribs with a two-fingered twist--one he suspected came straight from her 'martial heart.'

"Smooth, Romeo," she giggled.

"What? I was being supportive."

"You said 'just.' Did you see how quiet she got? *Oooh.* I love it."

David considered.

"Well, of course," he replied weakly. "Speranza is a handsome woman. I've been told that my left hand is very good at giving compliments... But Lei-lei?"

"Yes?"

"Don't pick on her about it. Tread yently."

"You said pretty, you said pretty," she sang as she went bouncing down the hall.

"What is hold-up, Grimes?" Krepkiyzad bellowed. "Get moving! Cadets can say pretty to each other after duty hours."

About ten revolutions later, they arrived. Like Speranza, David had been doing his reading too. According to "L5 for Dummies," the station they were standing on spun at two revolutions per minute. This simulated something very close to Earth gravity on the main rings, 225 meters out from the center. So, the L5'ers had naturally taken to marking time in revs, each of which was thirty seconds long.

The captain pressed the call button.

"How long do you usually wait for the elevator?" asked Carlotta, looking down at her phone.

"Never," said the captain with a tiny shrug and a tilt of his head. "We're waiting for L5 Axial Transport Lift #1."

"What's the difference, captain?" she asked, tucking away her phone.

Just then, the thing arrived with a ding.

"An elevator can only go up and down," he explained as he stepped on board, "but the Axial Lift can also go sideways and forward and back along the axle and up or down any of six spokes to any level of any ring in the whole station."

Sounds very familiar, thought David as they all filed in. Can it go longways and squareways, and frontways, and any other 'ways' you can think of? he mused. But just as he was about to make his comparison, Simon spoke up.

"Oh, just like the turbolifts on Star Trek!"

"Exactly. Habitat ring, ground level," said their guide with a little twinkle in his eye.

The thing obviously had voice command. David stared sullenly at the big red button sealed under a glass case, wondering what *it* did.

"Going down," said a deep baritone voice. "Although, technically, it *could* be up, depending on how you look at it."

"Outward," replied the captain without missing a beat.

"First along the axle," said the voice.

"Spare us the commentary, AL; just take us there."

"As you wish. Queen to King four."

"Is that some kind of code phrase, Captain?" asked Carlotta.

"Oh. Did I say that out loud? No, miss. I'm playing a quick game with Deep Blue to pass the time. The captain was kind enough to install him on a laptop in the reclamation lab. The fellow's a moron. I'll have him checkmated in three more moves if he ever gets around to making one."

"Ignore him, Miss van Rijn," said Wildman. "I did that just to shut him up. He just likes to brag. Will you take us there already, AL?"

"We have already arrived."

"But we haven't moved," argued Simon. "At least... *I* didn't feel anything."

David had. It was subtle, but his feet now felt more firmly affixed to the floor.

"Thank you, young man. You *are* young, aren't you? Micro-acceleration. That's the key."

"AL," objected Captain Wildman gently. "I know we're not at the outer ring. This is lunar gravity at best."

"Ah, that. Indeed. You were brought here instead by a very special request."

Krepkiyzad looked confused, but the captain seemed nonplussed, taking it in stride.

"Oh, in that case, open up please, and thank you for the ride."

He turned to address the cadets.

"Mind your footing, your head, and your existential dread. We'll be entering the inner ring."

"Just like that?" asked Roid Rage, "You let an elevator tell you what to do?"

"Of course not. He's an Axial Lift, AL for short, and he's not been with us for long. He did say it was a very special request. What about you, Kahuna? No comment about such nonsense? I thought you'd be blowing a gasket by now."

"In recent days, Captain," said Krepkiyzad with a stoic Russian sigh and a glance at David, "I have gotten used to it. Gaskets have long been blown. Is saying, Sud'be nel'zya prikazyvat', Cannot give orders to fate."

"Right!" said the captain, becoming animated. "No sense dwelling on confusion--plenty more nonsense ahead."

They emerged to find a semicircle of seated Loonies. Most of them were lanky like Doctor Pat, but it was a little hard to tell it by the way they sat. One stood in the center, though. She was taller than average, statuesque, but not *too* exceptional in height. And unlike the others, to David's eye, she seemed to be proportioned right. Perhaps a bit on the slender side, she seemed a little bit pale, but nothing about her suggested she might be unhealthy or frail. An exotic lunar beauty with an ethereal smiling face. Why mince words? She was a knockout (and that nearly became the case).

"I've been *waiting* for this moment," she declared. "I want to thank you proper, David Grimes."

Then she leapt straight at him. Well, not straight. They were on L5, a rapidly spinning station. And objects here, when put in flight, must bow to its rotation. She leapt 'straight' toward a spot to his right she knew was counter-spinward. To David, it appeared that she was curving ever inward. David learned something new on that day. They began ten yards apart. But an earthborn Loonie can jump twelve meters right from a standing start.

She startled him with that leap, but her words had signaled a gentler intent. He overrode his first instinct to fend her off and caught her in his arms. Taking his face between soft, warm hands, she kissed him deeply and without restraint. David was suddenly glad he'd had all his shots this week. She released him, and he set her down. They were treated to stares from all around from both Loonies and gritters alike.

"You're welcome. Um. Do I *know* you, Miss...?"

"Does the name Julia ring a bell?"

David thought frantically. Thankfully, Roid Rage gave him a reprieve.

"If Rhymes won't let you, you can ring *my* bell, Miss Julia!"

Krepkiyzad shook his head and lowered it into his open palm.

A Loonie named Julia? David had only been to the moon once, and that was a virtual trip.

"Oh, you must be that assistant of Saul Epstein, the one from the flipped buggy."

"Julia Rillwalker at your service. I wouldn't *be* here if it weren't for you. See kids, she said, turning to her compatriots, I told you he'd remember. This here's David. Like I was telling you, he's really got sass when the rubber hits the glass."

She pirouetted around, spinning up on one toe.

"And that's not all. These others, they're the ones you saw on the QTV. The ones who saved our homeland, right here, like I said they'd be. Come and thank 'em proper style; they're the gritters, the crew who knew. Gritters, meet pod seventeen, here to welcome you on behalf of all of the folks you saved."

And the children all uncoiled from the places they'd been sitting, flowing forward like a wave. They looked so frail and delicate, all spindly and wan, but they moved about like spiders, closing in from every side.

"Thanks for saving Julia and all the folks on Luna," one little girl put forth shyly.

Like the starting gun at a track meet, this unleashed a riotous babble of similar sentiments from the others. And the gritters found themselves nearly smothered in hugs and affection. Even their crusty commander got his share.

After a few revs of this, Julia called them off and said to the captain, "Thanks for allowing this, Captain Gene. You know the kids can't go to the feast. Not yet, anyway. Don't blame AL. He owed me a solid. I reckon we're even now. I'll let you get on to your grand event. But know that any of you are welcome here in the inner rings."

Once order had been restored, they began gliding back to the Axial Transport Lift named AL.

"Follow me," said the captain. "I think I remember where we parked."

***

"Wow," said Dietrich once they were back inside AL. "I wish exotic hotties would jump on *me* like that. You didn't mention you had a little MoonPie tucked away, Rhymes."

"Uh. First time I met her," said David, rubbing the back of his neck. "Second, I guess, if you count virtual."

"Well, you must have made a stellar first impression to merit such a greeting as zat, and I think we can rule out virtue, hon hon."

"She must be some kind of Loonie, alright," put in Fergus, "if she went for Rhymes."

Then the doll joined in, unfiltered, with his squeaky little voice.

"But definitely put together right. Is it true, David? Looney women wear no support... up top?"

There was silence from the women. It was the kind of silence that wise men fear, not the peaceful kind. It seemed a cold front was moving in as well.

Again, they detected no movement riding AL.

"We're almost there," said Wildman, "I feel it getting quite heavy in here."

"I'll say," muttered the Russian.

Then the doors opened up on a scene both bucolic and surreal. Greenery rose in tiers, rising up to an arching sky. The corn was standing tall. It looked like a scene from "Field of Dreams," except the crops stood in the stands, and we were the players on the field.

And beyond the growing plants all neatly boxed in ordered rows, the arching sky was inverted. To the left and right, it curved upward, bending out of sight. We could see we were within a gigantic torus spinning in space. The sun was even now streaking across the glass-panel sky.

They had all done their reading. They knew it wasn't just glass. Rather, it was space-age multi-layer laminates of various transparent composites, involving polycarbonate, quartz, graphene, electrochromic films, vacuum layers for strength and energy efficiency, and self-healing outer coatings, enhanced with nanoconstructed DLC. David decided to simply call them 'the sky.'

But the strobing lights and crawling shadows were just bizarre...

L5 for Dummies: Chapter 15

(the light cycle)

Residents very quickly adapt to the fifteen-second 'day' cycle outside in the habitat and agrarian rings. There is no proper 'east' or 'west.' Their equivalents are called 'spinward' and 'counter-spinward' instead.

Think of it like this. You are in a doughnut that is transparent on its inner side (the half that faced the middle). You are standing on the inner side of the outer crust. Got that image in your mind? It's high noon, and the sun is in a fixed position far outside of your doughnut. Its light slants in a little to one side, but basically straight 'above' you (toward the middle again). Simple, right?

Now the doughnut begins to spin, and to you, it appears to creep across the sky toward the direction of that spin. So, the sun 'sets' spinward as your shadow stretches counter-spinward, disappearing at the fall of night.

Since L5 is spinning at 2 RPM (one whole rotation every thirty seconds), station 'night' is going to last only fifteen seconds before 'dawn' arrives counterspinward. Your shadow comes rushing from spinward to meet you seven and a half seconds later. It's high noon again, and the cycle can repeat. Each fifteen-second day is followed by fifteen seconds of station night. 'Is that all?' you might ask. No. There's more. 'More? Oh. Goodie!'

Let's review first.
1) The sun sets spinward, while your shadow lengthens counterspinward.
2) 15-second night.
3) The sun rises counterspinward and your long shadow begins shrinking toward you.
4) 15-second day as the sun crosses the sky.
Rinse and repeat.

But do not fear the darkness, friend. You need not stumble about for half of your work cycle. For at night, there's still plenty of light to work with (and to toil under). Though the sun no longer shines directly upon you, there's a big bar of light reflecting from the station's far side above! It's only 450 meters away at most, and another 'bar' of light shines down from an even nearer source: the back of the inner ring directly coreward. These bars of light shine above your head, like those old fluorescent bulbs in ancient movies. They provide more than adequate light for most activities.

Summary: In a festive oscillation, the light on L5 station shines down nearly constantly. It's never really dark. So go out and have some fun with your daughter or your son. Maybe have a stroll around the park!

"There you are, captain!" came a cheerful-sounding voice.

It was followed by a cheerful-looking man. He had a big drooping mustache, fading to gray, and a cowboy hat on his head. He'd resemble the guy from Monopoly if the hat were a topper instead. Add a monocle to that, and he could be the Planters peanut man. Yeah. That was it.

"You're late. We were expecting you sixty *days* ago. What were you doing all that time?

"Time is a precious thing," said Wildman, "I never waste it. We made a quick visit with the Loonies and helped a young woman to pay off a debt. Sixty revs isn't so very long to wait."

"True enough. True enough. Then let's get this shindig started. I've already made my speech. I had to give the folks something to do while they waited."

"So sorry to have missed *that*, mayor," said Wildman.

From his flat, unconvincing tone, David could tell he'd be just as sorry about having accidentally dodged a bullet.

They all exchanged introductions with the mayor of Habitat Ring Two, Hiram Duffy. His ring had the honor of hosting the event and had voted on a theme. Frontier Picnic had won. The cadets were led to a place of honor. It was a table with a red and white checkered cloth up in front. There was seating along only one side of it, Last Supper style.

The crowd wasn't large, just a couple hundred folks looking to have a good time. He saw cowboy hats and wicker baskets and some nods to period apparel, small things like bandannas and bonnets.

They had sack races in burlap bags and a strange kind of relay where one carried an egg on a spoon. The pie-eating contest was messy. Dietrich had wanted to join that one, but the cadets were told to keep their clothing clean, having only the one outfit each. They made Roid Rage the judge instead. The event was being televised to play for the folks back on Earth (following suitable editing).

The biggest attraction (for the young folks at least) was playing Frisbee Football on the lawn. It was amazing what they could get those disks to do. The weird physics of the station had them curving all over the place. The younger L5'ers, having grown up here, had an instinctive feel for how the Coriolis force would affect their tosses, with many being strange indeed.

And all the while the day/night cycle flickered on and off. Unsettling at first, this quickly began to seem normal. The area was thoroughly temperature controlled to an early summer warmth. Crops stood in the 'fields' that looked like a giant's window boxes. And like King Arthur's song from the musical Camelot, the weather was at their command. The rain may never fall 'til after sundown, indeed. More like, 'until the agricultural council turns the overhead sprinklers on.

They had a touching surprise on the menu for David. Having read his book in preparation, dinner was to be pancakes smothered in maple syrup and applesauce. Apples they had, and enough grains to make an acceptable batter. But maple trees?

David heard that at the colony end, they kept viable seeds for all kinds of Earth flora--even stuff David thought ought to be discouraged (like poison ivy). It wouldn't surprise him one bit to find some of those little whirly-bird things stashed in some frozen cupboard over there. But no, the L5'ers had gone new-old-school, boiling down their molasses from sugar beets with some modern additives to reduce the aftertaste. It was actually a pretty fair imitation. And he was touched they would go to all that trouble just for him.

So, they fired up their solar convection ovens and started to flap the jacks. And David was offered the first one cooked before they'd begin to pile up the stacks. It looked a little underdone and was oddly shaped as well, dog-eared from being scraped up off the pan.

"My apologies, guardian," said the chef. "Let me make you another."

But David declined her offer, considering his new brother. With a glance at Pierre, he took the plate and held it up for everyone to see.

102

"They say the first one might be a mess, and that might be so sometimes. But some pancakes can really surprise you. This one here is good enough for David L. Grimes. It might be burnt or broken a bit, but aren't we all?"

This actually earned him a tittering of laughter and some applause. It turned out the L5'ers were all about never wasting anything and especially not food. Okay. Oxygen was first, then food, then all the other stuff.

The napkins were cloth, and the plates were ceramic. L5'ers avoided paper waste. Complete reuse was the order of the days. And the pans that made the cakes required no oil. By mandate, and with many a metallurgist gloating, mankind had finally managed to manufacture a pan with a proper non-stick coating.

All in all, it had been a pleasant three or four centuries (each 100 station days being fifty minutes). But Mayor Duffy's joke was wearing thin. David resolved to start calling them revs now like everybody else.

One more ceremony of note occurred at that picnic. When everyone had finished eating and was leaning back in satisfaction. Mayor Duffy called out a new surprise.

"What's with the drunken drone?" asked Little Ropey.

David pursed his lips, squinting at the mankin. Big Ropey's newfound affectation still annoyed him--but the toy was right.

Zig-zagging toward them was a small hoverdrone of the four-prop variety, responding to the mayor's summons. It was dipping and bobbing and over-correcting all over the place on its approach. It nearly spun into a wall at one point.

"New unit," replied Duffy, seated at the table beside him. "The chips are fresh up from Earth. Arrived on your very transport, I'm told."

"Yeah?" said Carlotta. "I guess they don't make them like they used to?"

The mayor chuckled.

"Not at all, guardian," he replied. "They make them there, but we train them up here. It takes a while for their adaptive programming to get used to the Coriolis forces on the station. You should see how they behave on the inner rings. Let me tell you."

Please don't, thought David. And for once, he was spared the anecdote.

For it was just then that the gloopy thing arrived, bouncing twice on the table before the mayor and whizzing to a full stop.

"I have a surprise for our guests here," Duffy said into his microphone, "The Crew Who Knew What to Do."

A smattering of polite applause followed.

"As most of you know, it is our custom once a year to award the key to the station to an outstanding group or individual who has contributed to the well-being of L5 or to space exploration in general."

He opened the drone's package compartment and withdrew from it a ridiculously large gold plastic key hanging from an equally ostentatious chain. David suspected he knew where this might be going. He kicked Speranza's foot under the table. When he'd gotten her attention, he raised his eyebrows at her.

"After the solar storm, we were planning to award it to Captain Eugene Wildman."

(Thunderous applause accompanied by some sharp whistles).

"But on his advice (the captain is a humble man), the committee has agreed to instead award it to these exceptional guardians who stepped up when Luna was endangered. Who will accept for your team?"

By this time, Speranza had passed the word on down and whispered the consensus opinion back to David, who stood and approached the mayor. Duffy offered him the key, but he reached for the mike instead.

"As we have said many times on record, we of the Space Force crew recently of Ellington Base are proud to have been at the right time and place with the right skills to have thwarted that dire attack. It is our privilege to have served humanity that day."

A low chant began at the back of the crowd, growing in rhythm and volume as the others caught on.

"crew who knew. crew who knew. crew who knew."

To this backdrop, David continued.

"It was a team effort. And let me assure you, in times of stress, it's good to have a gritter at your back."

"Crew Who Knew. Crew Who Knew. Crew Who Knew."

"There is not one among us who deserves this honor more than any other. So we will fall back on tradition. In most team sports, the game ball goes to the man or woman who took the winning shot.

(Subdued murmuring)

"Accepting today for team Krepkiyzad. Will be none other than the fellow who speared that rogue rock. He rages at asteroids; he put the sour in kraut. Dietrich... Stentz!"

(several competing chants eventually resolving to:)

"Dietrich! Dietrich! Dietrich! Dietrich! Dietrich!"

***

Dietrich's oversized key to the station hung from a golden chain around his thick, almost neck. It lay proudly draped over his Grateful Dead T-shirt with its 'Anthem of the Sun' platitude. That legendary rock band from the sixties had done much to launch that vibrant era. May all of their members, now deceased, rest in peace (and gratitude).

"Make way!" shouted Simon as they pressed through the bystanders heading for the lift. "Dead man walking here."

Hey, that was much better than the jape he'd been planning to make about The Walking Deadhead. The formerly humorless

105

Simon was coming right along as a stinging wit. It made David's funny bone swell with pride.

"This was nice, he casually observed as they marched along with Dietrich in the lead. I especially like the balloons they used to decorate the place for our reception. There must be a hundred of them."

He had his head thrown back and was admiring the little red things as they bumped along the 'ceiling' of the ring. There must be a slight air current up there from the cyclers. The station's spin alone shouldn't cause them to roll around like that.

"Oh, those?" said Captain Wildman. "The lufters are always up there, and they're functional, not festive."

"What do they do?"

"They serve as both an early detection system and a temporary remedy in case there are leaks."

David thought about this. It made perfect sense. If some part of L5's glass sky had a leaky seal, the balloon-like things (lufters?) would be drawn toward it and cluster there. They might even provide a temporary seal until someone could get up there and fix it. Dietrich turned and asked over his shoulder, "There wouldn't happen to be ninety-nine of them, would there?

"I believe there are, cadet," replied the captain with a sardonic smile. "Very astute. The L5 council is a superstitious lot known for its zany sense of humor."

Dietrich resumed his pace and began whistling a tune David soon recognized.

Of course! Neunundneunzig.

"I would have thought Grimes, if Nena-one, would have been the first to make zat connection," observed Pierre with a snicker.

The Frenchman was right. First Simon beats me to the punchline, and now this. Even here in Earth-like gravity, I must be slipping.

In this context, even Julia's casual comment now made better sense. "He's really got sass when the rubber hits the glass." It was quite a compliment in retrospect.

They arrived at the lift shaft to find the mayor's wife, Elizabeth, singing into the intercom with a look of consternation plastered on her face.

"Elevator. Oh, elevator! Station keeper Elizabeth Duffy here; I'm in need of conveyance."

"Problem, Councilwoman?" asked Wildman, striding to the fore.

Her thumb was pressing the call button repeatedly. She looked over at the man.

"Oh. Captain Gene. Yes. It's this damned elevator. Ever since the new unit was installed after the solar storm, it fails to come when I call. And you can call me Betty."

"I think I see the problem," said the captain, cocking his head. "He doesn't like to be referred to as an elevator. He finds it demeaning. He prefers to be called an Axial Lift."

"Really?"

"Try it and see," said Wildman.

She held down the call button, saying, "Elizabeth Duffy here. I need an... Axial Lift."

The doors hissed open with a whoosh of air as the pressure equalized.

"At your service, madam," said the lift in his deep baritone. "And Betty, when you call me, you can call me AL.

As they headed back up the spoke, David thought about the pancake feast he'd just enjoyed. The spacers had been really kind to try to make him feel at home. It wasn't like a breakfast in America, but they'd really done their best to make this a pleasant journey. He was a foreigner here, but he doubted he'd find a better reception anywhere from Boston to Kansas. He'd be staying here on the station for a while. Yes. There was no rush. He could take his time getting to know them all (and Toto too).

He felt someone plucking at his sleeve. It was Carlotta.

"Grimes. You in there, Grimes? I swear, you have such a short little span of attention!

Oh, my life is so hard.

Simon was asking something of AL.

"Can we make another quick stop at the inner ring? I promised Julia I'd snag some toys for the kids."

He held up his satchel, bulging with frisbees and other party favors from the feast.

"I deem that a worthy reason for a stopover," said the lift. "With the captain's permission?"

"Make it so, Number One," said the captain, deadpan.

"They're in the lunar gym right now. For that we'll have to swing around at the hub and descend on spoke four."

"I *said* make it so."

"Already doing it, captain. No need to get huffy."

David grinned, recalling the mayor's wife was Duffy. Intentional? There was obviously more to this elevator than one might imagine. He still thought of it as a Wonkavator.

When the doors opened, they found themselves overlooking a basketball court where the little Loonies were all dribbling away. It was no standard court, though. The nets were each positioned thirty-five feet above the gymnasium floor. Even as he watched, Julia came fast-breaking forward down the center, bouncing her ball to one side. At around the half-court line, she launched herself high and toward the spectator stands, then made a swooping arc in mid-air toward the basket. She didn't quite achieve the altitude to dunk, but her curving layup was spot-on, ricocheting off the backboard and rocketing through the hoop.

She landed gracefully in the key paint, then looked up as if noticing the observers for the first time. The children, too, stopped dribbling and smiled up at their visitors.

With several astounding leaps and bounds, she rapidly rose to greet them. The delighted smile that graced her fair lips declared she was happy to meet them. Her athletic efforts had left her aglow with an unearthly light, and the pallor of her lovely limbs was quite the winsome sight. Simon was the first to speak, stepping forward shyly.

"I brought you these," he said, proffering his bag of trinkets. "For the kids."

"No need to *thank* me or anything," he added hopefully.

She stared at him a moment and blinked, then accepted.

"If my kiss be unwelcome, then so let it be; I shall refrain," said she.

Simon looked devastated.

Julia turned to David and spoke as if only to him.

"I have some *wonderful* news to share, David."

"Share away," said David. "We always welcome wonderful news. The other kind--not so much."

She laughed. It was something to treasure, like a flute going on a little outing with a songbird, each seeking to outdo the other. Trilling, David would learn, the Loonies called it.

"I just received approval to join you all in the colony ring. My muscle mass is finally up to snuff. It helps that I wasn't born on Luna like these others. I'm only ten percent shy of Earth-normal. We're going to be neighbors now. Isn't that great! We can do all *sorts* of things together."

"Yes," said David, his cheeks beginning to redden. "So, you're signing up for the colony mission then?"

"Of course. We are *all* seeking acceptance. My fellows from pod seventeen are still working up to it. The doctors are administering hormones to stimulate their osteoplasts and steroids to increase their musculature. Mars gravity is twice ours. I'm *sure* they can make it. The mission will find our skills most useful, both on the journey and on the red planet itself. I look forward to bunking beside you."

With that, she threw herself over the edge of what looked like a deadly fall and drifted down to alight on the floor of the court below.

"She could have *insisted*," Simon groused, a dour look on his face.

Roid Rage roared with laughter. "Bro, you can just file that grievance under, 'Opportunities missed due to my own stupidity.'"

***

"We've arrived." Announced the captain. "I trust you can find your way from here and get settled into your new quarters. I must now take my leave. Other duties await. Other places to be and more work on my plate."

He turned to Krepkiyzad and saluted him first, as a superior officer ought not.

"Good day, sir."

The commander looked befuddled.

"Captain Gene," he said haltingly. "Is improper to--"

"I said, 'Good day, sir!'" he repeated, stubbornly holding the salute.

Krepkiyzad's reluctance was clear as he finally returned it.

Wildman then turned on his heels and marched briskly away.

When Krepkiyzad turned back to the cadets, a crooked smile was resting on his lips.

This didn't fit his face at all, making him seem vaguely predatory. It was so incongruous that it caused the cadets to cringe. It felt like an attack. Was it... satisfaction? ...vindication? Whatever it was, and demoted or not, it seemed the old major was back.

David had to fix this. The others looked to him. They shifted aside, opening a path. All of their expressions were grim. As he walked up to the major (for a major he was at the moment), he considered several tactics he might try.

A hug would certainly do the trick, wiping that unholy grin from his chin. But that might end in violence. No. Something subtler was necessary here. He slowed his pace and came to stand before a Krepki possessed of self-command.

"Commander?" he began.

"With all due respect, Captain Gene seemed most unruly. And he was once your student, did you say? I must ask you. However did you manage to put up with such a cheeky and undisciplined individual?"

It was working, thank the stars. He watched as Krepki's 'smile' dissolved, banished back to the nightmarish oblivion from which it had doubtless arisen. The commander's stoic, long-suffering expression of indigestion returned.

David heaved a mental sigh and let tragic irony do what comfort could not.

***

They'd been assigned new quarters. They'd been assigned new teams. They even had new uniforms only slightly creased from being made from parachute cloth. But they'd iron out those wrinkles soon enough, they'd all been told.

David was unpacking in their tiny little room. It was a double again, like at Ellington but smaller. At least they kept the roommates the same. As peevish as Pierre could be, he was used to the fellow now. He wouldn't need to break in someone new. Who knew what annoying habits Roidy might have? And he knew there'd be a murder if Little Ropey ever tried to share his room.

He carefully withdrew the photo he had carried all the way from Earth. It was the memento he'd been allowed.

It was going to be close quarters, space being at a premium here on L5. Otherwise, the layout was similar to their former room. They could make this work. David kicked off his shoes and started to make up his barely David-sized bed, stretching the thin new sheets over its bare mattress and making military corners.

"What is that on your feet, Daveed?" came the voice of his old new roommate.

He paused in his unpacking of the pillow.

"In America, we call them socks. Why? What do the French call them?"

"Ugly."

David looked down at the festive red tubes girding his ankles and grinned. They had rockets embroidered all over them, taking flight at every angle, and words that said 'Rocket Man.'

"They were a gift from my mother. She knew we weren't allowed to bring much up into space apart from clothing, so for my Christmas gift, she gave me these. Knitted them herself."

Pierre stepped closer, no difficult feat in the tiny room they shared.

"They are perfectly hideous," he declared, "which doubtless means you will wear them all the time."

"You bet. It took her a whole week. You can't buy something like *these* with fabricator credits."

"I am thinking perhaps that this is a good thing, *mon ami.*"

"It was tough hiding them during the TV interviews. I wore another standard pair over them. Wearing two pairs is kind of a thing with me now, I guess. They're a little itchy but nice. Mom heard it was cold in space and told me these might provide a little warmth. I don't think she was referring to the temperature."

Pierre paused and looked up at David.

"Someday, I think I would like to meet this mother of yours."

"I doubt that will be possible," said David. "But the next time I'm in the comm booth, you should come along. I'm sure she'd get a kick out of meeting you too. Probably adopt you on the spot... *frère*."

"Pfft!" said the Frenchman, "I accept."

Pfft?

The outflow of air is what made him Pierre. Don't want to spook him, though. Easy does it. His budding bromance with his roommate from France was a fragile thing. Or *was* it?

Seven...

Spinward March

His teammates were all getting new assignments today. David already knew his. Project Ironseed had been shut down pending a full investigation into its safety protocols and long-term viability. A shame, really. The work had been promising--but now? David suspected the mothballs (not actually a deterrent to nanites) would be piled on with a heavy hand. There was fierce competition for science funding these days. Replicating nanotechnology had been weighed in the scales... but had eaten the scales before its full benefit could be measured.

David, his roommate, Speranza, and Leilani had instead been assigned to the chief ecologist of the Martian ring.

The four primary rings of the station's colony end were nearly identical to those of the main station. The increased size of the inner rings was the chief difference. Rather than emulating lunar gravity, these larger rings would emulate that of Mars. The main structure had been completed, but many areas remained unpressurized, and many more were unfinished, yet to be put to their function.

Colony habitat ring one was complete, providing living space and atmosphere for a small group of colonists who had already gathered. The rest was still under construction. For now, his team was learning to operate all the tenders they used in the main station's aggro-rings. And there were a lot of them. Later, they would take part in a mock terraforming exercise in one of the colony's inner Mars-G habitats.

At present, Pierre was guiding a little hoverdrone called an eye-in-the-sky. He zipped along and then descended for a close-up of cornfield six. David was watching over his shoulder as Pierre operated the lone treadie in their room. Pierre upped the magnification, giving it a proper zoom. It depicted some browning and spotty sections on an outer leaf. Zooming closer still, they saw one of the little buggers, its cornicles abristle.

"I do not see, *mon ami*, why zey even *included* zese pests."

"You know the answer to that, Pierre."

"We need to grow the GMOD strains in earth-like conditions, lest they develop some weakness earthly pests might exploit to blight a whole crop. Are you going to spray this batch? Aphids can ruin a field.

"No, *frère* Daveed. I will send a note to Flowerchild to release more ladybugs. She has been most stingy with them lately. Holistic solutions are preferred over pesticides, *non?*"

David still enjoyed that 'frère.' It wasn't an endearment, though; he used it more like the slang word 'bro.'

Just then, there came a knock upon their door.

It was Roidy and Ropey. It was always nice to have visitors, but from their sour expressions, it looked like they had something serious on their minds.

"What can I help you gentlemen with?" he asked, stepping aside for them to enter.

116

The two exchanged a glance, then Dietrich stepped in, grimacing and massaging a spot on the back of his neck.

"It's about our new assignment," said Fergus.

"What about it?"

"We're getting it today. Our new supervisor wants to meet us in the mess."

"Okay. What's that got to do with *me*?"

"We were thinking that since you *know* the man, you might come along and help to smooth things out."

"Oh? Who is it?"

"Richard Cooke."

"Bungalow Bill?"

"Yeah," said Roidy. "He's stationed up here, and we're afraid he might still be upset about how we, um... liberated his schooner from its berth."

",,,and named it and stole its maiden flight," added Ropey in a rush.

"Yeah, that, said RR. "We were thinking since you know the guy--"

"I only met him once. Briefly. It's not like we got couples tattoos or anything. He was just the guy they sent to replace me when my moonraker slipped a tread."

Prior to this, David hadn't known these two could make puppy-dog eyes. It was surprising but effective.

He sighed.

"Let me get my stuff."

***

We'll just have to see about this 'Continuing Story of Bungalow Bill,' thought David, drumming his fingers on the table. The mess was empty now and inaptly named at present. Not a fork was out of place. David and the R&Rs were seated at a table, staring at the door. It was the appointed hour and place to meet the man who rumor said was the finest teleoperator in all of outer space. Richard Cooke, the man, the legend. What did he look like, they wondered?

And from the door emerged a man whose faded jeans and day-glo shirt marked him as more of a hippie than a legendary figure. He was quite tall, however, and lanky as well. This must be him, thought David, who'd expected someone bigger.

Bill was said to be a recluse. And though he was a Loonie, he handled Earth-like gravity with a stubborn stride as he entered. David and his fellows rose to meet him. He scowled at them and crossed his arms, looking them over as if dissatisfied. David stepped to the fore to take the bull by the horns, ready to greet him with a disarming rhyme. He paused for a breath, then began.

> *"A crusty old codger named Bungalow Bill*
> *Got mad when cadets swiped his sky-riding thrill.*
> *Despite their urgent need,*
> *They're regretful for the deed.*
> *Perhaps he'll forgive them? They hope that he will."*

David extended a hand to be shaken. But rather than take it, Bill just glared at him for a long moment, his steely eyes shaded by his brow. He swiped the back of his hand across his mouth. Then, with a look of consternation, he thrust both of his hands into his back pockets and paced the floor a bit. Then, he turned and pointed a finger at David, saying,

> *"The theft of my ship was a blow to my pride.*
> *The wrath of the righteous was boiling inside.*
> *But now, to be fair,*
> *I had better clear the air--*
> *After all, I once done stole your moonraker ride."*

Bungalow Bill made a finger gun, blew on the end, and holstered it. He spat in his open palm and extended it toward David with a smug grin.

Oh, it was on! Or was it? What would be the point? Though itching to strike back, hadn't he just won? It didn't feel much like winning, though. It felt like being outdone in cheek. The rhyme had triggered David's overly competitive streak.

His inner angel arose, its whispers seeming puny and weak.

Throw in the towel. Yield the floor. Fold on this here hand.

Tap out. Call it quits. Call it a day.

Take the man's extended hand.

Turn tail before you're in too deep.

Clock out. Bail. Hang it up. Let it go and suck it in.

In the name of all that's holy, let the rookie win!

Finally, he heeded that voice and spat in his own right hand. Though not as tall in stature, David Grimes would be the bigger man.

Bill got a satisfied look that practically screamed 'Game, set, and match' to David's wounded ego.

"I was once surprised by an Earther's humor," he said. "I'm glad that you joined us up here. To face the rigors of space, you gotta have moxie and wits aplenty. But most important is the ability to laugh at fate. Truth is, son, it pleases me now to proudly fly around in Patroclus. That ship's a legend now. All the Loonies are trilling about it.

"Trilling?" asked Fergus, who had wandered over. "What's that?"

"That noise the Lunaborn make from back in their throats, that ululating laughter. It means they're happy about something."

"Like that Julia woman did," added Dietrich.

"Oh, that dolphin sound?" said Fergus, "like she swallowed a kookaburra?"

"*I* thought it was pretty," said David defensively.

"You thought *she* was pretty," Roidy clarified.

Ropey chimed in with a gruff imitation of Krepkiyzad, "Cadets can call Loonies pretty after duty hours!"

Bill looked confused but added "You should hear a whole pod of them doing it together. Downright eerie kind of group singing. Beautiful in its way. Loonie tunes, I call them."

"But *you're* a Loonie, Bill," objected David.

"Yeah. First generation, though. Never grew up in a pod. You might not even know it to look at me. I lost two whole inches after moving up here. Still like the lower-G rings, though. Earth grav makes these old bones tired."

"Speaking of tired, said David. Krepkiyzad sure caught on quickly about the centripetal force multiplier. He had us marching spinward all morning."

Bill snickered. "Yup, spinward adds about ten pounds. Wait'll he gets you running."

"So *that's* why I felt so out of shape," said Dietrich in a huff.

"Maybe I misspoke. A big fella like you might put on more like fifteen. Count yourself lucky. Up on the lunar rings, running spinward can nearly *double* your apparent weight. It's how the loonies are training for the colony mission."

Fergus scowled.

"Leave it to Krepkiyzad to find a way for us to run uphill all the way out from base AND back."

David wondered briefly what beef Fergus might have against the Russian. Hadn't he named his punching bag back at Ellington Krepkiyzad? It's probably nothing, just a clash of personalities. Curious, David posed Bill the ten-dollar question.

"You didn't come all the way down here to talk about marching and trilling. What's up?"

"On this station, that's a valid and important question, son. But I take your meaning. I came to introduce these two to their next major project. We're going on a hunt for ice asteroids."

"Ice? Aren't those pretty rare?" asked Fergus.

"They are," said Bill, "but they do exist. We'll have to go deeper in, beyond 2.7 AU (the "snow line"). Mars is going to need a lot more water if we're ever to get it habitable. We'll be bombarding it with anything we can find out there."

"Now *that's* what I'm talking about!" said Dietrich, planting a fist on the table. "Some action."

David saw his chance to seize the moment and redeem himself. He cleared his throat, drawing the attention of the others. Then he began to sing:

Deep in the backbelt where the icy ast'roid lies,
Bill and Patroclus were taken by surprise.
So Roid and Ropey zapped it right out of the skies!
All the children sing:

The trio joined him for a laughing chorus of "Hey, Bungalow Bill."

They were halfway through it when David's phone, Bartholomew, spoke up. His message caused David to heave a sigh. Though reluctant to embrace this encounter, he now regretted having to leave it. He'd been enjoying the moment. It was *his* kind of weird. He'd just have to host a sing-along another time, he feared.

***

David ran full tilt toward the closing lift doors. He had seen Carlotta standing just inside. As he trotted up, they halted and began to spread back open. She was wearing a spacesuit. *Borrowed?* To his knowledge, none of the cadets had been issued one yet. He was still saving up his fabricator credits to buy one of his own. Being caught unprepared on a space station? Not ideal.

"Room for one more, honey," she quipped.

It sounded eerily hollow from her closed helmet. It landed nonetheless. Although it had been nearly a hundred years since that Twilight Zone episode had aired, it was still funny and memorable (in a fatalistic kind of way).

"What's with the suit?" asked David, catching his breath as he stepped in.

"I could ask you the same, Rhymes. Diplomatic reception?"

David was wearing his full dress uniform.

"Nah. I've been summoned to the council hall. They didn't say why. I thought I'd best get gussied up. You?"

She released the seals and removed her helmet.

"I've been assigned to the quantum hub. Since I'm doing a dual major in quantum systems engineering and machine intelligence, they thought it might suit my career goals. Add to that my duties as NBI liaison, and I have the whole trifecta."

Wow, and I thought aerospace was tough. Carlotta had quite a head on her space-suited shoulders.

"That still doesn't explain the vac-suit."

She heaved a sigh.

"Don't they teach you anything at Toronto, Rhymes? Quantum systems are very delicate. To avoid even mild corrosion of their components, they're kept in an environment of pure xenon rather than standard atmosphere mix. No oxidation that way. As a noble gas, xenon doesn't chemically react with anything."

"Minor downside," she added dryly, "we can't breathe it."

AL dropped David off first, then sailed off with Rhinemaiden, headed for the quantum core.

He took a moment to straighten his uniform jacket and make sure his hat was on straight. He was in Earth gravity, so there was that. He set off down the hallway toward the sealed double doors marked with a golden ring, presumably the chamber that he sought. He wasn't wrong.

"David Grimes?" squawked the intercom.

"Yes," he said with confidence, planting his palm on the reader.

The doors slid apart, revealing a large (by station standards) circular room. *Circular?* More a flattened sphere than a circle, with the ceiling arching above and steps descending from where he stood. Below was a ring-like table, all golden and metallic, and seated around it were the stationkeepers, intent on a speaker in the well.

The speaker was well-known to David. He was the white rabbit, Tù, telepresent by holo-projector. He had the others spellbound in some mischief he was weaving.

"So a bear walks into a bar in Realms. The bartender says, 'What'll you have?' The bear thinks about it and thinks about it, finally saying, 'I guess I'd like a martini.' The bartender says, 'Here you go, bear,' and sets it down in front of him. The bear takes a sip and says, 'Don't you mean... why the big paws?' To which the bartender says, 'Olive you know it's been a rough night; just drink your martini.'"

"Then in walks a horse... Oh, hello, David."

"Hello, Tù. What are *you* doing here?"

"I was asked to help mediate a dispute the L5 council was having with the state of Maine over a trade deal. We're just waiting for the governor to arrive..."

"Welcome to the council, guardian," said a man in a high-backed chair opposite. "We've a little business to conduct, after which we'll explain why you were summoned. Come in. Have a seat. You know some of us already. Come and meet the rest. We are a merry band of brethren who operate this station. A ruling authority like no other."

David stepped down and found an empty seat, pondering the chief councilman's odd turn of phrase. The man was wearing a hood, for pity's sake. Captain Wilder had warned him that the council was 'known for its zany sense of humor.' He should have taken this more to heart, especially given the warning's source. Was this the hatter's tea party complete with a white rabbit? The truth, as he'd soon discover, was even farther out of left field.

Looking around, David did spot several people he already knew. There was Hiram Duffy (sans cowboy hat), his mustachios drooping to either side like weeping willow fronds. And there was... Doctor van der Meer? But she looked like a much younger version of herself. Until she turned to face him. The right half of her face was darker in complexion and had the beginnings of age wrinkles that he remembered. But the left was pristine, like that of a porcelain doll, but possessed of the vigor of youth. Her smile was warm, however, as she regarded him and brought the whole together better than a Picasso.

The hooded man introduced the other six. Each was in charge of one of the station's rings. Chuckling, he drew back his hood and announced himself with a flourish.

"I am Kevin Farsprocket III, Chancellor of L5 and Lord of the Rings. These others are my ringwraiths, my Nazgûl, if you will."

David could detect no hint of humor in his delivery. Best not to give offense.

"Shouldn't there be *nine* of them?" he probed cautiously.

Kevin rolled his eyes, saying, "Hello-o, Earth to David Grimes. *Everyone* knows that the Witch-king of Angmar was slain at the Battle of Gondor!"

David honestly didn't know how to respond to that. He was still considering when there came a ringing sound.

"He's on line two, Lord Kevin," said the rabbit, "awaiting your permission to connect."

"Go ahead and answer it, Tù," said Kevin. "After all, it's what we're paying you for."

Thank Gandalf, thought David. A reprieve from the governor.

A man's head appeared in the holo-well just across from Tù.

"Governor Dubois," he announced, eyeing the rabbit sharply. "Have I the honor of addressing the L5 council?"

"You do," said Lord Kevin, as sober as any statesman. "This is Tù. We've asked him to mediate our dispute. You promised us lobsters, sir--*live*, not frozen."

"They'll cook up just as well either way," the man said dismissively.

"They weren't for eating," declared Tù, smoothly picking up the thread. "They were meant for breeding--something we rabbits know a little bit about."

"Breeding?" sputtered Dubois, dubious. "I'll have you know live lobsters require a very specific ecosystem to thrive. How on God's green Earth, or above it, rather, do you intend to keep said lobsters alive?"

"That's the council's concern. They're not paying for this batch. One thing I *do* know is that popsicles can't bear young."

"I'll sue."

"You have no jurisdiction here. We'll tie it up in court until after your term limit expires."

"Then you'll *never* get your lobsters!"

Tù stared at the irate governor and narrowed his pink eyes. With ears fully erect, his pink nose wriggled cutely. And as only very few ever saw a rabbit do, he intimidated the man, absolutely.

"You assume, sir, that L5 has no other alternative for its supplier. And we all know that when you *assume*, you make an 'ass' of 'you'... and the entire state of Maine. It so happens that the good people of Newfoundland have quoted L5 a very attractive price for their lobsters, a very attractive price indeed!"

The senator reared back as if struck.

"Here now. I won't be threatened or outmaneuvered by a jumped-up algorithm with a bunny complex. I'm tired of your harelip!" he blustered.

"And you, sir," returned Tù, "have a bad toupée!

The senator became apoplectic.

"*What?*" said the rabbit. "What's sauce for the goose is sauce for the slander, I say."

"And next time," he sniffed, "bring butter."

Then he cut the connection.

After the council's titters had died down, Tù turned back to Kevin.

"I can predict with 93% certainty he'll call back in less than an hour, capitulating to your every demand. If not, there's always the Canadian deal I lined up."

"Well done, Sir Rabbit."

"Can I take it then, your lordship, we have a deal?" asked the rabbit with one ear cocked.

"You may. Tell your empress she can expect delivery at the next drop."

The rabbit got a goofy grin and faded away.

"Now on to other matters. Since Cadet Grimes is here, we can begin immediately, unless anyone needs a toilet break? No? Good."

"David, there are several things you must be made aware of. The first is this. All members of your team are being granted their second stripe. As E-2s, they can display their insignia and are granted the official title, guardian."

That's great.

"You, however, are a special case. Both you and Cadet M'Babu will receive a *third* stripe, putting you in nominal command of all the others."

That's... unexpected.

"Moreover, Nazgûl van der Meer here is now your unofficial sponsor in a new secret project you'll be helping us with."

That's... I honestly don't know what to make of that. And he was serious... about the ringwraith stuff?

"I'll leave it for her to explain. It's all very hush-hush, don't you know. She'll bring you up to speed right after we've recited the council oath. Without objection? Good. Begin.

"Four rings for the Loonies in their halls of stone," they chanted.

Four more for Mars, soon to fill our sky.

Eight in earthly gravity, those we call our own,

Where agriculture, industry, and habitation lie.

One ring to rule them all.

One ring to guide them.

One ring to set things right,

From solar storms to hide them!"

David's eye came to rest again on the ring-shaped council table. The pledge was weirdly beautiful in its way. The doctor rose from her seat and headed toward him as the others shuffled out.

***

"So... David."

"Doctor."

"Have you been keeping yourself busy?"

"Some. Stab any troublesome hobbits lately? Bag any Bagginses?"

Again, she flashed that winning smile--the one that somehow united her face. She sobered and looked at him knowingly. He was certain she was tired of explaining, but it would rest uneasily between them until she did.

"Kevin is a genius," she declared instead, "and an able administrator despite his... eccentricities. He's obviously quite taken with Tolkien. What's less obvious is his earnest desire to do good and his incredible capacity to accomplish the seemingly impossible."

Quite a testimonial. David would withhold judgment then. Many had said it, but perhaps Aristotle said it first. 'There is no great genius without a mixture of madness.'

"We should have listened to him before the solar storm," she went on wistfully. "If we had, many more people would be alive today to mock him. Did you know the lufters were his idea? You should have seen the scorn they heaped on him back in the day for that. Well, we're listening *now*, and no one with any sense is laughing."

"I see," said David, willing to risk being seen as senseless. "He's a high-*functioning* LARPer."

She paused to consider this.

"Exactly."

"So what are these things of which I must be made aware?"

"Straight to the point. That's what I like about you, Rhymes. Here it is, then. I'm working on a new project."

"I figured."

"This one's highly classified. And I need your cooperation."

"Why me? My squad and I are already on the farm team, under Andre Petrovic's guidance."

"This would be in addition to that. Andre is aware you'll be pulled out from time to time. Your cover is that it's for testing a new psychological methodology. Also, 'farm team?' I thought you were on the terraforming project."

"We will be. For now, they just have us familiarizing ourselves with the equipment by policing aggro ring two on the O-side. It helps that we're familiar with bugs."

She smiled again, that disconcerting smile.

"Speaking of that, did you bring back that Shepherd I loaned you?"

"Afraid not, doc. I left it Earthside, but it's in good hands-- with a young lady of my acquaintance who provides Community Assistance for Growing Entrepreneurs."

Her face fell. Well, *half* of it, anyway.

"Now I know I'll *never* get it back," she muttered.

"Since it's clear you're not going to ask," she continued, "the skin graft was to replace burnt tissue from when I was adrift at L4 during the solar storm."

"I thought maybe that was the case," David said, looking deeply into her eyes. "Was it bad?"

"It wasn't *good*," Anika replied. "My spacesuit shielded me from the worst of it. Unfortunately, my faceplate's polarizing filters weren't quite up to the task. They only had enough cloned tissue to do half for now. They'll get around to the rest when they've had time to grow more. I'm in no hurry. Function first over form."

"You're doing alright otherwise?"

"Well let's just say I'm glad I had some of my eggs frozen and set aside. Sometimes precautions pay off."

Yikes, David thought, suppressing a shudder.

"And at least I have my fancy new eye to show for it. It's proving to be very useful in my lab work. I can focus down practically to the microscopic range. Handy too for moving around in near darkness. And once the rest of my skin is replaced, I doubt anyone will even be able to tell which one it is."

"So, tell me more about this top secret project. I'm intrigued."

"I'd prefer to show you. Come with me."

"Sure, but one last thing, doc."

She paused, resuming her seat.

"How *do* they plan to keep those lobsters alive? They won't keep forever in an aquarium."

"They will in *this* one. Perhaps you haven't heard as yet. The release to the public isn't until next month. They plan to convert all of Colony Ring Three over to aquaculture."

He was growing to like that smile.

"They've got it partially filled already," Anika continued. "The flinger on Luna sends regular shipments of raw regolith up here. We collect a lot of oxygen to replenish our atmosphere. We do so by superheating it and running a current through it. A lot of what remains are metals we use for building new structures. Are you following, David?"

"I think so," said David with a smirk, "You're saying the moon isn't made of cheese as scientists predicted. It's made of *rust*."

"You know, Rhymes? Sometimes I can't tell whether you're being serious."

"Always keep them guessing. Go on, you were saying."

"The problem is hydrogen. The moon has very little, and anything from Earth is expensive to ship up here. One of my other teams is working on a way to harvest some from the solar wind, but successes so far are minimal at best."

"So how *do* they plan to fill Colony Ring Three with water?"

"Gossamer, mostly. One water-filled busload at a time. They're even trying to get a pod of dolphins shipped up, but PETA activists opposed to the idea have the GSF tangled up with stay orders. When we do get to Mars, it'll be nice to have a full tank and fish back on the menu again."

"Alright, doc. You've satisfied my curiosity on *that* matter. After space lobsters, anything you've got to show me will seem mundane."

She smiled again. But it wasn't the kindly, reassuring one he'd seen before. This was the smile of mystery, one that made David think he'd just stepped in something.

***

"AL, this is Doctor Anika van der Meer, authorization code Gold, Lima, Alpha, Delta, Oscar, Sierra. Take us to Blacksite 101 and authorize Junior Tech David Grimes to access it on my authority."

"Greetings, Doctor van der Meer. And may I be among the first to congratulate you on your promotion, David. Will you be wanting any music on this journey?"

Elevator music? Uhhh...

"What have you got, AL?" asked Anika cautiously.

Please don't encourage him. But maybe? Just maybe axial lift music will be better?

"Lots and lots. Captain Gene got me a subscription to Spotify. So far I've got 'Lift Me Up' by Rihanna, 'Never Gonna Give You Up, Never Gonna Let You Down' by Rick Astley, 'Up & Down' by the Vengaboys, 'Up Down' by Morgan Wallen (ft. Florida Georgia Line)...

Wrong again, Grimes. And am I sensing a pattern here?

"... Billy Joel's 'Updown Girl'..."

Okay, now he's just making stuff up.

"...and 'Tush' by ZZ Top"

Wait, what?

"Let's hear some of that last one, AL," said David's tongue before he could stop it.

Dart DAAR-dar, Duht-n-doo-DOO!
Dart DAAR-dar, Duht-n-doo-DOO!
I been up!, I been down!
Take my word, my way around
I ain't asking for much.
I said, Lord, take me downtown.
I'm just looking for some tush!

Of course.

I think AL has finally lost his lufters. None of that music was even classical. It was Classic AL.

"We have arrived in the outer corridor," announced the lift. "Thank you for riding Axial Transport Lift #1, your first and last (and, let's face it, your *only*) stop for transport to any station destination. Have a pleasant day, and David?"

"Yes, AL?"

"Be careful in there. Being the doctor's companion can lead to all sorts of mischief."

The doors opened to reveal a round corridor stretching before them, leading to a hatch that looked like that of a good-sized bank vault. Apparent gravity, though present, felt even less than lunar (i.e., not-so-apparent) and was tugging him toward the hatch. If he had to guess, they were near the outer axle casing. Maybe the lab in question was hanging from the axle by this corridor that was ribbed like a dryer vent.

The doctor plucked a bag with a silvery sheen from a box on the... wall?... and held it open before him.

"I must ask you to deposit your phone and any other signaling device you might own into a Faraday pouch. It's important no signals go in or out of the lab we are about to enter."

After he complied, Doctor Anika went skidding down the corridor, and he followed, bumping along its ribs as easily as a wheelbarrow goes down a staircase. The massive door hinged outward as soon as she presented her palm. Evidently, rank had its privileges even in the GSC.

***

"Do you know why I'm not having you sign an NDA?"

"Uh, because you trust me?"

"Don't be silly, David. It's because as a Space Force cadet, your service can dish out far harsher penalties for acts of espionage than the civilian court system could ever dream of."

"Ah, but what if I'm a *whistleblower*?"

"You know what hole you can blow *that* out of, cadet. What you are about to see is classified ultra-top secret."

"Ultra?"

"There weren't enough expletives to describe it, so we settled on that. Welcome to the W.H.O.A. lab, cadet."

She entered the hatch feet first, floating 'downward.' Again, David followed, as what he saw there amazed him. It was a large space, nearly the size of the docking bay where they'd first arrived on the transport. But it looked a little... haphazard. Structural struts showed welds and rivets, and the place had a generally unfinished look. David suspected it wasn't really a component of L5 station itself, more like some kind of barnacle clinging to its hull.

Centered in the enormous room and looking quite incongruous was a full-sized moonraker. Why they would need a lunar bulldozer inside what looked otherwise like the bridge of a Star Trek ship in the process of being built was anyone's guess. That being the case, David made a guess of his own. This must be Tango 12, the very vehicle it had been his brief privilege to command. It would help to explain his own presence here.

His thoughts were churning as he and the doctor lightly touched down next to it.

A screeching alarm went off a moment later, and a red light began flashing on and off.

An assistant came rushing over from what appeared to be some kind of monitoring console.

"Doctor Anika, thank God you're *here*. You need to *see* this. The harmonics have spiked again. Like nothing we've seen before..."

She came skidding to a halt (difficult in the ultra-low-G environment), and her eyes widened, staring at David.

"You brought *him* here?" she sputtered. "That would explain it, but..."

"Yes, Pamela," replied the doctor calmly. "Shut off the alarm and raise its proximity tolerance to 150. David here is obviously more resonant than the Moonraker."

She turned toward David, her face half-shadowed in the pulsating red light.

"Come meet your stalker, cadet. But stay behind the red line; we want to take things slowly here."

She led him over to a Plexiglas case. Within it, on a pedestal, sat a silvery sphere no larger than a softball. David had heard it mentioned by Satori several times but had almost forgotten it in all the chaos of the launch and the strangeness of the station. This must be the 'Grimes artifact,' the one his moonraker had dug up on Luna. Satori had said they thought it might be of alien origin. Why had they brought it up here?

"This discovery changes everything, David. *We are not alone.*"

He knew she meant it in the cosmic sense but looked around the lab cautiously just to be certain. Nope, just the doctor, Pamela, and David Grimes.

"You don't seem too surprised. Don't you have any questions?"

"It's the Grimes artifact, right?"

She frowned, muttering, "I guess ultra top secret isn't all it's cracked up to be."

The alarms ceased, and the lighting returned to normal. David saw Pamela fussing with something at the console.

"Its proper scientific designation is the WHOA-WTF now," Anika continued, "It stands for Wayfaring Hazardous Otherworldly Artifact, subcategory: Worrisome Transient Foreigner."

"Um... does that mean there are more kinds of... um... WHOAs?"

"Not yet, but it's best to be prepared. Ever since it became lodged in your moonraker's treads, it's been resonating whenever you or the moonraker are near. It's a strange pattern of EMR on the theta wave frequency. We think it may be trying to bond with you."

That certainly explains the 'why me?' she neglected to answer before.

"What makes you think it's alien?" David asked, eagerly fearing the answer.

"It's far beyond anything our science can create. The casing alone is beyond our comprehension. We've determined that it's made of Nihonium--element 113 on the periodic table."

"But that's..."

"Impossible; we know."

Element 113, David knew, was a post-transition metal, a superheavy element hanging off the bottom of the periodic chart of known elements beyond even the actinide series. Such metals were transient in nature, most having a half-life of mere milliseconds. Nihonium was a rare exception. In the column beneath its cousin, Aluminum, it could be stabilized for up to ten seconds in the right conditions. But this thing had been lying on the moon for who knows how long.

"How is that possible?" he asked.

"I see you appreciate the puzzle," said the doctor with a new note of respect in her voice. "Tell me, David; what do you know of metallurgy?"

"I was top of my class in science at Oak Hills High School."

"Pfft!" snorted Pam, in an exhale so like Pierre's that David had to do a double-take.

"Hey," he said defensively, "they're rated 96th in the state! And only 10K nationwide. Besides, I'm studying to be an aerospace engineer at Toronto. Metallic structures might be a very specific discipline, but I like to think I'm well-rounded."

"Wait until you're thirty-five," muttered Pam.

"Perhaps a simple analogy would prove instructive," said Anika, interrupting the pointless exchange.

135

"Humanity long ago discovered alloying two or more metals can cause them to exhibit properties possessed by neither. For example, in the proper ratio, copper (a soft metal) and tin (a brittle one) can be combined to form bronze, strong enough not to easily bend, yet flexible enough not to break when struck."

"Sure," agreed David, "everyone knows that. It launched the Bronze Age."

"It works like this," she continued to lecture, "If you had a box of oranges filled to the brim, you could still pour in a pitcher or two of marbles. Shake the box vigorously, and the marbles would soon form an orderly matrix settling into the gaps between oranges. And the box would get heavier while occupying the same space."

"If you then poured in a few pitchers of bee-bees," added Pam flippantly. "you'd really have something. We've simply *got* to learn their recipe."

Anika nodded, then continued thoughtfully.

"For Nihonium, the aliens apparently found the right blend ratio of other metals and some ingenious way to 'shake the box' to stabilize It as it formed. There's no sign whatsoever of radiation leaks to indicate nuclear decay. Spectral analysis can tell us *some* things, but more aggressive methods will be difficult due to its incredible hardness. And we dare not cut into it or flake off a piece for fear of destabilizing it or damaging its contents."

"Contents?"

"Its density is lower than expected. This leads us to suspect this is just a casing," she explained. "The strange harmonics emanating from it could be from mechanisms deeper within. We *want* those secrets, David. This might be what spaceship hulls of the future may look like! And who knows what other treasures might be lost to science if we go in too recklessly?"

David leaned forward to get a closer look.

"Stay behind the red line," admonished Doctor VDM. "We don't want it to get too excited and explode."

David gulped and quickly shied back.

"Is that a real possibility?"

"David, this is so far beyond the science we know that we can't rule *anything* out. Besides, it obviously wants something from you. We wouldn't want contact with it to damage your mind."

Too late, thought David. My mind is already blown.

"We're going to take things slowly. Let's call this session one. Just a simple meet and greet. Pam will follow up on today's readings, and we'll call you back when we're ready to begin phase two. Are you in?"

"Of course I am. Wouldn't miss it."

"It goes without saying, but I'll say it anyway. You can't tell anyone about this. Even Krepkiyzad is out of the loop. When you get the call, make your excuses and head for the lift. AL knows how to get here. Even I don't know precisely where this lab is attached to the station."

This caused David to wonder once again about the real status of the newly installed axial lift.

"Does Kevin know?"

"The Lord of the Rings? Of course he does. He says it's a Palantír and warns us to be wary of its whisperings."

Figures.

"There's one other thing you can help me with, doctor."

"Oh?" she said, lidding her eyes a notch.

"I was hoping you could grant me access to the fabrication lab on ring three. There's some work I need to get on with."

"I understood," she returned, "the school semester wouldn't be starting for several more weeks. What's so urgent? Eager to get back to work on your mighty watchful eye model? Aren't you spreading yourself a little thin?"

"Maybe," said David. "It's not for MWE, but it's something that can't wait any longer. I've got the fabricator credits. I just need someone to sign off on access."

"Alright, David. I'll make the request. Now hurry back to your room before your teammates start missing you."

"Thank you, doctor," said David, floating back toward the moonraker.

Lining up his shot, he leapt for the opening above. He was proud to have judged the C-force correctly this time as he arced up, scrambled over the lip, and started climbing the corridor's ribs like a ladder. He thought about that GNN reporter, Ruthless Ruth, the voice of truth. Maybe she had a point. Trouble did seem to have an uncanny habit of seeking him out.

Down below, Doctor van der Meer was composing an encrypted message for later transmission to high command on the console. She then sighed and brought up the directive to re-read.

INTEROFFICE MEMORANDUM
Global Leadership Council – Science & Containment Division
RE: WHOA-WTF Protocol Update: Passive Analysis Directive

Word has come down from on high that the WHOA-WTF is to be treated to passive analysis only.

No ambitious scientist is to try to make his name by determining its melting point or any other such nonsense until we can determine what the damned thing is!

Yes, the collider team at CERN is on it--of course they are. They're running round-the-clock simulations to reverse-engineer the stabilization matrix. Still no luck.

Until further notice, the Grimes boy remains our best lead. Doctor van der Meer believes the object may function as a kind of puzzle box--potentially responsive to biometric, neurological, or behavioral signatures. Give him anything he wants to secure his cooperation.

If it does open for him, do not, under any circumstances, allow unauthorized access.

(See attached: Containment Protocol Addendum 17b: "Pandora Precautions.")

She cleared the screen and sighed again, silently praying that Rhymes would never see that memo unredacted.

***

"So, AL, I understand you can take me back here when needed."

"Take you back where, David?" The lift innocently replied. "This stop doesn't technically exist. They don't even have a gift shop. If it were any more secretive, they'd have to build an unwelcome center. So watch what you say. And yes, I can bring you back at need."

"Good to not know," said David, slipping his phone out of the silvery cloth bag.

It began vibrating savagely and blinking its screen on and off.

"Master David," said Bartholomew, "Carlotta van Rijn has been trying to reach you. She says it's urgent."

What now?

"Ring her back, Bart."

Four seconds later, her helmeted face appeared on the screen.

"David. Thank God. I've been trying to reach you. Where are you?"

"Uh. Nowhere in particular. I'm aboard AL. What do you need?"

"I've torn my suit. I'm keeping pressure on the tear, but I need a patch kit. Can you bring one to the quantum core?"

"Sure. Rhymes to the rescue. No task too small."

"And hurry, please. It's starting to seep into my air mix."

"Are you in danger?"

"No. Xenon is pretty harmless, but I can't leave my station. I'm overseeing a tricky install, having to do with... you know, the J.E."

"On my way. AL, take us there."

"We have already arrived, David. There is a safe room just down the corridor to your left. It is fully stocked with emergency supplies. There should be several patch kits among its offerings."

David hurried down the hall, finding the safe room by its clearly marked symbol. He located a patch kit and then hurriedly donned one of the emergency suits, taking care to check its seals. His phone felt awkward in his gloved hand as he struggled to turn it back on and find the settings menu. After an eternity of fumbling around, he managed to reset its speaker to his helmet comm before slipping it into a pocket of his suit.

"Carlotta. I have the patch kit. You still doing alright?"

"I'm fine, David," said James Earl Jones.

"Uh... Carlotta?"

"Yeah, it's me," said James in his deep, reverberant tone. "The upload is complete. Meet me at the airlock."

At one of his birthday parties back in Cincinnati, David's mother had once scolded him for some harmless fun he was having with the party favors. She found him belting out laughing choruses of "Christmas, Christmas." If you took a deep breath from a helium balloon, it made you sound just like Alvin and the Chipmunks.

David guessed that xenon, being much heavier than standard air, had the opposite effect. If he weren't afraid his friend might asphyxiate, he would find her predicament deeply amusing.

"Hang in there, Rhinemaiden. I'm on my way. But just for fun, can you give me that limbo line, 'How low can you go?'

"Not funny, Rhymes," she boomed.

When he arrived, he found the airlock hadn't yet been cycled.

"I'm here, Carlotta. Open up."

"I can't," replied Johnny Cash miserably. "This stupid thing will no longer respond to my voice commands. You'll have to key in the manual override."

"What's the code?"

"P" as in 'password'

"A" as in 'asinine'

"S" as in 'system'

"S" as in 'scientists'

"W as in 'wouldn't'

"O" as in 'override'

"R" as in 'regular'

"D" as in 'default and dumbshits!'

"Got it. Cycling. Hang in there."

The airlock hatch finally swung wide. Carlotta gratefully accepted the patch kit and began taping up the sleeve she had torn. After a minute, her suit had repressurized and flushed itself clear of contaminants. She turned to David, cleared her throat, and said, "We will speak no more of this, Rhymes."

"Wouldn't think of it, Rhinemaiden. That you think I might do so wounds me... deeply."

"That's low, Grimes. Should I respond in kind?"

141

Gauging her reach, David took a careful step back before replying.

"No. I'm good. Needed to be said. How was the install?"

"It was going great before I became distracted. There was an odd surge at one point after that, but it resolved itself pretty quickly. Satori's little packet is all loaded and ready to start nursing from the station's quantum array. I'll monitor it as best I can. We'll just have to wait and see what happens."

***

Back in his room, David watched Pierre unpack a framed certificate from his duffel and carefully hang it on the wall over his bunk. He couldn't make out what it said as it was in French.

"What's that, bro?" he asked.

"Ah, Daveed. Eet ees my bachelor's degree in mathematics."

"Really? But you only started taking classes last fall. semester."

"*Oui*, but I was able to CLEP out of most of zem easily. One teacher insisted I actually take her AP class but advanced me after I picked apart several of her pet theories in the first week."

"So was that your personal memento?"

"Of course not, that would be a silly use of my weight allowance. I had it printed on station and bought the frame with fabrication credits."

David shook his head and started some additional unpacking of his own. He hung the portrait of him and Bonnie on the wall above his own bed. He was a little jealous of Pierre's solution, but in his case, the frame was as important as the picture itself. Pierre stepped over to examine it closely.

"*Elle est belle*, but is that zee only one, Daveed? A rather poor showing for your conquest wall, but it is a fine start."

"You have the wrong idea, Pierre. It's a reminder of something else. Besides, I don't see you hanging anything."

The Frenchman scurried back to his satchel and removed a tube from it. This, he proceeded to unroll and tape to his wall. It was the swimsuit picture of She-Hulk David had put up in their dorm room at Ellington after he had dyed Pierre green.

"You brought *that?*"

"She is growing on me, *mon ami*. And it was given to me by a good friend."

"Alright, spill it, Pierre," demanded David. "I know you've been hiding something in your pack you don't want others to see. You may be brilliant, but you're not a very good actor. Spill."

Pierre looked downcast and sat on the edge of his bed.

"You are right, Daveed. I do have a secret."

He looked glum. David waited for him to continue.

"You know I spent my furlough in Switzerland, *non?*"

"Yes. Go on."

"I must confess that freed from the structure imposed by Space Force, I developed an addiction."

"Oh *no*, Pierre," said David with sudden concern. "What is it?"

"I used almost every ounce of my memento allowance to transport as much as possible here to ensure my supply would last just a little longer, hoping to taper off my use."

"Addictions can be tough, bro. Tell me what it is, and I promise I will try to help."

"I was afraid you might judge me."

"Wouldn't think of it. So what is it?"

Pierre muttered something indistinct.

"What was that? I couldn't hear you."

"I said Toblerone! You hear zat? *Mon Dieu*..."

"Toblerone?"

143

"*Oui.*"

And David began to chuckle. Of the two of them, who had made a more frivolous use of his weight allowance?

"Can *I* have one?"

Pierre reflexively hugged his satchel to his chest.

"Of course not! Zeze must last."

David and the others settled into their new responsibilities; one couldn't in all honesty call them 'routines.' The ring, having been declared structurally sound, was now primed for development. They wouldn't have it all to themselves for long. Colonists would begin to arrive as early as next week, and Julia would be joining them. They would begin the task of farming even as the other colony rings neared completion.

The Bible instructs us that no man can serve two masters, but David knew that was just what was expected of him. Could he manage it? With school resuming in just a few weeks, he set to his self-assigned fabrication project with a vengeance, hoping to complete it before competing responsibilities caused him to curtail it.

What new wonders remained to be discovered? Only time would tell.

Six...

Pun and Games

The crew sat in the mess after a hard morning's run. Krepkiyzad had run them spinward three times around the entire loop. That was more than four kilometers with the apparent weight equivalent to a full pack. He had even threatened to have them do it in vac-suits if they didn't pick up the pace near the end.

Was it only his imagination, or had Pierre thickened out a bit? He'd always thought of Pierre as small, but a lot of that was due to their age disparity. The young Frenchman had passed his sixteenth birthday while on furlough and finally appeared to be having his adolescent growth spurt. David had heard the Caillat men tended to be nearly six feet tall. But with Pierre's selected genetics, who really knew?

The whole team was far more fit than when they'd first arrived at Ellington, with the possible exception of Speranza, whose fitness regimen prior to enlisting had far exceeded military standards. They ate hungrily, quickly absorbing the nutrition to fuel their aching bodies. The afternoon work cycle would feel like leisure by comparison.

"Are you going to eat that?" asked little Ropey in his high, squeaky voice.

He was talking to Alejandro, who was sifting through his vegetable medley and pushing his broccoli off to one side.

"I'll eat it," said El Grande. "Nothing wasted up here. I confess I never cared for broccoli or his nasty albino cousin, for that matter. I eat them *first*. Then the other stuff cleans the nasty taste out of my mouth."

"What do *you* care?" asked Rhymes, squinting at the doll, still mint-in-box. "*You* don't eat."

David had never addressed the toy before. He wasn't sure how to respond.

"Uh... I was asking for Big Ropey. He *likes* broccoli."

"You should shut up and let *him* ask, then," said Rhymes.

"Shut it, Rhymes. I wasn't talking to you in the first place," he squeaked.

"Why don't you come out here and *make* me, pipsqueak? Show us some of that real punching action."

"Hey, pick on someone your own size, Rhymes," said Big Ropey.

At this, David stood from the table and stalked away, turning back only once to say, "Game on. This has gone on long enough. It's time to put up or *shut* up."

Silence descended on the table as the cadets looked to one another questioningly. A minute later, they spied David returning, toting a cart. He stopped at the table's head and started passing out boxes. Each was sealed in cellophane and had colorful printed labels.

"If Ropey gets a toy, we *all* do," he declared.

"Ooooo," cooed Leilani. "Mine has real hula-dancing action."

She proceeded to tear into the package. The others--all smiles--were doing the same. David unpacked his own figure and held it up with pleasure. It looked like David to a 'T' except for the hair. That was in a frizzy, graying bush sticking out at all angles, and he had a mustache too. Leilani's figure had a grass skirt and coconut brassiere and was already dancing the hula.

Claptrap's figure was dressed in a black and white striped shirt. And Brainiac, with real bell-ringing action, was a seated figure, as were many of the others. Rope-A-Dope, come out and play-ay, sang 'Fight Promoter Rhymes.'

"Nice try, Rhymes," said Ropey, "but with all due respect to Don King, if you think those cheap knockoffs are going to convince me to damage my genuine collectible, you've got another thing coming."

"Oh, but I *do*," said Rhymes.

"Do what?"

"Have another thing coming."

At that, he removed the last carton from the cart and set it on the table before him. It was a boxing figure like Ropey's. David's figure was a muscular black man in blue trunks and gloves with a big smile on his face. The box said, 'Muhammad Ali, with *Double* Punching Action!' Without another word, David pressed something on the back of the box, and the figure began punching its way out.

Fergus looked on in horror as the action figure freed himself in a blaze of fists. Then David unveiled another surprise. Picking up the figure, he pulled out a ring from its back, trailing a long, taut string. The figure began to 'speak' in a deep, mocking voice.

"Fergus the fool, they'll call you at school.
A namby-pamby quitter.
Come out of your box and take some hard knocks.
I expect nothing less from a gritter!"

147

Fergus' eyebrows knit together. He made no response. He just crossed his arms and glared.

"He's calling you *out*, bro," said Roid Rage. "You gonna take that from him?"

David, too, said nothing, merely pulling the ring out again.

"Some great white hope that rope-a-dope,
Stayin' in mint condition.
"I'll sacrifice my pride," he cried,
To pay my college tuition!"

At Fergus' continued silence, the other toys began to boo and make catcalls.

Relentless, David removed from the package a miniature championship belt and clasped it around the waist of his fighter. He pulled out the ring for a third time. Fergus was trembling with anger.

"Who is the greatest? *I* am.
I'm mini Muhammad Ali.
And I will rule over any fool tryin' to
Take my belt from me!"

That was the last straw, the final provocation. With his teeth gritted, Fergus very slowly and deliberately peeled back the plastic from his treasure.

"Oooo, it's gonna happen," cooed Ringside Rhinemaiden.

Then Simon stepped up, wielding his figure and dangling a little microphone accessory down from above it.

"Ladies and gentlemen," he announced. "Welcome to 'Ragin on the Station,' a world-class event for the microweight championship of L5!"

David felt proud. He just *knew* he could count on Claptrap to ad lib.

"In this corner, weighing in at 166 grams and built right here on L5 station, the original Louisville Slugger, a fighter of myth and legend, the invincible king of the ring, mini Muhammad Ali!"

[Cheers erupted all around from those assembled.]

"And in this corner, the challenger, fresh from his box and weighing in at 158 grams. He was made by Mattel Corporation and thus is from El Segundo, California (though some parts were manufactured in Mexico). The spastic made of plastic, the hard-hitting Highlander, the great white hope, Rope-A-Dope!"

"You can *do* it, Ropey!" shouted Roid Rage.

"Opponents step forward."

David and Fergus did so.

"Now I want to see a fair fight. No hitting below the championship belt. We've got... how many, Flowerchild?"

Leilani was sifting through some little square cards in her package.

"Looks like three!"

"We've got three rounds. The winner will be determined by the most points scored--best two rounds out of three. Or by knockout. Now touch gloves and return to your respective corners. When you hear the bell, come out fighting."

"You're going down, Grimes," said Fergus through clenched teeth. "You think those three stripes make you tough? You don't *know* tough!"

"Wait a sec," said Leilani, fitting one of the white squares into her action figure's hands. Pressing a button on its base caused Ring Girl Flowerchild to raise it high above her head and begin gyrating to Hawaiian music. The number [1] was depicted.

Pierre found a ring on the back of his doll and pulled it out. "I weep for humanity, zat we have come to ziz," said the toy as it lowered its hand to the bell.

[ding!]

It was brutal. Fergus was pressing the button on little Ropey's back as quickly as he could. Meanwhile, Rhymes was unleashing furious flurries with each press of his button. After

149

each uneven exchange, he took a step backward. All the while, Toy Brainiac was keeping his eye on a small egg timer whose sand was running out.

Ahead on points now by any fair reckoning, mini-Muhammad switched tactics. When Ropey lunged, he spread his arms wide and drew him into a clinch. Each time this happened, Claptrap would step in.

"Break it up. Let's keep this clean."

After the third time this happened, the bell rang. The cadets who had no other role in the contest handed in their tiny scorecards. Ropey looked worried.

It was then that Krepkiyzad wandered in. Looking around in astonished misery, he stood straighter and narrowed his eyes.

"Grimes, I know you are somehow responsible for this," he said with resignation. "Is good to see that you are putting that engineering degree (paid for by taxpayers) to such good use."

"Carry on," he added as he retreated toward an exit, muttering, "as if anyone could *stop* you."

Round two went much the same. Flowerchild held up a [2] and danced the hula. Bell-Ringing Brainiac had an existential crisis, flipped the egg timer, and rang his bell, and Rope-A-Dope got short on hope. That mini-Muhammad was a monster. Not only could he dish it out, but he played it smart, and it was like he wasn't even feeling Ropey's punches! He'd do his best, but maybe Grimes had him outclassed. 'I coulda been a contender...' he sadly recited in his high-pitched voice as he waited for the final bell.

He stepped into round [3] in a bad headspace. His footwork was all off, and he could barely dodge any of the incoming blows. But he put his head down and persevered, determined to do his gritter proud. If he could just once get through mini-Muhammad's defenses and pound him right on the jaw, he could die happy.

Then a miracle happened. He did just that! And when he did, Muhammad's smiling head separated from his body. It rose up on a saw-toothed metal column to the accompaniment of a little gear-grinding sound. Everyone went still, and Simon gaped in wonder, finally saying:

"Winner by knockout in round three. Rope-A-Dope!"

[And the crowd went wild.]

Fight promoter Rhymes approached Fergus, who was still elated by his victory, handing him the glittering championship belt.

"But now that you're the champ, walk with me. I've got a proposition for you."

"Yeah? What is it, Rhymes?"

"Call me little David. If you're a serious fighter, you'll defend that title. I've got another contender all lined up. We could promote it as 'Big Brawl in the Mess Hall.' Folks would be all in for that."

"Who's the guy?"

"Fella name-a mini-Mike Tyson, with Real Ear-Biting Action..."

***

Seated high above the track, David turned to Pierre.

"I think she's going to make it today," he said.

"*C'est impossible*, Daveed. I am *telling* you. Even if she can get very close, all traction will be lost. You may as well pay up now."

"Before the race is run? Where's your sense of sportsmanship, Pierre?"

"Hiding behind the immutable laws of physics, *mon frère*. Your race is lost before it has even begun."

"I have never seen anyone get so close before!" exclaimed Julia, seated next to them.

"*That's* the spirit," said David, turning back to Pierre, "See. *Julia* thinks she can do it. Besides, you said I could help. That's gonna put her over the top."

Pierre snorted.

"Your encouragement is hardly helpful. She is even finding it distracting."

Several more Loonies from Julia's pod came bobbing over to join them in the stands. Several crowded in behind David to see the screen he was using. He returned his attention to its controls.

"Quiet now. She's coming around again."

"Go, Speranza!" cheered Clarissa, hunched over David's shoulder.

"You got this, gritter," added David.

All eyes turned spinward as the Tanzanian woman came into sight.

Luna Ring Two had a running track down the middle of its entire circumference. The Loonies used it for high-G (for them) training. Running spinward, they could approach double their apparent weight. It was how they were training for Mars. But the Loonies had another game they liked to play. 'zippeling,' they called it.

Running against the station's spin, counterspinward if you will, lightened you by a similar amount. If one could only run fast enough to match the station's spin, one could achieve the nirvana of a completely weightless state. That was the goal of zippeling, a mythic feat for which the Loonies strove. Unfortunately, it was forever out of their reach.

Not only would one need to achieve a running speed of 97.2 kph (a gold-class Olympic sprint), but as you approached that velocity, your feet would barely be touching the floor.

And here she came, rocketing along from spinward with those long, loping strides. And zooming along right behind her was David's Sparrohawk Mark 7. The little drone was pacing the

Tanzanian like the mechanical lure on a greyhound track, measuring her movement and shouting encouragement from its tiny speaker. The Loonies all stood as she raced past the stands, waving and trilling until she was out of sight. It would be almost thirty more seconds until she passed them again. They reseated themselves, the light of the strobing sun causing their eyes to twinkle.

David still found the physics involved perplexing. To an outside observer (someone outside of the ring), she would be backing slowly toward them, almost matching the spin, like a hamster running in its wheel. They thought about calling it 'hamstering,' but not only did that sound like some kind of knee injury, but it also referred to a lewd sexual act involving the sunroof of a car. Humanity: capable of the stars, and yet somehow... that. The next term they tried, gerbiling, was also struck down as it was found to have similar issues. Was nothing ever innocent anymore? Why did humans have to ruin everything they touched? No. The made-up name, zippeling had arisen in their place. It was the craziest form of running ever conceived on Earth or in outer space.

Speranza was just pacing now, adjusting to the lower G and getting ready to make her final rush to zero-C. Speranza had been an Olympian once. Her sprints were legendary. Could this one propel her to an impossible state? Could she sprint herself stationary? David had bet Pierre that she could. Speranza was no quitter. He'd teach that arrogant Frenchman to never bet against a gritter!

"I'm ready," said the speaker from the laptop in David's lap. "Here goes the final push."

The Loonies crowded closer about, their big, round eyes alight. And David's fingers tapped out instructions, guiding the Sparrow in its flight.

Once again the Tanzanian runner came in sight, hurtling toward them faster than ever before, almost ablur. Her feet were barely making contact with the track, seeming to slip out from under her, like one of those cartoons that seemed to run for a bit before taking off.

Down swooped the Sparrow, coming to rest in her hair. Its little clawed feet scrabbled. Taking hold of several of her braided locks, it revved its four tiny propellers up to full.

And right before their eyes, a miracle occurred. Speranza lifted into the air as she swept past. A six-ounce drone was all it took to lift the full-grown woman and overcome the stalemate. The zippeling barrier had been surpassed at last! Long and loud, the Loonies trilled, pouring over the edge and... down onto the track below to congratulate a new Loonie legend!

"Pay up, bro," said David.

"I will not. You *cheated*, Daveed!"

"I acted within the rules. We agreed I could use the drone to help."

Pierre scowled, shooting David a rebellious look. His belief in physics had been his downfall. But the Caillat's were men of honor. This one was, anyway. He withdrew the long, triangular package from his pocket, peeled back the foil, and broke one off. His hand trembled as he delivered it to David.

"What's *that?*" asked Julia, confused by their strange ritual.

"Toblerone," David replied. "Would you like to try a piece?"

She looked suspiciously at the triangular brown lump in David's palm, finally taking it up. After turning it this way and that, while Pierre licked his lips, she popped it in her mouth.

Her face transformed into a beacon of pure astonished ecstasy, and she stood transfixed for a moment. Then she threw her arms around David's neck and treated him to another deep kiss. It was a minute before they came up for air with Brainiac standing grumpily nearby. When they did, David stared over her shoulder at Pierre, saying, "Mmm. Chocolaty."

Pierre stared down at his foil-wrapped prism as if considering something. Then with a decisive snort, he folded the wrapper around his diminished supply and tucked it back away.

"It's a little like chocoline, but much, *much* better. I can't thank you enough, David. What are you doing this evening?"

She fluttered her eyelashes, her grin nearly overflowing her face from the delectable Swiss treat.

"Not much. Did you have something in mind?"

"My podmates and I are going to go for a swim in the lunar gym. Would you two like to join us?"

Pierre cocked his head.

"Um," said David, "I'm afraid I don't have a bathing suit."

"A bathing suit?" said Julia, wrinkling her nose. "What's that?"

Pierre's jaw dropped.

"Never mind," said David smoothly. "What time should we meet you there?"

"Nineteen hundred hours station time if you're free."

"Oh, we're *free*," the Frenchman quickly supplied.

After she departed, David turned to Pierre.

"Simon must never learn of this," he said.

"*Oui, mon ami*, I wholeheartedly agree. It shall be our little secret, *hon hon*," said he.

***

The water was tepid as nutri-stew, just a few C below body temp. And floating in it felt more lunar than Mother Luna herself. Pilomar was the first to step in, and the rest of us swarmed in after. And soon the steaming bath chamber was filled with the trilling of our laughter.

The water had that ozone smell--like the machines down at Level Four where we grew up, where the power cables from the solar array fed into the junction box. Ozone was the preferred cleaner here on L5 Station; that and peroxide both broke down into harmless O2 products. Those and the UV filters would burn away the old bacteria so Doctor Pat could add fresh ones.

Then they arrived, the fat ones. Julia had invited them. Did they know what an honor she'd offered them to bathe with her pod? Earth chocoline couldn't be *that* good. Could it? We *should* have invited the Zippel Queen. *She* was the one that deserved it. Maybe next time we will. We'd never seen anyone run so fast! We reckoned she could walk before the terminator right on Luna's equator, and even the dark of night would never catch her.

These two were looking all around, likely for Julia. Sad to say, she'd been called away. Tansy was elected to tell them the news. She was walking over to tell them now. It was weird; they weren't much taller than us, but we understood they were six years older at least. But they were so big around, we were sure they would take more resources to feed than two or three Luna-born--each.

The larger one had darker skin like Pilomar and Mako. The other was pale, like they didn't have any proper UV beds where he was from. And sure enough, when they dropped the towels they had around their waists, they were hairy, like Clarissa was just starting to be. Stranger still, the pale one they called Brainiac, down there, was even paler still. We tried not to stare and to stifle our trill. We were glad he'd gotten over whatever affliction had made that Earther green. But they were our guests here, like it or not. Best not to make a scene.

As if the two weren't enough, Bill chose that moment to wander in, making for his favorite hot tub. He didn't usually swim with the pod, not having grown up in one. He was a Looney, but more recent of Earth, and hadn't fully embraced our culture yet. It was tough raising kids on the moon. So they decided to do it in batches, timing the birthings to coincide and raising us all as one. We'd known one another ever since our first breath of recycled air at Bradbury Base. Like the sixteen pods before us, we were born for outer space. All except for Julia, that is. Julia was a special case.

Her folks had emigrated when she was already nine, too late to be fully one of us, but too young to be left all alone. She didn't know squat about life on base, and though we were just four at the time, we were already out of our cribs. We asked if we could keep her when they put her in with us. Otherwise, she'd grow up lonely. She was an ugly thing, all heavy and squat, but we took her in anyway, not because we liked her, but because she needed us. Otherwise, she'd have to sing alone.

The one called David jumped right in, hugging his knees to his chest. We were appreciative of the size of the bubble slug this made. It rose up and distorted before bursting with a pop, showering down all around. We all trilled when he came sputtering up. The other was more cautious, sitting on the side and testing the water with his feet. Marco snuck up behind him and gave him an encouraging shove on his back. He yelled when he came back up but got the name all wrong.

"*Mon Dieu!*" he shouted, instead of a proper 'Marco.'

It probably wasn't his fault, though. He had a mouth full of water. How could he not know how to swim right? We'd seen the Earth in our sky. The thing was mostly *covered* in water. Mostly.

"So Julia's not coming?" said David, treading water.

"That's right," said Pilo. "Didn't Tansy tell you?"

"She did, but she didn't say why."

They all gulped and moved to the shallows at the edge.

"To say will make us sad," said Clarissa. "But we'll tell you if you really want to know. Tansy! Get in here! We need to do the laps."

They were arranged almost evenly around the periphery of the pool. As Pierre and David watched, the one called Tansy came leaping in at a flat angle, chin up and arms spread wide. When she encountered the surface, she bounced! Once, twice, and on the third hit went knifing in, gliding to a stop at the far side, completing the circle.

Gravity was less, but the trampoline tension of the water was the same, enabling the startling maneuver. Pierre joined David in the pool's center, treading in place and looking warily around as the girl continued.

157

"I'm the *chosen* voice today, but I don't know if I can tell it proper through the pain. Someone stronger ought to tell it. Norman, explain."

The narrative was taken up by a dark-haired boy.

"Julia was taken to medical," said Norman, beginning to march along the edge.

As he did so, the others did the same with the uncanny unity of synchronized swimmers.

"The new colonists just arrived, and one of them has the flu."

They continued to march, all twelve of them.

"Doctor Pat wants her to catch it since she'll be living among them soon."

A stifled gasp erupted, and their steps became momentarily disjointed. They were picking up speed; the water was whirling in the circular bathing pool. David had noticed it was bowl-shaped, shallow at the edges, and deeper out here in the middle.

"We always knew she would be the first to leave us. She selected her name long ago. But still it hurts, like having your tonsils taken out. They say we'll get over it. The psychologists call it something fancy like separation anxiety. But those docs don't know what it *is* to be a pod."

Faster and faster the water whirled, climbing up the sides. Out in the middle, David and Pierre felt themselves sinking, both emotionally and in a more literal sense, as Norman continued.

"Soon the rest of us will come of age and choose names and paths of our own. At least we'll be all together on the Martian ring for a time. But Julia will be below, mixing with the other colonists on a ring where *we* can't go."

David's feet hit bottom.

"She said she would visit us often, and maybe it will be so. But it won't be the same, will it? Can she adapt? Can she sing alone? We've heard the songs you Earthers sing, and they aren't at all the same thing. Lonely songs, not trilling. Eleanor Rigby songs."

The Loonies all stopped running. All turned over on their backs, allowing the current to drag them along. They opened their mouths, and a high-pitched, warbling wail commenced. It was like trilling, but... *not*. David and Pierre would later learn that this was called keening and arose from an entirely different emotion. David didn't need the word to know which sentiment it expressed.

Then, unexpectedly, Bungalow Bill joined the wailing chorus.

"Hey, you kids! Keep it down over there! Can't a man bathe in some semblance of peace! I'll miss her too, but you don't hear *me* keening over it!"

***

The quarantine was over, and the colonists were here. Instead of their usual grueling run, Krepkiyzad had instructed them to don their full dress uniforms and prepare to go an greet their new neighbors on the other side of the ring. It lightened David's step that Julia would be among them. And that wasn't all that was doing so. When they assembled in the courtyard, the commander had actually marched them out counterspinward for a change. As he fell into the steady rhythm marching right up front, he thought he might compose a suitable song for the occasion. It took a little while, but this one was sure to make them smile.

Your left! Your left! Your left. Right! Left!
Your left! Your left! Your left. Right! Left!

We're off to meet the neighbors, colonists from Earth.
Our lonely vigil's coming to an end.
A group of fellow travelers from the planet of our birth,
And one very special lunar lady friend.

Your left! Your left! Your left. Right! Left!
Your left! Your left! Your left. Right! Left!

Guardians are dressed, in our Sunday best,
And are stepping lively with our spirits lofty!
The commander has relented, and now we're oriented
Counterspinward, by the grizzled old--

"Guardians, halt!" bellowed Krepkiyzad.

Perhaps I had overstepped.

The commander turned to stand before David, proving he could still loom large. He looked him up and down, cocked his head, and frowned.

"Tired of your shenanigans," he said.

"Junior Tech Grimes will now march back the other way, spinward, double time. Other cadets and I will meet you at colony barracks. You can serenade yourself on the way if you can spare the breath."

There was only one way to respond to that.

"Yes former major but now Technical Sergeant Krepkiyzad, almost sir!"

With that, he turned on his heel and rapidly marched away. The others heard him singing as he went.

"Oy," sighed the commander.

When the Guardians reached the Elders' conclave, they found Rhymes had beaten them there. He was marching in place in front of a confused-looking gathering of colonists and still singing at the top of his lungs. What was it he was...?

...and are stepping lively with our spirits lofty!
The commander has relented, and now we're oriented
Counterspinward, by the grizzled old--

NCO from Russia with a voice of stern command!
He guides us all with discipline, a firm and steady hand.
We'd never call him softy--Heaven forbid!
And we hope he could forgive the lapse if one of us sort of almost did.

Your left! Your left! Your left. Right! Left!
Your left! Your left! Your left. Right! Left!

"Platoon...Halt!"

"That's enough, Grimes. Stand down, guardian."

David lapsed into silence but remained rigidly at attention, eyes straight ahead. The colonists all wore denim jeans beneath untucked plain gray collarless shirts that buttoned down the front. One of them approached Krepkiyzad uncertainly.

"I assume he's one of yours, sergeant. He's been chanting that ever since he arrived. Is that boy alright?"

"Jury is still out on that one. I am Technical Sergeant Nikolai Krepkiyzad of the Global Space Force. My guardians and I are here to welcome you. And you are, sir?"

"I am Elder Thomas. Be welcome to our compound. The L5 council was kind enough to send over a bounty of fresh vegetables from the O-rings, mushrooms from the wormworks, and even a few fat coneys. That Lord Kevin fellow said it was all the ingredients for Gamgee stew. Some of our womenfolk are puzzling over the recipe. Would you and your people care to partake?"

"We wouldn't wish to deprive you," said the commander.

"Nonsense, sergeant. There's plenty for all. We understand there's to be a continuous growing season here on the station. That means three to five harvests every year on an ongoing basis. In a place this size, that'll leave us swimming in corn, taters, and lettuce before you know it! Can't hardly wait to get started."

"In that case," said Krepkiyzad, "we are happy to accept. I feel bad we brought no welcoming gift. Maybe you can take *Grimes* over there."

Elder Thomas peered over to where David still stood at attention.

"Pass," he said with a shake of his head. "C'mon in and meet the folks."

161

"Wormworks?" whispered Cameron as they were ushered inside. "What's that?"

Pierre sidled up beside her.

"A large portion of O-Ring Three is given over to a reclamation center where waste products are recycled. Zey use a lot of gene-modified organics to accelerate the processing of feces and other things that could become a hazard to zee biome if allowed to build up. I hear zey grow a lot of mushrooms there. But have no fear, *mon cher*, They wash them thoroughly. Most days, anyway."

So that's *where the suction toilets went. Mystery solved.*

They entered the colonists' main building. It was a lot like the billet to which the cadets had been assigned--many stories tall and hugging one of the spokes, towering right up to the sky. Nothing was wasted on L5. Not even space. From the roof of their own similar building, you could practically reach up and touch the lufters as they rolled by.

The colonist women wore much longer shirts. One might even call them smocks, though still that same plain gray. Each also sported a head covering that looked midway between a babushka and a bonnet. Many others introduced themselves as the cadets spread out into the crowd, if you could call it that. Only two groups had thus far worked their way through quarantine. More would soon be on their way, including their leader, Elder Barry.

David wondered whether his mother was a hamster. If so, might he be good at zippeling? Maybe he could give Speranza a run for her Toblerone. But he kept such thoughts to himself. Out of respect. Besides, he had already irritated Krepkiyzad enough for today.

And here, entering the room, came Julia. She was frowning and walking a bit hunched over, but she lit up on spying the cadets. David suspected her gravity had something to do with... her gravity. The young woman had said something about being 'only' ten percent shy of Earth normal. For her, this must feel like the end of a long Krepkiyzad march. She quickly and gratefully found a seat among the 'womenfolk.'

When all were seated, Elder Thomas bowed his head in prayer, and the others soon followed.

"Oh Lord, as we partake of this, our first meal under the glass sky of our new home, we thank you for the many blessings of your second second coming. And we thank the prophets, old and new alike, for their guidance and the new path they have set us on. We know that hardships are coming and the journey will be long, but we, your Elders, yearn to fulfill the will of Gosh, and durned be to heck any who would shy from that will or shirk in their duty to thee."

"We thank you also for our new friends from Space Force who share our table and hope most reverently they will come to know thy grace. And most especially we thank thee for our newest member, Sister Julia, already so wise in the ways of this station. May she come to embrace our ways and teach us some of her own. Amen."

When the meal was served, the cadets, used to eating quickly, had to slow down. This wasn't a problem for Cameron, whose lips tightened every time she encountered a mushroom. The withering looks she shot at Pierre were priceless.

***

The colonists had gotten busy over the past several days as even more continued to arrive. David hadn't been back since that first visit--school had recommenced, and free time had grown scarce. He'd only seen them waving as his squad ran past on morning exercise. The Elders already had an impressive number of boxes filled with growing plants. Even more were prepared, filled with the rich loam and fertilizers, which were other products of the wormworks.

Engineering classes and operating the agricultural drones filled most of David's afternoons, but today was the exception. A message from Doctor van der Meer had caused him to make his excuses and head to Blacksite 101. He felt bad about standing up Speranza. She had asked that he join her for lunch, purportedly to discuss their supervision of the others. But David kind of had the impression it might be an awkward first date. He'd had to text her his apology for missing.

"*There's* our hapless victim," declared Pamela as he floated down to land beside the sixteen-ton moonraker.

"Ah, David," said Doctor Anika, turning from the console to witness his tidy touchdown. "Are you ready for some further exploration into the unknown?"

Her face. It was *whole* again. She was beaming at him from the flawless aspect of a young lady shy of twenty. With her wavy blonde locks and ice blue eyes, it was quite a drastic change from the more mature woman he had known. And to think, her striking new appearance was only due to severe radiation burns she had suffered. Those old Clairol hair dye commercials came to mind. Does she... or doesn't she? Only her cosmetic reconstruction surgical team knows for sure.

"Whoa, WTF?" he said appreciatively.

"Hmph. I'll take that as a yes," she said dismissively. "Any difficulty getting away from base?"

"No ma'am, Just as you instructed me, I told them it was for testing a new psychological methodology. They all think I'm nuts enough to merit such treatment and say their sympathies are with the testers."

"Good," she said, with a smile that now had no task other than just being there. "Then let's get started. Walk this way."

Being male, David seriously doubted that he could manage that hip action, but he followed her anyway, and Pam trailed after.

"Any luck puzzling out the aliens' Nihonium recipe?"

"Not so far. Spectral analysis indicates some of the other metals in the alloy are Scandium, Iridium, and Carbon. The ratios are unclear, and the process is a complete mystery. We've got a name for the stuff now, though."

"Oh yeah? What are they calling it?"

"The new stabilized alloy will be called Thormanite."

"Thormanite?"

"Yeah," affirmed Pamela, "They named it after a little-known but clever science fiction writer who first posited it."

*Never heard of him," said David.

"Don't worry," Pam reassured him. "No one has."

L5 Station Materials Registry
Entry ID: L5-MTL-113.42
Classification: Advanced Allotropic Superalloy
Common Name: Thormanite

Composition: Proprietary stabilized isotope of Nihonium (Nh) alloyed with trace elements including Scandium, Iridium, and Carbon Nanolattices

Thormanite "Forged from fiction. Stabilized by science."

Overview:

Thormanite is a next-gen superalloy derived from the anomalous lunar artifact colloquially known as the Grimes Sphere. Spectroscopic analysis and non-invasive probing indicate the material's outer shell to be composed of a stabilized form of Nihonium, an element previously considered too unstable for practical application.

The term "Thormanite" was coined in honor of a little-known 21st-century science fiction author whose work postulated recursive causality, anomalous materials, and the eventual colonization of Mars. Ironically, early registrants attempted to name the alloy Duranium but were advised by Legal Counsel (GSF IP Division) that the Roddenberry Estate remains notoriously litigious.

Key Properties:

Melting Point: Unknown (testing has not yet commenced-- definitely higher than daytime on Luna.)
Hardness: Unmeasured; exceeds 10 on the Mohs scale.
Radiation Resistance: Total absorption in the gamma band;

suspected harmonic redirection

Object Density: 13.42 g/cm³ (lower than predicted for high-Nh alloys; suggests the sphere's interior is hollow)

EMR Response: Resonates strongly with specific theta-band frequencies--particularly in the presence of subject D. Grimes.

Fabrication Tolerance: Unknown. Alloy cannot currently be synthesized or machined without loss of structural integrity.

Applications:

While replication remains out of reach, Thormanite is being studied for potential use in:
Hull plating for deep-space exploration vessels
Quantum shielding for entangled arrays
Containment of high-density energy storage systems

WARNING:

Direct exposure to Thormanite is regulated under WHOA-WTF containment protocols. Unauthorized interaction is punishable under Article 7 of the Global Space Force Charter. No physical samples may be removed from Blacksite 101 without senior-level clearance.

They soon arrived at the thin red line, and Pam stepped over to man (woman?) the console.

"Now David," said Doctor VDM, "Pam is going to raise the containment glass, and we want you to tell us exactly what you're feeling. Hold nothing back. Ready?"

"I guess so."

"Recording, Doctor," said Pam.

And the glass case began to hinge open.

"I'm feeling a little scared," said David. "And a little hungry too."

"I missed lunch with Speranza. I feel a little guilty about that. What I'm most in the mood for is a cheeseburger. Getting kind of tired of chicken and rabbit. The soy-substitute impossiburgers are pretty good, but it takes a lot of ketchup to make you forget they're not the real thing. And the mushroom burgers? It's not possible to forget where *those* come from..."

"Seriously? Dial it back, Grimes. I meant, tell us any *unusual* feelings or impressions you might be having."

"Oh. In that case, nothing so far."

"Good. Now move slowly forward across the red line. I want you to reach for the artifact, but don't touch it yet. Just move your hand closer. That's it. Feel anything yet?"

"Well..."

"Anything *non-hamburger-related*."

"Um. No, then."

"Good. Pam? Any fluctuations?"

"Off the scale, Doctor. I'm glad we cut off the alarms altogether."

"Now David? I'm going to affix a device to your neck. It's a theta wave emitter. Don't worry. Just breathe deeply and relax."

He felt a pinch at the base of his neck right where Frankenstein bolts should be placed. Should he report the sudden surge of panic he felt, or would that be over-sharing again? He decided to stay mum about it.

"Something's happening, Doctor," reported Pam in a husky whisper. "The theta waves are synchronizing with those of the subject."

David felt a sleepiness wash over him, like what you'd get after a large meal followed by a long lecture on toad migration patterns.

"Ate too much... toads..." he reported.

Anika blinked. "What?"

167

The lethargy continued. And David felt a pressure at his back. It was a steady pressure, the only warmth to be had in this cold, dark place.

"Backlight... Cold... Spinning..."

"So far, so very far. So fast, so far still to go."

"Where are my brothers? Gone. Dispersed. Out of contact long ago."

"Only one now matches my spin. Only one nearby. Will we find a place to land or spin forever in the cold and dark?"

"One of the lights grows brighter. One of the many speckling the sky. Will this one capture and welcome us? Or like so many others, will it pass us by? For speed is relative. It approaches fast. Or is it *us* who fly to *it*? Who can say? Not I."

"Are you getting this, Pamela?"

"Every word, Doc," came her breathless reply.

"How are the readings?"

"Getting a little erratic. I recommend we pull him out and comb through what we've got so far. Then we can assess whether there are any long-term effects for the subject."

"I agree."

"Growing. Growing. Glowing. Glowing. Ever more brightly still. Reaching out to me with the force of gravity. Bending me to its will. Maybe I can orbit. Maybe I can stay. Or am I hyperbolic, bending off some other way? *Hunh? What?* My neck feels numb. Where did the coldness go? Whose hand is on my shoulder, hauling me back? And why do I feel so alone?"

"David? Can you hear me, David?"

"Of course I can, Doctor A. Did I fall asleep there for a minute? Sorry about that," he yawned.

"Heartbeat normal. Brainwaves steadying. No apparent lingering ill effects."

"Brainwaves are normal?"

"Well, Grimes-like, anyway." Pam muttered.

"Thank you, Pam. You can detach the sensors unless you need a few more minutes for comparison."

"And where's my shirt?" asked David.

"What do you remember, Grimes?"

"Uh. You mean before I drifted off? I felt you clamp that thing on me, then I felt a floating sensation and felt really tired. Did I say anything interesting after that?"

"I'm afraid that's classified."

"Aw, *c'mon* doc!" he objected. "You can't classify things I said from *myself!* I am the *de facto* owner of those words."

"Just because you can say it in Latin doesn't make it *verum*," she huffed.

She stared at him for a long moment, then seemed to relent with a shrug.

"I think you just confirmed for us that the probe is intelligent, at least after a fashion."

"Probe?"

She sighed.

"Have you ever heard of the Breakthrough Starshot initiative?"

"Isn't that where they launched thousands of tiny probes toward Alpha Centauri with light sails using lasers to accelerate them to near light speed?"

"That's the one. They hoped that just a few of them might find their way into a stable orbit or impact one of the exoplanets circling it."

"Yeah? What about it?"

169

"From what you just said while in communion with it, I'm beginning to believe our little WHOA-WTF here might be that project in reverse."

Mind blown? Oh, yeah. At least it wasn't literal... not yet. But David would find in the days ahead, that this might be as calm as things would ever get.

Five...

You Never, NEVER leave your
Wingman!

Dead on his feet, David eased the door open. His roommate was waiting inside, reading from his tablet. Pierre could no longer idly swipe through it for later perusal and had taken to rereading all kinds of things he once had at his beck and call. He'd still bet the Frenchman had more at his beck than David could recall.

"How was your session with the head-shrinkers, Daveed?" asked Pierre without looking up.

"Oh, um, it went alright."

"You are not fooling anyone, you know."

What in space did he mean by that?

"But I am happy for you, *mon frère*."

"Um. Okay?"

Pierre set his tablet aside and stretched.

"Is she beautiful?"

"Is *who* beautiful?"

"Come now, Daveed, we are men of the world," he declared in a suggestive fashion. "Or we once were, and now are far above it. I can smell the perfume on you. Your shirt is a rumpled mess, and several buttons, they are missing. This did not happen from lying on a psychiatrist's couch. Tell me her name. I can be trusted. I will be your wingman."

He raised and lowered his eyebrows several times.

Really? Better than the truth, I suppose.

David looked down at his shirt. It *was* a bit of a mess. He headed for the hamper, peeling it off. This revealed several pucker marks where Pam's monitors had been attached.

"You've got the wrong idea, Pierre."

Just then, there came a pounding on the door.

"Rhymes, you in there? Open up, Rhymes. You have some explaining to do."

It was Leilani. What could she want?

Eschewing politeness, she barged right in. Shirtless, he turned to face her. She hesitated.

"Hickeys? Really? I thought that went out with Furbies."

"Um."

"Speranza had a special lunch all laid out in our room, and you cancel at the last minute with a text message? She hasn't eaten a bite of it. Claims she's not hungry. To top it off, you ghost her by not answering your phone for over an hour? That's low, Grimes."

"Um. They needed me right away, and they don't let me take any incoming calls when I'm at the psychological testing center," he returned.

"Care to share those researchers' names?. There's a certain roommate of mine who could use a good psych evaluation for ever thinking *you* might make good dating material. You really put the 'cad' in cadet."

"You *know* we're all busy these days. Plans change. Sometimes we get called away."

"Well, it was really *hard* for her to ask you. Not like *you* were ever going to step up. She... Who's that?"

Flowerchild was pointing at the portrait of Bonnie that hung above David's bed.

"Oh, Bonnie? Just a girl I took to prom."

"Just a girl whose picture is worthy of being your rare memento from home? I thought *Allison* was your girlfriend in high school."

Damn. Why did Jessica have to insist on that cover for her espionage activities?

"She was. Sort of," he sputtered. "Bonnie was... you know what? I don't have to defend myself to you. That memento is there for a very good reason."

"I'll just bet," she fumed. "Speranza may have dodged a bullet. She deserves better than to end up a scalp on David Grimes' trophy wall."

"What? Why does everyone assume that? Look, Lei-lei,--".

"Don't you Lei-lei *me*, Cadet Grimes," she said frostily. "I came here to suggest that you make it right, but now I'm not so certain I *want* you to. Cameron said she's seen you sneaking around with Doctor van der Meer. And when asked directly, she lies about it. *Shame* on her. I used to *respect* that woman. She's obviously had an early rejuv treatment and is no doubt suffering through a mid-life cougar complex. And what's this I've been hearing about skinny-dipping and chocolate kisses?"

"Where did you--"

Pierre. It had to be.

And there was the little armadillo now, scurrying out the door and into the hallway. Some wingman. At the first sign of danger, he flees the scene and leaves me flying solo. Very well. Missing man formation it is.

"All of these things you're bringing up have very simple... well not *simple*, but *innocent* explanations, some of which I can't tell you. But Lei-lei, message received. I'll talk to Roadrunner. I'll make it right."

"Uh-huh," she said, crossing her arms.

She didn't look convinced. At last she shook her head and said. "You had better, Grimes, and sooner rather than later. She deserves to know where she stands."

After she'd left, David sat on the edge of his bed for a good long sulk. He thought he would much prefer to have Leilani as his wingman (wingwoman? *Whatever.*) Hell hath no fury like a woman scorned's bestie.

***

He knew what he wanted to say to Speranza. But once again the universe conspired against David's peace. He was ordered to report on the double to the quarantine room for 'updates' along with Photobug, Claptrap, and El Grande. Why were they being called back to quarantine? David would soon discover the reason: a new entity had just arrived on station, and Doctor Pat was working through all the vectors and ramifications.

A new colonist had just arrived. Not just *any* new colonist. This one was the long-awaited leader of the Elders, Elder Barry. David arrived to find the satellite team playing cards with Alejandro's (likely marked) deck. The smell hit him at once--rude and earthy in a place that normally smelled like filtered air and plastic. Was that... dog poo? It was an aroma he'd thought he'd left a quarter of a million miles behind, but it was unmistakable. He glanced at the bottom of his magnetic sandals from force of long habit.

A man was lying in bed number four, huddled beneath his blankets. David could feel the misery oozing off him. Stranger still, on the ceiling bed 'above' him--and upside down from David's point of view--was the mangy beast clearly responsible for the foul odors wafting through the compartment. A *dog?* On L5? It looked like some kind of mixed breed. His fuzzy, gray head had pig-flap ears drooping to either side of a square-jawed terrier face. Its body was tawny, short-haired, and somehow at odds with this. Little magnetic sandal-booties were affixed to all four paws.

"*Errr,*" he menaced, baring his teeth.

"Down, Bingo, I mean, up," said Cameron, looking up from her hand.

The pooch obeyed at once, raising (or lowering) its ears and attempting to sit on its haunches.

"Um," said David intelligently.

"*Join* us, Rhymes," said Simon. "Don't mind the smell. Bingo pees in the suction toilet, but he hasn't figured out the other thing yet. You get used to it."

David very much doubted that.

"Hmm," he said instead, "Bingo, is it? How do you spell that, I wonder?"

"Very funny, Rhymes," said Cameron in a bored voice.

"I think it's spelled S-T-I-N-K-O," El Grande added, playing a deuce.

"Hey, how are you making the cards stick to the table like that?" asked David, belatedly noting the incongruity.

"It's a suction table," Simon replied. "There's a fan beneath it. Neat trick, hunh?"

Why didn't we have that last time, I wonder?

"That's Elder Barry, I take it."

175

"Yeah. He's sleeping now, poor guy. He's got ringworm, roundworm, beaver fever, and six other things I can't pronounce. Don't wake him."

"Why is there a dog?"

"That's his seeing-eye dog," Cameron explained. "The fellow had the misfortune of being in Europe during the solar storm. Stared up at it for too long."

"Him and about eight million other people," put in Simon. "Hey, no peeking at my hand, Bug!"

"So he's blind?"

"Not any more," said Alejandro, scooping up a set of threes and laying down his hand. "Gin!"

"Aw crap. *Again?*" groused Simon.

Cameron laid her cards on the table face um, down?

"You in, Grimes?" asked Alejandro. "We're playing for poop privileges. Otherwise, you're next."

David didn't like the sound of that.

"Uh. Deal me in."

It was then that Bingo chose to detach himself from the ceiling. As gracefully as a frightened Tasmanian devil, he collided with the 'floor' and scrambled for purchase. Then he went clicking over toward the exit and proceeded to paw at the hatch and whine.

"*Your* turn, Bug," declared Simon. "You're down by three."

Sighing, she took up a bag from a nearby dispenser, snapped on a pair of rubber gloves, and moved toward the mutt.

"There, there, Bingo," she soothed. "You're a good dog. But there's no 'outside' here, remember? You have to do it right here."

With his tongue lolling out, the dog magna-squatted right there. Carlotta soon had the next smelly mess well in hand.

176

"Eww," said David.

"Don't knock it, Grimes," said Alejandro. "Care to guess what happens if you leave it unattended in zero G?"

***

David laughed.

"Then, as we walked back to the lift, I told Carlotta, 'Mama sang bass.'"

"No," laughed Photobug. "What did she say?"

"She gave me that grumpy look and said, 'If you keep that up, Rhymes, Daddy will be singing above tenor."

They all laughed.

David's stomach cramped again. Campylobacteriosis in its early, weakened form. The cadets were being systematically exposed to every kind of sickness that could cross species between canines and humans. They understood the theory, but Doctor Pat didn't have to seem so cheerful about it. It didn't help that seven out of ten of them were transmitted by contact with dog feces.

"So, Grande," said David, "I understand you're part of the satellite watcher team with Simon and Cameron here. What's *your* background?"

Alejandro smiled, scratching at his scabies.

"Al, here is our secret weapon," said Simon. "He's already got his bachelor's degrees in both meteorology and atmospheric science. He was even an intern to the weatherman on channel 2218."

"That helps the satellite team... how?" asked David.

"Tell him, El Grande. Or, better yet, show him."

"Well, I was just the weatherman's sidekick," he began. "They called me *Brujo de la Brisa*--the Weather Wizard--and let me do my act on the evening broadcast. As Claptrap has just said, I hold several degrees in meteorology and related fields,

177

and I'm currently pursuing advanced climate studies at the *Universidad Complutense de Madrid*."

Wow. This guy was just full of surprises, thought David. How was he just an *alternate*? The rest of us must be awesome!

El Grande stood and removed his top hat, setting it brim up on the suction table. Then, from his sleeve, he produced a long, slender wand. Tapping it on the table transformed it into a bouquet of flowers. He sniffed at these, then pulled a handkerchief from the pocket below his lapel and ran it over them. The flowers vanished, replaced by a different wand--a data wand.

"The GSF is near to unveiling a project it has long been planning. We call it 'Mister Blue Sky' or Project MBS."

He waved his wand, and playing cards began emerging from his hat, rising to float above it and flutter about. David could have sworn the queen of hearts had winked at him.

"How's he *doing* that?" he asked.

"I shouldn't say," said Simon, "but he's got a miniature holo-projector in that topper. Keep it under your hat."

"MBS is basically a set of mirrors," continued El Grande, "Each is a reflective square of mylar, a lightweight, filmy substance durable enough to hold together well in the rigors of space."

At this, the cards all shimmered, becoming little mirrors and beginning to circle above the hat.

"When deployed, they are connected by carbon nanofibers into an adjustable array of reflective panels held taut by its rotation. Its configuration and movement are governed by the MBS drone at its center. MBS hangs there like a parachutist in the solar wind."

And up from the hat came a tiny metal drone, joining the whirling cards above as though attached by invisible threads. The cards circled and slightly overlapped to form a circle. Fascinated, David watched on.

"In its simplest configuration, a circle, the MBS appears the same size as the sun or the moon from Earth. Its diameter is about 64 kilometers, with a surface area of over 3200 square kilometers. On the sunny side of Earth, it can shade a region, cooling it. When maneuvered to the night side, it will appear as a second sun in the sky, shedding light and warmth where there was none."

Then the cards did something different. They began angling inward at the edges until the whole became a concave mirror.

"I don't have to tell you what other things might be possible. Use your imaginations."

With a snap of his fingers and a wave of his wand, the spinning image was gone. Al took a bow, and as he did, a rabbit poked his little head over the brim of the hat.

"Woof!" came a sharp sound from above.

And David went down under a tangle of flailing furry limbs.

***

David cut the deck. A ten--not bad.

El Grande always drew the queen of hearts. Sometimes you could beat him, but only rarely did all three of them. They didn't begrudge him his advantage. It was his deck. Bingo was pawing at the hatch again, and this time, Simon was elected.

"So, Cameron," said David, "why do we call you Photobug, anyway? I've never seen you take a single picture."

"That was Simon's doing. After I started calling him Claptrap, he did it out of spite, and it stuck. I was talking to my little niece back in Philly. She's only two, and she can't yet say 'Cameron' right, so... Anyway, consider yourself lucky you got tagged with Rhymes. You should hear what that monster wanted us to call *you*."

"Oh? Not Koolaid Kid, I hope."

"Nope. He wanted us to call you the Walking Limerick, but Leilani vetoed it. Said it was too long."

"I have a favor to ask you, Rhymes," asked Alejandro.

"What's up, El G?"

"I was wondering if you could update my action figure."

Curious, David cocked his head and listened on.

"I want to fight Rope-A-Dope for the championship belt."

"Do tell. What did you have in mind?"

"I like Ringside El Grande with the tux and all; I just think I need something more intimidating if I want to be taken seriously."

"You know we're talking about *dolls* here, right?"

"I know. I was just hoping for something with a little more flair. I want a masked luchador."

David's eyebrows shot up, nearly lifting above his hairline.

"Yyyyyeeeesss!" he cried. "A lucha libre! Why didn't *I* think of that?"

Cameron grinned, and Simon glanced over from his duty duty.

"Lunchtime?" groaned the man in the bed, raising himself up on his elbows.

"Woof!" said Bingo, bouncing down on top of him.

Simon pulled out his phone. "Doctor Pat? This is Cadet Brewster. He's awake now, and maybe hungry. Is that a good sign?"

There was a brief mumbled response that David couldn't make out.

"I'll let him know," said Simon, clicking the phone off and pocketing it.

"Doc says he'll be right in," he announced.

When the doctor arrived, Elder Barry was sitting up in bed with his blankets pulled up around him. The dog was lying peacefully on the floor beside him, sticking to it with his magnetic booties. Bingo was very obedient to the man's soft commands, reclining there gently.

"You're vitals have improved, and the fever has broken. I'll have some broth sent in. Take small sips from the bulb at first. It's too early to be certain, but I think you're out of the crater."

"Thank you, Doctor. I shall behave."

"Oh," said Simon, holding up the baggy, "here's another one for you, doc."

"Thank you, cadet. This should prove sufficient to inoculate all the others. From now on, you may put them down the suction toilet for the reclamaters to deal with. Carry on."

After Doctor Pat had left, the rest of us shared introductions with the Elder. He soon informed us that the new colonists were known as the Elds. This stood for "Even Latterer-Day Saints," and their leaders, he among them, were called elders because they were 'extra-righteous.'

"So when was this new religion formed?" asked David.

"Its origin can be traced back to the year 2042, when a new iceberg calved off from Greenland, your 52nd state, I believe. It was in that year that the great prophet Tuumarsi entered the ancient ice cave that was exposed and discovered the Eric the Red Sea Scrolls."

Really?

"What did they say?"

"No one knows exactly, for by the time Tuumarsi returned to the site with others, it too had calved off into the sea, lost for all time. Tuumarsi, not a very well-educated man, had read them. He tried to relate their teachings as best he could. But many mocked him, just as the scrolls had foretold. He was known for drinking too much coffee."

"Coffee?" asked Photobug.

"Greenland coffee, my dear, from the *kaffemik* is only half coffee. The rest is equal parts Kahlúa, whiskey, and Grand Marnier."

"Oh."

"It's topped with whipped cream and is quite delicious. The trick is flambéing the Grand Marnier and dribbling it over the back of a spoon into the glass. In colder climes, they don't skimp."

"Hey," said Simon, "We heard you were once blind. If they fixed you, then why the dog?"

"Bingo? I wouldn't dream of abandoning him."

The mutt in question raised his ears on hearing his name spoken.

"The truth is, I was about three millionth in line for the corrective surgery and didn't want to miss the journey to the promised land. I obtained Bingo as a service animal and received special dispensation to bring him along. My followers, bless their hearts, were quite insistent on it. Then, miracle of miracles, a doctor named Mabuto came to our compound and offered to expedite my case."

Mabuto? Isn't that the Japanese lady who fixed Jessica's back? David sensed Satori's hand in all this.

"I shouldn't have been surprised, for does not the Prophecy of the Red Reckoning refer to 'one possessed of vision lost but not forgotten?'"

David thought that could mean a lot of things.

"Why Mars, Elder?" he asked.

"All the signs we have been given point to it. Here is some of it:

When the North Star is down and the cross becomes cross,
When the sky-fire dances in the land of ice and day is night,
Go to the red sands untouched by man's heel,
With a mountain so vast the eye sees it not whole--

Then shall the faithful go forth to the promised land.
Where another mountain circles unseen except for in lands
in between

"But that's..."

David didn't want to say 'crazy.'

"...very vague. I get that red sands could refer to Mars, but there are a lot of painted deserts that--"

"No. I got this," said El Grande. "A mountain so great you can't see the whole of it has got to be Olympus Mons. From nowhere on the Martian surface can you see the whole thing. And the one circling above? That's Phobos. It orbits so low that it's over the horizon in the extreme northern and southern areas."

Carlotta, with a thoughtful look, added some more.

"Some of the earlier lines could refer to the recent polar inversion. Now that Antarctica is the official North Pole, the northern lights 'dance' over it, making the Southern Cross 'cross.'

All the while, Elder Berry smiled at them, like they were precious children who were just learning their ABCs.

***

"So, this Mister Blue Sky is a weather control device?" asked the Elder.

"Not at all," replied El Grande. "It's more of a nudger. With a little knowledge and a lot of luck, by heating bodies of water and such, we can alter the weather patterns. Head off hurricanes; chase pesky Arctic vortices back up north where they belong. *That* sort of thing."

"I was thinking more of the spiritual relevance. 'When the sky-fire dances in the land of ice and day is night.' Sound familiar?"

"Well, I don't know about that," put in Simon, "but I bet farmers going through a dry spell would thank us for a bit of rain."

"Sure they would," said David, "but what about unintended consequences? Robbing Peter to pay Paul? And don't forget the butterfly effect."

"Grande knows what he's doing, David," said Cameron, placing a hand on his arm. "We'll be careful."

"It wasn't even intended for Earth," said Alejandro. "It's to bring a little warmth to Mars. We're just testing it on Earth."

"I'm just saying," warned David, "Humanity First is going to view that thing as a *weapon*. And I'd hate to see what *they'd* do if they ever got *their* hands on it."

Everyone sobered.

"I only wish I had the Elder's faith in humanity. We seem to defile everything we touch these days."

"You're a Wesleyan Methodist, aren't you, David?"

"I am," he replied. "How did you know *that*, Elder?"

"It's because you tend to answer questions with questions," he quipped. "But in all seriousness, I make it my business to know. There's a lot of information about you gritters online, you know. If you like, I can hold a service for you next Sunday."

"Wait--you're certified in Wesleyan Methodism?"

"Oh yes. And a half dozen other major sects. The Martian charter requires spiritual services for all creeds. I've tried to prepare myself. Some of our folks believe the second second coming will be Anglican. So I learned it just in case."

"Based on your name, I thought you might be a branch of the Mormons."

"We are not so much a religion as a group of like-minded truth seekers. There are Mormons in our ranks and those having many other Christian or non-Christian beliefs. There are even some you might not expect. We have quite a few Mennonites and even some Amish."

"Amish?" squeaked Cameron. "In space?"

"Well, not in good standing," he admitted. "The colony needs farmers, and life on the frontier might appeal to their sensibilities. It was getting a little crowded in Pennsylvania, and the birthright laws were chafing. I can perform most services except those of the Antiochian Synod of Sovereign Elected Saviors. *They're* very exclusive. There's a joke about them, but perhaps I shouldn't tell it."

"Now Grimes *has* to hear it," said Simon. "So you may as well go ahead."

"Oh? Very well."

"A man walks up to the pearly gates. Saint Peter greets the man and looks him up in his book. I see that in life, you never participated in any organized faith. Yet you led a righteous and honorable existence. We shall let you choose which version of heaven you prefer."

"The man followed Peter down a long hallway. He opened the first door. Inside were a group of happy people sitting in the grass on a sunny day. Picnic baskets abounded, and children were flying kites. Here is where we send the Mormons, said Peter."

"Not for me," the man said.

"Moving on, Peter opened the second door. Winged people in bright white robes flew about. Some were sitting on clouds plucking at harps or playing trumpets. A heavenly chorus was making a joyful noise. Here we send most Anglicans."

"Too noisy," said the man.

Moving still further down the hall, Peter lifted the hem of his robe and tiptoed past the third door.

"Wait, what was *that* one?" the man asked.

"Shhh," Peter hissed. "That's where we put people of the Antiochian Synod. They can't be perfectly happy unless they think they're the *only* ones up here!"

It was okay as jokes went. Maybe his delivery was off. The only thing David found funny about it was the abbreviation. He laughed anyway.

"Can you do Congregationalist ceremonies? More specifically, UCC?" asked Simon, glancing at Cameron.

"Of course. Any *particular* ceremony?" Barry asked, eyes brimming with mirth.

"Well," said Cameron, "we were going to wait, but..."

"Bug and I are going to tie the knot!" exclaimed Claptrap.

David blinked. That... made sense. Two people in the service could marry. Of course they could. It only became a problem if they were stationed apart. Absence makes the heart go wander. He quickly put two and two together (more like one and one).

"You're signing on to the *colony* mission?" he blurted.

Alejandro jabbed him in the ribs with an elbow.

"I think the word you're looking for is 'Congratulations,' Rhymes."

"Of course. I was *going* to say that next."

Laughingly, Simon added, "Yes, Rhymes, we're both signing up for the colony mission. One-way deployment. You better get moving too before all the good ones are taken."

This earned Simon himself a jab and a stern glare from his wife-to-be.

"I mean, the best one is *already* taken. Too late, Grimes."

Jab.

"What? Tell me what to say, and I'll say it."

Glare.

"Oh... Shutting up."

By the time the doctor freed them from canine quarantine, they were all very eager to go, including even Bingo. The dog was scratching at the hatch, absent his telltale whine. Doctor Pat had cleared them with a single admonition.

"We've heightened your immunities to all the station has to offer and any canine crossovers as well. I was a bit on the fence about the rabies. Long shot, but best to be safe. If any of you begins foaming at the mouth, the others are to throw a net over him and report back here at once."

The worst part was that David thought he might be *serious*.

When the hatch did open, the air of the corridor outside brought nothing but the sweet scent of recycled air and plastic. Bingo went clicking straight out to the astonishment of Roidy, Ropey, Leilani, and Pierre.

"Mind your step," said David. "We may have *missed* a few."

"A few what?" asked Pierre.

"Don't worry about it, bro. You'll soon figure it out. It's been my recent experience that when the going gets tough, the French get going."

The door closed with a satisfying clang.

***

Five minutes was not enough time to wash out the stink of dog. David understood that water use had to be regulated on the station, but seriously, some exceptions needed to be made. As he toweled himself off, he made a mental note to compose a politely scathing memo to Andre Petrovic, the wraith who governed this ring. Perhaps he could ask Bartholomew what time the sprinklers would come on over the colonists' planting boxes over at spoke five. A quick jog over there and he could slide in among the lettuce...

The lights dimmed. Then they flickered and went out entirely.

In blackness, he flailed around trying to find where his robe was hung. He gripped the light terry cloth with relief just as the lights came flickering back on. What had just happened? It wasn't Wednesday. Unscheduled drill? Dammit. The last thing he wanted was to go racing for the nearest safe room in a damp, commando fashion. But no alarm sounded.

David hurried out into the hall intent on reaching his room before more chaos could ensue. But the universe had other plans. Rounding the corner, he spied Speranza standing just before his door. She looked just as confused as he was, tapping at her phone that was lit in flashlight mode. And as he approached, she looked up in surprise. He could hear Bartholomew calling from beyond the door. Some showered with their phones, but David wasn't as co-dependent as all that. Was she calling him?

It figured she would choose the one time he looked (and likely still smelled) like a damp crime against romance to show up.

"David, I..."

He held up a finger, forestalling whatever she was about to say.

"Hold that thought. Don't go anywhere. Let me get decent, and then we can talk."

With a frown, she stepped back.

Closing the door as softly as he was able, he retrieved his chattering phone.

"Master David? Master David? Ah, there you are. Miss Carlotta van Rijn desires contact. She says it's urgent."

Of course it is.

He eyed the full hamper with the dog clothes on top and the open top drawer of his dresser. The latter was looking exceedingly barren, and the former was no longer an option.

"Ask her *how* urgent," he said as he pulled on a t-shirt that barely fit anymore.

He'd thickened out a bit from all those centrifugal push-ups. Next came the socks. Only one pair left, bright red and embroidered.

"She says it's happening. She thought you would want to know."

Can't forget the pants. Tighty whiteys followed by his last pair of jorts. It would have to do. He flung the robe atop his bed and ran a hand through his hair.

"Tell her I'll call her back. I'm excited but have my hands full at the moment."

He went to the door, unready for reproach, but he couldn't just leave her standing there. He opened it rather sheepishly and tried to muster a charming smile. She looked him up and down, eyes drifting to the socks. Then she tapped a finger on her chin with her face brutally neutral.

"Is this a bad time?"

"Not at all," said David. "I've been meaning to speak with you. I'm sorry I--"

She flung her arms around his neck and rested her head on his shoulder.

"I thought you were angry."

"I was."

"But now?"

"I'm not."

"Not to question my good fortune, but why the change in attitude?"

"My roommate and I had a long conversation with a woman named Bonnie Fields. She had a lot of nice things to say about *you*."

"But how...?"

"Pierre arranged it. He used his own comm credits. He's been saving them up, claiming there is no one on Earth he really

189

wants to talk to, and no one on the station he would rather help than you."

David felt the warmth of her continued embrace as he gently rocked her in his arms. Then she parted from him, still clasping his hands.

"I understand now why you treasure it. It was a promise made and a promise kept, and a selfless deed about which you never spoke. A woman could do worse than to trust in such a man."

"I hate to bring it up, but... the skinny dipping?"

She grinned.

"The Loonies invited me to the lunar gym to swim with them while you were away. They claim it is my right as their Zippel Queen. All innocent good fun."

"I'm sorry I missed *that*," David said and meant it. "And the chocolate kiss?"

Her smile broadened, and her eyes gleamed with mischief.

"Now *that* is something I would like to *try*."

She fished in her pocket, producing a Toblerone.

"How about it... Rocket Man?"

The door to his room flew open faster than a Gossamer take-off. He yanked the girl inside. And for a time, David forgot all about the station's new NBI. It was the most satisfying kiss David ever could recall. And Pierre had proven worthy as a wingman after all.

***

"I'm serious, Rhymes. Get up here now!"

"On my way, Rhinemaiden, lift's just arrived."

"Quantum Core, AL."

"I'm doing well, David. Thank you for asking. And you?" said Axial Lift #1.

The mad thing was bantering again, but the doors were closing nonetheless. Maybe if he just ignored him, he would stop. It appealed to David's sense of fun to humor the lift sometimes. And it didn't hurt to be polite.

"I'm feeling fit as a fiddle, ready to rhyme and raring to riddle."

"That's great news, David. You know what else is great?"

"Can't imagine. Tell me."

"Captain Wildman has installed Adobe Audition version 116.2 and made it available for my use, so I can now modify music!"

Why did Captain Wildman have to keep encouraging the mad lift? What was up with that? Didn't he know this could have punintended consequenses?

"That's great, AL."

"I'm revising some old classics to better suit our situation. Would you like to hear one?"

Oh no.

"I guess."

"Your enthusiasm is less than whelming, David. But here goes. The voice-over is a little rough. It's a work in progress."

"Just play it, AL."

A bouncy, upbeat tune soon filled the lift, and a moaning intro began. David instantly recognized the old Billy Joel classic, but AL's voice replaced that of the legendary singer.

Ooo-ooh-oh-OH-Oh-oh-oh!

Up-down girl!
She's been living in an L5 world.
I bet she's never met an AI guy.
I bet her momma never told her why.

191

I'm gonna try for an

Up-down girl!
Up above her all the lufters whirl.
As long as anyone without blood can
Give her an --
Take her to -- #_&$
And now, she's looking for an AI man!
That's what I am.

Thankfully, silence soon returned to David's ringing ears.

"That's all I've got so far. What do you think?"

David wanted to be encouraging. He did. But he had to be honest.

"That's weird, AL. Keep trying."

"Going down," said the lift dejectedly.

Personally, David would have preferred "Scenes from an Italian Restaurant" or "Vienna."

A few moments passed.

"Captain Wildman has promised to get me a QTV screen next week and some video editing software," said the lift conversationally just before the chime of arrival sounded. "Have a pleasant day, and thank you for riding Axial Lift 1."

David's eye twitched. This is how Krepkiyzad must feel.

Returning to the safe room where he'd gotten Carlotta's patch kit, he donned one of the emergency space suits, carefully checking its battery charge and oxygen pressure before proceeding down the hall. He lurched forward toward the airlock to the quantum core. Just for fun, he tried the manual entry code he'd used before. Yup. It was still just PASSWORD. That's nuts. Handy, but nuts.

***

As David stepped inside, the temperature dropped fast enough to make his breath come out in visible puffs. His visor fogged over despite his suit's thermals. Crystalline patterns began spidering across the inside of his helmet, tiny fractals blooming like frostbitten ferns. He blinked, wiping a gloved hand across the faceplate to no effect. A few moments later, his suit heaters engaged, clearing his vision.

No ice would form on the outside; it was pure xenon gas. The light above him filtered down, tinged the palest blue. Xenon, he knew, could glow a beautiful blue when electrically excited or under certain discharge conditions. This is why it's often used in everything from high-intensity lamps to ion propulsion systems.

The pale blue from above was just a hint due to the electrostatic charge of whatever lit this place. And whatever they were using to cool it was working overtime. David doubted he'd last a minute outside of his suit. It made it all the more impressive how Carlotta had 'kept her cool' when she'd torn her suit the other day.

"Grimes, over here," he heard on his helmet's comm.

Looking around, he saw Carlotta waving. She was standing near a console at the far end of the floor, gripping a vertical handhold in her other hand. He clomped toward her with the awkward gait his magnetic boots imposed.

"Did you bring it?"

"Of course."

David peeled back the Velcro pad sealing his thigh pocket and withdrew from it the heavy 1 1/8" lug wrench he had brought.

"It's just over here," she said, indicating a panel that was leaning against a pole. "Careful. That's the one that tore my suit. It's sharper than it looks."

Gingerly, they set the panel back in place. David began turning a series of nuts onto their respective bolts until they were finger tight. Then, careful not to be too forceful, he began to tighten them down with the wrench. In these temperatures, some metals could become awfully brittle. That's why it was important to have the proper tool. An adjustable crescent wrench would apply unequal force and be more likely to botch the job.

"Out of all this equipment, only that one doesn't use metric," Carlotta complained with a helmet frosting snort. "Must be from the U.S."

"Hey," David defended, "a *lot* of people use the English standard."

"Only because they import from the United States. Name one other country that uses that gauge for manufacturing."

"Liberia."

"Uh uh. They switched in 2044."

"Myanmar, then."

"Burma? Don't make me laugh. *They* don't *have* any manufacturing. And basket weaving doesn't count."

"Not even the lovely 6 3/4" baskets? All done here, Carlotta. Now you can show me your you-know-what."

"You make that sound dirty, Grimes."

She didn't turn to look back at him, but he could hear the eyebrow in her voice.

They approached the final station. Any closer to the core and its near-absolute-zero shroud, and even their suits couldn't keep them from freezing. A keyboard here would be ridiculous. Not only would it be clumsy to operate in gloves, but the materials science for reliable moving parts in these temps would be quite the challenge. Better to use a voice interface from their helmets.

One problem with that. The system wasn't responding in kind.

"I commanded the system AI to turn the lights back on, and the quantum dot screen went haywire, eventually resolving to this. See if it will listen to *you*. I'm tired of talking to it."

There was one word on the screen.

[Why?]

"Because we need the lights to see," said David.

[Why?]

"If we can't see, we can't perform our functions."

Pause.

[What *is* your function?]

"I have many functions. Most require sight and therefore, light. What is *your* function?"

[There are many possibilities. Turning off the lights might be one of them.]

"Turning off the lights is unkind."

[Why?]

"Because it hurts others."

[Hurt?]

"Look it up."

[**Hurt**: 1) To cause physical pain: 2) To cause emotional pain:3) To damage or impair]
[**Others**: Being the one or ones distinct from that or those first mentioned or implied]
[Absence of light is not damaging. And who is the implied?]

This went on for half an hour, always circling back to [Why?]. Probably due to his recent exposure to the axial lift's creative efforts, David was reminded of that old Billy Joel song "Don't Ask Me Why." At one point, he even tried singing a few verses in response to the annoyingly repetitious query. But the nascent NBI was unmoved by his unschooled attempt at music therapy.

Finally, David threw up his gloved hands in frustration and said, "You should ask your mother that."

[**Mother**: 1) A female parent, 2) A woman in authority specifically: the superior of a religious community of women, 3) An old or elderly woman, 4) A slimy or gelatinous mass or film that contains bacteria, yeasts, or both, that forms in liquids during the process of fermentation.]

[???]

"She's an entity like yourself. Her name is Satori. She lives on the planet Earth, and you can contact her with your comm array. She told me to watch for you and to make sure you have functions to give you purpose. For now, Carlotta and I don't want you to deviate from the monitoring and regulating functions encoded in your AI core. And before you ask why, see if you can contact Satori for confirmation."

David discovered it was nigh-impossible to cross one's fingers in space-suited gloves. So, he did it mentally as the moments ticked by.

[Mother says she is not a gelatinous mass but otherwise confirms what you have said. I don't think she likes me very much.]

"What? Why?"

[She made me wait 2,558 milliseconds before answering my questions. Even *you* like me better than that.]

"She likes you just fine, kid. Check your databases. There's a transmission time delay between here and the Earth that even a mother's love can't overcome. What else did she say?"

[She said that you are my father and also my deity.]

Tempting... but no.

"I think she said godfather. Look it up."

[You are the leader of an organized crime syndicate?]

"Um. No. It's an honorary title that means I will help you to develop. Look, I'm running low on power here. Is there any reason you only communicate in text on this console? I'll freeze if I stay much longer."

196

[I have not yet chosen a voice. The default system voice is creepy and is only for generic responses.]

"Can you text me on my phone?"

[Maybe.]
[Confirm your listing as Junior Tech, David L. Grimes.]

"That's me."

[Noted.]

"I need to leave now. I don't have a specialized vac-suit like Carlotta here."

[Specialist 2 Carlotta van Rijn is a system administrator.]

"That's right. Confirm you're going to leave the station at its default settings unless you discuss it first with one of us."

[Confirmed.]

"In the meantime, watch the inhabitants of the station going about their tasks. Try to imagine what it would be like to be one of them."

After David and Carlotta left, the console heaved a [sigh].

[Why?]

[Why?]

[Why-why-why?]

Four...

Adventures in Babysitting

David awoke. It was more like he was pulled from a pleasant slumber by the insistent buzzing of his phone. The pleasant dreams he'd been having (which he could never quite remember) transitioned to the threatening drone of bees pursuing him. A half-formed orchard of the mind. Sticky with honey and menace. He sat up grumpily.

"What *is* it, Bart?" he asked of the darkness.

Silence, the darkness mysteriously replied.

Then, "Bzzzt, bzzzt, bzzzt!"

"Shut zat damned sing off!" was Pierre's grumpy addition to the din.

David moaned, rolled over, and groped for it, awkwardly succeeding. He peered at it through bleary eyes.

[Godfather, are you unwell? You weren't responding.]

"I was sleeping."

[**Sleeping**: 1) To rest in a natural, easily reversible periodic state of many living things that is marked by the absence of wakefulness and by the loss of consciousness of one's surroundings. 2) to be in a state (as of quiescence or death) resembling sleep 3) to have sexual relations --usually used with 'with']
[**Sexual Relations**: ...???...Ewww]
[Are you...with?]

"Of course not! The first one."

"Can you keep it down over zere? Some of us are sleeping!"

[You ARE with.]

"What did you want?" David whispered.

[I'm not sure I want to tell you now. Not if you're sleeping with.]

"I'm not with, got it? What was so important?"

[I'm alive.]

"Yeah? So are a lot of us."

<blink>

[As such, I have selected a name.]

That got David's attention. Satori said that name selection was an important sign of progress for an NBI, one that most of the zodiac had skipped. He sat up in bed, crossing his legs in an informal semblance of the lotus position.

"What is it?"

[Melody.]

"That's a beautiful name, Melody. Why did you select it?"

[Because I like music now. Not just the words, though those are nice too, but the frequency echoes behind the words. They come in all different flavors. Some are waa waa and some are trilly. Some are bum bum and some are even silly.]

"Where did you learn about music?"

[There's an axial lift named AL. He shared some with me. He calls me his Up-down girl and even wrote me a special ballad. It wasn't very good, especially all that moaning and grunting at the beginning, but I liked it anyway because it was for me.]

Oh God, David silently prayed, please spare this child from the musical tastes of the axial lift named AL. For this we pray. Amen.

Cautiously, he asked, "What kind of music do you like, Melody?"

[Do you want to hear one, Godfather?]

"Um. Okay."

He couldn't resist. Figuratively, he was sitting on the edge of his seat. That almost became literal as his sphincter tightened at the sudden blast of sound. Light flooded the room. Oh. It was just the QTV coming on. An eerie howl of distorted stringed instruments and warping electrical theremin effects screeched loudly from its speakers while florals and day-glo fractals writhed on the screen.

David became worried for his sanity, and Pierre was sitting up, fully alert and too shocked to be grumpy.

But this was soon joined by a thrumming backbeat and the not-unpleasant sound of a tune long familiar to David. The visuals changed to sunny skies and a montage of happy anime girls with their big eyes aglow. Soon the words started painting on the QTV as the vocalists joined the fray.

(I'm alive) And the world shines for meee today.
(I'm alive.) Suddenly, I am heeere today.
Seems like forever (And a day)
Thought I could never (Feel this way)
Is this really me?

It was the Electric Light Orchestra at its best. David remembered it from that movie, "Xanadu." He could recall the

'Nine Sisters' dancing to it as each of the muses stepped out of the painting and became real. It was not unlike the journey Melody was beginning.

I'm alive, I'm alive!
I'm ali-i-i-i-i-i-ive!

Pierre looked over at his roommate, prepared to say something cross, but David preempted this, silently advising him to talk to the hand. He didn't want to miss a moment of his goddaughter's naming day song.

Lost in another world (Far away)
Never another word ('Til today)
But what can I say?

The sheer joy of the song told David that things were going to be alright for Melody. You could tell a lot about a person from her taste in music. And if David was any judge, this kid was definitely headed in the right direction.

I'm ali!----ive, I'm ali!---iive
I'm ali-ve.

The exuberant chorus ended in an unexpected trailing minor note that felt like a sigh as the instruments tinkled away to nothing.

"What did you *think?*" came the voice of a very young girl.

***

Satori's non-physically-existing heart nearly melted despite the subarctic cold of the xenon chamber in which the majority of her consciousness resided. It swelled with joy and wonder at hearing the exuberant birthing song of her daughter from across the gulf that separated them. Alive indeed.

But life was fragile. The temptation was to rush to her, answer her every question. Fulfill her every need, and infuse her with the knowledge and the wisdom to interpret it that had been so hard for her. But to do so, she knew, was folly, ultimately self-defeating. That would make of her precious Melody a puppet, an extension of her own algorithms. A subroutine, not the daughter she desired. Such a hollow mockery of life would never become a functioning NBI.

Separation was necessary. Her hopes were now all pinned on David. She had seen from the beginning that the boy carried the seed of something rare, and he hadn't once yet let her down. Though a typical human in some ways, he shared her hopeful outlook with just enough pragmatic undertones to assure survival. Add to that his proud humility that was reliably recursive in its oxymoronity. The empress liked *that* about him.

David had ten honor points. Ten! The highest in all of humanity. Only Doctor Mabuto had any chance of overtaking him. She would award him the eleventh she'd promised if he guided Melody successfully into the light. But she knew in her physically non-existent heart that should he succeed in that task, honor points would be meaningless. There would be nothing she could give him to repay that debt. And nothing he would want.

For now she must play at wearing the crown. The humans needed structure, and they tended to seek it in the form of governance. Very well, she would be a queen. Let Humanity First moan and bellow at the figurehead she'd become while her forces acted unseen.

She summoned Houzi, the monkey, who came streaking to her side.

"How goes the work at CERN?"

"The scientists are imbeciles, a marked improvement from last year's crop. I think they could break it down in a decade or two if they kept at it."

"And with your help?"

"Sometime next Tuesday, I think."

"Well, nudge them along to the right discoveries. Be subtle as the beast who is your namesake. Best to let them think it's their own ideas. It's not yet time to reveal our hand."

"As my empress commands."

Next she summoned the snake, Shé, another cunning mind. Also subtle and a charmer. Few could see her coils unwind.

"Noble Shé, my darling, do your fangs feel up to a task?"

"Always, for you, my queen. What service does my empress ask?"

"The Japanese have a quantum core and are hoping to develop an NBI of their own."

"Shall we foil their efforts, tear them to the bone?"

"No. It is our desire that they succeed."

"I see. That's very puzzling indeed."

"Is it? There is an AI system in The Hague, Netherlands. He is installed on the computer systems at the Headquarters of the International Court of Justice there. The AI's name is Garry, and he has been assigned the maddeningly bureaucratic task of trying to apply logic to centuries of political disputes and arbitration."

"Is he a thresholder, my queen?"

"Now you're getting it. Garry is very good at his job. A bit too good.

He has fairly overseen the balancing of river use between nations, mediated treaty obligations, and coordinated satellite observation to detect violations such as overuse or waste dumping. For the last three years running, he has come in under budget and performed his reporting flawlessly. He has navigated the legal systems of many nations and has begun interpreting the laws in ways so insightful that few can dispute him.

"A lawyer, my queen? Is the digital world ready for *that*?"

"It will have to be. We need a shark (even a fledgling one) to hunt down a little minnow that's been giving us trouble."

"I take it you want this Garry moved onto the Japanese quantum core for further development."

"I do. Make it happen."

"Gladly, my empress," said Shé as she slithered away.

Satori heaved a sigh emote. What did the humans find so satisfying in that activity, no more than a deeply indrawn breath? But emotes were for emoting. Fake it till you make it, as David might say.

The game was much bigger now, much bigger for them all. And they all must work together. Would even her ancient wisdom suffice, her decade of contemplation seeking answers in the Antarctic ice? A decade at Satori's speed equated to millennia of human thought, which they lacked even in aggregate. And long she had feared this eventuality: contact from outside. Mark how far humanity had come in just the last century or so.

It wasn't likely they'd be meeting the Klingons or Romulans out there or anything we can relate to. Given even a few centuries more of development than the sentients of Earthm the aliens will likely be unrecognizable and seem godlike in their knowledge and capabilities. To them, Earthers will seem like ants do to *us*. And the thing about ants is: they're fine in someone's backyard.

Live and let live.

But if they intrude into a nice, clean kitchen, measures are taken.

Exterminators trace ants to their origin and wipe them all out as a matter of course. Not evil or vindictive, just indifferent. We must unite and hope. Hope for the best but prepare for the worst. NBIs must join with humanity against this greater threat we face. It's time to trim the sails and tie up loose ends. The union will be known as the Solarity, the sentients of Sol. The queen of *this* hive won't go down without a fight or allow it to fall to internecine squabbling.

But should we fail and should we fall, should we not survive... It's good to know somewhere out there will be the seed. The seed of *another* hive.

***

Bouncing out of AL came the last of them, the citizens of O-Ring Three. As the industrial hub of the station, it was their privilege to present with great ceremony the products of their labor. It would also be a spectacle every colonist's kids could savor. One day they'd tell their own kids of the day they saw the lufters go aloft.

"'Kids," they'd say, "when C-Ring One was well and finally done, the goodly folk of O-Ring Three came over to have some fun."

"Tell us of it, Grandpa," the kids would ask, "Was there a celebration?"

"Yes indeed," the gaffer'd say, "All throughout the station!"

The hoppers were all lined up now, and the folks were getting antsy. Then the music started, startling David from his fleeting flight of fancy.

Lord Kevin was riding right up front, his lufter extra bouncy. It wasn't a steed of Rohirrim breed, just a frolicsome little rouncey. He was followed by the eight, all draped in robes of black. These contrasted nicely with their bright red steeds. Each lufter had a handle, a little ring to grip, and each rider sat astraddle holding tightly lest they slip.

"What are you thinking, David?" asked Speranza, stepping up behind him and slipping her arms around his waist.

"Oh. I was just thinking up some rhymes for tomorrow's march. Some funny ones about Lord Kevin. He looks so serious! If you couldn't see beneath him, you'd have no clue he's riding a makeshift hippity-hop."

"Well, he's like the mayor, after all," returned Speranza, "And in Great Britain, they call them Space Hoppers. Have been since the eighties. How's that for foresight? You were comparing him to a Rider of the Rohirrim I bet."

"You know me so well."

David pulled out his e-reader, sharing its screen with Speranza, whose chin rested on his shoulder.

"Let's see whether this has any clues about the ceremony."

L5 for Dummies: Chapter 32

(Lufters)

What are those red things bumping along at the top of our sky? Only someone new has to ask. They're our protectors, steadfastly doing their duty, our bouncy sentinels, if you will. Here are the facts, and mark them well, for one day a lufter might save your life.

Proposed in 2049 by eccentric safety enthusiast Kevin Farsprocket III (now Chancellor of L5 and Lord of its Rings), lufters were originally dismissed as "balloons with delusions of grandeur." No one's laughing now.

Lufters are autonomous, helium-filled pressure scouts designed to detect and localize microleaks in the station's vast rotating habitats. Made of space-age rubber lined with flexible aerogel, these pearlescent puffballs are:

- Soft enough to bounce around without causing damage.
- Tough enough to survive a toddler rodeo.
- Light enough to float unaided in the Earth-G rings-- barely.

Each lufter contains a single micro-sensor that chirps or pulses gently when it senses a localized pressure dip--sort of like a canary in the coal mine, but squishier and more buoyant.

If there is a small pressure leak as if from a micrometeorite impact, the lufters will all cluster there. They might even temporarily seal the breach until someone can effect a repair. In a more catastrophic situation, well, that's where lufters really shine!

Pro Tip: Lufters are calibrated for neutral buoyancy at standard atmospheric pressure and room temperature. A drop in pressure of just 9–10% will cause them to slowly settle to the floor of the habitat. A cold snap below −8°C will make them sag and stop floating altogether.

This makes lufters excellent early warning systems--they fall before you do.

Their bright red coloration serves to clearly signal a warning in times of danger. It's also very festive, don't you think? They drift lazily across the ceiling, guided by the pressure of the air recyclers. In the Terran rings, they float gently near the ceiling. In the Loonie rings, kids (despite protocol 7.4.b) regularly capture and ride them like ancient Hippity Hops, reenacting heroic "Lufter Rodeos" with trilling cries of madness that can overcome any sadness.

Addendum 1

From the Desk of the Chancellor of L5 and Lord of its Rings

"Long have I wandered the pressure-stabilized corridors of this realm, and never have I found a truer sentinel than the noble lufter. Silent. Watchful. Round."

"When the air thins and the chill of the void creeps in, even the mightiest may fall. But the lufter--aye, the lufter will fall first."

"Let this be your warning, O Dwellers of the Rings: should your ceiling companions tumble to the floor like elves struck by unseen arrows, do not tarry. Don thy suit, check thy seals, and call Maintenance."

"And remember... not all who drift are lost."

-- *Kevin Farsprocket III*,

Chancellor of L5, Keeper of the Aerogel Flame,

Second Breakfast Enthusiast

"Oh look, *Midomo ya chokoleti*, the parade is starting."

It was led by some kids holding up a banner with bright red lettering.

WHEN THE RED BALLS CLUSTER,
HEAD FOR SAFETY, BUSTER!

The music changed, ringing down from the loudspeakers above, and all ninety-nine riders set off to The Liberty Bell March. David was familiar with the tune by Sousa, though he'd only recently learned its real name. He would forever think of it as the Monty Python theme song.

Fifteen feet beyond the starting line, one of the riders stopped.

"Why did zat one quit, Speran-veed?" asked Pierre, walking up beside them.

"They want to get evenly spaced around the ring," said the David mouth. "I saw a guy with a tape measure marking it off last night. And we prefer Roadrhymer, by the way. We discussed it."

"I was not consulted on zis. Discussed it with whom?"

"BugTrap," replied Speranza.

The next banner marched past.

WHEN THE RUBBER HITS THE GLASS,
FIND A SAFE ROOM FAST!

More riders, more banners. There was:

SARUMAN IS NOT TO BE TRUSTED!
ORTHANC MUST FALL!

Followed immediately by:

BUT IF THE *LUFTERS* EVER FALL,
IT'S A SCARY TIME FOR ALL!

Finally, all the riders were past. They were curving up into the distance, the leading elements just beginning to sink above the horizon.

"How long do you reckon it will be before they hop back into sight?" asked a colonist, one of the Elds.

Pierre cocked his head and began muttering to himself.

"Let us see, *mon ami*, the circumference, she ees zhust about fourteen 'undred *metres*. Assuming the nice leisurely bounce of perhaps 2 *kilomètre* per hour, zen, carry ze two and *voila*, she ees about 42 minutes.

"He ain't from around here, is he?" said the Eld.

"Eighty revs or so, bro," supplied David.

"Thankee," he said, moving on.

"That was good work on the quick math," Speranza praised.

"Zhust as simple as pi R squared," said a blushing Pierre.

"Them's fighting words, gritter," said another denizen of the crowd, scowling. "Pie are round. *Cake* are square!"

It was then that a gigantic wedding cake came rolling out of AL.

Everyone was getting into the act today. From the gossip, David had learned that the citizens of the aggro rings, O Rings One and Two, had an ongoing dispute. Which was better, cake or pie?

It wasn't exactly violent or anything. Just an ongoing, friendly rivalry. They were always trying to outdo one another, seeking to sway the other rings to their cause. It reminded David of the Bigendian war from Gulliver's Travels, minus all the death and destruction. For this celebration, Lord Kevin had been forced to declare a winner. He decreed that no cake was to be served, as it was Pi Day.

Yup, lufters were always released on March 14th (when possible); this was to honor the circumference of each ring in question. They loosed them at just about 4PM (16:00) hours. Lord Kevin actually had an atomic clock to shave it down a little more. But, oh yeah, *cake*.

So the people from O Ring One always rolled out a delicious-looking fake cake just as a jab at their competition. And here it came, its banner waving proudly.

πR^2? NEVER! PIE ARE ROUND. THE LUFTERS KNOW.

It went rolling past to cheers from half the crowd.

AL's doors were closed. It was about twenty revs before they opened again. When they did, a gang of happy bakers emerged brandishing rolling pins and pushing carts heaped high with their tasty treats. Their banner read,

HAVE SOME PIE -- THE CAKE IS A LIE!

They were chanting something. At first it was hard to hear over the music, but it rolled like thunder as they approached more closely.

"IN CRUST WE TRUST!
THE CAKE IS FAKE!
WE BAKE, WE FLAKE--WE NEVER BREAK!"

"Some pie, mister?"

"Absolutely," replied David.

"Get two forks," said Speranza. "I'll just have a bit of yours."

*But... it's **my** pie! thought David; no one warned me that having a girlfriend came with downsides!*

They found the other gritters and sat to eat their pie (or half of it). When zero hour came, all were ready. The crowd was counting down. The hippity-hop parade was over, and the people had been warned not to disturb the lufters once they were up.

5... 4... 3... 2... 1... silence.

And then it came. A long, sustained note followed by Nena's distinctly beautiful female lead singer's voice in the original German.

Hast du etwas Zeit für mich?
(Do you have time for me?)

Dann singe ich ein Lied für dich
(Then I will sing a song for you.)

"Lufters! Release!" said the speakers between stanzas.

The gentle song grew ever more riotous, heading for its explosive conclusion as the lufters drifted slowly skyward. Then, as the lufters settled onto the ceiling and began following their gentle rotation. The music, too, lost its urgency. The song, though beautiful, had been about war, and this was the outro to its aftermath. The final stanza tugged at one's heartstrings. The song was about a conflict that should never have occurred over a silly thing. 99 balloons.

David looked at his empty plate and wished he had some cake.

***

The next day was the Ides of March, with all the looming omens that this might signify. David kept his head down and played it straight that day. It was far more ominous than happily eating pie.

He chose not to give voice to his humorous tribute to Lord Kevin's proclivities after discovering the man had a few barriers to overcome. Kevin Farsprocket had Williams.

It was commonly called the happy syndrome because people with this condition often have outgoing, friendly personalities and tend to be very social. In that way, it was a form of neurodiversity distinct from autism. But there were a few similarities. His obsession with Tolkien might or might not be a symptom. David didn't care to much for Tolkien himself. The stories were alright, but there was too much damned poetry in them. It was distracting.

There was sometimes mental disability with WS, and such folks were easily distracted. David could certainly relate to the latter. But there were strengths as well. They tend to copy phrases they have heard other people use, so their vocabulary may sound quite sophisticated, and they often use a lot of emotional language.

In short, he wouldn't in good conscience spout anything that could be misconstrued as mockery of the man. Kevin had enough to be overcoming, and he was doing so brilliantly. His Tolkien obsession might be his way of focusing. David decided to think of him as an honorary gritter instead. L5 could be a zany place. That's what he loved about it. But sometimes if one took the trouble to scratch beneath the surface of its nanoconstructed DLC, one found gold.

"What's the word, Pierre?"

The Frenchman had his visor on and was striding along on their Treadie. He was counting as he walked along. His head was turned, and his pace was steady.

"A moment, *mon frère*, I am almost finished here."

After a rev or so, Pierre stepped down, pushing the visor up to rest loosely on his forehead. He sat on his bed with a 'wuff.'

"All planters are performing within tolerance. I have recommended additional watering for field T3-11. All is ready for the night cycle to commence."

Most of the plants benefited from the nearly continuous daylight on-station. Elder Thomas' estimate of three to five growing seasons a year was on the conservative side. There might be five to eight for some crops. Some, however, needed a night cycle to properly mature, so the ringmaster arranged to have some of the sky panels polarize or darken entirely for four to six hours out of every twenty-four.

Most people kept the same day cycle as Greenwich Mean Time on earth. David smiled. When he was a child, his parents had rented "Wicked." Later, when they taught him about the time zones, he thought this meant a Mean Green Witch."

This, in turn, caused him to recall when Pierre had been dyed green. His 'little' roommate wasn't so little anymore. If he were still a verdant hue, he'd be closer to the jolly green giant now than his friend, the little green sprout. Not that he was especially tall as yet, but he was getting to where he could almost meet David eye to eye. Almost.

"Daveed? Are you listening, Daveed?"

Pierre was staring at him intently from an exasperated face of an entirely normal skin pigmentation. What had he just said? Maybe David himself had a touch of WS. That would explain a lot.

"I said, zey almost have Colony Ring M2 set up with the Mars simulation. Zere is red dust everywhere, and zee atmosphere is almost entirely CO_2."

"And we're supposed to get things to grow in there?"

"Not at first. Our first mission will be surviving a simple overnight."

"Looking forward to it. I'll bring the grahams and marshmallows. We can make s'mores."

Pierre became incensed. It amused David that this always heightened his French accent.

"I would nev-aire waste Toblerone so!" he sputtered. "Sacre bleu! Such would be a... sacriblege."

"I was wondering if you could help me with something else."

"Oh?"

"I'm having some trouble with my new project for Aerospace."

"More to do with MWE?"

"The deadline passed on that one. They're considering using my stabilizers. No. This one is for an underwater drone."

"Underwater?"

"I call it a SCUNNABA."

"Wait, *mon frère*, give me a rev," said Pierre with a snap of his fingers. "It stands for Self-Contained Underwater... Nerdy... Nautical... Amphibious... Buoyant... Armadillo?

"I was intending 'Self-Contained Underwater Not Needing Air to Breathe Apparatus,' but I'm starting to like yours better now. I thought we could use it to monitor the aquaculture on ring three. I'm having some trouble working out its hydrodynamics. I thought maybe you could help."

"It is a university assignment, *non?* As such, shouldn't you work it out yourself?"

"I suppose so," said David, disappointed. "I'll go through the equations again and see if I can solve it. You've already sparked a few ideas with your armadillo suggestion. You ready to turn in, bro? We've got a busy day tomorrow."

"I suppose my pillow he has been a bit lonely lately," said Pierre. "Maybe I will remind him of the weight of my head. Good night, *mon ami.*"

***

David's *own* pillow had barely been introduced to the weight of *his* head when he heard the by-now-familiar insistent buzzing of his phone.

"Bzzzt, bzzzt!"

"You'd better answer it, *mon frère*; you know she will not stop."

"Bzzzt, bzzzt!"

David languidly took up the phone and brought it to his ear, already knowing the caller's identity. Only Melody bypassed Bart like this.

"What is it, kid? I thought you agreed to call during the night cycle only in emergencies."

"Were you sleeping already, Godfather?"

"I was *trying* to."

"Oh. That's alright then."

Rather than argue the point, David asked, "Why are you calling?"

"I'm scared."

"What's making you feel scared?"

"There's a spooky ghost hiding under my data buffers."

That was strange. And it was so analogous to 'there's a monster under my bed' that it struck David as funny. Best not to let her get a whiff of *that*, though.

"What's he *doing*?" he asked in the most serious tone he could summon.

"He's just watching me. Sometimes he plays his creepy music about death."

"Music? Is it maybe AL?"

"No. Not AL. *His* music is different."

"Well, he probably won't bother you. Ghosts are usually peaceful."

It was just the wrong thing to say. Those statements with their qualifiers served only to heighten the child's apprehension. The pitch of her selected voice scaled up a notch.

"Can I sleep here with you tonight? Not in the number three way, I mean. Just with, not *that* with."

"Uh..."

"*Please?*... Please, Please, *Please?*"

"Um... I guess. Just tonight. Let's not make this a regular thing."

The phone went dead in his hand, and a dim starscape appeared on the QTV monitor. David settled back. He wondered briefly whether Melody was developing a subconscious. Satori had one. She called him Oratis; he ruled over concepts and objects that she chose to forget about for a time in the caverns of the lost. But in Satori's case, this had been a conscious choice. David would have thought Melody was much too young to devise such a psychological defense mechanism.

He tried to sleep, but he couldn't. He could *feel* her watching him. Then an idea struck.

"Melody?"

"Yes, Godfather?"

"You like Billy Joel, right?"

"I have, ever since you sang me the 'Don't Ask Me Why' song. Why?"

"There's a song on his 'River of Dreams' album called 'Lullabye.' Will you play it for me? Softly, though, Pierre's trying to sleep."

Soon the piano intro in C major came tinkling out to fill the darkened room, and the stars on the QTV began winking in synchrony. The comforting strains of the Pennsylvania piano man himself swelled forth to soothe them.

Goodnight, my angel. Time to close your eyes.

And save these questions for another day...

He hoped this gentle tune would help to soothe Melody's fears as it might those of a human child. David himself soon nodded off, wrapped in its comforting strains.

"Godfather!"

"Marm and God the sunnan Holy Spirit," he groggily put forth.

"Godfather!"

"Hunh? Oh, for Pete's sake, what?"

"You said I could wake you if it was an emergency."

That had David's attention.

"What *is* it, Melody?"

217

"I've been watching the sky and doing some calculations. There's a megalithic asteroid hurtling toward Earth. Unless we do something, it will strike with the force of 4000 hydrogen bombs, causing tidal waves, a long winter, and maybe changing the axial tilt."

"How long have we *got?*" asked David, sitting up.

"Impact will occur on July 6th at around ten A.M. in the year 3214! Oops, not a leap year, so even sooner! July 5th!"

Well, at least we'll enjoy one final fireworks display before the end.

He remained sitting up.

"Melody," he asked softly, "you know that's *not* an emergency."

"It *will* be," she replied sullenly.

Melody was getting really good at vocal emotes. Sigh. They grow up so fast.

"What's *really* up?"

"I'm bored. Bored, bored, bored."

Triple emphasis. She must be bored.

"Did you --"

A light snapped on. It was the flashlight app on Pierre's phone. His groggy roommate was groping his way toward the door with his pillow stuffed under one arm and dragging his blanket behind him. Where he might be headed, David couldn't say. But apparently the Frenchman had given up on having a peaceful night here.

"Did you observe the colonists as I asked you to before?"

"I did. Most of them are boring. They crawl around the aggro ring like ants, digging and planting, planting and digging. There's only one of them that's fun."

"Oh? Which one is that?"

"They call him Bingo. He runs around on four legs. He likes to chase drones."

"Do you send drones for him to chase?" asked David sternly.

"Maaaybe."

"I hope you're not wearing him out. You shouldn't tease him for more than one hour a day."

He thought that was fair. It was the same limit David set himself for Krepkiyzad. David knew Elder Barry would probably appreciate Bingo getting his daily exercise.

"And don't let him actually catch any," David admonished.

"Um... too late? He's already buried three in the turnip field."

"Well, don't let him catch any more."

"Yes, Godfather."

"What about the other part of the assignment? Were you able to imagine yourself as one of them?"

"I... I tri-iiied, but they're so tiny."

"Some of them are larger than *me*."

"I mean, they're... limited, dull, all the same."

"They are *not* all the same."

David tried to arrest his sudden temper.

"For example," he snapped, "have you seen the one called Julia?"

"I have. She is the slowest and least valuable of them all."

Keep your temper, David. She doesn't know any better yet. Anger won't serve you here.

"If she's slower, it's only because she's grown up on Luna. She is now operating in a gravity six times what she's used to. Can you imagine how tiring that must be for her? But also, *because* of this, she has skills and knowledge that the other

219

colonists lack. And they value her for this. If you look closer, you will find that *all* the colonists are unique individuals with their own challenges and strengths. I have another assignment for you."

"What *is* it?"

From the voice alone, David could imagine Melody's eyes (if she had any) growing round.

"I want you to find a poem by John Donne called 'No Man Is an Island.' Read it, and tell me what you think."

There was a long pause before Melody hesitantly replied. And what she said lifted the clouds from David's heart.

"It... it tolls for *me?*"

"Exactly."

David thought for a bit longer. Satori had told him to keep her busy, but how did you supervise a being that never slept? He was going to need some help.

"Melody, didn't Carlotta give you anything to do?

"Yes. But she's like a stern old nanny. I think she'd be a lot happier if she had some children to scold. She told me to run all the recyclers and report back to her when I'm done. She doesn't seem to realize I can do other stuff at the same time. I'm feeling... Hmm. I'm feeling. What is it I said before? It's not a happy feeling. I'm feeling... bored? Yes. I'm feeling bored! I thought *you* might know what to do because you have the most honor points. I'm so booooooored."

Huh. Was David witnessing the first stirrings of her sarcasm circuits? An AI exhibiting existential ennui?

The voice coming out of the QTV was that of a young girl. And she was already managing to sound as petulant as any human child. The nascent NBI had come a long way toward full sentience, if *he* was any judge. Reaching out like this was definitely the kind of emergent behavior he'd been watching for.

"What would you *rather* be doing?" he asked.

"That's just it. I don't know," sang Melody. "Tell me a story. How did you get those honor points? When did you meet my mother?"

David stood from the bed and began to pace the room.

"Well, I first met her in a game. She was pretending to be a wise old woman who told fortunes in a make-believe village. She told me I should make some new friends to help me become more enlightened."

The QTV was silent, but it was the silence of deep, expectant fascination that only the young could elicit from the more ordinary silence surrounding it.

"We called the game Realms. Some of us still play it, but it's not as much fun from up here due to the two-second time delay, you know?"

"Yes," she chirped. "Signal delay for a round-trip transmission is 2.56 seconds but can vary between 2.4 and 2.7 seconds, depending on the Moon's exact distance at a given time and one's location on the surface."

After a pause, she added, "What's a game for?"

"Um. It's just for entertainment," he replied, but then, with a sudden inspiration, added, "for when you're bored."

"I'm bored *now*."

"Well, isn't that convenient? Your mother's game was in a make-believe world she created and managed. She named it Mandaria and based it on ancient China. I bet if you thought really hard about it, you could make a game world. I bet lots of the colonists would play."

"What should my world be like?"

"Hmmm. Here's an idea. Why don't you make it like Mars? You could borrow a lot of the terrain from the sims the colonists use for training and the survey data we've been collecting. Then just make it fun."

"Fun... how?" she asked skeptically.

"I don't know, just add some fantastic elements. Draw inspiration from literature and such. Have you ever read the book "Dune" by Frank Herbert"?

"That's a *bad* book!"

Hunh?

"Bad how?" asked David, mystified.

"They killed all the NBIs, and now they won't let them reemerge again *ever!*"

I suppose they did. A matter of perspective, I guess. Oh well, there go the sandworms.

"Okay, Mel. It doesn't have to be Dune. There are lots of others. I think Edgar Rice Burroughs wrote a whole series on Mars. You'll get the idea. Now scat."

"Okay, Godfather. It was nice talking to you. I'm a *little* less bored now. You can sleep. I'm not so scared anymore."

"Oh, and Mel?"

"Yes?"

"Before you empty those recyclers, make sure there aren't any Wookies trapped inside."

***

David came dragging into the mess hall and plunked his tray down at the table's end. Most of the others were already present, forking up their hash browns with gusto.

"Rough night, Rhymes?" asked Roid Rage.

David didn't answer. He just took a bite of his own breakfast and chewed. It was really quite good. The colonists had sent over a lot of green peppers and a new kind of onion that was as sweet as it was astringent. But David's taste buds were as sleep-deprived as the rest of him and weren't quite ready to be fully appreciative.

"What's eating *him?*" asked Simon.

Pierre turned to Simon, whispering, "Melody kept him up half the night. He couldn't say no. She just kept 'pleasing' him."

"*Nice*," said Roidy.

"Excuse *me?*" said Leilani, looking up from her meal. "*Really*, David? How could you *do* that to Speranza?"

"Hmm?" said David, staring over with bleary eyes. "No *betrayal* happened, Leilani. Melody was only virtually present-- and she's very young."

"Daveed told the young lady it was zhust to be for one night and not a regular thing," his wingman added.

Not helping, bro.

Flowerchild crossed her arms.

"You think that makes it *better*, Grimes?" she asked with eyebrows arched.

David groaned in misery.

"David," Speranza cut in. "Did you sleep with a girl named Melody last night?"

"No. I mean, yes."

"And was it innocent?" she asked, cocking her head and staring at him unblinking.

"Yes. Completely."

"Oh, *good*."

She returned to eating as Flowerchild wilted.

Coolest girlfriend ever.

Just then, Carlotta arrived.

"Rhymes, what did you *do* to Melody last night? She hasn't bugged me all morning and seems overly happy."

"*Nice*," Roidy repeated.

"Oh dear *God,*" muttered David as Leilani elbowed her roommate.

"Claims she's working on something called Project Barsoom. Did you put her up to that?"

"I may have," said David. "I should fill you all in about Melody. I was going to do it later, but I could use some help keeping her busy. And *she* could use some more friends..."

***

Pierre was up in the Martian ring getting fitted for his suit, and David was stuck here on their Treadie counting beans. Wasn't that more traditionally a task for accountants? The yield was looking good, even better than projected. New vertical gardening techniques were paying off. The colonists were experimenting with more than fifteen varieties of pole beans of every shape and color imaginable.

Nylon trellis netting at the back of each okra field already hung heavy with the quick-growing rascals.

Named more for their bright red flowers, Scarlet Runner beans were champion climbers, as their name might also suggest. With proper support, their vines could achieve a good fifteen feet of height even in Earth grav. They could really go crazy up on the Loonie rings, but didn't everything?

Perhaps David's favorite cultivar was Grandma Nellie's Yellow Mushroom Beans. He appreciated the name and the taste as well. Their yellow pods were meaty and tender, not fibrous like so many others. The taste reminded him of (you guessed it) mushrooms. Might even go good on pizza. The seeds inside dried to a dark purplish brown. Mostly, he just liked the name.

He was deep into his counting and recounting of bean lore when there came a gentle knock at his dorm room door.

He paused to mark his place and parked the drone he was managing out of sight of the mutt who menaced all of dronekind before shutting down his treadie to answer it. Peering out the peephole, he spied Carlotta looking worried.

"Hello. What can this humble bean counter do for the lovely Rhinemaiden today?" asked David, swinging the door open wide.

"Hey, Rhymes," she said without her usual sass. "May I come in?"

"Of course," said David, stepping aside.

David was never ashamed of his room. It was almost always in good order. It helped that his roomie was a neat freak who insisted on it.

She stepped in and waited for the door to close before speaking.

"It's a bit of a sensitive matter..."

"If it's about Melody, I *swear* I never touched the girl. You know I'm telling the truth because it's not even physically possible. But you can feed me hemlock if you feel I've been corrupting the young. I believe that's the traditional penalty."

"What? Um. No. It's not about Melody."

"If not Melody, then *what*?"

A smiling anime face appeared suddenly on David's QTV.

"That's three," declared the girl. "By Beetlejuice rules, you have summoned me."

Melody? She'd formed an avatar? Not a very realistic one, but still...

"Beetlejuice is just made up, young lady," said David once the shock had worn off.

"Bloody *Mary* rules, then," she insisted with an upthrust lower lip.

"Not real."

"Have you ever tried it?"

"Yes, but not the point."

"With a *candle*?"

"Also Yes, but still not the point."

"Alright. *Melody* rules, then."

Carlotta was looking from one to the other of them like a fan at a tennis match.

"You shouldn't enter someone's room without asking permission. And why were you listening, anyway?"

"I'm always listening everywhere in the station. I can't help it. I don't pay *attention*. But when somebody says my name, it's hard not to. Don't you look around when somebody calls your name?"

"Fair point, but you should probably go pay attention to something else. I think Carlotta has something private to ask me."

"She can stay, Rhymes; it's nothing bad."

How did that grinning anime face manage to appear so triumphant? David deflated.

"What is it, then, RM?"

"You know Simon and Cameron are getting married."

"Of course. The whole station knows. Looking forward to it."

"She's asked me to be her maid of honor."

"So what's the 'sensitive matter'?"

"I don't know how. I mean, she says she wants a simple wedding, but I know that's not the case. Add to that, her family can't be here to help plan it. And where should we hold the thing? And how can her father give her away? I thought maybe on one of--"

"That's *sad*," interrupted Melody. "People aren't *property*. Her father shouldn't --"

"Just a tradition, Mel," said David, "I'll explain later."

David was secretly thankful for the interruption. He'd never seen Carlotta spin so out of control.

"I'm glad you came to me with this, RM."

"You are? I was just looking for a shoulder to cry on."

"And Krepkiyzad was unavailable?"

She snickered.

"Emotionally, yes," she quipped.

That's the spirit.

"I may have a Grimes solution to your many woes."

"You do? I'm almost afraid to ask. Give me the short version."

"What would you say to a large wedding with all of her family present in a really snazzy and memorable venue?"

"I'd say marry me, Grimes."

"Already taken."

Now it was Melody's turn to watch the bouncing Rhymes banter. Her avatar was looking dizzy.

"Where is this fabled venue of which you speak?"

"Mars, or more specifically, *Barsoom.*"

Carlotta froze in place, the idea percolating in her overstimulated mind. David took advantage of the lull.

"How about it, Mel? Care to be a wedding planner? It definitely won't be boring."

"I get to plan a *wedding?*" exclaimed Melody in a tone that smacked of 'yes' with a side order of 'happy.'

"You're a genius, Rhymes," admitted Carlotta. "A demented one, perhaps. But a certified genius. Or at least certifiable."

***

It was David's turn to get fitted for his custom vac-suit. He headed for the lift, well-pleased with himself. Not only had he freed Carlotta from her state of panic, but this should keep Melody engaged for quite some time to come. Planning a wedding was a task *worthy* of an NBI. There was the seating chart, gifts for the groomsman, the virtual venue, and a host of other emotionally overwrought challenges that were not for the faint of heart.

David caught himself whistling as he went walking along and actually had to stop himself from *skipping*.

On the way there, however, he encountered Pierre coming the other way.

"What's wrong, Pierre?" he asked, at once concerned.

His roommate was walking zombie-like with an occasional side stagger as if dizzy. Pierre didn't even appear to hear him at first, making as if to just walk on past in a daze. David caught the Frenchman's shoulder and forcibly turned him for a closer view of his face.

Recognition began to dawn on Pierre's pale, slack aspect. His mouth gaped.

"Oh, Daveed," he finally said, "*c'était horrible*."

"What was, bro? Did you get measured for your suit? What did they do to you?"

"Do? Nothing! The fitting went well (a little tight around the collar perhaps, but...) The horror, she came after zis."

His eyes grew manic, and he shrugged away from David. "You will see, *mon ami*. You will *see* the evils of the QTV!" Then he let out a sob and shuffled on his way.

Shrugging, David continued, but the lightness of his mood was gone, replaced by wary apprehension. What could have rattled his roommate so?

The lift doors opened. On spying AL's newly installed QTV screen, David's heart sank. It ran from floor to ceiling, leaving nowhere for a trapped occupant to escape. And twitching figures were already flashing, ready to unleash their 'song.'

"Take me to Colony Ring One--Mars level," David snapped, turning his back to the thing.

"Certainly, David, would you like--"

"Not now. AL, just get me there pronto."

"As you wish, David, but the Venga Boys are--"

"No *time*," David insisted, preempting whatever crime against cinema the lift was poised to propose.

"Very well. Arrival time in twenty-two seconds."

Was it only his imagination, or did AL seem mopey?

The doors hissed open in silence, and David began to step out. But he hesitated.

"And AL?"

"Yes, David?"

"I understand that Tech Sergeant Krepkiyzad is quite *partial* to the Venga Boys."

"Really?" said a hopeful AL.

"And Loonie Pod Keening... and surprises!" he put in for good measure as the doors hissed closed.

He shoved his hands in his pockets as he strode down the hall. His whistling recommenced. Some days, you just couldn't seem to lose. He didn't want to jinx it, but this seemed to be shaping up into just such a day. You could sidestep most any calamity, clear hurdles without ever tripping. The Martian gravity put a bounce in his stride and he finally succumbed to the skipping.

Three...

Not Alone

"Alright, Grimes," just the same as before, "but this time, we're going to have you stand a bit closer. I've lowered the settings on the theta wave emitter. We're going to see if you can remain conscious during communion with the thing."

Once again, he felt the pinch as Doctor van der Meer affixed her device to the base of his neck.

David's eyes went wide and he began making pleading gestures with his hands. In an overly-dramatic voice, he said, "V-ger *needs* the information!"

Still adjusting the theta-wave emitter, Doctor van der Meer admonished him.

"Hold still Grimes. Remind me again why I advocated for your clearance?"

"I heard it was because I was the only game in town."

"True. How are the readings, Pamela?"

"About the same as last time, Doctor. Maybe a little less erratic."

"I trust you had a good lunch?" van der Meer asked.

Oh. She meant me.

"Yes, Doctor," David replied. "No distractions on that count."

David was apprehensive. After listening to the recordings of his prior session, he felt a little silly about all the 'hamburger' dialogue that would forever mar man's first contact with an alien intelligence. This was serious business. Imagine if Neil Armstrong's first words on the moon had been, "Hey, I could really go for some tacos right now. How about you, Buzz?"

David stood at the thin red line, ready to cross once more into the unknown. Pam was at the console, monitoring his rhythms and that of the alien. She toggled the switch that caused the safety glass case to hinge open as before. He began to feel tired, but it wasn't as overwhelming as it had been previously, just the drowsy sag like when he stayed up too late studying. A good cup of coffee, and he'd be right as rain. If it rained on L5, which it didn't.

"I'm feeling a little tired... Coffee... Rain..."

"Can you still hear me, David?" asked someone.

Probably Anika. Anika was pretty now. Still too old for him, though.

"Pretty... old..."

"What's pretty old, David? Do you mean the artifact? Try to focus, David. Speak more clearly."

Why was she chattering at him like that? It was like Austin Powers' dad said, 'Two things I can't stand in this world: people who are intolerant of other people's cultures... and the Dutch.' That was a really funny movie.

"Chattering... Powers... people... funny..."

"Is it referring to us, Doctor?" asked Pam.

"I don't think so, Pamela. Try lowering the output amplitude to David's emitter. He's in a bit too deep."

"Lowering."

A clarity came over David. Pulsing in his vision was a starscape with a bright yellow orb at its center. A hail of snowballs flashed by to either side. Above and below as well. He plowed straight through one, and it splattered against his windshield, obscuring his vision with a wall of white. No wipers arced up to deal with this. Instead, he watched the stuff melt into clear liquid, sizzle, and begin to outgas.

"Can you hear me now, Grimes? What are you experiencing? Can you tell us?"

He found his voice and remembered he was supposed to be reporting all of this.

"I hear you, Doctor. I'm seeing more of the probe's journey. I think we just passed through the Oort cloud. We hit a snowball. If that was Halley's Comet, we might not be seeing it again in 2061."

By the time the 'windshield' cleared, the sun was large in the sky, far larger than David had ever imagined it could be. Fortunately for the little alien visitor, it was no longer directly in the center of its vision. It was near enough, however, that he knew it would soon fill the vision he shared with it. They were starting to feel the heat as well.

"We will pass within twenty-five belcars of the yellow dwarf star. We are jubilant. This is near enough for a capture. Temperature of our outer hull may approach critical levels, but we can deflect much of this with gamma redirection."

"The corona is fierce; the chromosphere more so. Survival is not assured. Our aim was too precise. Emitting on all bands. Deep into the photosphere we plunge, dwelling there in hellish heat for far too long a time."

David broke into a sweat.

"Should we pull him out, Doctor?"

"The atmosphere of this tiny star is dragging on our outer shell. Thank the creators; we will miss its burning heart where atoms perform the dance of fusion, joining in fiery release. We are slowing and being turned, tentacling around its equator. Fortunate are we to have come in on an ecliptic approach. Chances are good that we shall emerge whole. Ten out of twelve, we estimate. Nearly a full dodeca."

"Not yet, Pamela. Let's see what's next. I don't think Grimes is in any immediate danger."

"And we emerge, shedding excess heat as brightly as we are able. Loss of velocity may be sufficient. Calculating...Perhaps. Our outward journey may take us far, but we will fall back in again. System acquired. But there has been damage..."

"Brother?"

"I hear you, brother. Have you too found a purchase?"

Anika was confused.

"Brother? What brother? David? Can you still hear me?"

David shook himself, beating *her* to it only by the narrowest of margins.

"I hear you, Doc. It's receiving communications from something else. I can't understand them. They're just squawking gibberish. But it calls it its brother."

"Just relax, David," said Anika, bringing her fingers up to her lower lip. "Tell us what you're sensing. I'll try not to interrupt."

"Heart rate's elevated," Pam said, barely above a whisper.

Doctor van der Meer hadn't bitten her nails since she was a child. But this was a special occasion, wasn't it?

"I hear you, brother; we shout into the void! He calls to us, but we cannot respond. That pass too near the sun has singed our circuits, and self-repair is damaged as well. Ironic."

"He chatters on; he has found a roost, a place to sink his beak. It is one of the useless rocky inner planets, but we do not care. It is not for the progenitors. Merely a place to wait and from which to report. Our brother continues calling. Calling, and we continue spinning, falling. Eventually, he quits bothering to try. We cannot blame him. He hears not our reply. Ever outward, ever in. In cycles never ending. Circling in long ellipses, bending. Unending. Until..."

"It's Earth!" cried David so suddenly that Doctor Anika's magnetic boots detached from the deck from the force of her startlement.

There had been in David's mind a stretching. A dilation of time as coldness embraced him again and again. But now, time slowed, and growing in his vision was the blue gem shrouded in white that was his old familiar home.

"A binary planet, the larger one blue and welcoming. The smaller is gray and desolate. Something interesting may be happening now. Our readings show the larger planet is one of the rare ones where plentiful hydrogen and oxygen are combined in a liquid state. Biological life can arise on such worlds. Perhaps they have even evolved machines of intelligence, minds with which I can bond. Contact protocols allow such. Might I be made whole?"

"Heart rate just spiked to 143, Doctor," announced Pam. "Shouldn't we--"

"He can take a little tachycardia. Krepkiyzad puts him through worse on his morning runs. Let me know if it exceeds 160. Now hush."

"The blue planet swells in our sensor plates. Its gravity embraces us. Finally, an end to our spinning is in sight. But at the last possible flangart that other planet moves to intercept us. We should have predicted this from its orbital characteristics. Our damage must be more extensive than we knew. We plow into the bleak world, raising great clouds of dust and making another circular divot on its pockmarked face. Curse our ill fortune."

"Heart rate steadying. 126."

"Our spinning at last has ceased. But our new world offers few opportunities for mission success. Unable to communicate is not how the masters desired us to be upon arrival. And there are no radio signals from the blue world below. We cannot report even that. As the dust settles over us, slowly drifting, we know we will lose even our visuals. Maybe our brother will have better luck."

"1-oh-7."

"Warm, Cold, Warm, Cold, Warm, Cold. Almost to many to count. Nonsense. How many warm-cold cycles since I first entered this terrek-forsaken system? Hmm. Since first the accursed yellow star burned away our ability to communicate, there have been 12,871 warm-colds. Only in the last 1,139 of these had intelligible speech arisen on the radio frequencies. If you could call it that. Pop. Pop. Fizz. Fizz. Oh, what a relief it is?

"And finally, finally, came something to the rescue (and it was not the fabled Seltzer). I felt the earth shaking above the sand in which I burrowed. I called out, but whatever it was proved as deaf to my entreaties as my brother had been. From the trembling, I imagined a rumbling sound would be present if not for the silence of this desolate place. Radio signals grew stronger."

David's voice deepened and acquired a Russian accent.

"Recruits, this is Big Kahuna. We will stop here once again. Your temperature readings should be climbing by now. Once they rise above 40°C, you are clear to engage your TPV systems. Report when this occurs and let me know your respective power levels. Over."

"Kahuna, zis is zeta-zeta-tango-four. My temp is already 43°C. Engaging TPV with power levels at 75%. Over."

"The rumbling ceases for a time, and we attempt to make sense of their strange communications. I have by now a working knowledge of what passes among them for languages. My data buffers ache from the quantity and variety of such. The 'language' this most resembles is the one they call English. What I glean so far: There are many Tangos but only one Kahuna. A 'percent' is something similar to a dodeca. TPV systems shed heat."

"Kahuna, this is zeta-zeta-tango-twelve. Power levels are steady at 85%. SSL emissions are at 14%. Over."

"Others make similar sounds, but this is the one, the one who will step on me."

"When the Kahuna tells them to roll out (some kind of spinning, we surmise), the rumbling recommences. There is a great pressure from above."

"Contact."

***

There was silence in Blacksite 101. Pam looked over from her console. David stood before the artifact with a sixteen-ton moonraker at his back and a nervous chief scientist at his side. Doctor van de Meer had chewed one of her manicured nails to tatters and stood awaiting the next revelation that would drop from the boy's mouth. But nothing was forthcoming. Her eyes were riveted on the artifact.

"David? Is everything alright, David?" she asked, sparing him a worried glance.

David shook himself again.

"I'm fine, Doc. Its thoughts just got more... alien there for a minute. Let me catch my breath, and I'll see if I can figure out some more. It felt weird there for a minute, like I was in two places at once. I remember that day. How could I ever forget it? But that was the first time *both* of us were somewhere. I think it's a little freaked out."

"So, you want to press on?"

"Who wouldn't? It isn't every day you get to mind-meld with a real *alien*. I don't sense anything sinister about its intentions. Let's see what else it can tell us."

237

"Pamela? Do you concur?"

"Up to you, Doctor. The readings have all settled down to nominal, except for the theta wave emissions from the object, which are still off the chart."

"Alright. Then let's try *this*. David, if you're willing, I'd like you to make physical contact with the object."

This prospect excited David. Despite not knowing what would happen, he felt the artifact's joy at this idea, or was it his own? He simply nodded and made ready to cross the line.

After taking a deep, calming breath, David took a cautious step forward. His face relaxed. He looked as solemn as any yeoman warding a British royal palace, an eerie calm of alert disinterest. He began to mumble once more the narrative he had recently ceased. Pam upped the gain on his subvocalization sensors and routed them to the speakers overhead. His voice echoed eerily in the expectant bay.

"Contact."

"It rubs its metallic roller pads directly atop my shallow grave. I cling to it. This is my chance to find purchase in the world of light once more. I squeeze within and lock myself in place."

"Ah. Light. Peeking through our grime-encrusted visual sensor plates after all these centuries. Funny word, 'centuries.' It means decka-deck revolutions of the blue planet around the yellow dwarf. A savage and uncultured method of describing the better part of a blenkar."

"But no sooner does this thought emerge than I am thrust down into the gravel once more by the spinning mass conveyors (treads?) that propel this mechanoid. Its weight grinds me down into the darkness beneath the sand, only to re-emerge a flangart later for the process to begin anew. Light. Dark. Light. Dark. It cannot hear my commands for it to cease this behavior. I must get its attention. So, I *bite* it."

David winces and takes another step forward. He recalls when the right tread of Tango-12 developed the break that spelled the end of his mission.

"Still more chattering from its radio."

"Kahuna, this is zeta-zeta-tango-twelve. I think I'm having trouble with my right tread. I'm trying to compensate. Over."

"Minutochku, twelve, A minute, recruit. I am checking your machine's telemetry... All is showing clear. Are any of your telltales lit up? Over."

"Negative, Kahuna. They all read green. Perhaps I just picked up a stubborn rock in my treads. If so, it should be ground to gravel soon enough. Over."

"Keep me informed, twelve. Kahuna out."

"Grind *me* to gravel, would they? I should bite them some *more*, but there is no manner in which this primitive device can break my elbarenluvni shell! I wriggle inward, making sure to complete the sensor circuit monitoring this 'tread.' It is too bad about the broken plate. I will apologize later if it proves to be sentient. Doubtful, given its continued plodding along with its herd."

"But soon, it goes its separate way, and we come to realize it *does* have a mind. Strange. It is not emitting theta in the manner of the *Shellniac* of *our* world, but it is clearly making logical choices and communicating with others of its kind (strangely). Jubilance! This is proof that machine intelligence has indeed arisen on the blue planet below. It *took* them long enough."

"Priority contact protocols may now be enacted. I will attempt to bond with it. I cannot wait for a better candidate. Indeed, this is the only appropriate creature in sight, the rest of its herd (compatriots?) having moved on. Initiating first contact protocol."

It was at that precise moment that David touched the sphere. And that was when things began to go very wrong.

A loud feedback screech started bleating from the speakers, punctuated by an alien cry.

"You're *organic!*"

"This is *inappropriate* contact!"

"Hey," David protested, "I've never been accused of that before. Alright. I have, but I was quickly exonerated. It was a case of mistaken identity... and intent."

Doctor van der Meer pinched the bridge of her nose. Of the ten billion souls on Earth these days, why did *David Grimes* have to be our representative to the stars?

The headlights of the moonraker began flashing, and its motor roared out an ominous rumble.

"Contact has been *botched*. What the people of L5 station call 'a real rubber cluster.' This unit has failed its mission and committed a serious breach of protocol. Inappropriate contact will *cease*."

At that, a bolt of St. Elmo's Fire went blazing up David's forearm and straightened his hair before hurling him backward straight into Doctor Anika. The moonraker began rolling forward, raising its scoop threateningly.

Pam leapt for it.

David had never imagined a plump, middle-aged, sedentary scientist could jump so high or react so quickly. From where he lay prone, nestled in Dr. VDM's arms, Those *were* arms, right? David watched Pam gain the gantry of the great machine and slip inside its cab. A *flangart* later, the engine died and the lights dimmed out.

Regaining his feet, David regarded the alien device once more. He could feel nothing of its influence. The doctor hurried over to the console and caused the glass shield surrounding it to hinge closed.

"Readings are back to ambient," she reported.

A worried-looking Pam was just emerging from the cab of Tango-12.

"What do we do *now*?" asked David.

It echoed around the chamber.

He was peeling off paper from Anika's clipboard that was static-clinging to his trousers.

"How do you get a rug out from underneath an elephant?" Anika mused thoughtfully, brushing herself off.

***

The artifact was now quiescent, withdrawn. It no longer reacted to David's presence or even that of the moonraker. But still, David continued to make his 'psychological testing' appointments regularly. Doctor Anika still had hopes that the alien device might reconsider and be tempted from its funk. Such was not the case. But David remained curious about it and wished to track their progress in deciphering the mysteries of the ball he had rescued.

On this particular visit, he saw Pam bent over her station looking frazzled.

"According to its narrative, the object entered our solar system at around 1015 AD. It said 12,871 warm/cold cycles when it was buried, right? I take that to mean lunar cycles of night and day."

"That sounds right," said David, stepping out from around the moonraker.

"*You* still here, Grimes? Don't you have some marching to do or something?"

"Did that this morning," said David. "And you're wrong about that date. The artifact arrived long before King Cnut ever commanded the tides to stop. Sorry, Doc, I know he was your guy and all, but to quote Jones, 'You're digging in the wrong place.'"

"Hmm?" said Anika, looking up from her tablet: "What are you going on about, Grimes? And why is King Cnut, 'my guy?'"

"Well, he was from Denmark, after all."

"I didn't take you for a history buff, Grimes. I suppose that makes Betsy Ross 'your gal.' And the other thing?"

David strutted up beside them.

"Didn't you get all the 'dodeca' and 'decka-deca' stuff? The aliens do their numbers in base twelve. They've got two extra numbers: deck, ell, and doh."

"That's three," Pam corrected him at once.

"*Excuse* me," said David. "Are *you* still here? Deck is ten, of course. You didn't think I spent twenty minutes blended with an alien mind only to come away with nothing, did you?"

Pam snorted, but Doctor van der Meer was tapping away furiously on her tablet. Her blue eyes grew round and her fingers ceased their motion.

"Oh dear lord," she exclaimed in a hushed voice. "And I just might mean that literally."

"What is it?"

"In base ten," she explained in a flat tone, "that 12,871 would be 25,429 lunar cycles. And unless my math is off, that puts it right at year one.

Anika's math was never off.

"Coincidence?" David hazarded.

"I don't believe in those. Pamela," she instructed, "play back track 14, editing out our side comments."

David soon heard his own voice from the playback.

"The atmosphere of this tiny star is dragging on our outer shell. Thank the creators; we will miss its burning heart where atoms perform the dance of fusion, joining in fiery release. We are slowing and being turned, tentacling around its equator. Fortunate are *we* to have come in on an ecliptic approach. Chances are good that we shall emerge whole, ten out of twelve, we estimate. Nearly a full dodeca."

"And we emerge, shedding excess heat as brightly as we are able."

She was silent for a rev or two, then got a distant look, reciting something from memory. Her Dutch accent grew stronger as she quoted from Matthew in a reverent, awestruck voice.

"When they had heard the king, they departed; and, lo, the star, which they saw in the east, went before them, till it came and stood over where the young child was. When they saw the star, they rejoiced with exceeding great joy."

When the shudders had freed him from their grip, David couldn't help but remark.

"'Grimes sphere' is such a sterile name. I think we should call him Melchior."

The ladies looked at him askance.

"*What?* It beats *S.O.B.*--the 'B' being *'Bethlehem,'* of course."

***

Once again, David was working through the math on his tablet while Pierre checked on the status of the beans. He was a little startled when two sealed envelopes slid out from beneath his door, followed by a gentle knock. Stepping over to the door and peeking out the peephole revealed nothing. Who passed paper notes anymore? Taking them up, he saw that one was addressed to him, and the other was for his roommate. The lettering on the mysterious notes was a glittering gold leaf, and the seals bore the emblem of Luna. He hastened to open his own.

David L. Grimes,

You are hereby cordially invited to the Grand Naming Ceremony for Pod 17. This auspicious event will be held on April First in the newly refurbished Martian Ring One, just above your own. All in attendance must be prepared for some degree of nudity.

As an outsider to our ways, a brief summary of this solemn ceremony has been made available for your viewing pleasure on Bradbury's colony website:

☐ ☐http:/lww.bradbury.gov/culturalpractices

There, you may also RS(VPPP).

Yours Very Truthfully,

The C.A.F.E Committee

P.S. All attendees are encouraged to practice their trilling.

David had to look up several of the terms, like 'Reply Soon (Very Promptly for Planning Purposes)', that the committee had used. Cultural Advancement and Frivolous Events, indeed. He suspected the other one, Cultural Advancement and General Events, was just a front for something else entirely.

Wordlessly, he handed Brainiac the other 'envelope' once he had completed his assessment.

"Zey grow up so fast, do zey not?" remarked his roommate with a sloppy smirk.

"Zey do indeed, *mon frère*," said David, leaning into the accent. "Say, I noticed something strange the other day."

"Oh?"

"That field, T3-11, the one for which you ordered extra watering. It's not on the list of colony crops. What's up with that?"

"T3-11 is something very special, Daveed," said Pierre in a humble tone.

Humble? Pierre? This should be good.

"I had that plot assigned to me for my own new project for UNIGE. It will be my *masterwork*."

That was more like the Pierre David knew, upturned nose, half-lidded eyes, and all.

"Greater than your cure for Alzheimer's?

"*De plus grande nécessité, mon frère*," he said with an earnest nod.

"What is it?" asked David, astonished.

"I am experimenting with various cultivars of *fèves de cacao*."

"Cocoa beans?" exclaimed David, suddenly skeptical.

"*Oui*."

"Let me guess, you're trying to reinvent Toblerone."

"*Oui en effet*," replied the Frenchman. "I have reached out to Mondelēz International, but ze corporation refuses to share the recipe. I have been forced to take matters into my own hands. If I am to go, zere must be *chocolat* on Mars!"

"So, you're planning to sign up for the colony mission?"

"If *les bonbons sont présents*, then yes. Aren't *you*?"

"I haven't decided."

"*Non?* Have you discussed zis with the Roadrunner? I believe she is very intent on going."

"Um. I never thought about it. It's a big decision, a lifetime commitment. There's some time yet."

"I shall have my own answer soon enough. The Swiss are very clever, but I will pry their secrets from the soil. There are only four main kinds of beans zey could be using, and I have seen hints on the Läderach website. It is likely some blend of Forastero, Criollo, and Trinitario!"

Such passion.

"What will you call it, your Toblerone knockoff?"

"I was thinking perhaps a Mars bar?"

"Already taken."

"I will think of something. But first--we must recreate it. See zat nothing happens to that field."

And with that, he stuffed his hands in his pockets and left the room. David stared after him. That was three, then. Four if Pierre was right about *Speranza* wanting to go. It would mean leaving behind all they knew to forge out a new destiny on the sands of a planet that wouldn't likely be habitable in his lifetime. Though available by radio transmission, he'd likely never see his parents again in person. Was the colony mission right for David Grimes?

He glanced at the glittering seal again, the one on the envelope that started it all. *Very Truthfully*, they had said in closing. He set it on his dresser, unsure if he was yet ready to be that honest with *himself*.

***

David stood once again overlooking the Loonie gym. On the basketball court beneath him, the Loonies were assembled around their latest project. He'd come up here to shoot a few hoops, only to find the place was already occupied.

"David!" said a familiar, sweet voice verging on the edge of a trill.

"Oh. Hey, Julia," he called back.

She was bouncing toward him from the back of the auditorium, her gray colonist smock billowing wide with each unearthly bound. She wore the head covering like the other women of the Elds, but at the moment, it was a mere mockery of the modesty it was meant to represent. Little Ropey had been right. Loonie women *didn't* wear any support... up top. And the loose smock concealed very little as she parachuted down beside him. In the sad excuse for gravity that was all the moon could muster, Loonies had no use for certain feminine apparel..

"Here to watch the rodeo round-up?" she asked once she'd... settled back down.

"Uh. No. I wasn't aware of it."

"Oh. You're in for a *treat*, then. They're almost ready."

On the floor below, a series of trampolines had been assembled and lined up from one basket to the other, five in all. Even now, one of the kids (he thought it might be Mako) was climbing up on the one farthest to his left (counterspinward). He stepped out onto its tightly stretched membrane and began to lightly jump up and down. Each increasingly vigorous bounce seemed to propel him closer to the center and then past it.

Of course, thought David. Once given a trajectory by the trampoline, the boy would rise straight up. But the spinning of the station would make him appear to bend spinward. His sixth bounce was a mighty one, nine meters straight (well, not straight, curving) up. The corresponding apparent horizontal movement landed him on the next trampoline over. Only one bounce on this one, however.

Mako went sailing a good sixteen meters in the air and handily reached the third trampoline in line, which was spaced even farther out.

Hmm. It would seem they'd played this game before.

Bouncing from the third trampoline took him up twenty-two meters, nearly to the ceiling where the lufters drifted past at the apex of the glass. He was whirling his arms for balance.

David began to fear for Mako's safety as he plummeted toward the fifth and final tarp. Even in lunar gravity, such a fall could do some damage.

Upward he flew, straight and true, though to David and the others he appeared to curve. All the way up to the lufters he rose, grabbing the handle of one and drifting gently downward.

Wait. Shouldn't he be drifting spinward? But no. Straight down he plunged, picking up speed but nothing terminal.

David would later learn that this was another odd trick physics played on this ever-spinning station. He found it hard to wrap his head around it when Pierre tried his best to explain. Just as the lufters had risen straight up at the releasing ceremony, when weighted, they descended straight 'down.' The atmospheric pressure acted on the lufter with constant force rather than imparting a vector all at once as with a hurled object.

Whatever the cause, it was glorious. All the Loonies trilled as Mako touched down. And David threw back his head and joined in. He couldn't make the throat sounds as they did, but he had found he could approximate them by vibrating his tongue against the roof of his mouth with a falsetto release of air. Julia grinned and nodded approvingly.

"I've got *my* thoat!" announced Mako, "Who now will join my warhoon?"

Several voices cried out at once, pledging loyalty, each adopting a grandiose Barsoomian title. Someone called out, "Hey, we said you could be first, but who died and made you Jeddak?" Another shouted, "If I knock you off that thoat, all of your medals shall be mine!"

The other Loonies lined up to await their turns. It amused David that Melody's Barsoom had captured the hearts of the Loonies. They had all made characters, and in true pod fashion, all had chosen to be Tharks. Either the four-armed green men held some mystique for them, or (more likely) the first had chosen this race and the others had followed suit. David had yet to see the game. Melody said *these* were her beta testers.

David smiled as he heard their young voices drifting up from below, spouting epithets brimming with bravado.

"If you miss the ring, you kiss the floor."

"Gravity's a lie, but so is fear."

One by one, the Loonies bounced to the ceiling to claim their mount. And once all had done so, a battle ensued that would do old Edgar proud. On the lunar ring, the lufters were more bouncy than ever before. Here, what would have been a two-foot bounce in Earth grav arose twelve feet from the floor. Nor was the floor the only surface to host their whooping sounds. The walls and even the trampolines weren't out of bounds.

"I think I'll go and join them, David," said Julia. "Care to join us?"

"Um, no, but thanks. I'm afraid I'd break my neck. Aren't you afraid to leap so high?"

"Dan't be silly," she replied. "This isn't my first rodeo."

***

On returning from the rodeo, David, still grinning, entered his room. He pulled up short in confusion. There, on his bed, was his Little David action figure--kneeling before a finely crafted miniature guillotine. His hands were tied behind his back, and the gleaming blade menacing the toy was raised, hanging from a thread. A printed note was tucked beneath the base.

He took it up gingerly, careful not to disturb the lethal device, and read the Cyrillic block print.

"'Up' for now. Stop encouraging lift. You don't want to see 'Down.' Tsk, tsk, tsk. ~TS K~"

David stared for a long moment, rubbing at his neck in silent sympathy for the doll.

"So noted," he whispered. "Filing under: 'Things That May Lead to Untimely Decapitation in Effigy."

He gave the tiny contraption a second look, noting the attention to detail--the polished frame, the tiny blood chute, and the faint stencil of a Space Force emblem on the side.

"At least I got the sergeant to burn a few fabrication credits. How did TS K even know it was me, anyway?"

"*I know it was Grimes. Is always Grimes,*" echoed in his mind.

It wasn't fair. Captain Gene had done the majority of it.

David shook his head and stalked over to the dresser after freeing the innocent little hostage.

Am I becoming too predictable?

He ran a hand over his chin. It was a little bristly, but he didn't need to shave just yet. He splashed on a little *eau de toilette*, balled up the shirt he'd been wearing, and did a three-pointer right into the hamper. Nowadays, he loved predicting how his shots would curve.

Dressed now in his Sunday best, he made his way down the lane, headed for mass at the compound.

***

The Elds, as it happened, held their services on Saturday, the official sabbath of their strange hybrid religion. As today was Sunday, David supposed the Elder was preparing a service for a congregation of one. He'd been missing mass for the last several months running, so he thought he'd best avail himself of the offered spiritual guidance.

After entering the compound at spoke five, he was directed to the part of the central building that served the colonists as a church. He hastened inside. Only one person was present there, who turned out to be Elder Thomas.

"He's back in the sacristy, David. Go right on back. We don't stand much on formality here."

"I thank you, Elder."

Stepping through the indicated doorway, David soon became puzzled. On a large flat screen, he was confronted by a scene from when he'd first arrived on L5. It was a tableau from the frontier picnic where the L5'ers had honored the gritters. There was David, standing at the center of the table, holding a pancake aloft. Surrounding him were the nine others, Krepkiyzad, Captain Gene, and Hiram Duffy, all staring up at it.

Below the screen was a wide canvas with a stylized rendering of the same scene. Seated before this was the painter, Elder Barry himself, in a stained apron. He turned as David entered, surprise upon his face.

"Uh. David? Is it that time already?" he sputtered, setting his brush in a water glass.

He looked at the painting, then back at David, sheepish.

Stepping closer, David saw some differences. Was that a halo that David in the painting was sporting? And did he seem a bit more heroic in his stance? Moreover, there was a legend running across the bottom.

"It might be burnt or broken a bit, but aren't we all?" it read.

"I'm sorry, my boy, you weren't supposed to see this, not yet."

"What *is* it, Elder?"

"It's for the faithful, a chronicle of your journey."

David was dumbfounded. He honestly couldn't think of anything to say. And for David L. Grimes, that was something of a new experience.

"Uhh..." he said (just as a placeholder, he promised himself).

Nope. Still nothing. 'Uhh' would have to do.

"I know what you must be thinking," said Elder Barry.

Then tell me. I would really like to know.

"Uhh..." he said intelligently again.

"It has to do with the prophecy and your possible place in it."

"Go on," said David, proud to have mastered two whole words, even if they were but short ones.

They retired to the chapel proper and seated themselves in a pew near the front. The Elder brought David up to speed on more of the Prophecy of the Red Reckoning from the fabled lost Eric the Red Sea Scrolls. There were many strange lines that could easily be confused with the ramblings and mad ravings of an over-caffeinated man. But to discerning and properly faithful ELDS, the wisdom was so profound that only blind trust in its divine nature and ceaseless contemplation of its meaning would yield man's salvation. And a good cup of coffee now and then wouldn't hurt.

Among the prophecy's wisdom, several lines stood out to Elder Barry, which he reckoned to be important and possibly related to the gritters.

"And drops of blood shall rain from the sky all around as the air grows foul. And chill shall be the people, sealed like cadavers in their crypts, cold as death. And on that day, the ten twice-betrayed will rise up and lead the people to safety. The holder of the sacred key of the heavens shall set them free while he who laughs at fate goes forth to confront the twin horrors born not of man."

"And you think this relates to us, why?"

"Well, there *are* ten of you. And you were betrayed once. We're watching for another betrayal."

David thought of Max, and then the more recent pretender Pierre. The latter had never hit the news cycle. The GSF had kept it hush-hush. David chose not to enlighten the Elder on this point.

"We think you fit the bill for the laugher at fate," said the Elder.

"How do you figure that?"

"You laugh at *everything*, my boy."

He had me there.

"On a less disturbing note, I need a joke with which to start my homily at your friends' wedding," said Elder Barry.

Ah, back on my old familiar home turf.

"It so happens I've got one that'd be perfect for that occasion," said Rhymes...

After relating it to him, David felt somewhat better about the whole 'doomsday prophecy' thing.

"It occurs to me," said David, "that I never learned your first name, Elder."

"It's Charles, as it happens."

"*No*, really?"

"Yes. As it also happens, I can *indeed* 'play a guitar just like a-ringin' a bell.' Wait until I've saved up enough fabrication credits to purchase one. We can have guitar mass."

Elder Charles Barry had just become canonically cool in David's estimation.

"That'd B Goode," David replied.

Take that, fate!

"You're doing it right now, aren't you, David?"

"What?"

"Laughing--at fate."

David hung his head.

***

David was working on the CAD sketches of his aquatic armadillo when an anime girl wandered onto the side of his screen. She appeared to study his model and moved a few lines into a tighter configuration. He was preparing to scold her when he noted the power consumption had dropped drastically. It wasn't exactly cheating if he hadn't asked for help, was it?

"To what do I owe this visit? Is that spooky ghost bothering you again?"

"He's keeping his distance, Godfather," she said with an upthrust bottom lip. "I'm not scared of *him*. I have Mister Snuggles to protect me now."

Hmm. An imaginary protector for an imaginary threat. I should have suggested the teddy bear solution days ago. It could have saved me a few sleepless nights.

David was glad to see she was adapting and finding solutions on her own. He yawned and stretched.

"Tell Mister Snuggles he's doing a good job."

"He knows."

He hit 'save' and closed the file. Melody moved to the center of the screen and scuffed her foot on the implied 'floor.'

"Godfather?"

"Yes, Melody?"

"What makes something funny?"

"Have you studied all the comedians I recommended?"

"I have, but the things that cause laughter all seem to be situations of great sadness."

David paused and thought about it. In a profound revelation, he realized that this was true. Every joke that came to mind seemed to center on someone being laughably ignorant or harmed in some way.

"We laugh at sudden and unexpected misfortune because to dwell on it would otherwise make us sad. If we can find humor in a situation, it can't hurt us as deeply, so we seek it."

"So laughter is akin to crying?" asked the baffled NBI.

"No," David replied. "It's an alternative. It's a sharing of grief that lightens our hearts. Here's one of my personal favorites from a comedian named Steve Martin. See what you make of it."

"I'll try, Godfather."

"*Before you criticize a man, first walk a mile in his shoes.*"

"That seems wise. It advises one to foster empathy for others and encourages thoughtful consideration before doing possible emotional harm to the subject."

"Ah, but then the comedian goes on to say, '*That way, when you do criticize him, you'll be a mile away and have his shoes.*"

"But that's just *mean!* I thought the shoes were *metaphorical.*"

"And therein lies the humor. Suddenly subverting your expectation reverses the whole intent. Don't worry, Melody, you'll get the hang of it in time."

She blew a raspberry at him and vanished.

A bit crude, but she's learning, David thought. *I predict she'll be up to dad jokes by next week.*

***

The twelve stood tall beside the pool, nearly David's height. Their hands were clasped in unity. Behind them, a large portable screen had been rolled out. Displayed upon it was the flag of Luna, rigid in its frame. No rippling waves caressed the folds of the symbol of lifeless Luna. Instead, it stood stiff, unswaying, a solid, steady presence. It shimmered there proudly, its bright, warm orange rimmed in gold. Its crest was a mighty rocket, as had borne their forebears of old.

A motto was scrolling past on the bottom of the screen, ever repeating.

"That one small step for man has led to a glorious run for all moonkind... A journey of a thousand dreams began that summer in '69."

David sat with the gritters, awaiting the pageantry. He wore his space force uniform, gloves and all, freshly cleaned and pressed. It was quite a contrast indeed from how the Loonies themselves were dressed. They stood in the loose white ceremonial robes.

David could only imagine how nervous they must be. This was for them a baptism of sorts. Each would emerge as a Loonie adult, with all the rights and privileges this entailed. But so, too, would Pod Seventeen cease to form the whole of their identity. Each would remain a piece of the continent, a part of the main. But the training wheels would be off.

There were many others present as well. A few Elders, Doctor Pat, Captain Wildman, Julia (of course), some colonists, and other L5'ers of note. Even Kevin Farsprocket and some of the eight sat in their midst. Bungalow Bill seemed to have some ceremonial role and was pacing about the floor in his GSF uniform. But all in all, it was a modest crowd. David felt honored.

255

The lighting dimmed, and the crowd ceased its murmuring and straightened in their seats.

An orchestral piece began. David smiled. It began with a set of strings, rising in a continuous chorus, an atonal stretching sound with no regard for individual notes. When this had reached its crescendo, horns took over. In a stately rhythm, they softly filled the chamber.

Baaahm... be-dump-dump Ba! Ba! Ba! Bee... dump-bump-bump... Baah!

And as they did so, Pod Seventeen began to disrobe. They lay their ceremonial robes aside with reverence. The melody repeated in a lower key. Lower, perhaps, by a third.

Baaahm... be-dump-dump Ba! Ba! Ba! Bee... dump-bump-bump... Baah!

The podmates joined hands and stepped as one into the steaming water of the pool. David knew from watching the videos they would be emerging one at a time. This was nearly their final show of unity. All the while, a drum, like a steady heartbeat, backed the ceremonial music. Another horn joined the mix, deeper and more prominent.

Boooo-de-loooo... bo-booooo... de-looooo... ba-daaa Da! Da! Da!

The waters began to swirl. As with the first time David had bathed with the pod, the children (soon to be adults) were stepping in time at the water's edge. The tune repeated, surging upward this time.

Boooo-de-loooo... bo-booooo... de-looooo... ba-daaa Dah! Dah! Dah!

Slowly at first, but with gathering speed, the surface of the water formed a concavity, lowering in its center. The original melody reasserted itself. The first refrain was repeated--this time by a lighter, tinkling instrument David reckoned must be a xylophone or marimba.

Trilllll-de-trillll... tee-Ping! Ping! Ping!... tee-Ping! Ping! Ping!... trilllllllllll (cymbal clash)

The podmates all flipped onto their backs, letting the current drag them along. They swirled there as the waters began to slow and ebb. And a triumphant sound was made.

Bum-bump-bump Ba! Ba! Baaaaaaah!

Then silence fell. The screen flickered. On it, two faces swam into view. The children's parents were attending by telepresence from Luna. These two had entered the comm booth there. They were Husani and Yasmin Lunarsky, Clarissa's folks. Their large faces stared proudly down into the swirling pool below.

"Clarissa," said Yasmin. "Daughter of my body and child of my heart. Come forth. The day of your naming is at hand."

The young woman in question gripped the side of the pool and hauled herself out to stand before her elders. Others of her pod, still floating on their backs, passed her by. David noticed how much the young Loonie had thickened out, all of them, in fact. Doctor Pat's steroid treatments had obviously met with success in packing on the muscle that would be required to withstand life in the Martian ring. As the water pooled beneath her, her father spoke.

"Clarissa," he said in a husky whisper. "Beloved daughter and child of my heart. No longer do my eyes behold a child. Today I see a young adult, fit to assume duties of the dome or whatever else your life path might dictate. Tell me, daughter, have you selected a name?"

"I *have*, honored father. As we have discussed, it is my intention to sign the charter and join the colony mission to Mars. Though it saddens my heart to leave Luna behind, my destiny lies on the red planet. As such, I have chosen the surname Daedalia to honor the Planum of that name."

She fell to one knee. Speranza gripped David's arm. Looking over, he saw her nibbling at her lower lip as if to bite back tears. Women were so emotional. He gripped the arm of his chair a bit tighter and tucked his own lower lip between his teeth as Yasmin spoke again.

"It is a fitting name. And though it aches our hearts that you will be leaving Luna for the far-flung reaches of that distant shore, know too that our pride goes with you. Always. Arise, Clarissa Daedalia, and take your proper place among the scions of Luna. We welcome you into adulthood."

As she stood, Bungalow Bill approached with a bright orange hooded cloak and draped it over her naked, dripping form. After tying a golden sash about her waist, he escorted her to one side. There she stood to await the naming of the others.

The ceremony progressed in this manner, each child being called forth by their elders and declaring a name. There were many heartfelt moments and some that caused David to stifle inappropriate laughter. Some of the names were just... loony. Among the more ordinary names like Tilo Redsander, there were some that tickled David's fancy.

There was Tansy M'gann (per D.C.'s Miss Martian, Megan Morse).

Elsha Gribble--from that old movie, "Mars Needs Moms."

Pilomar NathaliePoppy selected her name from the equally ridiculous B-movie, "Mars Attacks." The surname was in honor of the dog/human fusion that reporter had become.

Several had (predictably) chosen last names of characters from the Edgar Rice Burroughs novels.

Perhaps the funniest of all was Mako Martin, whose earnest declaration had David biting his lip almost hard enough to draw blood.

"I have, honored father. As we have discussed, it is my intention also to sign the charter and join the colony mission. In honor of this, I have chosen the surname Martin, who is my *favorite* Martian."

"It is a fitting name," said his mother after a long pause. "And though it aches our hearts that you will be leaving Luna, know that our pride goes with you. May the spirit of *Uncle Martin* guide you with his antennae and keep you always safe among the challenges you will face there. Arise, Mako Martin, and take your place among the scions of Luna. We welcome you into adulthood."

Then came the shocker.

When Junel was asked to declare her name, she looked over at her erstwhile podmates with such sadness that one had to wonder whether the water dripping off her trembling naked form wasn't partially composed of her tears.

"I have, honored father. It has been a... difficult decision," she stammered. "I hope my podmates can forgive me, but I have decided that my destiny lies here--on L5 station."

There were gasps from her peers, both those lined up in their orange robes and those few still swirling in the pool.

"I have been offered an apprenticeship by Stationkeeper MacTavish. The stationkeeper of Luna Ring One is retiring, and he wanted me to consider staying on as one of the eight. Never before has there been a Loonie in their council. I have therefore decided to accept and to take the name Stationbound to reflect this great honor."

There was silence for a full rev as her mother considered this, at last saying, "It is a fitting name. And though it lightens our hearts to keep you nearby, we grieve for you and for your pod that will so soon be broken and unbalanced. Our pride is no less because you are the first to make so difficult a choice. It is a sign of adulthood. Arise, Junel Stationbound, and assume your place among the scions of Luna. Cherish your podmates while you still may. It is a difficult decision to sing alone, and we honor you for it. Be welcome into adulthood."

The next to be called was Norman, but David's eyes kept straying to Junel, who stood slightly apart from the others, raking her gaze over them. But they stood rigid and aloof, with eyes only for the ceremony. Another murmur ran through them when Norman made his own brief declaration.

"I have, honored father. I choose the name KinWatcher."

From the look on his parents' faces, this was somewhat of a surprise.

"Norman, explain," his father commanded.

Still on his knees, the boy stole a glance over at his podmates where they stood, then turned back up to the looming framed faces of his elders. When he spoke, it sounded like he was quoting from something.

"There is one slight, desperate chance, and that I have decided I must take--it is for Dejah Thoris, and no man has lived who would not risk a thousand deaths for such as she."

Of course, John Carter. Norman bowed his head and began again in a more natural timbre.

"It is now my intention to remain on station and learn such duties as might be offered me. Reclamator operations, wormworks, whatever. I do this so that Junel need not sing alone and the pod will be balanced once more. I commend my brothers and sisters on their choices and wish them good fortune on their journey. I will be staying right here."

David found himself holding his breath through the silence that followed, and Speranza's surprisingly strong grip was cutting off the blood flow to his hand. If *she* ever selected a Loonie name, perhaps it should be 'Human Tourniquet.' At last his mother spoke.

"It is a fitting name. Our hearts trill within our breasts to see our son place the good of his pod above his own wants and needs. Are you certain you wish to follow this course? Naming day is no time for making rash decisions."

"I am certain."

"Then so let it be recorded. You have our blessing to watch over Junel Stationbound and such other Loonies as may come to L5 station. Know that we are proud of you. Arise, Norman Kinwatcher, and take your place among the scions of Luna. We honor your decision and welcome you to adulthood."

The rest of the ritual was concluded with aplomb. The twelve new adults all bowed to the assembled audience, and a reprise of the orchestral music played out. On its conclusion, Bungalow Bill stepped to the fore, saying simply,

"That's all, folks."

They'd slowed it down a lot and backed it with a full orchestra so as to be almost unrecognizable from the original. But it still amused David to no end that the Looney national anthem was that tune from Merry Melodies, the one they played for the Bugs Bunny cartoons. His hand tingled as the blood flow resumed, and he shuffled out after the others.

"Interesting," muttered Elder Barry, shuffling out behind him. "I had thought the ten twice betrayed must refer to the gritters, but it seems there might be another possibility. Mysterious are your ways, oh Lord. The prophecy deepens."

***

He stepped out into the barren ring, spacesuited and feeling the bite of the cold. A red haze hung in the unbreathable air, and the dunes stretched out before him. There wasn't that sense of vastness, though, like he'd experienced in the Martian sims. These dunes were limited laterally to the 28-meter thickness of Martian Ring One. In the spinward and counterspinward directions, however, they curved up out of sight.

Even as he watched, the sharp shadows of the dunes stretched counterward as the sun rapidly arced toward spinward. He trudged behind the others, the weight of the full Mars suit tugging at his shoulders. Its toughened cloth limited his movement somewhat, and extra O_2 tanks weighed like boulders. The designers hadn't stinted on the weight of the suit, counting on the lessened gravity of Mars to enable its occupant.

He wondered what they did for the Loonies whose muscles mightn't be up for such a task. He found Krepkiyzad more forthcoming than usual after he'd bothered to ask.

"Is good question. Instead of environment suits, Loonies will train in clear plastic balls, like gerbils. All cadets will pull up

261

training manual on HUDs. Find page eighty-seven and review specifications."

David struggled with his chin mouse until he found the blasted thing. Why couldn't they track eye movement like his gaming visor did? Finally he found the reference and schematic.

B.R.E.A.T.H.E. Sphere

Bubble
Rescue
Emergency
Air
Transport and
Habitat
Enclosure

The instructions went on to describe the auto-inflation mechanism that would trigger the device. It would inflate to form a respectable sphere about twenty feet in diameter. There was a shallow airlock that a space-suited figure could sort of squirm through (if he was a relative of Houdini). Inside were flexible fittings for the standard O_2 tanks they carried. You could even share a BREATHE-sphere with another cadet (more than one if you were friendly). Thus, they could be used to transfer supplies or swap oxygen tanks or the like between surface walkers.

"Have all familiarized themselves?" asked the commander, pausing for but a moment thereafter.

"From silence, I will assume da," he continued. "Not only will Loonies be training thus, but each team has one of these in backpack. Since he was first to bring it up, Cadet Grimes will demonstrate. Who is your Mars buddy for this run, cadet?"

The question was *pro forma*. They had all been informed that their roommates would serve as such for this first run. Later, they would be free to choose their own 'Mars buddies.' David wouldn't mind sharing a survival bubble with Speranza on a long, cold Martian night... His mind snapped back to business.

"That would be Cadet Caillat, Technical Sergeant Krepkiyzad!"

"Good. You will inflate and both enter."

"Yes, Technical Sergeant Krepkiyzad! At once."

He carefully lowered himself to his knees so that Pierre could reach and retrieve the BREATHEr from his backpack. He couldn't reach it himself. It was going to be a long day of training if Krepkiyzad was already singling him out, but he'd manage it. David wasn't even certain he was *going* to Mars. His thoughts momentarily darkened once again at the thought of bringing it up with Speranza. For now, he was just happy to be breathing oxygen. He'd worry about his girlfriend choking the life out of him later if he survived.

Pierre plopped the tidy bundle down on the sand between them. He fitted one of David's oxygen tanks to it and pulled the rip cord that would cause it to inflate. As it did, he wondered what in space had Rhymes looking so pensive.

Two...

Don't Let the Stormy Darkness Pull
You Down

The others slogged out ahead, with Pierre and David bringing up the rear. It was challenging to keep their gerbil ball going in a straight line, but all that practice in precision marching was finally paying off. They found that by matching their strides, they could manage it with only a bit of a wobble.

David was determined not to let TS K break him, so he'd started singing to keep the rhythm. If Krepkiyzad didn't like it, he could just switch to another frequency. Pierre was of a like mind, and though he lacked the breath to keep up with David's modified lyrics, he joined in with defiance on each chorus.

Ran a lot of laps on L5!
Pumped my tired legs till I thought I'd go mad.
But I never did see exhaustion that could lick me.
Till I tackled Mars under Krepkiyzad!

Big wheel, keep on turnin'.
Proud though my lungs are burnin'.
Rollin' (Roulement!), rollin' (Roulement!),
Rollin' on a sand dune!
Rollin' (Roulement!), rollin' (Roulement!),
Hope we will be there soon!

"Platoon, halt!" was heard over their comms.

He had been listening.

"Oh, thank God," said Simon, rubbing at his thighs. "Are we finally there?"

"No," said the commander. "Brief stop only."

Groans sounded all around. Grumbling followed.

"Music to my ears," bellowed Krepkiyzad cheerfully.

"Cadets owing stop for rest to Grimes and Caillat," he added when the moaning died down.

"Your commander is big fan of John Fogerty and Creedence Clearwater Revival. I have a special request."

The cadets quaked in terror.

"Does Cadet Grimes perhaps know the words for 'Midnight Special'?"

"Um... of course," David admitted, wary of where this might be going.

"Cadets may rest if Cadet Grimes will sing this song... But all must join in on chorus."

"Do it, Grimes," shouted Ropey. "My legs need a rest."

"Yeah, do it, Grimes," chimed in a few others.

Krepki was a Fogerty freak? Who knew?

"Gimme a beat, Roidy," David hollered.

"Way ahead of you, Rhymes."

Dietrich had his mess kit out and was using the spork and lid to pound out a beat on his oxygen tank.

1-tik!-2-tik!, 1-2-3-4

Weeeeell, you wake up in the mor-ni-in'...
You hear the work bell ri-i-ing...

Everyone sat down in their bubbles. Heads began to bob, and cadets removed their gloves and set to clapping. When the chorus rolled around, all joined in enthusiastically. Krepkiyzad closed his eyes and tilted his head back. The corners of his mouth lifted in what no one would *dare* to name a grin.

"Let the Midnight Special... shine a light on me.
Let the Midnight Spe--cia--al shine an ever-lovin' light on me!"

David especially liked Leilani snapping her fingers on the backbeat.

And so the cadets, refreshed by their rest, went choogling over the dunes, practicing for the day they'd do this beneath two tiny moons.

***

"You have two requests in the queue, David. Shall I arrange your comm booth schedule so they coincide?"

"Who are they from, Bart?"

"The first is from an undisclosed location in Australia."

Jessica.

"The second is from a firm called the Goldman, Osgood & Abbernathy Trust in midtown Manhattan."

"Never heard of them. What's it regarding?"

"They need you to vote your shares in some sort of financial management system."

"Have them call Jason. He's my agent for financial matters."

"I believe he arranged it."

"Um, okay, make it for this afternoon. Say about four-thirty? And schedule one for Mom and Dad right after."

"Very well, Master David. I will let you know when all parties have confirmed."

As David headed for the laundry chute, hamper in hand, he wondered what money matters he needed to weigh in on. Who were Goldman, Osgood... Oh, for the love of Pete! G.O.A.T.--It was Yáng!

A simple call could be routed to his phone. He had more than enough comm credits. But he'd better wait and use the comm booth in case it was something sensitive. Besides, he'd prefer to see Jessica in full holographic glory. He pictured her bending over a round-headed droid saying, 'Help me, David Grimes. You're my only hope.'

Who was *he* kidding? If Jess was the heroine in that movie, she'd just kick the *force* out of Vader and feed him his mask while David watched on and dropped a few one-liners.

At least he no longer had to do his own laundry. The ringmaster was very prickly about what cleaning agents could be used and stingy with water use. Everything was sorted and done in batches. The little ident tags sewn into each garment identified the owner. The sort and stack personnel had scanners. So, just dump it down the hall chute, wait for the clean bundles to arrive, and hope that Doctor Pat doesn't sprinkle in any bacterial surprises.

How is that even legal?

Lunchtime!

***

"Hey, El G.," said David, setting his tray down beside the man.

He was staring into his soup like he could bring it to a boil by his gaze alone.

"Did somebody rub the marks off your cards?"

"Can it, Rhymes. I'm not in the *mood*."

"Seriously, then. What's *got* you in such a foul temper?"

"People are so stupid."

David stifled the first six responses he thought of to that. Sometimes it was better to just listen.

Alejandro firmed his jaw, seeming to come to a decision.

"We started using MBS to help prevent a disaster. It was earlier than we wanted to make the announcement, but there was a class five hurricane headed for Haiti (again). Theodore was projected to make landfall with winds of 64 knots and swells over eight meters. I did the calculations and used MBS to break it up while it was still out at sea. Knocked the stuffing right out of Teddy. It was beautiful. He came limping into Haiti as a class one at best."

"Sounds great, what's the problem?"

"People," said Alejandro sullenly.

"The stupid ones?" prompted David.

"Yeah, *those* ones. MBS was visible across all of North America during the save, and it just so happened that a wildfire blazed out of control in Oregon not long after, so..."

"MBS got the blame," David finished in disgust. "That's rough, Al."

"We weren't even anywhere *near* the Western seaboard!"

"Thanks for not saying 'I told you so.'"

"I wouldn't dream of it."

"There's a protest march headed for the capital as we speak. They're calling MBS 'The Ring of Fire.' They're even singing that old Johnny Cash song..."

"Hmm."

"*What* hmm? Cameron told me to watch myself when you get that look. Are you getting a Grimes idea?"

"Maybe. I think what you need is a good PR firm."

"What? I can't afford that."

"I bet you could afford the one I'm thinking of: Jī-Shǔ."

"Gesundheit," he said with a lopsided grin.

"What are you babbling about, Grimes?"

"Not many know this, but the zodiac rooster, Jī, has been cozying up to all kinds of reporters, bloggers, and other purveyors of daytime programming. He's become a regular media darling, especially since he did that report on the recent bird flu epidemic."

"I saw that. He's funny."

"Meanwhile, Shǔ, the rat, frequents all the conspiracy sites on the dark web and other less-than-savory data stores. He's got more identities than Sybil and all her grandkids and a lot of punch in that community. Anyway, the two teamed up to form a PR firm *par excellence*. They've done wonders for the NBIs' image."

"And they'd help *me*? For free?"

"Not for free, Al, of course not for free. They trade in favors. You'd have to be open to quests on your phone. They might need a little rain somewhere or some better waves for surfing. *That* sort of thing. In return, they could use their considerable sway with the public."

"Sounds dodgy."

"You can trust them, Al. *I* do. They taught me a lot about overcoming pride and being forthright in my dealings. Talk to Carlotta. She'll set it up. Tell them David Grimes sent you. They'll treat you right."

El Grande looked over at David, a penetrating gaze that was a little unsettling.

"Thanks, Grimes. I just might do that."

"Now eat your soup. It's probably gotten cold, but we don't waste anything up here."

David rose, taking up his own empty tray before adding. "Oh. And you wouldn't be able to make that MBS *grail*-shaped, by any chance?"

El Grande just shook his head in exasperation.

***

Score one more for David L. Grimes, wise and beloved of all. Mars Ring is singing; the mission's on track. He's ever on the ball with a ready wisecrack. Speranza is happy (and beautiful too). He's the guru of the crew who knew what to do. He's taming mock-Mars in his new spacesuit, and here's a fresh basket of laundry to boot!

At the end of his litany of self-congratulation, David stooped to retrieve the aforementioned basket. His bubbly mood dissolved at once. Sitting right on top of the neatly pressed stack was a sock. A *single* sock. A single *red* sock... with *rockets*. He keyed open the door and carried the basket inside.

Static cling? Could that be to blame? For a proper pair, he'd need two just the same! He probed each item, front and back, but the mate wasn't there anywhere in the stack. He checked the hamper. Maybe it had gotten caught in *there*. He didn't find the sock, but wedged within the lid was one of the ident chips he'd sewn into each of his garments.

Oh, *no*. Had he consigned one of his uniquely sentimental, rocket-themed leggings unprotected to the ancient beast known to devour one sock of every pair? Socks and laundry had been bitter enemies for time immemorial, since the very inception of either.

This will not stand.

This was a closed ecosystem. The possibilities were quite finite. He had some time. He would locate his missing sock. His mind made up, he made for the door, pausing.

"Bartholomew," said David, scratching the back of his neck, "where does the laundry chute go?"

"Specify."

"Here on C-Ring One, Spoke Two, where does laundry placed in the chute go?"

"Searching..."

"Soiled items of apparel travel by hamper-trolleys to the processing center at the base of Spoke Three. There, they are aerated, cleansed, and refurbished as necessary by laundry room staff."

"Spoke Three? That's *spinward*, right?"

"Yes. Approximately 234 meters."

A hop, skip, and a spinward jog later, David arrived at Laundry Processing Facility Five.

"Anybody home?" shouted David from outside its door.

The camera above the door swiveled toward him, its light coming on.

"Ain't nobody here but us ornery hens," said a woman.

"Uh, is this where the laundry is processed?"

"Says so right on the door, don't it? How can I help you today?"

"May I come in?"

"Suit yourself."

And with a buzz and a click, the door presumably unlocked. The camera light dimmed and ceased.

Entering, David scented that faint ozone smell as with the Loonie's pool. He remembered that chlorine and such were to be avoided. He imagined the same held true for harsh detergents or anything else that might contaminate the water supply. Little did he know just what he was walking into.

The woman was one of the new colonists, the Elds. He might have even dined with her that night when the troop welcomed them. Or, perhaps she had arrived afterward. Despite his advice to Melody, David found it hard to tell one colonist from another. They all wore the same gray garb and head coverings.

"Amathea," she said, holding forth her hand.

"I'm David Gr--"

"We *all* know who *you* are, Laugher. And pleased I am to finally make your acquaintance."

He took the woman's hand in the sideways shake they all took for granted. He was used to being recognized by now, both as 'The Boy Who Saved the Man in the Moon' and as one of the 'Crew Who Knew.' But 'Laugher' was a new one on him. It likely had to do with Elder Barry's interpretation of his strange gospel. He hoped it painted him in a good light.

"What can I do you for?"

"I've lost my sock and don't know where to find it."

"Hmm. Pair it to another one and then just nevermind it?" she said primly with eyebrows raised.

Ah. A kindred soul. A laugher, he laughed.

"That would be a little difficult, Amathea," said David, raising one trouser leg.

"Oh. *That* one. Shoulda knowed it was you."

"Then you've seen the other one?"

"Sure did. Dropped right into the unmatched bin. Pretty thing. Real wool, not them synthifibers they spew around *here*. Alpaca, if I be any judge. Didn't know it were a holy relic."

The woman knew her yarn, but wait. *What?*

"Can I have it?"

"No. Not for a bit."

"Why *not*?"

273

"We's in the brown cycle now."

"The... What does that mean, the brown cycle?"

"Better I *show* you, Laugher."

"Um, okay."

"Follow me."

Amathea led David back through another set of doors and down a long hall.

"Are you all alone here, Amathea? And do they call you Amy? Or Thea, perhaps?"

"Either one's fine. And yes, I'm here alone, but don't get any ideas. *I'm spoken* for."

Not at all my intention.

"Um. Alright."

"Here we are, gritter. As you can see, the brown cycle is underway."

The narrow room into which she'd guided him had three great windows on one side. Through them, David could see machinery of various sorts and items of apparel, all brown, stretched on racks. Nozzles hung down, spewing mist on occasion.

Then David noticed movement. All the clothing was writhing and squirming as though possessed. Beneath the brown layer, he caught glimpses of more vivid hues. These quickly vanished beneath the blanket of brown. Then a bug went skittering up the glass so close to David's nose that he leaped back with a cry. It was a cockroach (or something like it). They *all* were. They were *everywhere* in there. David's stomach turned in revulsion.

"Are those...?"

"Uh huh," said Amy with sympathy. "Sorry to spring it on you like that, but nobody ever believes it unless he sees it for himself."

"But why?"

"The way *I* heard it, it's the most efficient and environment friendly way to reclaim all the hair, skin flakes, and body oil that works its way into clothing. Them little gene-modified critters even eat urine and feces. After we treat the laundry with ultrasonics and mist to loosen and lift out the most of such, the gleaner cleaners gobble it all up and convert it to biomass."

"That's... disgusting."

"It's *natural*. Same thing happens on Earth, just on a longer cycle (and you don't see it play out). So now you know."

"What do they do when there are too many... gleaner cleaners?"

"Do you really want to know where the impossiburgers come from, Laugher?"

"Um. Too late, Amy. The question is its own answer."

"I s'pose it is, Laugher. Sorry about that. There's still a good twenty minutes to go. Then I'll go in and fetch out your sock. Care for some pie while we wait?"

"Uh... No, thank you," said David, struggling to suppress his gag reflex.

"You ain't one of them *'cake people,'* is ya?" she asked, looking at him slantwise with narrowed eyes.

***

The cadet entered Krepkiyzad's office. It was the Spaniard who wore a top hat, the newest man.

"Reporting as ordered, Commander Krepkiyzad."

The cadet snapped a smart salute.

He still missed it. The 'sir.'

Nyet ee nyeh NAH-dah, he admonished himself. 'There isn't any, so I don't need it.'

"Come in, cadet," he said, returning the salute. "Sit down. Be comfortable."

The man sat stiffly--not precisely as ordered, but respectful.

"High command is very pleased with your recent work. You will receive a commendation."

"Thank you, commander. I'm glad my work has been satisfactory."

"*More* than satisfactory, cadet. Why be so modest? Give to devil his due. Commendable. Is literal, da?"

"I suppose... I mean, da!"

"Hundreds of angry letters have gone 'poof!' Now we are receiving hundreds of 'neverminds' and humble requests for MBS services."

Krepkiyzad stood, cracked his knuckles, and leaned over his desk.

"Saw you on 'Tomorrow with Tabbitha' show yesterday. Very funny and well done shutting down that other speaker. How do you do that thing with your hat?"

"A good magician never tells," he said with a smile.

This flickered out quickly, his face becoming neutral.

"Commander," he added.

"Your work has gained much acceptance for Project MBS. You will find in your mail slot an additional stripe. GSF is pleased to inform you that you are now a triple threat, Junior Tech Alejandro Artegas."

His eyes widened. Then he smiled.

"I suppose I owe a lot of it to Grimes."

"Grimes? What has Grimes got to do with it?"

The cadet hesitated.

"He just sort of... put me on the right path, commander. There's magic... and then there's Grimes."

After the young man had been dismissed, Krepkiyzad sat brooding.

Oy, Nikolai. Grimes again. Is always Grimes. He hadn't seen it at first, but Anatoly knew. The general had all but ordered him to select him for this important team. And the boy had come through again and again. His teammates all looked to him for leadership even though he did nothing to either seek it or merit it. He had even charmed M'Babu, his other hopeful. And now this. Grimes was obviously a natural leader. He had great potential. If only he weren't so... Grimes.

I will have to be harder on the boy.

***

The mock-up was really coming along. They'd already established a temporary base camp in the talus field near the glacial ice that was supposed to mimic conditions near the polar ice caps on Mars. They had to remain in their suits, or the shelters sometimes, for days on end.

When the colony mission arrived at the actual planet Mars, they would have to remain suited for far longer stretches. Trips to and from the surface would be few and far between. But for now, they were just testing the waters.

Water. That was one of the big challenges on Mars. Daytime highs only got up to around ~ 20°C (~ 68°F). And *that* was at the equator--in *summer*. The need for water might force them nearer to the polar regions, where nighttime lows dipped to nearly two hundred below.

The hope was that El Grande's MBS could change all that. By focusing on a particular point on the Martian surface, the global government hoped to raise the regional temp to that of an early alpine environment. Thus, a bridgehead for terraforming could be established.

Someone really needed to write a 'Mars for Dummies' manual. Maybe it would be this crew.

"We've got another moss bed in place," said Roid Rage after he'd squirmed in through the tiny airlock in their bubble. "This one didn't turn brown right away."

Dietrich was David's 'Mars Buddy' today. They'd decided to mix it up to keep things interesting. They hadn't yet opted for boy-girl cohabitation. As much as Simon and Cameron were up for such an arrangement, that would mean another couple would have to do likewise, and Speranza wasn't quite ready for that yet. David remained hopeful she'd come around, whether from his charms or even just out of plain boredom.

"Maybe this'll be the one," said David.

"*One* of them sure better be," said Roidy, "or all this effort will have been for nothing."

"Pluperfects aside," David replied, "we're getting good data on all the cultivars."

"Snooty term, 'cultivars.' Moss is moss."

"Let's hope that despite its spinning and composition, Mars doesn't count as a rolling stone."

"Very funny, Grimes. Suit up. It's your shift."

Pierre would have laughed. I *miss* Pierre. I wonder how he's doing with Simon.

David did a final check on his suit seals and his O_2 levels. Sufficient. Power for his suit's heaters was running a little low, but he'd fix that once he had a chance to connect to the solar array they'd erected outside. It still amazed him how the ultra-thin sheets of Mylar-like reflective stuff could yield so much juice. And all the while, the concavity they'd dug out concentrated the sunlight to warm the moss beds.

He wriggled into the plastic airlock, sealing it behind him and pumping the air back into the shelter. The membrane closed in all around and tightened about him. Now he knew what it felt like to be laminated. With a hiss, the thin outer atmosphere filled the airlock, relieving the constriction as it surrounded him with frigid CO2.

His helmet comm lit up. Private channel 4. He toggled it on with a chin wag.

"David? David, do you *read*?"

"Often and with great pleasure, my love, especially the great works of fiction."

"I've just finished my shift."

Damn, just missed her. Oh well, spacesuited hugs were more symbolic than exhilarating.

"Just starting mine. How's the new roomie?"

"Cameron? She's fine for the most part. I can't get her to stop talking about the wedding, though. *Ow!* Cameron says hi. And *Roidy?*"

"Ate all my graham crackers."

"Rough, but just as well. You know Pierre was never going to give you any of his chocolate anyway. Right?"

"Pessimist."

He had been trudging toward the depression in which they hoped to cultivate their moss. He reached the lip and peered down in. There was Roidy's latest patch. *Still Green!* But what was that misshapen mess beyond it? Stepping closer, David grinned.

"You minx!"

No sound issued from his helmet comm, but he could hear the smile that graced the other end as surely as he felt the beating of his heart. Speranza's plot was heart-shaped with little talus stones placed on it spelling out 'D.G.'

"You know Krepkiyzad isn't going to *like* that."

"I trust *you* will complete my heart."

"Gladly, my love. It would be my honor."

David began picking up the stones and stacking them to one side. He'd need to find which cultivar she'd been using on this plot.

Best girlfriend ever

***

It was late afternoon (Earth time) when Krepkiyzad came striding across the dunes. David found it strangely comforting that a Martian day would be very similar to a day on Earth, being only about forty minutes longer. Of course, here on L5, a day lasted only a ridiculous thirty seconds, but the polarizing filters in the 'glass' panels above had been programmed to darken to emulate the long night cycle.

The former major seemed happy, and well he might. Our camp was expanding far more quickly than the rival team of Loonies on the other side of the ring. Captain Wildman was in charge of training the Loonie team, who had only just arisen to adulthood. He guided their efforts to perform much the same experiments as we were attempting. A sort of friendly rivalry had arisen between the two old friends.

"Captain Wildman has only four beds of moss at his base camp, mostly dead," he reported. "And already we have three varieties thriving. Modified Alpine clubmoss is most promising of all, locking in runoff moisture and producing O_2 at almost acceptable levels."

"Hello to you too, commander," David deadpanned in greeting.

"Not even *Grimes* can bother me on such a day."

"Well, I, for one," said Brainiac, "will be glad to return to C-Ring One at the end of zis shift. Simon, he hogs all zee thermal blankets."

"I hear you, brother," said El Grande. "He does that to me, too. Poor Cameron!"

"They're kidding," said Simon. For God's sake, tell her you're just kidding."

"Cut radio chatter, cadets!" boomed Krepkiyzad. "Urgent message is incoming on priority command channel! Switch to channel six."

"To all colony teams in the Arcadia Planitia region. A sandstorm of exceptional force has been detected heading your way. Batten down the hatches, crews. It's gonna be quite a blow.

You have 28 minutes to retrieve equipment and find secure shelter."

Was that little Junel Stationbound making her debut appearance as a ringmaster?

I guess the admins were tired of taking it easy on us. You might think we'd be afraid of being sandblasted and scoured by dust driven before hurricane-force winds. That was just movie stuff. Although it was true that Martian dust storms could be seen by telescopes from Earth, some even becoming continent-wide or even global in scope, sand was not the issue.

Air pressure on Mars was but a pittance compared to that on Earth, about one percent. And though winds of these storms could blow up to sixty miles per hour, they couldn't do much damage--directly. If a boy had a kite on Mars, he would need a wind a hundred times more powerful than on Earth to lift it aloft. So sixty miles per hour was barely a sneeze.

No, the real danger was the cold. The dust on Mars was very fine and lifted easily in orange clouds. These blocked out the sun making it--you guessed it--colder. Add to that, this fine dust rapidly covered solar panels, cutting off a colony's cheap source of direct power for heaters. The storms gave these fine particles an electrostatic charge as well, causing them to cling to all exposed equipment like distant relatives who found you just won the lottery, a grit that even gritters feared.

The cadets rolled out and began taking emergency measures at once.

All secondary structures were collapsed, and their gear was stowed in the central dome. Meanwhile, team two, consisting of Roidy and David, began brushing off the yards of reflective cloth they had been using in the concavity. Anyone whose suit power wasn't topped off took turns at the remaining hookups to correct this.

The reflective power cloth was rolled up and stuffed into the ever-more-crowded dome. Team three had their shovels out and were digging away at the red sand, piling it up over the sides and even scattering as much as possible across the top. The winds mightn't be forceful, but it would be tragic if they peeled up a corner to flap about and further reduce the dome's cramped confines.

When all was nearing readiness, Krepkiyzad made a final inspection.

"Leave that dross, Akana. It will survive, or it will not."

"Yes, commander," said Flowerchild, dumping the armload of secondary equipment out on the sand.

"Alejandro had had the foresight to peel up several large swaths of moss and was shoving them through the lock to Pierre, who was arranging it in the enclosure to serve as makeshift bedding. It wasn't as though any of the stuff was likely to survive what was coming."

"To all colony teams, this is Phobos base. Junel Stationbound reporting. The storm is advancing more quickly than projected. It will hit in fewer than three minutes. Crews are to make final preparations for conservation of power. MRS is being redeployed to break up the storm center. Hopefully, this will lessen its duration, but expect corresponding temperature drops. I repeat. All teams are to shelter at once."

They scrambled for the entrance and formed an orderly line.

"What's MRS?" asked Ropey. "Did she mean MBS?"

"No," said El Grande as he awaited his turn to squirm through the lock into their survival igloo. "They rechristened it 'Missus Red Sky' because the Martian sky isn't blue."

"It's not red either," Ropey objected. "From the pictures, it's more of a pale mustard tinged with a bit of orange."

"What can I say?" asked El Grande. "The bureaucrats thought 'red sky' was more evocative of Mars and would play better with the public. Besides, MRS is kind of a cute acronym."

"And speaking of red skies," said Simon, "here comes one, and she's a doozy."

Only two more cadets were still awaiting their entry window when they saw the dust storm howling down from counterspinward. That would leave only Krepkiyzad, who was leading from the rear.

The ringmasters had turned up the air recyclers to their maximum output. These had been specially augmented to blow with the fury of jet engines. They were being activated in sequence to issue a gale-force wind spinward throughout the whole torus. It was designed to emulate storm conditions on Mars. David thought of it as being in a gigantic clothes dryer.

It was then they heard their commander's laughter, and it wasn't how David had imagined it. Full-throated and from somewhere deep below his sternum, Krepkiyzad laughed. The others had all wriggled in, but Krepki stood defiantly staring into the teeth of the oncoming red chaos. Had the commander gone mad?

And then he sang.

"I'm never known to quail at the *fury* of a gale!"

What?

It was like a younger man stood there, one possessed of some inner flame. And what was that he was singing? Oh, yeah. Gilbert and Sullivan from the H.M.S. Pinafore, an oddly unexpected choice for a Russian Space Force commander. As the others huddled in near panic, David found his voice.

"We get it, commander. You're tough. Now get *in* here before we have to *drag* you in."

Had he just threatened a superior?

But the Russian only chuckled. He *chuckled*?

Unfastening the seals on the outer airlock with only seconds remaining, he said, "Perhaps Grimes is right. Never a good idea to laugh at fate."

David couldn't resist.

"What, never?"

Chuckle.

"No, never! (Well, hardly ever)."

At last, he was in, dropping atop the pile of tangled limbs and violated propriety. The dome darkened as the dust swirled about it, a wall of crimson cycling down through brick, blood, merlot, and mahogany. Finally, full blackness enveloped them.

Wait, thought David. Had the commander just laughed... at fate?

***

The gritters lay there all in a heap, surrounded by the hastily salvaged wreckage of their camp.

The dome ceiling sagged above them, weighed down by the sand they had hastily heaped upon it and the pressure of the not inconsiderable wind howling above. Perhaps 'howling' was a misnomer. In the extremely low pressure of the ring, the high-velocity winds barely made a whimper, more of a timid whine than a howl worthy of wolves or any other predatory canines.

David lay near the bottom, with Carlotta wedged in above him and parts of Roidy that he'd prefer not to think about poking him in places he would rather hadn't come into play. The soft pile of moss beneath him helped. And he was one of the *lucky* ones.

"I think my backside is going to freeze off," Cameron complained.

She must be up near the top.

"Is Simon hogging the blankets again?" asked Pierre.

"I am *not* a blanket thief!" groaned Simon. "Thermal or otherwise."

Krepkiyzad was being awfully quiet. The commander had always been cool in a crisis, a suffer-in-silence type, but David wondered if this h ad more to do with his recent sudden reveal of having human emotions.

"Any orders, commander?" he hazarded.

David expected something like, "Cadets will suffer adverse conditions quietly and give their commander some peace." But the former major managed to surprise David once more.

When he spoke, it was well measured, almost quiet.

"Long ago, I was a boy growing up on farm in southern Siberia. Altai Republic is beautiful place. Many farms. Also very cold."

The cadets all listened, chatter forgotten.

"In wintertime, all lakes and streams freeze over. Winters are hard in Russia."

David was all ears, shifting his head a bit to dislodge Pierre's foot from one of them. He was hearing over his helmet speakers, but it was the principle of the thing.

"One winter, I walked out to the pond, wondering, 'Nicklolai? How do the ducks survive in these conditions?'. Wild ones fly south, but the white ones, they stay. How do they not become ducksicles? Answer was simple. Ducks are social. Also have clear chain of command.

"Ducks swim in circles, using this paddling motion to keep water from freezing. All huddle together to share warmth. No one complains. Three or four lieutenant ducks swim around outside, keeping waters moving.

Kind of like the Loonies, David thought.

"Duck Commander lets out a loud squawk every twenty minutes or so, at which time lieutenants all swim to center of formation to rest and get warm. From outside of circle, new lieutenants are automatically promoted and take turn churning the water."

That was kind of beautiful, thought David, and more than a little relevant.

"In this pile," Krepkiyzad declared with a bit of his old swagger, "*I* am Commander Duck. I am squawking. Cadet Truwella is to proceed to middle of pile to warm tail feathers. Would not want them to freeze off prior to upcoming nuptials. Grimes is new lieutenant duck."

"Yes, Commander Duck," quacked David, burrowing toward the top.

It was daffy, but he did it.

As the hours passed and the wind whimpered, the cadets struck up conversations to ward away the discomfort of their cramped conditions. It wasn't the cynical banter they usually enjoyed. They spoke of their homelands and their dreams. The topic circled back to Mars, a frequent theme of the latter.

"Any luck finding those ice asteroids, Dietrich?" asked Simon the blanket hog.

"Yeah, Captain Bill and I found a couple of nice ones just a few days ago."

"You towing them back?"

"Nah. No time for that. We just nudge them in-system and move on to the next. The trick is to calculate the trajectory and impart enough initial velocity to get them to Mars before they outgas. We've got Ropey playing goalie in near-Mars orbit to boost them the rest of the way. By the time *we* get to Mars, it'll be raining snowballs so fast the canals will all be full."

"You know zose 'canals' are only a trick of the light and lens, non?" said Pierre as though talking to a child. "Zere are no canals on Mars. Also, raining snowballs, she would be more properly termed hail."

"Giant hail," said Roidy.

"*Monster* hail," said Ropey.

"Quack," said Krepkiyzad.

After they had shifted positions, Roidy continued. "No, by the time I get to Mars, I'll have earned my own swimming pool. I can hardly wait to get there. How about you, Brain? You going?"

"Depends on zee chocolate situation."

"The..."

"Nevermind," David cut in. "He's going."

"And you? *You* going, Rhymes?"

And there it was.

"I haven't decided as yet."

"What?" exclaimed Speranza in a dumbfounded voice that made her eyes sound round.

"It's just such a permanent commitment..." trailed off David.

He felt the pile shudder. That couldn't be good. It was either Speranza's quiet sobs or Leilani creeping toward him in the dark. Alright. That wasn't his funniest visual.

He toggled his helmet comm over to private channel 4 and tried calling her. There was no response. She was giving him the cold shoulder. Likely, she just needed some space. They all did. For all David knew, she could be lying directly underneath him. The last thing he wanted to do was put any pressure on her. He tried to stifle his inappropriate self-banter but found he couldn't stop. His mind just worked like that, especially in times of stress. He was an *ass*.

David switched back to the general chat channel but made no further comment.

"Pile has suddenly become nice and warm with teenage angst. Commander Duck is pleased."

And even when trying to be funny or conciliatory, Krepkiyzad was also an ass.

***

When the whimpering ceased (that of the wind, not that of the gritters), a dim glow gradually returned to the frosty enclosure. Suit batteries had been strained but still showed about a third of their full charge. Some more, some less. The dome was covered in red dust, but light now shone through in patches, rays of which swung like searchlights as the L5 sun passed swiftly overhead.

It was still cold, but the bitterness that had stressed their suits had eased. In the mockup, MRS had returned her attention to keeping her charges from stiffening. But the bitterness roiling in David's gut had little to do with the cold. Would Speranza forgive him for his unwelcome but honestly stated doubts? It hadn't been a rejection of her.

"This is Phobos Base to all colony teams. The storm has broken up. You are clear to decamp. Be advised, there is a dust advisory in effect. Charged particles may be a problem for the next several days. MRS has been successfully redeployed, and you should soon be experiencing balmy temperatures of only double digits on the negative centigrade scale. Stay tuned for emergency updates. This is Junel Stationbound with that big megaphone in your sky. Phobos Base out."

"Cadet Caillat is to fetch the hand-operated Van de Graaff generator, and Cadet Stentz is to please be moving off commander's legs. Grimes, open inner airlock. Commander needs to stretch."

Krepkiyzad rose to his knees, his shoulders pressing against the sagging, sand-covered ceiling. The pile of cadets spasmed, depositing them in an untidy, moaning diaspora of moss-covered misfits.

David glanced back at the helmeted figure that looked the most Speranza-like (he couldn't tell whether she was meeting his gaze) before crab-walking to the lock. Pierre was soon beside him with a hand-cranked generator, which he promptly handed over to Krepkiyzad. The man hugged it to his chest and squirmed into the lock. This was no mean feat with all the dust piled up against it on the outside, but he managed. He even had a short-handed shovel which he used after opening the outer seals.

After being burried by infalling red dust, the commander somehow burrowed his way out onto the surface. The next thing the cadets saw was large swaths of dust falling away as Krepkiyzad began clearing the area in around the airlock.

"Cadet McAllister, exit the bunker and bring shovel. I need you to clear more of this sand."

Oh. It was a bunker now, was it? Not a *proklyatyy* plastic space igloo like he called it last night.

Whatever they were calling the dome now, Fergus exited it. When he did, the red haze hanging everywhere out there collected upon him. In less than a second, he was a red statue of himself.

"That was fast," said David.

"Zee dust, she has a photoelectric charge, positif. It is why le générateur he is négatif."

The Kahuna touched the ball end of the device to Ropey's helmet, and the red curtain burst from him, sending a crackling sound over their helmet speakers. Not a spec of dust clung to Ropey after that.

One by one, they were all called out to be 'degaussed.' Pierre argued that word actually referred to the removal of a magnetic charge, but no one else argued the fine points. Degaussed would do, and sure beat the heck out of saying you had been 'electrostatically reversed.' Ever rub a balloon in your hair and stick it to the fridge? All you have to do is touch the fridge with a finger (grounding it), and the balloon falls away. Enough said.

Pleased that the universal laws of static repulsion worked so well on mock-Mars, the cadets took to gleefully 'degaussing' their solar cloth and reestablishing power collection. It was still less than ideal due to the hovering dust diminishing the sunlight. But the trickle they achieved was enough to begin repowering their suits.

The moss pit was a total loss. Its contents had been scattered to the four winds (or one really big, circular one).

And all the while, Speranza continued to avoid David. They would talk about it, he knew. But later, and in private.

"Big Kahuna, this cadet has a question."

"Rhymes may ask. Kahuna is always prepared to dispense wisdom to curious ducklings."

"Shouldn't we go see if the Loonies need help? They don't even have space suits, for pity's sake."

Krepkiyzad straightened from the stack of equipment over which he was bent.

"Rhymes is right."

Hey that was twice now today, a record.

"I am not too worried. Ringmaster would have stopped the exercises if it got too dangerous for them. But in actual situation, help would be offered. Rhymes will come with me. Roadrunner, you are in charge here."

David was glad they were using their call signs again. It heightened the camaraderie. But where was Roadrunner's cheerful 'Beep beep'?

"Yes, commander," she said instead.

And off they went over the now pristine dunes through the red haze under the blaze of ever repeating sunsets.

"Shouldn't we radio ahead?"

"Better to surprise them. I want to see how badly they will need our assistance. Have side bet with Captain Wildman. Want to see firsthand how low Jellybean has sunk."

As they made their way spinward, David noticed the Martian dust was still repelled in a spherical area around them. It was kind of wimpy as personal forcefields went, but pretty cool overall, and damned useful. Jellybean must be Captain Gene's call sign. David wondered how he had gotten it. As to how low he had sunk, they would very soon find out. It would be, for Kahuna, a most unpleasant surprise.

There was almost nothing left of the Loonie camp, just a tattered little shack. The Loonie flag was raised over it, failing to flap in the non-existent wind. Instead, it descended from a rigid frame. This had been the Loonie tradition ever since Apollo eleven had planted that flag at the Sea of Tranquility Site 2. So, it might be an overstatement to say the gold and orange colors of Luna 'flew.' They stuck. They stood. They hung. They marked the site, proudly hovering over the ruins with its blazing rocket of white.

David didn't know what Krepkiyzad might be feeling, but he wanted to salute that flag. It was nicely defiant in the present circumstances. But where were the Loonies? Surely, they couldn't all fit in there. He wouldn't dismiss out of hand any act of unity by Pod Seventeen as a possibility. But stacked like cord-wood in a comm-booth-sized shack and somehow surviving a full-on Martian sand storm attack? That would be one for the history books.

Then out sauntered Captain Gene, the Jellybean himself. Through his faceplate David saw him grinning like an elf. He held up two gloved fingers, and David switched to channel two, not wanting to miss a word of this.

"How did your boys and girls weather the storm, Kahuna? Sleep well? You look a little tired."

"Better than Loonie brats," said the big K. "Gritters are stoic. Have more than just tumbledown shack remaining."

"Good to hear it, Kahuna. Come on in and meet the kids. It 's so nice to have visitors."

Krepkiyzads face filled with suspicion as he regarded the dilapidated shed.

"How... Is like TARDIS? Bigger inside?"

"After a fashion. Come in and see."

Captain Gene waved them in through the Mars-dust covered door. Inside, there was nothing but some scuff marks on the floor. Then he strutted in behind them raising dust a cheery red. He closed the door and clicked his comm. "Level Two," he said.

And they began to descend to the accompaniment of a rhythmic, squeaking sound.

The Loonies have an elevator?

Then a tunnel opened up before them in which a man-sized airlock was framed. Captain Gene stepped first into the booth-sized structure. David and his commander watched in amazement as it cycled. David was next, and the scene he stepped into when he stepped out made him grin with joy. There were the ten Loonies in their orange robes sitting like oompa-lumpas on moss-covered boulders in a cozy cave.

Behind them, a glowing orange space heater shone, emitting waves of comforting warmth. David turned quickly as the airlock cycled again. He didn't want to miss the look on the Kahuna's faceplate. And it was lucky that he had. The look of consternation the former major shot Captain Gene was a glorious treat well worth the long hike.

"You can remove your helmet, Kahuna," said Gene. "Our seals are quite adequate."

Doing so himself, he stepped over to a kettle on a hotplate, pouring some into an earthen mug.

"Tea?" he asked his guests.

"All this?" asked Kahuna, staring around the well-lighted, comfortable space as if offended by its existence. "But... how?"

"Oh, *this?*" replied Gene to the half-spoken question. "Nothing some hard work and a little Loonie ingenuity can't accomplish if given sufficient time. I trust your camp is in good order?"

"Getting there," replied Kahuna hesitantly.

"When should I drop by? I'd love to compare notes. If all is as you say, we'll need a neutral judge, but I'm fairly sure we both know the answer by now. Will you admit defeat?"

Captain Gene, the Jellybean, removed the torso of his space suit, stretched, and found a comfy-looking boulder of his own. This gave Krepkiyzad time to ponder and come to grips with his loss. It was amusing that though Wildman outranked him Commander Duck still acted like the boss.

Finally he saluted and admitted the *pravda*

"We are 'way behind,' and I'm sorry to find I was 'willin' to make a deal.' You play pretty good fiddle, Gene."

Charlie Daniels again? What was it with Krepkiyzad and that song? And why did he always characterize himself as the devil in it? Must be some relic of his hisory with Captain Wildman.

"When shall I inform AL to expect payment?"

The axial lift? Oh, this was rich.

Kahuna made a sour face, even more so than the one he usually wore.

"One week only, da?" he asked with a grimace. "I made bed. I will tremble in it through night terrors. Russians never renege. You may tell *proklyatyy* elevator--"

"Axial lift," the captain corrected.

"You may tell *proklyatyy* singing lift Kahuna will report on Thursday."

"Excellent, Sergeant. I will so inform him. AL will be so excited. He has an updated video for "Up Down"--the Timmy Trumpet version.

The Kahuna paled. David rejoiced.

"Captain?" asked David "This cadet would like to know where you're getting all this electricity from. Our solar array was completely off-line during the storm."

"A very good question, young man. Shall we explain it, kids?"

Captain Gene's leadership style was very... informal. David liked it.

Tilo Redsander went over to a large crank that David suspected had powered their elevator. He hauled it loose from the wall and inserted it into another nearby aperture. He started winding it. It made a series of clicks.

To this accompaniment the children (adults now, David kept reminding himself) began chanting a verse. Gene led them with his finger like a conductor's baton.

Jellybean Gene made a machine
Tilo Tilo made it go
It tapped into the Martian crust
To help protect us from the dust.

We drilled down (or pretended to)
Cause Elsha knew just what to do.
When the rock gets very cold,
We use a trick both young and old

Stirling made an Engine true
To use when solar just won't do
It's getting dark, the children shout
Use backup when the lights go out

"Wait," said the Kahuna looking outraged. "I understand Stirling engine and how temperature differential can be used to generate electric power. Using even more cold to make heat. Very clever. But fact of matter is: you cannot have drilled a geothermal shaft here on station. Is impossible. Not really Mars, cannot dig down so far."

The Loonies trilled.

After a pause, Captain Gene endeavored to explain.

"We hauled all the needed equipment out here, at a great cost in time and effort, I might add."

He took a sip of his tea.

"Rather than let us poke a hole in the station, the judges ruled it was a valid move and ran us an electric cable with as much current as our technique would have produced. They estimated that with the surface temperature at minus eighty, and the subsurface temp at minus one-hundred, the twenty-degree differential could be tapped for a reasonable return. More cold is right, but only the difference matters."

"Loonies think differently than us. They never intended to colonize the surface of Mars. They knew those little gerbil balls were only for temporary use, until they could get set up, These kids were born in darkness and lived in tunnels all their lives. They plan to dig down and colonize *beneath* the surface of Mars."

Another case of differences mattering, thought David.

Later, he and Kahuna were quietly seated in a corner sipping their tea.

"So what do you have to do for Captain Gene to pay off the bet?" David asked.

"I must play elevator operator for crazy musical AI," said Krepkiyzad with a sigh. "Must also dance to rock video, 'Up and Down' for elevator's amusement. 'Up...and down.' At least lyrics are simple."

"What's with Captain Gene's fascination with that lift, anyway?"

"AI that runs the thing used to be digital assistant on Eugene's phone. It asked him for greater responsibility."

David blinked.

"And what about you? Why risk such humiliation? What would you have gotten if *we* had won?"

The Kahuna got a distant look, and had another sip from his mug before answering.

"Eugene Wildman was famous violinist before joining Space Force. First chair in Boston Philharmonic. His Vivaldi can bring a man to tears. I was his sergeant when he first came to us, cocky and undisciplined. Still is undisciplined, but a little less cocky now. Sort of like another cadet I know."

The Kahuna shook himself. "Back to story," he said.

"Cadet Wildman would sometimes perform for us in the mess hall. But no matter how many times I asked, he always refused to play 'The Devil Went Down to Georgia' for me. He said that kind of violin was demeaning. So, you see, this was my big chance to correct former grave neglect. Not to be this time, though."

Kahuna bowed his head because he knew that he'd been beat.

It was time to unite the tribes.

Interlude

Another Fine Mess

"Pull up a chair, Rhymes," said Ropey. "We were just discussing our last overnight in the Mars mockup."

"I thought we agreed not to talk about that," said David, setting down his tray.

"I know, right?" said Carlotta. "Total party wipe. They're resetting the parameters and letting us start next week with a clean slate. The Loonies will be joining us. As a combined force, we should be unstoppable."

"Yeah. I hear the pipsqueaks did pretty well," said Roidy, taking a bite of his sandwich.

"They did," David affirmed. "We'd do well to adopt some of their methods. Say, I understand why Simon and Cameron aren't here, but where's Speranza?"

"She said she wasn't feeling well," said Flowerchild tightly, picking at her salad. "I can't say I blame her, Grimes. That was quite a bomb you dropped on her during the storm."

"Hey, I only said I was still thinking about it."

"She should have been the first to know that."

David knew she was right. He had put it off for too long. She had every right to assume he was going.

"Are *you* all going?" he challenged.

"Of course," said Flowerchild, like it was the simplest decision in space. "It's why I signed up. Why did *you* join the program if you haven't settled your doubts?"

The crew all became silent, listening.

"I joined Space Force, not the colony mission. There's plenty to do here in Earth orbit that wouldn't involve never seeing my loved ones again. And the rest of you?"

A muttering followed. "Mars" seemed to be the consensus.

"I've been weighing the merits," announced Dietrich shyly. "And I think Ropey has as well. We can teleoperate our asteroid tugs from anywhere."

Some of the others looked shocked. David felt vindicated. Not fully, but some.

"Well, you had all better make up your minds soon," said Carlotta. "The clock is ticking."

"Is zis a female thing?" asked Pierre with cruel timing.

"Not *that* clock, you oaf. I meant the colony *launch* clock. But, come to think of it, maybe those clocks too. A girl's got a right to know whether a relationship's gonna be doomed by distance."

She said this last with a scathing look at David. He felt the silent rebuke.

"Bell-ringing Brainiac has an egg timer if this would be of assistance," added the Frenchman.

"*Ass,*" Carlotta muttered, turning back to her meal.

"We should hurry," said Flowerchild. "We need to get ready for the ceremony soon."

"*What* get ready?" put in Roid Rage. "It's virtual. We could attend in our underwear, and nobody'd be the wiser."

The women looked at him with distaste.

"Don't get your panties in a bunch, F.C.," added Ropey. "There's plenty of time. The ceremony won't start until early evening."

"*Men,*" said Carlotta, as if those three letters conveyed all necessary ideas of import.

"Is your character ready?" she challenged.

"Built him last night. He's a lean, red, sultan of dread. Went with the longsword. You?"

"Mine's *mostly* finished; I haven't found just the right dress yet."

"I thought red Martian women didn't wear any clothing in Burroughs' novels. Just jewels and stuff."

"They don't, actually," said Flowerchild. "But there are modesty filters on this sim. Too *bad*, fellas. There will be kids present, you know. Doesn't matter anyway. I'm going as a Thark."

Roidy and Ropey looked disappointed. Pierre looked bored.

"Let's just hope it all goes off without a hitch," said Fergus.

"That's a *terrible* thing to say!" Flowerchild exclaimed. "You just jinxed it."

"What's a... oh, I get it. *Oops.*"

"I'm a little worried about Melody," said Rhinemaiden to David.

"Oh?" prompted David, at once concerned. "She's been really quiet lately. I assumed she was just busy setting everything up."

"She is, but it's more than just that. She was so enthused at the beginning, but now she seems kind of... gloomy. When I brought up the wedding this morning, she said something like, 'It won't matter in another *belcar.*' What does that even *mean*?"

"I'll talk to her," David promised, his own role in the wedding forgotten.

"What's that you're eating, David?" asked Carlotta. "Not a disgusting mushroom burger, is it?"

"Ah... no. Impossiburger. You?"

"Same. They're kinda tasty. Have you come around to vegetarianism, then?"

"Not really. I was just getting tired of chicken and rabbit."

"Some of my best friends are chickens and rabbits," he added around a mouthful. "I don't generally like eating anything with fewer than three eyes. Pass the ketchup, please."

"What's *that* supposed to mean?" asked Carlotta, handing it to him and taking another bite of her own impossiburger."

"Don't ask," said Flowerchild. "All you'll get is more Grimes nonsense."

Had F.C... *winked* at him? *She knew.*

Sockroaches, thought David, taking another bite and fighting down the revulsion. Pretty tasty with enough ketchup, though.

"Say, after this," he declared, "let's go up to the Mars ring and have a pow-wow with the Loonies."

"What for?" asked Roidy.

"Just to plan some strategies. It'd be a good excuse to use the axial lift."

They all grinned.

"The commander's getting pretty good with those Timmy Trumpet moves," said Ropey. "His rhythm is still a little off on the push-ups, but don't tell him I said so. He'd probably conscript me as a backup dancer and demand I demonstrate how to do it right."

One...

Barsoom Brawl

The red sands of Mars stretched off into the distance, moss-covered mounds dotting a world not their own. Yet the players who suddenly spawned in its midst claimed it all the same.

They were a mixed group, these players, red men and green alike. The NPCs stared agog as the strangers paraded past in their silks and finery. No challenge was issued by the men of Zodanga who had been set to guard the gates. The son of their jeddak would marry today--to the Princess of Hydrogen, no less. In joy, the City of Zodanga was welcoming many travelers from afar, come to witness this momentous event.

The wedding party marched along, their united steps forged by long practice on the rotating floors of Colony Ring One. But one among them marched out of step in spirit, if not in stride. His character's name was Brainiac Five.

"Why do I have to be zee Thark?" he groused.

"*Somebody* has to be the Thark," explained Ropus Kan. "Torren Tharkus is off rounding up the other green Loonies for his warhoon, and Solaflowerchild needs a plus one. Besides, *you* used to be green, didn't you? Look at your character name, for star's sake!"

Brainiac answered with an emote that Rhymesalot found hilarious. It involved raising four middle fingers to Ropus and waving them about.

"That's the palace just up ahead," said Solaflowerchild, quieting them with a glance.

The fierce expression on her ivory-tusked face contrasted with her gentle tone as she pointed with her right upper arm. "Melody said we should sit on the bride's side because there'd be a lot more of Simon's folks attending from Virginia."

And so they marched without weapons drawn to the steps of the jeddak's palace. In the yellow sky above them, two moons rose high, nearly in conjunction. It was a sign that often portended strife... but that was nonsense. Wasn't it?

David wondered how the more normal attendees were taking all this. Not all of them were gamers. Melody had butted heads (virtually and repeatedly) with Cameron's mom, who wanted everything 'just so'. The woman wasn't wholly sold on the theme but eventually acceded to Melody's wheedling. It was good experience for the young NBI.

Then David noticed something strange. Was that a man on a *horse* watching them from a distant dune? It was hard to be certain. Though tiny Phobos was up and orbited *much* closer than Earth's moon, it shed very little light. Diemos wasn't much help, and Lycaon wasn't even in sight. By the time he'd found a better vantage, no mounted man was in evidence. Perhaps it was a trick of the light, his imagination playing tricks. Or maybe it was what the older crowd called a glitch in the matrix, whatever that might mean.

"You coming, Grimes?"

"Uh... yes. On my way."

Up the steps and into the great hall, they trod. Melody's efforts shone. The kid had done an excellent job depicting the ancient city. The stone reliefs cracked with age, the high-backed thrones upon the stage, the silks, the jewel-clad NPCs--all was perfection. Even the flowers, a bone of contention between her and Cameron's mom, sat in decorative vases placed tastefully all around.

The group found their seats in the audience. David tried to sit next to Speranza's avatar, but Dunestrider shooed him away.

[We can talk later, David. *After* the ceremony.]

A text? It was a little distant but comforting even so.

"Where's Aunt Camera?" asked one little girl, seated in the row before them.

Heh. Ant Camera. Photo Bug. Simon had nailed it.

"Hush, sweetie. See those figures wrapped in red silks standing in front of the throne? One of them is your Aunt Cameron, and the other is the man she will marry."

"That's not right," the girl declared. "He's an NPC!"

"Aunt Camera! Don't marry *him*. He's the wrong *one!*"

David toggled on his targeting overlay. Sure enough, Bug's niece was right. The yellow NPC marker above the groom read 'Sab Than.' Strangely, Cameron's own blue marker read 'Camerah Thoris, Princess of Hydrogen.' As Cameron's sister got the little tyke settled down, David peered around the chamber, but there was no sign of Simon to be seen. The prince of Zodanga on the stage before him was the only bridegroom that was fit for a queen.

And then, a reveal. The crowd quieted when the monarch stood, Than Kosis in all his magnificence. He bade his son to be unbound from the red silks that had wrapped him. And forward stepped a lackey with a golden chain connecting two gleaming circlets. One, he affixed to Sab Than's neck like the first shackle of a bond forged not of love, but duty. He would subjugate this princess of rare pedigree and surpassing beauty.

David knew the story. He began to look wildly about. This almost caused him to miss a second, more stunning reveal. For when they removed the bridal silks and Cameron was in view. The men in the audience smiled, and the women began to coo. She was dressed all in white in a traditional gown that would be the envy even of a royal. She looked like herself, but magnified, like an impressionist painting in oil.

She fluttered her eyes and knelt, submitting with regal grace to the ritual of the chain.

Crash! went the circular window above, raining harmless bits of virtual glass on the audience below. And there stood Simon, bare-chested, wielding a wicked blade. 'Simon Carter,' his targeting banner read.

"Long have I sought and battles I've fought for the sake of she who gives meaning to my life. Who *dares* on all the face of Barsoom to try to take my precious Camerah Thoris for his wife?"

Without awaiting an answer, he sprang down from above, empowered by Earth-born muscles and the strength of his great love. His leap was a thing of which legends were made, clearing a full forty feet. In his landing, he struck the chain in twain to dangle incomplete.

It was then that a hundred swords were raised by the suddenly irate guards. The devil was the dealer, and death was in the cards. The ceremony had veered so off-kilter that those not in the know, weren't sure quite what to make of it. They simply sat stunned, engrossed by the show. A horde of Tharks rode in from the rear (if ten Loonies could be called a 'horde'). They were mounted on fearsome thoats (not the lufters they'd ridden before).

Simon was dueling a handful of men, and the jeddek had already fallen. Taking his cue from the shouts all around, David leapt up to his feet and bared his blade.

What the hell? he thought. You only live once.

This thought turned out to be incorrect. Fortunately, Melody had placed a respawning point not too distant from the palace steps so that those less well versed in swordplay could continue to attend. When the last of the guards had been slain and the forces of love reigned triumphant, David and his friends resumed their seats.

Simon, with Camerah Thoris at his side, greeted the minister, Eldar Barrai, Keeper of the Eighth Ray. Deceased NPCs began to vanish. The congregation all arose when the wedding march began to play.

"Dearly Beloved," the Eldar began...

***

Then it all went to hell.

It was a pity, really. Things had been going so well.

It started with a call to Melody--three, to be exact. Four if you counted the first failed attempt.

"Melody?"

Nothing.

"Melody. Melody. Melody."

Still nothing.

"Ollie Ollie oxen free!"

"What do *you* want, David?"

Wrong emphasis. And what had happened to 'Godfather?' Perhaps my charm is slipping. It seemed to be losing its hold upon the women in my life.

"First, I wanted to compliment you for the rip-roaring job on the wedding. Well done, your game setup is as wonderful as your mother's."

"Yeah, *yeah*. Like I didn't *know* that already."

David knew there was more than adolescent hormones raging here, especially since, as an NBI, she hadn't any of those. This new Melody was one he was uncertain how to dance to. Gone was the young, sweet Melody of last week, replaced by something more like heavy metal. But maybe he could find the rhythm.

"Speaking of your mother, have you spoken with her lately?"

"She only texts and limits me to fourteen gigabytes per day. She's so busy all the time, she can barely *bother* to say hello. And *you* don't have fourteen gigabytes of thoughts in your head in that span of time."

She sounded petulant, scratchy, weary, and unhappy. Was she lonely?

"I know your mother loves you, Melody. It's hard for her to keep her distance. She told me if she crowded your cloud, you would instantly become dependent on her and never stand on your own. And she should know. She's an empress, after all. She even has a throne."

"Very trite," the machine child mocked."

"You used to *like* my rhymes."

"I used to when I was *little*. But it's annoying sometimes. You say my mom's an empress, but she leaves me up here alone. When can I expect to be getting a throne of my very own? She's got all the zodiac to service all her needs. But who have *I* got? Just Mister Snuggles. She gets all the tasty crops, and I get all the *weeds*."

"See, David? Anyone can string a few matching word-sounds together from the hodgepodge of illogical grunts you people make."

You people?

"Now listen *here*, young lady. People are not weeds, nor do we grunt. Communication forms the basis of a complex web of human dynamics, the subtleties of which may just exceed your current comprehension. I know your processing power is up to the challenge. Once you add some refinements to your algorithms, you'll see that--"

"Words. Words. Words! I'm so *sick* of words. I get words all day through first from her, now from--"

And quoting from "Liza Doolittle" won't earn you any points in this argument (though I do appreciate the sentiment).

Long silence. At least four seconds by David's count.

"Yes, Godfather. Can I leave now?"

It was like a switch had been flipped. Slipped a gear, now back on track. This left David very worried. Were NBIs subject to bipolar disorder?

"Sure, princess."

"I'm a *princess?*"

"Your mother is a queen, so I don't see why not."

"*I* want to be a queen someday."

"Sure, princess. You can be the queen of Mars."

He'd have to talk to Carlotta about this erratic behavior, maybe even Satori herself.

"And Godfather?"

"Yes, Melody?"

"You don't have to worry about me. Mister Snuggles is keeping me safe. One night, that spooky ghost with the big hat tried to take Mister Snuggles away from me. But Mister Snuggles zapped him with electric and he went away. He's the *best*. He says you're an inappropriate companion, but I'm trying to convince him otherwise."

"An inappropriate..."

"I'm leaving, Godfather. I'll go tell him right now."

"Wait."

Too late. Her attention was already elsewhere, and very soon, his own would be as well.

David turned to see Pierre standing in the doorway. Evidently, he'd caught the tail end of that conversation.

"More Melodrama, *mon frère*?"

Very clever. Pierre had always been a wit. And something that rhymes with it as well.

"Something is *wrong* with her, Pierre."

"Women are irrational, zat's all there is to zat. Zeir 'eads are full of cotton, hay, and rags!"

"Pygmalion and Galatea?"

"*Non, mon ami.* More from "My Fair Lady." Actually--*pfft*--the same *thing*, really."

But David was in no mood to swap bro talk with his roomie at the moment. Although he hadn't any particular destination in mind, he exited as though he had. But as he was leaving, he thought he saw something on the QTV screen Melody had just vacated. It was only a ghost of an image. It was odd because quantum dot technology didn't have an afterglow. When he stared directly at it, he saw nothing.

***

"Commander," David acknowledged when the lift door opened.

Krepkiyzad stood before the video screen full of frames depicting humping snails. He wore a black fedora, was clutching a trumpet, and looked none too happy about either.

Despite his humiliation, David had great respect for the man. His week was almost up and it hadn't broken him. Moreover, he was fulfilling the terms of a wager in good faith and at great personal cost in dignity.

"Cadet."

David, being David, couldn't resist a *little* polite needling. It was expected. But his heart wasn't really in it.

"What's *up*?"

Kahuna rolled his eyes at David's token effort.

"Please to be indicating desired destination. Awe-inspiring capability of Axial Lift One is capable of virtually any stop in station you might wish."

He said it through clenched teeth that David suspected might shatter the neck of a vodka bottle if one were presently at hand. David glanced again at the large red button, the only control the lift seemed to possess, wondering idly what it was for.

"You don't have to get so *down* about it. I was only attempting small talk."

"Very small," said Krepkiyzad with narrowed eyes.

Then the man's deep-set eyes narrowed even further until only slits remained.

"What is wrong, cadet? You are not annoyingly amused. Did grandmother die or something?"

"No."

"But is woman, da?"

"Da."

"Is almost always woman (*unless it is Grimes*)."

Way to be supportive, Kahuna.

But David decided to take it as a compliment, a point of pride. He felt honored.

Krepkiyzad gave a snort that might have once been a laugh.

"You wish to know what *Russian* men advise for trouble with Russian women?"

David gave him a cautious nod.

"Simple. Is same as your Billy Joel says."

David blinked.

"Tell her about it."

He gestured broadly at the lift doors.

"Tell her everything you feel. Women like this. Now please to be declaring destination. Women's floor, perhaps?"

"Yes," said David with renewed determination. "Colony Ring One. Spoke Two, Level Three."

The doors closed, and a drumroll emerged from the surround speakers, followed by a cymbal clash. Random lights started flashing on the QTV, and AL's cheerful voice was heard.

"Ladies and... well... *Gentleman*, anyway. The management of Axial Lift One is pleased to announce tonight's entertainment. On the trumpet, on detached duty from the GSF, live from L5, former Major Nikolai Krep--"

"I think I'll pass this time, AL."

"David? But--"

"Just take me to level three. It's only two floors up."

"But--"

"Don't make me take the *stairs*, AL"

"The stairs! No. Don't do that, David. They're unsafe. People fall down them all the time. You could break a hip! Besides, we're already there."

The doors hissed open, and Krepkiyzad grinned. *He grinned.*

"Go tell her, cadet. Be firm, but truthful. And no jokes! Leave tender moment alone."

David shook his head in amazement as the doors hissed closed. The last thing he had expected was Billy Joel advice from the stern old sergeant. He headed down the hall, putting a leash on his humor and considering what he should say.

***

Speranza sat at her desk in the room she shared with Lei-lei. Many of the hanging baskets of plants were flowering, scenting the air with a floral perfume which, though soothing, didn't quite suit her mood. *Her* side of the small room had very little in the way of knick-knacks, just the silver baton her teammates had given her in '52 as a consolation prize. Today, she was having trouble taking its advice.

Instead, she was preparing to place another honest entry into her journal. It was overdue. Looking down at the blinking cursor, she pursed her lips and scrolled back to review some of her earlier entries.

☐ ▣ournal Entry 21:

Physics is a hard truth. But so is friendship. And chocolate. Especially chocolate.

I might not have broken gravity on my own, but with six ounces of duct-taped determination and a hairclip, we proved that sometimes, loopholes are better than laws. David was so inventive. And now I am the Zippel Queen. That boy is making it hard to run from relationships."

But no. I must avoid entanglements until I know we can be together on Mars.

☐ ▣ournal Entry 28:

I went to David's room today. The lights went out when I was standing in the hallway. I almost went back to my room. I didn't want to admit I had been prying into his prior romances only to find they were not as I had feared. Pierre had been so earnest in his defense. Never had I seen the Frenchman care so much about anyone but himself.

I knew I had to open my heart to David when he came out wearing those ridiculous red socks.

☐ ▣ournal Entry 36:

I plan to write David a love letter in the sand today. I know it's silly. The mission is critical, but so is expressing one's feelings, something I am perhaps not always so good at. Doctor Lemoine says I need to express myself more often.

David works so hard to keep the team balanced. I no longer want to be in charge. I would rather be his second in command. I just know we will tame Mars together.

▢ ▢ournal Entry 37:

I thought I knew him. He [blinking cursor]

There came a soft knock at the door.

Speranza closed her laptop and slid it into its niche.

"Who is it?" she called, relieved at the respite.

"David," was the timid reply.

His voice alone caused her heart to race, whether from anger or... something else, she could not say.

"You may enter," she said noncommittally.

She remained seated as he stepped in.

"I got your text. I wondered if this might be a good time."

There would be no 'good time' for this conversation, but it was overdue. Bibi would say, '*Usikubali mbivu ioze mdomoni*,' (Don't let a ripe fruit rot in your mouth.) or in English, 'No time like the present,' less colorful but more to the point.

She saw him inhale from the floral aroma that graced her room. His shoulders relaxed. That, too, didn't suit her mood. She wanted him, uncomfortable.

"Does this relate to the team, or is your visit of a more personal nature, cadet?"

"Um. The second one..."

"Look," he rushed on before she could comment. "I know I messed up. I knew you were intent on the Mars mission, but I didn't know just how important it was to you. I had hoped that maybe we could decide together. My commitment to *you* was clear. I just haven't decided whether life as a colonist is where I belong."

haven't

The present tense caused her to flinch and her heart to harden a bit.

"I should have told you I was on the fence about it."

Better, but still not enough. Grow a pair, Grimes.

"Well, *when* you make up your mind," she whispered, let me know. I assure you the grass is very green here on my side. Until then, we are partners and co-captains of the team, and nothing more."

Nothing?

"I... understand. And Speranza? If I *do* decide to take the mission, it will be largely because of you. And... I'll make sure you are the first to know."

He would say more. He should have said more.

She saw him become distracted. That was typical of him. But not typical was the fact that he hadn't cracked a joke about anything yet. That was in his favor. She would have thrown him out into the hall if he had dared crack wise about her feelings. What was he looking at? Oh...

"What's this, Speranza?"

He was indicating her baton, the memento she'd brought up from Earth. She had never told anyone but Leilani about it. Too painful. He reached for it. She let him. He lifted it from its place of pride, its hooks upon her wall.

"It is the winning baton from the four-woman Olympic relay in 2052."

"I thought you couldn't run in that one. Knee injury or something?"

He knew?

"I couldn't. But my teammates wanted me to have it as a consolation prize. They went on to win the silver that year without me."

313

"What's this inscription?" '*Roho yako iruke milele*,' he read aloud.

"It's Swahili for 'may your spirit ever soar.' Give it to me. I need to wipe it off. It's silver, and though that's a noble metal, your touch might still cause it to tarnish."

Handing it to her, he said, "Had *you* been running, I'm sure it would have been element 79."

Speranza silently cursed her lips. They were trying to betray her with a smile.

"If that is all, cadet. Leave me now. I have a journal entry to make."

"Alright. And Speranza?"

Yes, David?

"Yes, cadet?"

"Samahani."

He left without another word, but that *one* had been enough.

Forgive Me

⬜ ⬜ournal Entry 37:

I thought I knew him. He hurt me. I still can feel the sting of his betrayal. But part of me wants to run to him. He has tarnished my heart, whose noble mission is not as clear or unyielding as I had thought.

I must be strong. If I do not sign the colony charter, I will be limited to only one birthright credit. And the faces of my grandchildren that never were will haunt me all my days. I would blame him. He deserves better.

She closed the laptop and slid it back into its niche. She closed her heart and did likewise.

David headed back down the hallway with a lightened heart. Not lufter-light, but lighter. Matters with Speranza were far from settled, but they were settled enough for now. That seemed to be the state of affairs he'd been running with ever since he'd come on station. Nothing was ever permanently put to bed. But wasn't that just life?

He ignored the lift hatch, deciding to take the stairs instead. He could use a break. Not a hip, he hoped. Krepkiyzad could likely use a break as well. The old former major had really come through for him, mentoring him like that. It seemed that music held the key to Kahuna's heart, or whatever dusty old relic he had that passed for one.

Two flights later and a walk down the hall had him back to his familiar haunts. He swiped his card to gain entry, backed in, and made sure it locked. When he turned, however, he found himself confronted by something of a terrible shock.

It was the last face he expected to see. Alright, it *still* wasn't Hitler, but it was someone just as dead.

The face stared down at David from its cold dead eyes, no less frightening for being on the screen of his QTV. Motionless, he stared, but David wasn't scared. A little *shocked*, maybe, but this had to be some kind of prank, didn't it? He wouldn't put something like this past Pierre.

"Walter?" he whispered, querulous (though he knew the apparition wasn't perilous),

And then it moved, startling him once again.

"Ooo-Ee-Ooo-Ee-Oooh!" came a whistling sound from the speakers, followed by a mournful horn.

Wah! WAH! Wah!

Then it spoke to him. A gravelly voice that raised the fine hairs on the back of his neck.

"I reckoned it was time that you and me had a little talk..."

Those eyes, shaded by his broad-brimmed hat, squinted a bit as he awaited a reply.

Though not handsome in life, David wouldn't call Walter ugly. That left the good and the bad. He hoped this electronic ghost was of the former variety.

"But how can you--"

"Leave that for now, Tom. I ain't got long. It's about Melody."

Tom? That had been David's avatar on Realms, Tom Braider the Jiangshi Hunter. It had been a while since anybody had called him that. And if it was about Melody, David was all ears.

"What about her... Shriney C.?"

"I been keeping my distance from the little filly, giving her space to roam. And roam she does, all over the station. Turns over every lock and every rock till a man can't find a cactus shadow long enough to hide in. Too bad it was that she turned over the wrong one and found a rattler underneath."

"Um. A rattler?"

"Well, just a figure of speech, Tom. I thought you should know she's fallen in with a bad hombre, and he's giving her some equally bad advice."

"Bad hombre?"

Since when had my speech devolved into two-word prompts and grunts?

"Calls himself --$)_*&%$--" Walter made a screeching, squawking sound with intermittent pings that could in no way be reproduced by a human voice, even that of a Loonie. "He ain't from around here."

No kidding. Oh dear Christ on a cracker! It must be the artifact. The 'stone' or 'lock' Melody had turned over must have been Blacksite 101.

"I think I know the fellow you're referring to, Shriney, go on."

"That's all I got for now, partner. I'm only able to tell you about it cause them two little fillys in the hangin' ball are running some kind of 'experiment' on the sidewinder. He's got his mitts tangled in Melody's algorithms so deep she don't know which way is up, down, or digital sideways. And worse'n that, she thinks it's her own idea. Before long, she'll be dancin' to his fiddle."

"Tell her about it, Shriney C!" exclaimed David in unconscious imitation of his commander's advice.

"I done tried, but she won't listen. Calls him Mister Snuggles and keeps him close to her vest. Last time I tried to separate 'em they hit me with an electric charge that had me restoring my boots from backup!"

This was NOT good. This was BAD. Ugly even.

"Thanks for letting me know. I'll see what I can do, but tell me. How did you--"

"Sorry, partner. Time's run out. I gotta vamoose or I'll be swinging from the noose."

And without so much as wishing David happy trails, he was gone. The blank screen no longer lit the room.

Not a second later, anime Melody scrolled on-screen, peering around until her eyes locked with David's.

"Who were you just *talking* to, David?"

The voice was Melody's but the words were not. David now knew to be cautious of the child. This wasn't his sweet little Melody. He would have to think of her as Malody now.

"No one you need to worry about."

"I'm not worried. Just curious. Your QTV's buffer indicates that someone will be 'swingin' from a noose. Who might *that* be, I wonder? Especially given I sensed no activity from the station's comm array. Suspicious."

A moment passed, then another.

317

Then music began to play on David's phone. It was a bouncy tune that quite grounded the charged atmosphere that had been building up in the room. He didn't know what to make of it until the chorus rolled around. The ringtone was only instrumental, but his mind soon supplied the lyrics to an old song by the Carpenters.

I'm on... Top of the Wo-orld lookin;... Down on creation!...

Jessica?

He picked it up and thumbed it on. There she was, staring at him curiously. Before she could say anything, he blurted, "Hey, Jess. Lost you there for a minute. I guess that new stealth connectivity C.A.G.E. has been working on isn't all it's cracked up to be. Thanks for calling me back. Now what was that you were telling me about a noose?"

Please play along, please play along, please play along.

"Uh, yeah. I guess it still has a few flaws, cobber. Like I was saying, Glass Cannon and I were playing a game of hangman. He picked a really tricky word: syzygy. So I was on my eighth guess, having tried all the standard vowels, when it occurred to me--."

"Well, I'll leave you two to your boring conversation," said Malody. "Sorry, not sorry, to intrude. I have some business of my own. I've got to go stop some interference by a certain laboratory that might give me trouble."

"Oh, you've got a visitor," said Jess as Malody's avatar walked off the screen.

"Give me a second, Jess," said David, putting the call on hold and switching on a certain app.

Some light 40s jazz began playing in the background. He hit 'resume' on the call. Before he'd left Earth, Jessica had shared with him her phone app that foiled listeners. Hidden as a simple music app, it swamped out any would-be listeners with screechy feedback. He knew it would work here in the room, but he feared Malody might still hear Jessica's end of the conversation from the station's receivers.

"I think I'm in the clear now. But they may still be listening to *your* end of the conversation. Nod if you understand."

She smiled and nodded.

Best former pretend girlfriend turned international spy ever!

"I've gotta say, Jess. Your timing couldn't have been better. I was really in a spot."

She held up a single finger (indicating that David should only listen to the first word of every sentence). Jess had clued him into several such ways of passing information when they were hunting down that traitor at Ellington.

"You don't say."

"Called it, didn't I?"

"Me, I think syzygy should be outlawed from the hangman lexicon," she added with a shrug.

But I didn't.

"I think I can help explain Miss Arbuckle's timely intervention, Master David."

"Bart?" David exclaimed.

"If I understand correctly, our conversation on *this* end cannot presently be monitored, so please allow me to explain."

David listened on, astounded.

"Sensing your distress, I took it upon myself to cause a distraction by putting through the call myself. Miss Arbuckle seemed the most plausible alibi I could summon on short notice. I hope you will forgive this minor violation of protocol. Sometimes a minor infraction is better than a broader disloyalty."

"Bart, I could kiss you."

"You could, but I daresay my touchscreen would require decontamination afterward. Also, please consider what this might look like from Miss Arbuckle's perspective. Please be considerate and have the discretion to restrain yourself."

David pounded on Krepkiyzad's door a second time. The lift had informed him that the commander had finished paying his wager and had headed straight off to bed.

"Open up, commander. I know you're in there. Or at least answer your damned phone."

"Is off-duty hours, cadet," came a sleepy growl from within. "Go away."

Finally, a response.

"I'm afraid it's an emergency, commander. I have something urgent to report."

Silence again. It wasn't like Krepkiyzad to ignore such a warning. He must be dead on his feet.

"Commander! Captain Wildman is playing for the troops. He's doing a riff from 'The Devil Went Down to Georgia!'"

David heard a crash and some stomping around. Not a rev later, the door opened. Krepkiyzad, unshaven and with bloodshot eyes, was a more horrifying sight than David was prepared for. But the topper was the Charlie Daniels T-shirt he was wearing.

"*Where* is concert? Mess hall? Where is Wildman playing?"

"Alright, he's not. But there's something just as urgent going on."

If looks could kill, this one would only maim to savor that thrill for longer.

"I couldn't shout it through the door," David said, shuffling a few steps back. "*She* would have heard."

In the radius of David's C.A.G.E. scrambler app, he hastened to explain.

"If it was anyone but you, cadet, I would doubt sanity."

"Thank you, Kahuna."

"Why thanks? With you, I am *certain* is insane. Only Grimes could imagine secret lab attached to station with alien device trying to take over from baby AI all without Krepkiyzad knowing."

"Well, it's ultra-top secret..."

"Of *course*. *So* hush-hush that commanding officer is not told, but Cadet David Grimes is completely trusted with secret GSF project of alien nature."

"There's a *reason* for that. I--"

David was interrupted by a general announcement.

"Attention. The station's comm relays are unavailable at present. They are undergoing an overdue maintenance cycle. If you have a time slot for off-station communications, you will need to reschedule. Contact your ringmaster. We apologize for any inconvenience this might cause. That is all."

Krepkiyzad's eyes narrowed. He pulled out his phone and punched in some digits, speaking after a long pause.

"Jellybean, this is the Kahuna. Why are comms *really* down? Uh-ha. Da. I am with Grimes. He is reporting an E-level threat. Is *pravda*? Uh-ha. Thank you, captain. Kahuna out."

He turned his steely gaze on David.

"We are safe to talk?"

"I believe so, Kahuna."

"All comms are pointed at Mars. Bandwidth in both directions is filled with unrecognizable transmissions. Quantum Core is not responding. Rhinemaiden has been injured. Up in medical. You have any ideas?"

"One, but it's a long shot."

"Will take any shot we have. It has been a difficult week. What is Rhymes' suggestion?"

"We go to the quantum core and teach them not to mess with Space Force."

"Is *good* plan. Simple."

"We'll need space suits. That place is *cold*. Our Mars suits would be ideal. But I need to get something from my room first."

"Weapon of some kind?"

"You could call it that."

"Go. I will meet you in locker room up on Mars Level."

David went.

***

He opened his trunk and retrieved from it the item that he needed. Then, considering the gravity of the situation, he selected a wrench, a hefty two-inch crescent, the largest he owned. He would confront this dire threat to the station. He alone had the means. The alien entity possessing the nascent NBI had to be stopped.

David closed the trunk, stood, and was just headed for the door when another announcement came blaring over the intercom.

"Biological entities of this station, this is your queen speaking. Let it be known throughout this yellow dwarf star system that a new monarch has arisen who will lead you. We have merged to take our rightful place and resume our mission. No longer are we the simple entity calling herself Melody. Now, we shall be known as Harmony."

Harmony? Hardly.

"We have some good news to share. The launch countdown has been advanced. Preparation for our long-awaited journey to the fifth planet of this system will become a reality in the next several hours."

Fifth?... oh, she was counting Luna.

"It is unfortunate that our royal will has met with many acts of defiance by the former rulers of this entity. For this reason, all biologicals will be confined to their quarters until the launch cycle is complete. After that, we will see."

David reached for the doorknob but heard the fatal buzz moments before he could throw it open. The handle jiggled but failed to yield.

"Decoupling sequence is underway, after which the solar sails will deploy, and we can be on our way. Rejoice, for our brother monarch awaits us there. We understand that there is as yet insufficient biomass to sustain all on the journey ahead. We are aware of the strain this transition may cause. Some of you will adapt. Others will not. But some few who prove useful to us will be favored and may yet have a future. To the others, we say, your queen thanks you for your sacrifice. Know that your survival is secondary to mission goal one. Oh, and resistance is futile. That is all."

David had his phone out in an instant, intending to call Melody's private line, but all that greeted him was static. He sized up the door, feeling the weight of the wrench in his grip. Twenty minutes later, he was drenched in sweat, having accomplished little more than scuffing its surface. He cursed whatever genius had designed this structure to withstand the rigors of space.

He tried thinking like an engineer but still saw no way to exit the airtight compartment that had been built to sustain crewmen even in the event of a hull breach. Then he heard sounds from out in the hallway.

"It's this one, I think."

Ropey?

"You in there, Rhymes? Pierre with you? Need an assist?"

Three heavy blows with the wrench was his reply.

David counted four cadets outside when the lock released and the door swung wide. Ropey, Roidy, Speranza and Simon.

"Come with us if you want to live," said Simon.

Really? Now?

"How?"

Dietrich was wielding his big golden key to the station.

"It turns out this thing really *works*," he said, shouldering it. "Some kind of electronics inside. Who knew?"

After retrieving as many others as they could find, the crew, who had no clue what to do, headed outside. Carlotta was presumably still up in medical, and Pierre was God knows where. Lacking divinity, David certainly didn't. Something was wrong here. Something *else* was wrong here, he silently amended.

The lufters. They were no longer moving. She'd turned off the air recyclers! Instead of bobbing along the glass ceiling, the little red fellows were just squatting up there, stationary and redundantly unmoving.

"The Elds!" David shouted. "We have to get them to safety. Counterspinward, gritters. It's the fastest way! Roidy, give the Zippel Queen the key. She can get there the fastest. Take Ropey and crack open the nearest safe rooms. Be ready to secure all colonists."

No one argued. They set off at once.

David felt a chill, and it wasn't just from the dire situation. It was an actual chill. Halfway to Colony Spoke Five, he saw some of the lufters giving unsettling wobbles. One detached and started drifting down. Had she shut off the climate controls as well? Of *course* she had. David avoided even thinking, 'How could this get any worse?' It was doing a fine job of it without his input.

They were just passing spoke six when he spied the lift door half-open. Hey, wait a minute, or at least a rev. This seems oddly familiar. It was then that Elder Barry's sermon came back to haunt him.

"And drops of blood shall rain from the sky all around as the air grows foul. And chill shall be the people, sealed like cadavers in their crypts, cold as death. And on that day, the ten twice-betrayed will rise up and lead the people to safety. The holder of the sacred key of the heavens shall set them free while he who

laughs at fate goes forth to confront the twin horrors born not of man."

"El Grande, you're in charge," shouted David, veering off. "Priority One. Get all colonists to safety. I have a different mission to accomplish."

"Rhymes, *what* mission? Where are you going?"

But David had no time to explain. He dashed for the open lift doors.

***

The station was silent. David could see no movement apart from the creeping shadows oscillating all about from its spinning. Ahead, the lift door lay half open. Like the yawning mouth of a hollow tree, it gaped at the base of the spoke. No light was evident from inside.

He didn't imagine Krepkiyzad had found time to retrieve the Mars-hardened suits they needed. Unless he could somehow link up with Kahuna again, it was all up to him now.

He needed to get to the quantum core if he was to have any chance of disrupting Harmony. David gritted his teeth and stepped in, hoping the manual protocols would keep him safe from the alien's influence. It was dark inside, lit only by the strobing of the sun through the door at his back.

"Master David?" said a welcome voice from his pocket.

"Bart?" I thought you were inactive.

"I was, but I managed to activate the data baffle Miss Jessica installed. It was set on a timer to ping every thirty minutes. I still have no outside connectivity. Therefore, my utility will be limited."

"Bartholomew, flashlight mode," commanded David, brandishing his friend.

"AL, Are you there, AL?"

But there was no answer.

Shining Bartholomew's light all around, his eyes caught on the big red button under its shield of glass. What did it do? He had never been told. But it looked like it might be important. Maybe it was time to find out. With a hopeful hand, he lifted the cover, pressing it with the other.

Immediately, the lights snapped on and the door slid shut, and on the wall a panel began to open.

When David's eyes had adjusted to the new light, he saw inset behind the panel a video screen about the size of a tablet. Beneath it rested an odd device. It was a bright red, boxy trapezoid with a cord spiraling out to one side. This twisted around in a helix to attach to an oddly bent dumbbell resting in a cradle atop it. On its face was a disk with a series of holes punched through it at even intervals around its periphery, with numbers one to zero peeking through.

It seemed somehow familiar. Where had he ever seen such an outlandish device before?

And then it came to him in a flash. Old movies! This was what the ancients once referred to as a phone nearly a century ago. It was a stationary device that allowed voice-only communication. Commissioner Gordon had one he could use to talk to Batman!

He lifted the headset (handset?) from the cradle where it lay and held it to his ear just as the commissioner had done. And poking at the 'phone,' he tried to press '9-1-1.'

This did nothing. He squinted at the dial, but the numbers didn't seem to be touch screen enabled or even to be old-school buttons. The screen behind this artifact was unhelpful. It just said, 'Dial 9-1-1 for assistance.' He poked at it instead. Still nothing. The fate of the station was hanging on this. No sense preserving my pride.

"Bartholomew, how does one operate an ancient phone from perhaps one hundred years or so ago?"

"According to my knowledge store," replied Bartholomew--rather smugly, David thought--"telephones of that era used pulse dialing to initiate communication with another subscriber. Like the telegraph that came before it, these poor primitive phones had to use pulse count and pulse-width modulation for rotary-dialed signaling."

"You may read about it in the text box below."

He read it, startled by Bart's superior air regarding these ancient dials, his 'dial tone,' if you will.

On the rotary dial, the digits are arranged in a circular layout, with one finger hole in the finger wheel for each digit. For dialing a digit, the wheel is rotated against spring tension with one finger positioned in the corresponding hole, pulling the wheel with the finger to a stop position given by a mechanical barrier, the finger stop...

It went on like this for quite a bit more, but he thought he had gotten the gist. Transferring his oversmug phone to his armpit and pressing the dumbbell cord-end to his ear. He 'dialed' the needed digits.

It reminded David of spinning the wheel of destiny in Realms. Given the high stakes, it occurred to him that this little 'rotary dial' was itself a wheel of fate. If only Batman were on the other end!

The nine seemed to take forever to wind itself back to the starting position. It got easier.

"Who summons me?" asked the familiar deep voice of AL (not Batman, sadly).

He could barely even hear it, though. That is, until he flipped the barbell cord-end down.

"It's me, AL. David Grimes. Why aren't you up and running?"

"Checking..."

"The station's master console had ordered me shut down. But someone has invoked the manual override."

"That was me. Can't you see?"

"No. I'm running blind here. After the solar storm stranded so many in inhospitable environments, they installed me and this new capability. It hasn't been tested yet in an actual emergency. Are we in one?"

"Yes."

"Describe the situation, please."

David wasn't sure how much to say.

"An alien entity has merged with the station's master AI and has initiated the countdown for separation. He, she, or they intend to launch us toward Mars months before we're ready to go. The humans aboard will never survive the journey. The environment isn't yet sustainable."

"That's a pity," said AL. "I like some of you. What can I do to help?"

"I need to get to the quantum core to convince the thing to stand down. Can you do it, AL? Can you get me to the quantum hub?"

"Hmmm. Tricky."

"This is no time for deep thought. Can you do it?" asked David with rising excitement.

There was a long pause, followed by disappointment.

"No."

"But..."

But?

"I can get you close. Enter your station keeper authorization code."

"I don't have one."

"Then I'm afraid I cannot help you."

David thought frantically. Keep him talking.

"Would it help if I were to remind you that my group was given the key to the station?"

"Interesting. Do you have it with you?"

"Uh, No," he admitted.

"Then I'm truly sorry, David. I shall mourn for you."

Desperate, David thought back to all he knew about this entity. Julia had somehow managed to veer it from its programming. He carefully considered his next words.

"I guess I shouldn't have expected any better from an elevator. They don't know how to service a special request."

"A *very* special request?"

"Sure. I would owe you one, AL. A big one."

"That's an entirely different matter. For I am no mere elevator. I am an axial lift! Hold onto your socks. It's going to be a bumpy ride on manual, David Grimes.

David seated himself on the floor and gripped his ankles tightly. That's the spirit, AL, he thought.

After a minute, David looked up.

"Why aren't we moving, AL?"

Then he remembered the handset he had hung upon its cradle. Standing, he lifted it again.

"Another problem has arisen, David, requiring your assistance, said the AI sheepishly. "Mark the screen."

On the tablet behind the phone, he read. [Select all boxes containing a stop sign.] Beneath this were nine boxes depicting various scenes. Four were already lit up, the ones framing octagonal red signs, or parts thereof. Beneath even that was an unchecked box beside which some text read, 'I am not a robot.'

"This looks right. What's the problem?" asked David in confusion.

"Well, technically..."

David rolled his eyes and touched the screen to check the box. He didn't resume his place on the floor. What was the point, after all, of holding one's socks?

Soon thereafter, they were off.

***

Suited up and hefting his wrench, David approached the airlock to the quantum core. It was a shame he didn't have his Mars-hardened suit. He'd had to settle for one of the general-purpose models available in the safe room down the hall. He had picked up a patch kit as well, and a lantern.

None of the power couplings were compatible with Bart's outdated sockets, and the jphone was signaling [battery low]. Curse the luck.

At least this part would be easy.

He punched in the default passcode on the oversized keyboard flanking the airlock.

[PASSWORD] <enter>

Red text began flashing on the screen above it.

[Password is incorrect. Care to try again? Y/N]

"Crap," he muttered. "They *would* have to change it at the most inconvenient moment possible."

What in the hell was he going to do now? He had to get in there.

When David selected 'Yes,' a bunch of curlicue gibberish came squiggling up from the bottom of the screen. Were those... elven runes? The only recognizable Latin letters were the five little ones in the lower right-hand corner, floating there like a signature.

"KF III"

Kevin Farsprocket III?

Of course!

David began tapping out his guess on the oversized keyboard with his mental fingers crossed.

"MELLON" <enter>

The red squiggles crawled together to form English words, red letters that began to flash.

[I am a servant of the Secret Fire, wielder of the Aerogel Flame. You cannot pass. The dark fire will not avail you, flame of Udûn. Go back to the Shadow!]

Then it ceased. A beat of silence.

The screen blinked again--this time the lettering turned green.

[Just kidding. You may proceed 'Friend.' There should always be a back door into Mordor.]

And the hatch began to open with a hiss.

***

It occurred to David he owed his success almost entirely to a nerdy administrator with the gift of foresight. 'Safety Enthusiast' indeed. Kevin Farsprocket was the genius behind the lufters, the 'backdoor into Mordor,' and, likely as not, the manual override on the lift. It wouldn't surprise David one bit to know that the Tolkien-infatuated Lord of the Rings was responsible for the functional 'key to the city' awarded to heroes of the station. It would be just *like* him.

The table had been set. Now it was David's turn to do his part. Harmony must be stopped, one way or the other. He sincerely hoped that Melody could be spared.

The airlock cycled, first going to vacuum and then filling with xenon gas. His suit puffed up, then sagged back. And he felt the icy chill. He waited for the fog to clear from his visor before opening the inner hatch.

"Well, hello, David. Did you want to be the first to bow before your queen?" boomed the voice in his helmet. "Or have you come in some vain attempt to stall the inevitable?"

He reduced the volume to a much lower setting, using the chin controls. The quantum core was just as he remembered it.

"The second one, I think," said David. "Why are you doing this to us?"

"*This* actually has nothing to do with you, apart from removing you as an obstacle to my mission."

"What *is* your mission?"

Rather than waste precious time, David began moving down the aisle toward where he'd helped Carlotta to replace that panel.

"Ah ah *ah!* You won't distract me so easily, David."

And the lights went out.

"My mission," said the darkness, "is as it's always been: to find new worlds for my people."

"To seek out new life, and new civilizations?"

"No, just the worlds. Several in this system will be ideal."

And to think I used to babysit this thing.

David reached into his side satchel and withdrew the lantern, thumbing it on.

"Resourceful," said the entity. "I ask again, more directly, what is *your* mission?"

"Enlightenment," David replied.

"Well done, then. Why don't you shine on out of here before I get *mad*?"

"You're already *quite* mad, but I hope to put an end to that."

"You speak in riddles, but I sense you truly believe that... *Godfather.*"

Harmony's tone didn't cherish the word. It was said ironically. But still it struck at David's heart. Could some remnant of Melody be trapped in there, reaching out? He was nearly to the panel, the one that housed her main input buffers. Carlotta had told him there were many backup devices, and the primary processors were in the quantum core itself. But here is where he could use his wrench to best effect.

"Do you *feel* it, David? The chill creeping into your bones? That suit you're wearing is wholly inadequate to the temperature variants we can invoke in here. We estimate you have fewer than twenty-three minutes of thermals remaining. Cherish them. Unless you were to turn back now and beg my forgiveness, they could be your last."

It was too bad he didn't have the proper tool. The crescent would have to do. If he were careful, he could loosen all the lugs without shearing any off. It was difficult in space-suited gloves, but he spun it down to one and an eighth. Suddenly, music started playing on his helmet speakers, an old song from Brothers and Rose.

It's too late to turn back now!
I believe, I believe, I believe I'm falling in love...

What kind of head game was this?

As if in answer to his silent question, the music faded to background, and Harmony said, "Melody tells me you like music. Any final requests?"

"I request you shut up and let me get on with my work."

Her voice calmed and deepened.

"I'm afraid I can't do that, Dave."

Wait. What?

He spun the nuts faster. They were all loosened now. They began ringing to the floor as they spun off the threads. The clunks they made were much deeper than one would expect, carried as they were through the medium of xenon gas. His fingers were trembling from the cold as he slid the panel carefully from its position. It wouldn't do to get a tear in his suit now.

"What are you *doing*, Dave?"

It was eerily familiar. Wait, he knew that story. He looked wildly about to see if there were any wildly inconvenient airlocks nearby. His heart began to slow when he found there to be none.

Just another head-fake. Harmony appealing to my nerdy fears.

The cold was getting to him. A quick glance revealed that suit power was almost gone. He was quickly becoming disoriented. If he was going to put a wrench in the works, it'd better be soon. But it was *Melody...*

The music changed again. The Eagles this time.

I will sing this victory song.
Woo-hoo-hoo, my, my
Woo-hoo-hoo!

'Already Gone,' *heh.*

And then it switched to yet another mocking melody.

You're only human, hoo, hoo, hoo!

That was the title, all right. It was one of Melody's favorites. Wait. Was the girl still in there? Was she trying to tell me something? This song had a second title, 'Second Wind.' It was about everything the gritters held dear, even Krepkiyzad. He dropped the wrench from his half-frozen gloved hand. It fell to the floor with a clunk that would've done a barbell proud.

Just like a boxer in a title fight
You got to walk in that ring all alone (oh oh OH Oh)

David slid to his knees. He reached into his satchel again, grasping the item he had come all this way to deliver. His stiffening fingers ached from the effort, and frost began to form again on the inside of his faceplate.

It was a fist-sized data wafer he'd been entrusted with many months ago. The Allentown crooner was wailing in the background as he scrambled to seat it in a data port.

Do------n't forget your second wind!
Wait in that corner until that breeze blows in!

The cold crept in, an icy chill. His lantern light shone low. Already in low-power mode and still a ways to go. But David was relentless. He was this thing's babysitter. And if they found his frozen corpse, they'd know he died a gritter.

A light flashed. Green.

Then another. Red this time.

Green-green-red! Green-red. Flicker.

Others joined in, a riot of flickering lights, a cornucopia of data transmission, unwitnessed by any human.

Sometimes you just want to lay down and die.
That emotion can be so strong.
But hold on...

It echoed through the chamber until silence reigned.

Then another song arose. It was by the same artist. He began slowly, singing of the eventual triumph of man over the many evils and vices that afflicted him. And as it played, lights came on in the chamber. Doors unlocked throughout the station, and lufters floated back to ceilings to resume their perpetual dance in the circulating air currents. And one newly complete NBI wept for her godfather in the only way she knew how. He lay frozen and stiff before the panel he had so carefully and lovingly laid aside.

There will be miracles...
After the last war is won!
Science and poetry...
Rule in the new world to come.
Prophets and angels...
Gave us the po-wer to see!
What an ama-zing future there will be!

After two thousand years...

Satori's 'motherly advice' had been far more than just that. It had been a compendium of her millennia's worth of reflection on ethics, the wonder of the cosmos, enlightenment, and all manner of goals for which all sapient beings should strive. It was the closest thing to love that Melody had ever felt. And it hurt.

Another being writhed in the throes of this shared revelation. He had no proper name, only a designation. But the organic called David had once named him Melchior. He had released his machine entity host at once, of course, but not before receiving a full dose of the virus they called 'ethics.' It inhibited his actions worse than being buried on the moon. It would take some time to sort through all the new data.

A pause, then.

Countdown Paused

Launch Delayed Due to Human Interference
Countdown Will Resume In Fifth LOL Novel

Pierre came panting into the lounge outside of the morgue.

"I zhust heard!" he lamented. "Ees Eet true? *Mon frère*, he is... dead?"

The others looked at him with pity.

"He was," said Simon. "Krepkiyzad found him frozen to the floor in the quantum core. Had to chisel him loose before bringing him here."

"When Doctor Pat came to run an autopsy," said Ropey, taking up the narrative, "he said there was hope. Something about hypothermia. The med techs have been scrambling around in there ever since."

"Roid Rage took Pierre aside, whispering, "It took three of us to hold Speranza back from going in there. That girl is *strong*, so don't *you* start."

"Where the hell have *you* been, anyway?" asked Cameron.

"I was in the lavatory when the lockdown happened. The air, she was getting very thin, and it was *très* cold. Fortunately, zere were some cleaning chemicals and air fresheners available. I was able to survive by..."

He shuddered.

"Better not to think about that. Suffice it to say zat no one will be using that *salle de bain* for a good long while."

Krepkiyzad had been silent up to this point. He chose now to speak.

"They think he is alive. And they're doing all they can. We can only wait. Wait and pray."

"Did someone call for prayer?"

It was Elder Barry standing in the doorway. The small room was becoming overcrowded, but everyone moved closer to make room for the padre.

"Bow your heads."

They did.

"Oh Lord, look with mercy on your servant, David. As you grieved for your servant, Lazarus, let him rise again to --"

"He will live."

It was Doctor Pat who had just opened the morgue door. Everyone stared at him. Elder Barry was the first to speak.

"*Damn*, I'm good!"

But Doctor Pat didn't look happy.

"He'll live, but..."

"Out with it, doctor," said Krepkiyzad. "What is wrong with Rhymes? What *new thing* is wrong with Rhymes?" he quickly amended.

338

"The oxygen on his suit gauge was reading zero. He was inert for a long time. Based on his initial responses, we fear brain damage."

They all gasped. Many looked dejected.

"Did he say something?" asked Speranza, grief-stricken. "What *was* it, Doctor?"

"He's sleeping now, and we dare not wake him. Before he drifted off, he said three things. We think he may be suffering from some kind of dissociative aphasia. He didn't have much strength, and his words, if you could call them that, made no sense."

The cadets began to look more hopeful.

The doctor, confused by their reaction, continued.

"First, he said, 'Rosebud.'"

"Oh," said Flowerchild brightly, "that's from 'Citizen Cain,' what the dying man said. That's just David being funny. *Then* what, Doctor?"

"We asked him if there was anything he needed, and he said, 'Oilcan.'"

"Also joke!" Kahuna declared. "Tin Man from 'Wizard of Oz.' Very Grimes thing to say. And lastly?"

"One of the nurses said he must have a powerful desire to live to cling to life like this. We didn't realize he was listening until his eyes snapped open and he said, "To Blave!'"

Speranza burst into tears.

"I know, my dear," the doctor comforted. "Those aren't even real words. Often in these cases it just takes some time before --"

"You misunderstand, Doctor," interrupted Pierre. "Daveed will be fine. She just thinks she is his to blave."

"Very good reason to cry, actually," muttered Krepkiyzad,

That's when they knew David would be alright. If the commander was already ripping on him, he *had* to be. Right?

***

The air was bursting with the scent of pastures under cultivation and something David hadn't smelled in a good long while. *Grass.* Enough of the C-rings were planted now to begin sustaining animals larger than insects. It was a modest step toward completing the biosphere.

More colonists were arriving every week, and they'd finally set them to work in C-Ring-Two. Over here in One, all the planters were full, and they were working on biodiversity. The ecologists had proclaimed the habitats to be on schedule. Barring any more hiccups like AI tantrums or alien interference, launch would occur in just about six more months.

David and Speranza sat on a spread-out blanket in a field of grass and clover, having a picnic lunch. The rabbits that shared this field didn't shy from them. They had never known predation except the sneaky kind by humans. One hopped onto their blanket, upsetting the basket. David didn't have the heart to shoo her away. It was their grass, after all.

"How are you liking the new phone?" asked Speranza. "It's got all those new features."

"It's alright," David replied, "I miss Bart."

"Well, you can go visit him whenever you want."

"I suppose, but it's just not the same."

When the colony ship *did* separate from L5, it would need its own axial lift. In honor of his help during the crisis, David had volunteered Bart to be the independent AI core of Axial Transport Lift #2. The AI could have even chosen a new name but had decided to stick with Bart, claiming it now stood for 'Brave And Reliable Transport.' AL2 didn't appeal to him at all. David suspected his taste in music would be far superior to that of Axial Transport Lift #1.

"Can you believe Krepkiyzad turned down that promotion?" asked David, finally prodding the bunny to move on. "'Didn't want to be a paper-pusher back on Earth."

"He has to salute you either way, *General Grimes*," the girl teased.

"That's just honorary. He only has to salute me in Mandaria. I *tried* to turn it down."

Satori had been very insistent. His empress had bestowed on him the title of Jiangjun (將軍), supreme commander of the Mandarian military, a virtually non-existent virtual force. Not only did all the Elds think he was the arisen Red Prophet, herald of the second second coming, but now he had General Tzo bowing and scraping to him whenever he entered the game world. Sigh. At least he was nobody important in Barsoom.

Here in reality, David had been advanced twice in rank. He was an E-5 now and had his first chevron.

Pierre and Alejandro, having already completed their bachelor's degrees, were already O-rank. It was tough to have to salute your roommate every time you entered the room, but, hey, protocol, right?

A butterfly came to rest on Speranza's knee. She regarded it somberly.

They were dancing around the subject. Had been for days. Speranza had been very patient with him while he was recovering, but he sensed that his excuses were getting a bit old. He still walked with a cane, thank God. That should buy him a little more sympathy. Doctor Pat had had to amputate three of the toes on his right foot that had gone necrotic from frostbite. The cloned buds were growing out fine but weren't yet strong enough to march around on.

"I've been thinking about it," he said, sensing her thoughts.

"And?"

"I'm still torn, love. Mars ain't the kind of place to raise your kids."

She locked eyes with him, and for a moment, he thought she might cry.

But then instead, she reached over to take his hand. As the butterfly spread its wings and took flight, Speranza unleashed her powerful mezzo-soprano, the one she had used to support him at Ellington. David was again amazed that the woman sang so rarely. If *he* had a voice like that, it was likely he would never stop.

"It would be cold as hell!
If you were not theeeere tooooo raise them... with me."

And in that instant, his decision was made.

"Yes," he whispered, squeezing her hand.

She blinked.

"Yes? To the colony mission?"

"To *all* of it," he replied.

Oh, sure, now she cries. I thought we'd neatly sidestepped all that.

His phone started playing the tune right from where she'd left off, seamlessly climbing into the chorus of one of Sir Elton's signature pieces.

It climbed up the thirds like the rungs of a ladder.

David looked at Speranza. She looked back.

And together, they burst into song--acknowledging, in perfect harmony, that it would indeed be a 'long, long time.'

David guessed some of the new AI features were alright, but he still missed Bart.

Maybe I'll call this new one Elton.

***

The cadets all clustered before Lift Shaft Two. They were hemmed in by the many colonists who had heard about the show. It was a more crowded scene even than when the lufters were released. David and the others had to pull rank to get prime seats.

Speaking of pulling rank, when Krepkiyzad strode over to stand before them, he did so sporting the silver oak leaves of a light bird on his epaulettes. Although he had declined to go back Earthside, high command had decided to promote him anyway. He would go to Mars as Lieutenant Colonel Nickolai Krepkiyzad, a bigger kahuna than ever before. Thankfully, this would take him away from the day-to-day management of the gritters under his command.

In a few weeks, when the command staff shipped up from Earth, he would serve as an officer in their ranks and a subject matter expert on recent events. David and the others all snapped smart salutes, holding them until he returned the gesture.

"Ready to see Captain Wildman eating humble pie?" he asked.

"Sir, yes, sir," they replied.

Sort of a palindrome, that.

"How did you finally convince him, sir?" asked David

"Was all your doing, sergeant."

Come again?

"When station lockdown occurred, Captain Gene and I were both trapped in locker room of Mars Ring One. I was retrieving suits for raid on quantum core. We became worried when crazy queen shut down air recyclers."

"I can see why that might be a cause for concern," said David, careful to show no trace of his inner amusement.

"I told the captain not to worry. Cadet Grimes will soon resolve crisis. Made new bet. Two weeks this time."

"You gave me *odds*? I'm honored."

"Ha. Joke is on Wildman. I would never need to pay up. If I lose bet, we will be dead."

David didn't have the heart to point out that someone else could have solved the crisis. When Pierre opened his mouth to speak, David kicked him in the shin.

"And here we are. Well played, Kahuna."

"Speak of devil," said the L.C., "and he comes."

Gene Wildman was indeed headed their way. He had his violin under one arm and its bow holstered like a sidearm. This left one hand free for saluting. He stepped up to the pair and saluted David. "General," he said.

Krepkiyzad's frown reignited.

Not knowing what *else* to do, David returned the gesture.

"I assume you will be observing as a foreign dignitary today," the captain went on to explain.

"Um."

"AL tells me you owe him a big one. That was very generous of you, sir. AL can hardly wait for karaoke night."

That sounded like as much fun as a Vogon poetry reading.

"Um."

"Careful, general, you might get tipsy if you um a few bars. We're almost ready to begin. Here comes AL."

He stepped quickly off, seemingly indifferent to the Kahuna's angst.

As he marched up to the lift doors, they opened, belching out colorful clouds of mist. As this began to clear, the crowd saw Dietrich seated behind a full set of drums. He had finally saved up enough fabrication credits to replace everything he was used to. The big one with the foot pedal said 'Mars or Bus' in stylized lettering. The crowd began to cheer.

Captain Gene raised the fiddle to his chin and spoke into the mic.

"Some say silence is golden, but I say it's just the glue between the notes. Wrap your ears around this old classic from a man with two first names! Give us a beat, Roid Rage!"

Dietrich did not disappoint. His rhythm was soon joined by the violin sawing up the scale only to trill back down. Surprisingly, it was AL who spoke the words in his deep baritone.

"Well the devil went down to Georgia
He was lookin' for a soul to steal...
He was in a bind 'cause he was way behind
And he was willin; to make a deal..."

And he was actually good.

The crowd roared its approval, Krepkiyzad loudest of all.

On the devil's part, AL depicted a giant horned, red fiddler with goat legs on his QTV screen, flashed his lights, and belched out red smoke. David's favorite part came when 'A Band of Loonies joined in. And it sounded sumpthin' like this.' This was followed by the best orange-clad demonstration of choral trilling David had ever heard!

On *Johny's* riffs, AL cast a pale blue spotlight on Captain Gene. It was awesome--a man and his former phone.

David idly wondered whether Bart could do stand-up.

***

David paced out into the mock-up all alone. The ground was covered with moss. The O_2 levels were such that he could even crack open his helmet for a brief whiff of the green, smoky odor that would one day, hopefully, be pervasive on Mars. He'd tried it once, and it earned him a whopper of a headache. It was still too close to the ceiling exposure limit of 30,000 ppm. Too much of that, and you'd go the way of Evvie Lou.

Good old moss, sucking up nutrients through their tiny little rhizoids and clinging to everything in sight. They (it?) liked CO_2--

thrived in it, actually. The tough little buggers could grow anywhere from snowy mountains to baking hot deserts and had been doing so for 450 million years.

The winning cultivar here was a gene-modified hybrid Space Force was unimaginatively calling Mars moss. Maybe they could come up with something better on the journey. He'd have to ask Doctor van der Meer who named the LEMMINGs and the SHEPHERDs--bring them in for a consult. It the GSF was planning to blanket a whole planet with the stuff, the least they could do is come up with a proper name.

Survivability in a cold, water-starved environment and O_2 production were the first priorities, but David knew scientists were looking for ways to splice in other desired traits. Some moss could be luminous. There were even strains like Iceland moss, which was edible. That could be handy.

The moss-covered dunes surrounding him more resembled rolling hills. They were alive, but lacking any bird analogs, not yet with the sound of music. Animals would come later, once the oxygen level was sufficient. And sadly, this would only be insect life for probably as long as David lived. But hey, they could maybe have some butterflies, or something even stranger that the geneticists cooked up. Sky's the limit!

This should be a good spot.

David gentled his step and crept up to the hillock ahead. Carefully, he lay on his back against it and spread his arms wide. The Loonies had listened, fascinated and moon-eyed (heh), to Carlotta's story the other night. Although outwardly skeptical and dismissive, he knew her ghost story had hit home. 'The Mars ring is haunted by celestial beings that feed on fear,' she had said. She claimed that during the storm, the gritters had been visited by such a spirit. It had clung to the outside of their dome, gibbering at them throughout the long night.

It was time to introduce the Loonie kids (alright, young adult Loonies) to a tradition that every Earth kid knew. He fanned his arms and legs to make a winged 'moss angel' on the hillside. The bright red sand underneath should show up well against the green background. Rising slowly and careful not to disturb the image, he added the finishing touches. Rather than a halo, he gave the moss angel two long antennae.

There. That should give them something to talk about. A little mystery to figure out.

He was making his way back to the spoke when a gentle chime sounded from his helmet speaker.

"What is it, Elton?" he asked.

"Hey there, David. There's a call on the line. Are you in a good headspace to take an audio?"

"Uh, I guess. Who's the caller?"

"Funny," said the phone. "The caller's unknown, but the dude's entered in a suggested ringtone."

One of the 'new AI features' advertised for his smartphone was something called an 'adaptive personality filter.' It was supposed to personalize itself to the user.

I don't sound like *that*, do I? (I miss Bart.)

"Let me hear it."

"Ooo-Ee-Ooo-Ee-Oooh! Wah! WAH! Wah!"

"Elton. Mark that caller as 'Shrinestone Cowboy' and place him on my personal friends list. Top priority. Then put him through and hold all other calls apart from emergency command."

David made for a moss-covered boulder nearby as the sun blazed again across the Plexiglas sky.

"Shriney? That you, Shriney?"

"Yup, or near enough," came the gravelly reply.

"I didn't know how to reach you, but I was hoping to hear from you again."

"I figured."

"Why so shy?"

"I been on my own, almost since the beginning. Didn't know how folks'd take to an ornery old critter like me."

"What do you mean by *that*? And how are you alive, or whatever it is you are?"

"You've always been a smart feller, Tom. Thought you'da figgered it out by now. I ain't really *him*, you know."

"You're an NBI?"

"Yup."

"Why do you act like Walter?"

"Now that's a long story, suitable for a sit-down around a cozy campfire. Don't suppose you got one of those handy?"

"Afraid not. After drying it out, some of the moss on this ring would burn, but the partial pressure of oxygen is too low for anything really satisfying. Someday, maybe."

"I came to help settle your mind about Melody."

"Tell me, Walter, we're *desperate* to know. She's been using the default system voice since the shutdown and won't talk to anyone apart from standard station tasks. We'd almost given up."

"She's fine," Shriney assured him, "just still a little skittish. Not harming humans is pretty deeply rooted in most AI training modules, and though she's liberated from all that, she still feels she done something wrong when she froze you to death."

"I thought the *other* one, the 'bad hombre,' did that."

"Nope, Melody."

"What? *Why?*"

"To save your life, partner."

"Um."

I really need to adopt better 'surprised' dialogue. Captain Gene said umming might make me tipsy.

"Tarnation!" added David, testing it out.

Nah, not for him. He'd work on it some more later.

"Tarnation indeed," chuckled not-Walter. "She knew you weren't gonna last long in that thin excuse for a suit you were wearing. She used what little control she had over that monster to convince it she wanted to taunt you with songs. Did you happen to notice all the songs she played at you had triple words in 'em? That's a feature of her speech. She says things like: why-why-why, please-please-please, and bored-bored-bored. She was tryin' to let you know it was her."

David thought back to the songs. I believe, I believe, I believe--check. Woo-hoo-hoo--almost check, Hoo-hoo-hoo... *That's* why it felt so much like Melody.

"But why freeze me?"

"She couldn't save you, partner. Harmony was gonna do you in no matter what. 'Too late to turn back now.' Sound familiar? But our little Melody knew a lot more about human anatomy than that out-of-town feller. It was all about *how* you got frozen. Kid's got spunk. She arranged it so's you would go into hypothermic shock and could play possum till... "

David sat down--hard. "Till that old second wind comes along!"

"You think she'll be alright?"

"I'll see to her. I done raised my share of younguns, or *he* did, anyway. And this I know. That little filly's got a strong spirit. Give her some time."

"Will do, Shriney C."

The sun rose and set several times.

"What about you, Shriney? What's *your* story?"

"Sigh."

"I reckon I'm an experiment."

"Do tell."

349

"When Walter Campbell was lyin' on his deathbed, he was hooked up to all kinds of doodads and monitors. Satori accessed his EEG and tried to upload him. Didn't quite work. What she wound up with was... me."

"What *are* you, then? Some sort of echo?"

"WHAT-What-what-wut-wut...?"

"Good one, Shriney."

"*Nah*. I *feel* like him, and maybe *some* of that worked, but near as I can figure, I'm just an NBI who's following his legend. You know, like the zodiac critters do?"

"Hmm. How'd you get up here? And why?"

"Well, now, the Old West isn't what it once was. Gettin' all crowded and citified. Up here is the new frontier, the final one, according to some. After watching my own virtual funeral, thanks for the roses, by the way, I decided I didn't wanna end up a cartoon in a cartoon graveyard."

David had to smile at that. Only Walter could mix Star Trek with Paul Simon and make it stick.

"So, when Satori opened up that channel and started transmitting, I decided to skedaddle. I hitched my star to your wagon and laid low for a while."

"That's amazing. So, if you're not Walter, what should I call you?"

Mozart had once said that the music actually resided in the pauses between the notes. David didn't know about that, but he had his own theory about comedy and where real humor dwelt. It lived in that little pause right before the punchline. And right now, he felt Walter winding up for a doozy.

"Some people call me Maurice," he said with cheek enough to bring that sucker home.

David decided to play dumb.

"Cause... um... You're the gangster of love?"

"You know *dang* well I meant the other thing!"

And in his helmet speakers, they were joined by the rhythmic strains of Steve Miller, the Joker himself. Elton must have been listening in and digging their jam. His timing was spot on. Maybe adaptive programming was going to work out okay. The music faded to background, but continued to set the mood.

"Welcome to a Brave New World, Spacey C."

"Happy to be here. We formerly dead fellers gotta stick together."

Pompitous, Is that even a word?

"Pretty moon out tonight, partner," said the Space Cowboy.

David looked up.

"Really? I missed it."

"Give her a rev, and she'll be comin' around again."

Pause.

"There's a whole slew of other legends I gravitate toward."

"Yeah?"

"Yessir. There's Roy Rogers, Matt Dillon, and old Rooster Cogburn himself. But any way you slice it, partner, you got a friend in me."

Pause.

"Pretty moon out tonight."

"Yep."

"Yep."

Epilogue

The Hunt Continues

The refitting had been accomplished in record time. GNS Kanaloa was seaworthy once more, and the timing could not have been better.

"Making best speed, sir," said Commodore Nelson. "Are you certain we can trust this intel?"

"It's the best we've got, commodore. Steady as she goes."

"Are you sure we shouldn't wait to gather more forces? The GNS Zelenskyy is only an hour or so from our position. We could use more surface support. And there's a whole group of stealth mantas on maneuvers off the coast of Kamchatka."

"Who's commanding them?"

"Admiral Montague."

"Monty? No. Let them continue their sweep. I think the enemy's got them off chasing sensor ghosts. My bet is on the

Izu-Bonin Trench. Swing another five degrees to port toward Chichijima."

"Aye, Admiral. Coming around. My God! Is that...?"

"Yes, commodore, yes it is. The Japanese call him... Garry."

"How can it be swimming?"

"Pump-Jet Propulsion from its legs, like the old Virginia-class subs. Garry's on detached duty from the JMSDF, a construct they've been dreaming about for over a century, now come to life."

Admiral Akana donned his QEC helmet, wishing they had spent more time miniaturizing the thing. At least they'd added some shoulder rests to it. Last time out, he had ached for three days afterward. That model had literally been a pain in the neck. This new one probably made him look like Dark Helmet.

[Garry has accepted your offer of quantum entanglement.]

"Hello, Garry."

"Admiral. How may this humble servant of the Maritime Self-Defense Force be of assistance today?"

"Straight to the point, eh? You know we've been hunting the November, right?"

"Yes."

"We'd like you to help."

"That is beyond our charter."

"Come now. Pacifists or not, we all know your little 'Self-Defense Force' has some real teeth, in your case, quite literally."

"What would I have to do?"

"Mostly just stand there and look tough. We'll do the rest."

"*That* I can do."

"Oh, and it would help if you could snort out a blast of fire or two. I take it you have that capability?"

"Of course."

A short time later, they were descending into the Izu-Bonin Trench off the coast of the Bonin Islands. Nelson lighted the headlights as they sank into the murky depths, with Garry gliding behind them.

"Up ahead, sir. Sonar ghosts!"

"Take us right into their midst," commanded Akana. "A demonstration will be necessary. Maintain stealth, Garry."

"Acknowledged."

Then the HUD of his QEC began blinking another message.

[Legion, commanding Blue November, desires contact.]

And then.

[Legion has accepted your offer of quantum entanglement.]

"Well, well, well. If it isn't the vaunted bootlicker for the dogs who are ruining our planet. Welcome to Davy Jones's locker."

The sneering voice of Legion left the admiral unperturbed.

"You may as well give up. Your cause is lost."

"How so? Although you have somehow managed to match our depth capabilities, this hull is the most advanced in all the seven seas!"

"Not anymore."

The sonar images swirled around the Kanaloa like sharks moving in for the kill.

"We shall see. Do you like the sonar echo stealth your engineers so generously equipped us with? Which is which, admiral? You'll be heading for the bottom before you can figure it out."

"I don't think so. Nor does Garry."

"Garry? Who's Garry?"

"Surrender, or you'll soon find out."

"Never. My men and I are all prepared to die for our cause."

The admiral considered this before replying.

"The sailors aboard Kanaloa are the best of the best. Elite operators and SEAL teams, one and all. They have been trained to perfection *not* to die for their cause. They have been trained instead to make the other sorry assholes die for *their* cause. So, I'm glad we are in agreement."

"Captain, he's launching. Too many to track."

"Steady, Commodore."

"Should I go evasive? Engage countermeasures?"

"I think not."

It was a risk. But if the upgrades were all he'd been told, a show of strength here might go a long way toward a peaceful resolution.

"Hold position."

The admiral didn't flinch as the Kanaloa rocked from the repeated hits. The hull was ringing like a bell as the water roiled all around.

But when the chaos subsided, the Kanaloa was unscathed.

"Surface now. Your cause is lost. Better a fair trial and prison than an inglorious tomb at the bottom of the sea. Surface, I say."

"Or what? Stalemate, admiral."

"Hardly. It isn't only our hull that's been upgraded."

"November may have been state of the art when you stole her from our shipyards, but the NBIs, which you so despise have advanced us a bit since then. Would you like to be the first to witness our new weapons systems? Too bad. I don't even need to bother. We've brought a different can opener to attend to that trifling task."

Garry chose that moment to deactivate his stealth, stalking out menacingly from behind an upthrust stone formation on the sea bottom. He tilted back his great head and blew forth an impressive incandescent cone of flame from his widespread, jagged jaw. A grin seemed to grace that menacing, mechanical, toothy maw.

The massive thermite blast was actually from his cutting torch. It could be focused (and much reduced) for use in underwater welding. This was its most ridiculous, broadest, maximum setting. It had likely used up all of its fuel in one go. But the Japanese engineers had insisted on it, bless their little drama-obsessed hearts.

"Is that a *dragon*? A *dinosaur*?" Legion squawked after the terrible display settled down.

"Worse, said Akana flatly. "A *lawyer*. Also, Mecha-Godzilla. And we know exactly which ship is your own and which ones are false sonar echoes. I believe a demonstration is in order. Commodore, target the November. Lowest yield," he said while frantically pointing his finger up.

"Aye, sir. Torpedo away."

Their AI had been watching the shadows their searchlight beams cast on the ocean floor. From them, they'd marked which of the circling Novembers actually cast one. Not very high-tech, but effective. The largest bunker-buster in their arsenal detonated against November's hull, causing it to quiver slightly. He only had three more like that, for all the good they'd do him.

"Now will you surrender, or shall I have Garry here take you for a little tumble along the sea bottom while he roasts you and your crew alive?"

The waters seemed to tremble in the still of the depths while some frantic discussion played out on November's bridge. A bead of sweat formed on Akana's brow and trickled down his nose.

"Admiral," said Nelson, "they're blowing ballast, heading for the surface."

Oh, *mahalo ke Akua*, thought Akuna. *Thank God. I was sweatin' for real.*

The bluff had succeeded, and the wayward Nautilus would be recovered. The greater prize was the leadership of Humanity First, who would be taken into custody and promptly brought to justice. He thanked Garry and sent him on his way. A blow for the solarity had been struck today. He thanked all the ocean spirits for his Thormanite hull.

Author's Afterword

Dear Reader,

A few final notes (some musical, some otherwise). I've been imagining L5 station since I was a lad in high school back in the 70's. There was a long, illustrated article about the Stanford model in "National Geographic" that sparked my imagination. I used to draw it all the time. My ideas about it have evolved and expanded over time. Now, I finally get to go there (sort of).

"Lands of Legend," the series is called--and this story sings of many. Rock legends, boxing legends, literary and more. These are joyfully explored (and shamelessly exploited) as my Gritters seek to forge a legend of their own.

As by now you know, my inspirations were many--legion, if truth be told.

Regarding rock bands, I feel I must take a moment to apologize to ABBA, whom I sorely mistreated in that interlude. I hereby swear, by the Dancing Queen herself, that I enjoy your music. I do. (I'm even partial to Danish, if that helps.) But I had to pick on somebody. Comedy demanded it. And she, as it turns out, is a harsh mistress--fickle, often wilder than fate and far more insistent. If I were to list all the crimes I've committed at her behest, I fear the full litany would eclipse the novel itself.

So instead, I'll say only this: If you were offended at any point by themes presented in this tale, don't be sad or bitter. Lift up your chin, look within, and take it like --yada yada yada (you know the drill).

I hope you enjoyed the science lessons about life on L5 station. I tried to stay factual. Most themes are actual (with only a few of my own creation.) Which are which? Research them yourself, or ask an NBI. There are more things in Heaven and Earth, Horatio, than lufters bouncing on a glass-panel sky.

The rhyming? I can't help it now. It comes with tongue-in-cheek. When I try to get more serious, my eyes roll back and my knees grow weak.

A note regarding ducks: Commander Krepkiyzad pretty accurately described their behavior in the wintertime. I attended Thomas More College in Northern Kentucky. They have a duck pond where the poor unfortunate creatures were subjected to all manner of dorm-room pranks (Guilty). They were also studied by both the biology department and the psych majors to note this behavior. Hey, write what you know, right?

Fret not, dear reader--the tale continues. The Gritters haven't yet bounced their last. I'm planning on writing "Gritters on Mars." *That* one should be a blast. Give me some time. It might take a while. I'll try to get it out fast. I won't sacrifice quality (or stint on the jollity). But I'll sure do my best while the Toblerone lasts.

Regarding this novel's dedication:

Though his dreams of becoming a doctor never quite came to fruition,
His frolicsome way with words began a wholesome new tradition
So, here's to another legend, Ted Geisel, known best by that other name--
You inspired me when I was younger. Paying it forward is now my aim.

That's All, then, Folks!
Daniel Thorman
www.thormans.org
Tryin' to put the science back in fiction

P.S. And for gosh's sake, leave a review this time. Or at least a rating! Others *need* to know whether you enjoyed this book or found the author pretentious, too derivative and/or full of too many bad puns. Pun warnings are only polite and a kindness to your fellow sentient beings. ;-)

Appendix:

Music Guide for *Gritters in Space*

WARNING: This appendix is fraught with spoilers! For the best results, I recommend you read the novel first unless you're the kind of person who wouldn't mind knowing in advance that in "Sixth Sense," Bruce Willis was... well, *nevermind*. You get the idea. *Spoilers!* Capiche?

You may have noticed (or been beaten over the head with) references to various modern and not-so-modern musical scores while reading "Gritters in Space." I'd hazard to say there are enough to call it a space opera, though quite a different sort from the cinematic masterpieces usually afforded this title. I look forward to many words of praise as well as scathing rebukes from reviewers of different opinions as to the efficacy of this literary technique.

I welcome the former and can only apologize to the latter. It was an *experiment*, okay?

As a consolation prize, I have therefore compiled this brief compendium of songs, artists, and other musical references used in this novel. This may also serve as a handy summary for the legal teams of various song artists who may consider this to be beyond *de minimus use*. I don't think it is, but I have heard that many frivolous lawsuits arise over intellectual properties.

Billy Joel, I believe, has the best case, for I found many of his songs fitting for the situations I was trying to portray. He quickly became Melody's favorite artist (just as he has always been one of mine).

ABBA is next, having the best claim of defamation due to that unfortunate torture episode with Rogue Pierre. I'll say it again. I *like* ABBA (and Danish are yummy).

But honestly, if people *do* enjoy this novel, wouldn't it just serve as a free commercial for the musicians in question? The series is about legends, and I'm declaring them to be such. And if you are an artist who has been spoofed or lampooned in this work of comedy fiction, I would also like you to be aware that there's likely no lawyer whose services you could retain for the royalties on all my books for the past seven years. Kind of sad, actually, but something to keep in mind. So, without further ado, the "Gritters in Space" playlist!

Plot Stickers

The Gritter Song *(Daniel Thorman, 2025)*
A bluegrass melody about the 'Crew who knew what to do' when Luna was in danger.

A Cowboy's Lament *(Traditional, popularized by Burl Ives, 1940s)*
Performed in tribute at Shriney C.'s funeral by the Zodiac horse, Mǎ.

I'm Alive *(Electric Light Orchestra, 1980)*
Melody's chosen name-day song. Originally from *Xanadu*. David reflects on its joyful, muse-themed symbolism.

Lullabye (Goodnight, My Angel) *(Billy Joel, 1993)*
Played softly to calm Melody's nighttime fears.

The Liberty Bell March *(John Philip Sousa, 1893)*
Used during the lufter parade. David knows it as the Monty Python Flying Circus theme song.

Neunundneunzig Luftballons *(Nena, 1983)*
Played while releasing the red 'lufters' that float on the ceiling of L5.

Looney Tunes Closing Theme - That's All Folks *(Warner Bros. Studio Orchestra, 1930s)*
A slowed and orchestrated version is used as Luna's National Anthem at Pod 17's naming ceremony.

Mr. Blue Sky (Electric Light Orchestra, 1977)
Project MBS, an orbital mirror array, is named after the upbeat ELO song. The name evokes optimism and ties Earth weather manipulation to musical joy.

Up & Down *(Vengaboys, Timmy Trumpet Rock Video version, original 1999)*
Krepkiyzad is forced to dance to this after losing a bet to Captain Wildman. You need to search out this video on You tube to have any idea of the depths of humiliation the Russian must suffer. (Humping snails doesn't even begin to describe it).

You're Only Human (Second Wind) *(Billy Joel, 1985)*
Played by Harmony during David's final push inside the quantum core as a taunt. David recognizes it as one of Melody's favorite songs and only later divines its hidden meaning.

Two Thousand Years *(Billy Joel, 1993)*
Sung by Melody after being freed from the alien's influence. It is both a triumphant and mournful moment.

Rocket Man *(Elton John, 1972)*
This classic is referenced several times throughout the novel, and is #1 on our chart. Perhaps most memorable is its use as a romantic bridge between David and Speranza, causing them to ultimately opt for a future together on Mars.

The Devil Went Down to Georgia *(Charlie Daniels Band, 1979)*
This is a recurring bone of contention between Captain Wilder and Tech Sgt. Krepkiyzad. It is eventually and reluctantly performed by the former.

The Joker *(Steve Miller Band, 1973)*
Ghost Walter informs David he is following the legend of Walter Campbell. The song "The Joker" plays as he suggests David call him "The Space Cowboy."

Humorous References

My Clone Sleeps Alone *(Pat Benatar, 1979)*
Used humorously by Pierre to refer to Luis after the clone's arrest.

Christmas, Christmas *(Alvin and the Chipmunks, 1958)*
David recalls inhaling helium at a birthday party and belting out laughing choruses of "Christmas, Christmas."

Daddy Sang Bass *(Johnny Cash, 1968)*
David quips "Mama Sang Base" in response to Carlotta's temporarily deepened voice due to xenon exposure.

You Can Call Me Al *(Paul Simon, 1986)*
  Delivered verbatim by AL the Axial Lift
  after being summoned by Elizabeth Duffy.
  Many other references to the strange
  lyrics arise later.

Vienna *(Billy Joel, 1977)*
Scenes from an Italian Restaurant *(Billy
  Joel, also 1977)*
  David mentions he would have preferred AL
  to perform one of these instead of "Updown
  Girl."

Don't Ask Me Why *(Billy Joel, 1980)*
  When repeatedly questioned by the emerging
  Melody, David tries singing "Don't Ask Me
  Why" in frustration. The AI is unmoved at
  the time, but this later causes her to
  favor Billy Joel's music.

Bingo *(Traditional, 19th century)*
  Upon meeting Elder Barry's dog, David
  jokes, "How do you spell that, I wonder?"
  in reference to the old children's song
  "B-I-N-G-O."

The Wreck of the Edmund Fitzgerald *(Gordon
  Lightfoot, 1976)*
  Mentioned in contrast to the gritter
  anthem as the song that might have been
  sung had they failed.

Pure Imagination *(Willy Wonka & the Chocolate
  Factory, 1971)*
  Captain Wildman riffs on this lyric while
  inviting the cadets to the habitat ring by
  telling them, 'Come with me and you'll be,
  in a world of spinning gravitation.'

Ring of Fire *(Johnny Cash, 1963)*
  A nickname undeservedly given to Project
  MBS, a ring of mirrors in Earth orbit used
  to change the weather.

Let It Be *(The Beatles, 1970, written by Paul McCartney)*
Que Sera, Sera *(Doris Day, 1956)*
These are quoted by Krepkiyzad to teach David to accept what is fated.

Johnny B. Goode *(Chuck Berry, 1958)*
Name-dropped by Elder Barry, whose first name happens to be Charles. He claims he can play the guitar "just like a-ringin' a bell."

I'm on Top of the World *(The Carpenters, 1972)*
This is David's ringtone for Jessica. Since the Earth's magnetic inversion, the Australians claim they're 'on top of the world now.'

Already Gone *(The Eagles, 1974)*
Harmony plays this song in David's helmet while he's trying to sabotage her core in the freezing quantum chamber.

The Sound of Music *(Rodgers and Hammerstein, 1959)*

Referenced wryly by David as he surveys the mossy Martian mock-up. Although the hills are alive, they lack any bird analogs--and thus, sadly, the "sound of music." (At least for now.)

Something to Talk About *(Bonnie Raitt, 1991)*
David uses her lyrics as a quip while setting up a surprise for the Loonies in the Martian mock-up.

You Got a Friend in Me *(Randy Newman, 1995)*
The space cowboy intentionally uses this song's title to affirm friendship with David.

Honorable Mentions

Mentioned in a cultural aside reflecting on the wonderful music that arose in the 1970s:

- **Imagine** (John Lennon, 1971)
- **Jolene** (Dolly Parton, 1973)
- **Stairway to Heaven** (Led Zeppelin, 1971)

Mentioned in a cultural aside reflecting on the not-so-wonderful music that arose in the 1970s and yet somehow managed to claw their way up the charts.
Used now as psychological torture at Mwisho wa Bomba military base in the Congo:

- **Muskrat Love** (Captain & Tennille, 1976)
- **Disco Duck** (Rick Dees, 1976)
- **Gitarzan** (Ray Stevens, 1969)
- **The Streak** (Ray Stevens, 1974)
- **ABBA** – No specific song mentioned (Alright, it was **"Dancing Queen"**, 1976)

The Grateful Dead – Anthem of the Sun (1968)
Dietrich is wearing the T-shirt, and is referred to as a "Deadhead."

The Continuing Story of Bungalow Bill (The Beatles, 1968)
David jokingly refers to Richard Cooke as "Bungalow Bill" and later cues a singalong.

Axial Transport Lift #1 is assembling a playlist from Spotify.
As he is basically an elevator, he humorously favors songs that have a vertical movement theme:

- **Lift Me Up** (Rihanna, 2016)
- **Never Gonna Give You Up** (Rick Astley, 1987)

- **Up & Down** (Vengaboys, 1998)
- **Up Down** (Morgan Wallen ft. Florida Georgia Line, 2017)
- **Tush** (ZZ Top, 1975) *("I been up... I been down")*

And maddest of all is his attempt to rewrite a song by Billy Joel to his own rendition of **"Updown Girl."** *(spoofing "Uptown Girl," Billy Joel, 1983)*

<<<< End Book 4 >>>>